RL AKERS

OVERTWIXT ™

WELCOME TO THE
WORLD OF BRIDGES

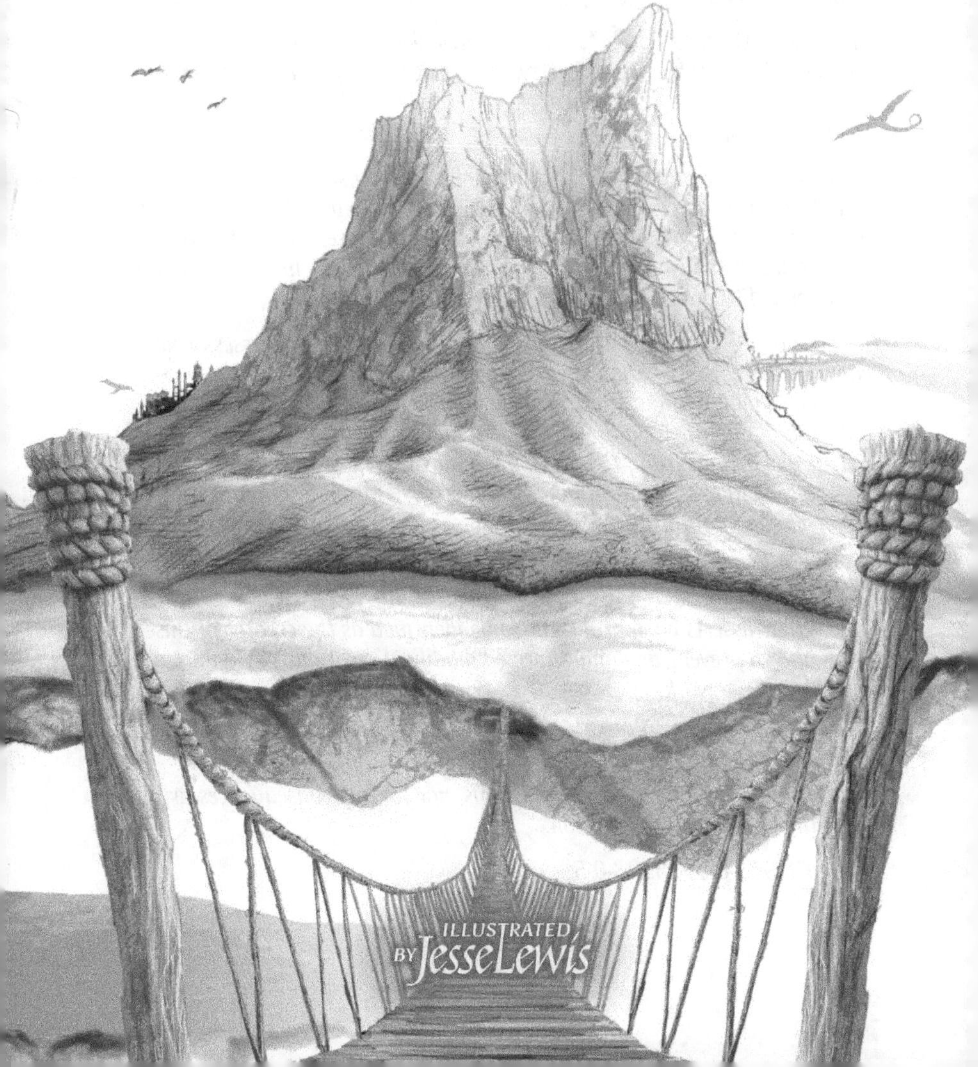

ILLUSTRATED BY Jesse Lewis

table of contents

prepared by the hand
of the Cartograp
on behalf of the Baron
in the 782nd human epoch

updated by
the Loremaster,
Nachton
Ollivaros

OVERTWIXT
The United Lands

0   15   30   45
miles

access to
Lugard

Maze
mount

LUGARD

HULAND

EQLAND

Quarry

HUCENTIA

CENTWICK

GNO-
CENTIA

access to
Gnobury

Capital
City

TWIXT

SHALAND

NAGLAND

SHANA
GRATLA

Alabaster
City

LEGEND

(H) port niland (portland)
(H) hub niland (hubland)
------ road or path
🜂 bridge to real world

CITIES & SETTLEMENTS
Pastoral City
The Grove
Castle of Hucentia

REPOSITORIES OF KNOWLEDGE
Grand Library
of Huland
Archives of the Eqmen

From what I've seen, the scale of these maps is
variable, often distorted by perspective. -N

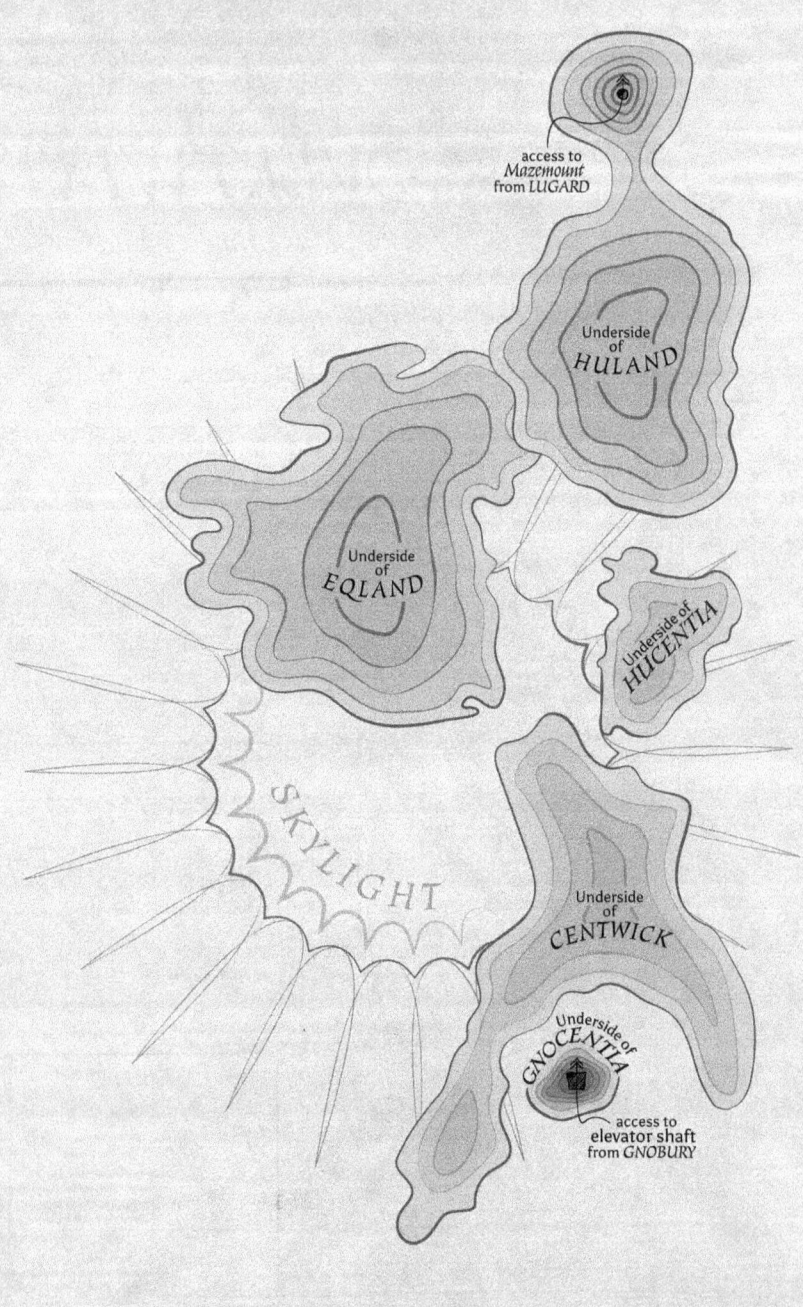

access to
Mazemount
from LUGARD

Underside
of
HULAND

Underside
of
EQLAND

Underside of
HUCENTIA

SKYLIGHT

Underside
of
CENTWICK

Underside of
GNOCENTIA

access to
elevator shaft
from *GNOBURY*

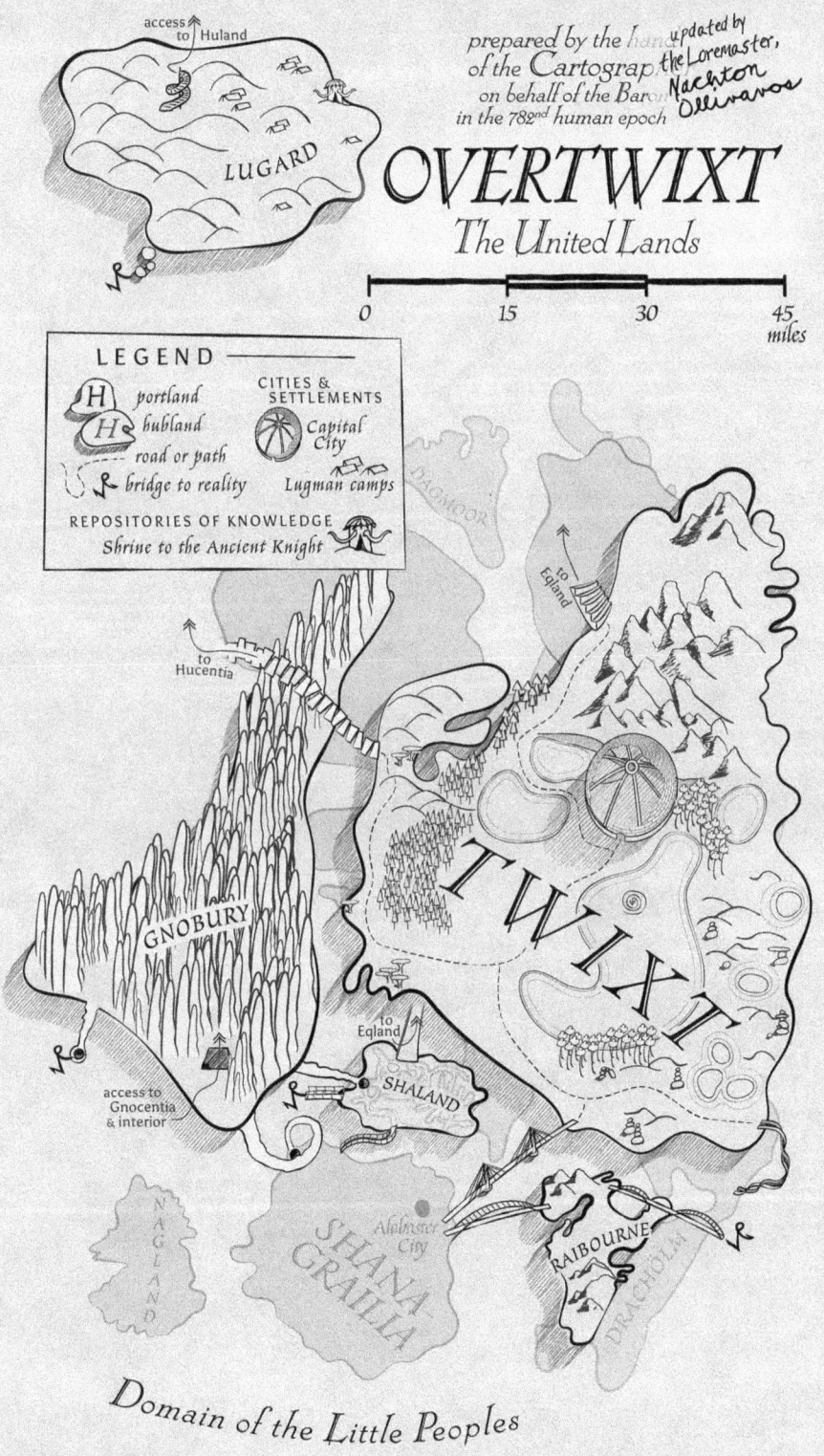

access
to Huland

LUGARD

prepared by the hand updated by
of the Cartograp the Loremaster,
on behalf of the Baro Nachton
in the 782nd human epoch Ollivavos

OVERTWIXT
The United Lands

0   15   30   45
miles

LEGEND

H portland
H hubland
road or path
bridge to reality

CITIES & SETTLEMENTS
Capital City
Lugman camps

REPOSITORIES OF KNOWLEDGE
Shrine to the Ancient Knight

DAGMOOR

to Eqland

to Hucentia

GNOBURY

TWIXT

to Eqland

access to
Gnocentia
& interior

SHALAND

NAGLAND

Aldinster City

SHANA GRALLA

RAIBOURNE

DRACHOLM

Domain of the Little Peoples

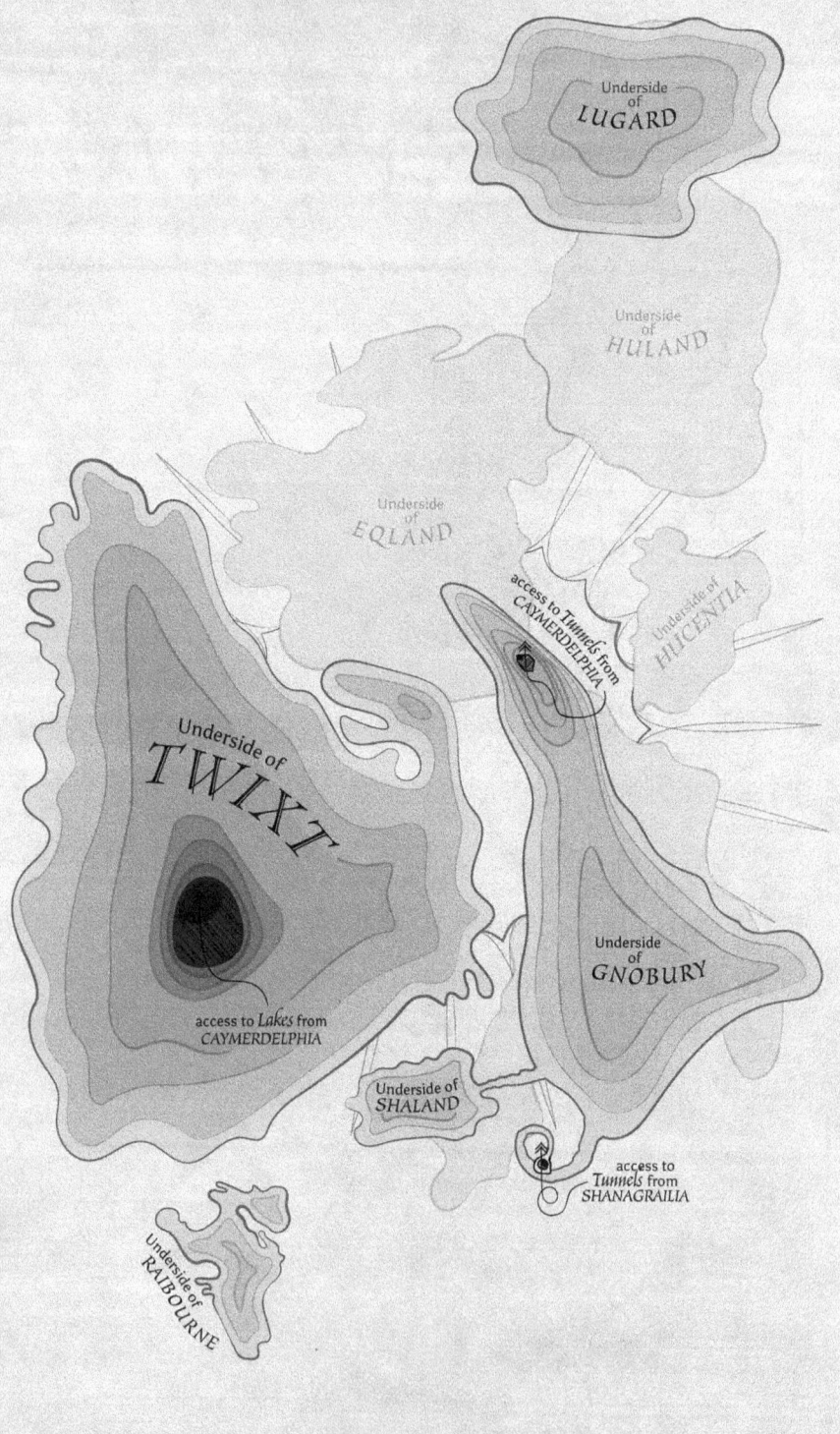

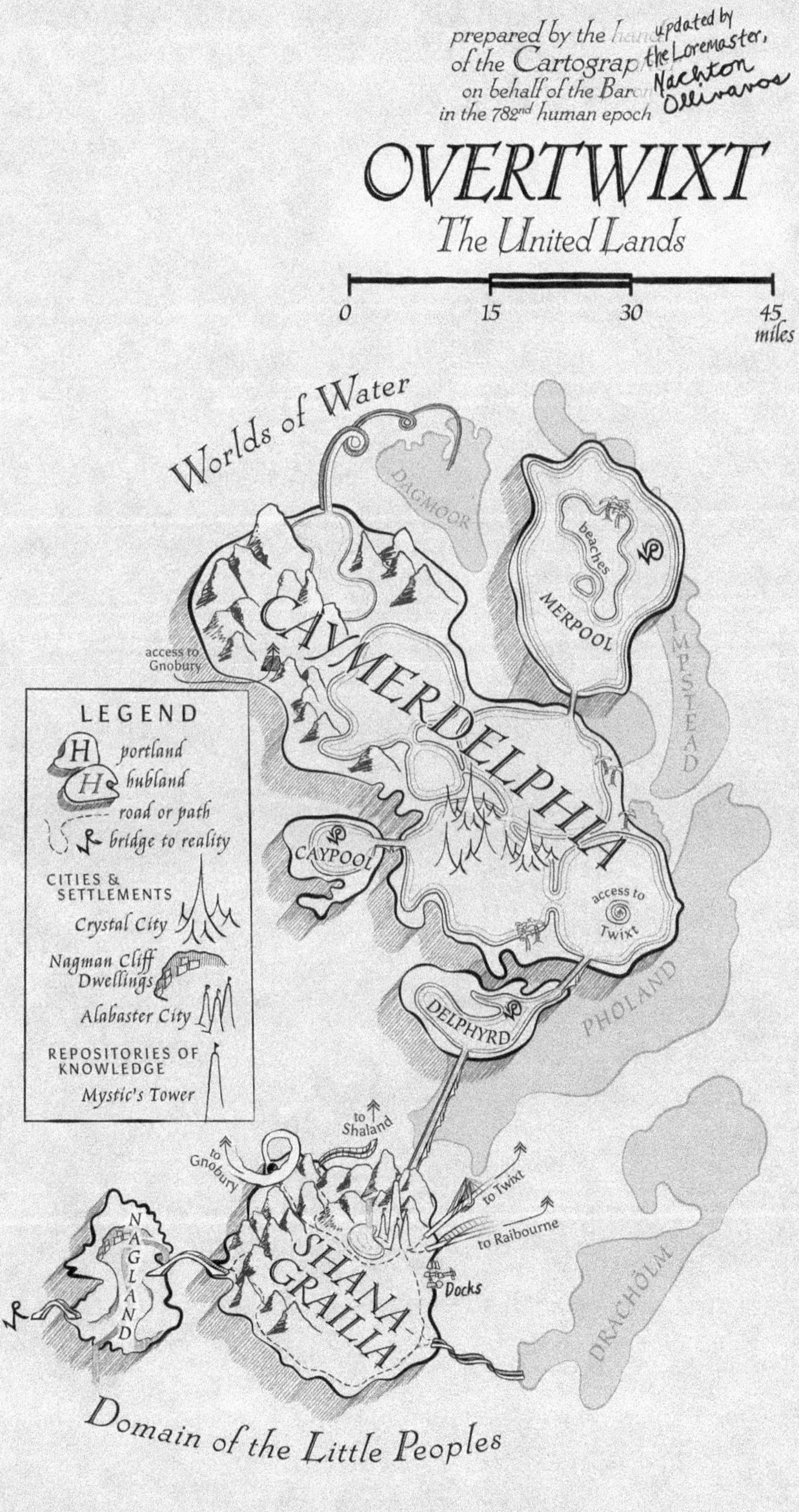

prepared by the han
of the Cartograp
on behalf of the Bar
in the 782nd human epoch
updated by the Loremaster, Nachton Ollivaros
OVERTWIXT
The United Lands
0
15
30
45 miles
Worlds of Water
DAGMOOR
beaches
MERPOOL
IMPSTEAD
CAYMERDELPHIA
access to Gnobury
LEGEND
portland
hubland
road or path
bridge to reality
CITIES & SETTLEMENTS
Crystal City
Nagman Cliff Dwellings
Alabaster City
REPOSITORIES OF KNOWLEDGE
Mystic's Tower
CAYPOOL
access to Twixt
DELPHYRD
PHOLAND
to Shaland
to Gnobury
to Twixt
to Raibourne
NAGLAND
SHANA-GRAILIA
Docks
DRACHÖLM
Domain of the Little Peoples

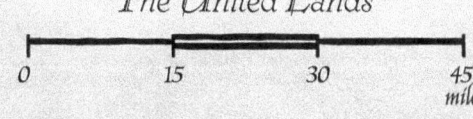

Underside of
LUGARD

Underside
of
MERPOOL

Underside of
CAYMERDELPHIA

Underside of
CAYPOOL

Underside of
TWIXT

Underside of
DELPHYRD

Underside
of
GNOBURY

Underside of
SHALAND

Underside of
RAIBOURNE

Underside of
SHANA-
GRAILIA

Underside of
NAGLAND

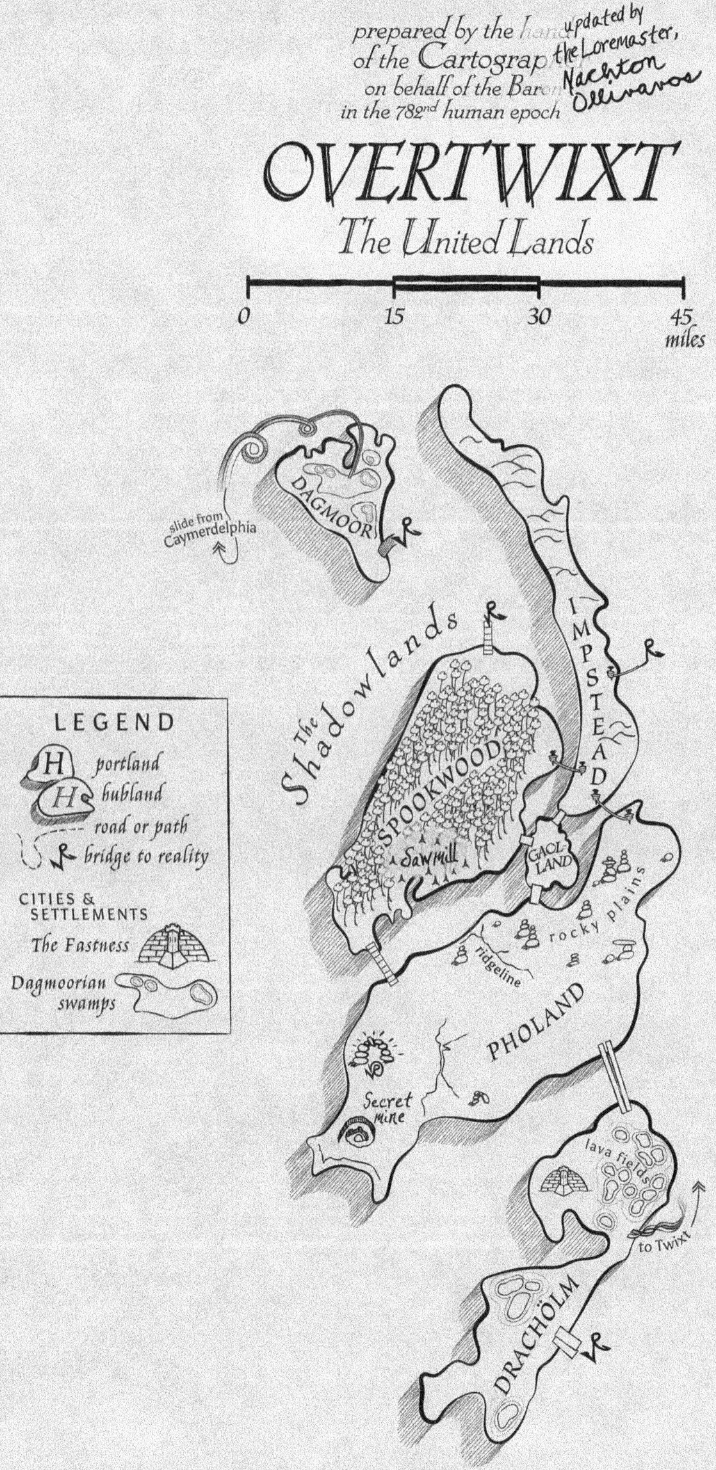

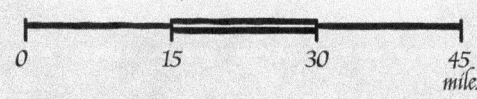

For Ian, Sadie, Emme, and Nate...

my own personal Knight, Princess, Empress,
and—yes—Loremaster

Author's Note

The main characters of this story were inspired by my four children (as they were more than five years ago now!). As such, these four characters reflect some of the traits I love best in my kids: their enthusiasm and wonder, their abilities and interests, their loyalty to one another.

As in all good stories, however, the heroes of *Overtwixt* suffer from character flaws. If they didn't, there would be no opportunity for character development and growth, and that makes for a boring story! While it's also true that real people suffer from character flaws too, the flaws in my main characters are *not* necessarily the same as my children experience. Rather, they reflect the sorts of struggles common among young men and women their age.

Therefore, as you embark upon this journey with Nachton, Amélie, Cécilie, and Ewan—and as you occasionally see them at their worst—don't wonder too much what this story reveals about my children; it's not meant to showcase anything but the best in them. Instead, ask yourself whether *you* identify with these fictional characters... and whether you yourself face the same opportunities for development and growth.

Welcome to Overtwixt! I hope your visit is meaningful!

OVERTWIXT™

· prologue ·

The Baron slumped on his throne, burying his face in his hands. He was a grandfatherly man, a good ruler, well-loved by most of his followers. How had it ever come to this?

Even as he asked himself that question, he knew the answer. While his intentions had always been good, he had not always been *wise*. "I'm only the *Baron...* I was never meant to be a king," he muttered.

"What was that, your majesty?" a strong voice called, echoing across the vast marble floor of the audience chamber. It was the Captain who spoke, the leader of the Baron's honor guard. He and his three soldiers were stationed at the tall doors on the far side of the room from the throne.

"Nothing, Captain," the Baron said wearily. He took a deep breath and pondered his next move. Then he spoke. "You and your men are dismissed."

The Captain half-knelt, inclining his human head in a kind of bow. "I will keep a man posted in the hall throughout the night. The rest of us will be in our chambers, in case you need us. You will remain protected at all times, my lord Baron."

The Baron offered his most loyal servant a sad smile. "You misunderstand me, Captain. You are not merely dismissed for the night." He hesitated. "You are dismissed *for good*."

The Captain stiffened.

The Baron sighed. "I mean you no insult, my old friend. Quite the opposite, in fact. You have served me well for many years, and I would like to see you rewarded for that. Therefore... I dismiss you, and all your men, from my service. Go home to your people."

"But... my lord Baron. You know what the Vizier* is planning."

The Baron squeezed his eyes shut. "Yes, I do. And brave though you are, my friend, your presence at my side will make little difference in that fight. It is far too late to change the outcome, I fear." He sighed. "Please, grant me this one final happiness, knowing that you are safe."

The Captain's face clenched, but he slowly nodded.

"Thank you," the Baron said, letting out his breath. "Besides, I have another task for you. I need you to pass the word on your way out of the city—*quietly*. I'm ordering the evacuation of all who remain loyal."

"I will see it done." The Captain straightened to his full height, as did his soldiers behind him. "It has been the greatest honor of my life serving you, my lord Baron."

"Go in peace, my old friend."

---

* Pronounced **viz-ZEER**. Find other pronunciation clues in the Glossary of Persons, Places, and Things that starts on page 271.

And with a clatter of hooves on the marble floor, the four guardsmen departed. The Baron was alone.

Well, *mostly* alone.

"You mean to go through with it, then?" a raspy female voice called from somewhere high above, its owner hidden among the rafters of the grand, vaulted ceiling.

"I do," the Baron responded. "And do you remember your part?"

"Of course," the voice responded. She did not speak to the Baron with the same respect as the Captain, for that was not the way of her people. But actions were more important than words. The Baron knew she would do the right thing.

"Get in and get out while I have everyone distracted," the Baron said, repeating the instructions he had given her earlier. "Keep going no matter what. Don't look back. Once you're away, hide those awful things where they'll never be found, and speak of them to no one."

"And destroy his research while I'm at it, so he can't simply make more of them," the raspy voice added. "Yes, I know what I must do."

"Very well."

The Baron waited an hour, enough time for the Captain and his men to flee Capital City, but not enough time—he hoped—for word of the evacuation to reach the Vizier. Then, with a feeling of dread, the Baron rose to his feet and strode out of the audience chamber.

The Vizier's tower was located on the far side of Capital City's huge capitol building, and it was almost as big as the Baron's own throne room. Unlike the throne room, however, the Vizier's chambers were full of servants and lackeys. A miserable, horse-faced creature strummed a musical instrument in one corner, while the Vizier's followers made fun of him.

"Summon your master," the Baron ordered one of the lackeys. He offered the musician a sad smile, then stepped to a nearby stained-glass window. Turning the iron latch, he pushed open the window to let in the cool night air. Then he stood there, leaning on the stone window sill, looking out at the night sky as he awaited the man who was supposedly his advisor.

Someone approached—a human, judging by the sound of his booted feet on stone. The Baron turned... and sure enough, there he stood: the Vizier. The only other human remaining in all of Overtwixt, apart from the Baron himself.

The Vizier had a looming, sinister presence. As always, he dressed entirely in black, a high-collared cloak draping from his shoulders to trail along the floor behind him. The color of a person's clothes meant little, of course, but why had the Baron never seen the evil in this man's *heart* before now? Back when the Vizier first arrived, he had quickly become a trusted advisor to all five rulers of this realm, not just the Baron; slowly but surely, however, the Vizier had worked to unite these lands into a single kingdom ruled by the Baron alone. Now, the Vizier was plotting to steal the throne for himself. Most likely, that had been his plan all along.

The Baron had been manipulated from the start. Well, it was time to return the favor, at least this once.

Striding away from the open window, the Baron spoke forcefully before the Vizier had a chance to get in the first word. "I've come for a report."

"A report, my lord Baron?" the Vizier asked lazily, raising one eyebrow.

"Yes. I've heard disturbing rumors," the Baron explained, frowning. "What exactly have you been doing these last few weeks?"

"Why, my lord Baron," the Vizier said with a mocking smile, "everything I do is for the good of the United Lands." This drew quiet laughter from the Vizier's lackeys. Ugly laughter. The music faltered, and the room plunged into silence.

Moving suddenly, without warning, the Baron bolted for one of the doorways that lined the Vizier's main chamber—the entrance to the Vizier's laboratory. He moved so quickly that no one tried to stop him until he was already through the door.

Inside, he found a long, silvery table lined with bubbling chemicals and wicked-looking tools. Behind that table, giving off a sick green glow as they hung from pegs in the wall, were the terrible inventions the Vizier had spent so many years perfecting: his collection of amulets.

The rumors were true, then. If only the Baron had found out sooner.

Someone coughed, and the Baron's attention was drawn to a small figure tied by straps to a chair in the corner of the room. What was this? One of the Vizier's victims was here right now? Dashing over, the Baron began unfastening the straps that held the creature in place—another of the little people that lived in this realm, like the musician outside. "My lord Baron?" the child-sized person asked in confusion. He was clearly terrified, his cheeks wet with tears.

"Run when you have the chance," the Baron whispered. "You'll know when."

"How dare you!" the Vizier thundered as he entered the laboratory.

The Baron finished with the last strap before turning around. "How dare *I*?" He began striding toward the younger, taller human. "What have you done to this poor creature?"

The Vizier spared a glance for the little figure the Baron had just rescued. "I was helping him," he lied smoothly. "He complained of headaches, and as you know, I'm a master of—"

"Enough lies!" the Baron shouted. Uncertain, the Vizier backed out of the laboratory as the Baron continued marching toward him. Soon, both humans were back in the larger chamber with everyone else. "I know all about the things you've done in my name," the Baron hissed. "The people you exiled, the others you imprisoned or forced into work crews. Your mining projects and your sick experiments..." He shook his head, disgusted. "And the bridges—it was *you* that destroyed them."

The Vizier straightened, and the expression on his face became ugly. He was done pretending. "Seize him," he ordered his lackeys, pointing at the Baron.

"You would dare to lay a hand on me?" the Baron cried indignantly, though he wasn't really surprised. The dark creatures who served the Vizier began closing in on him, reaching for him with taloned fingers.

"I will not suffer your bumbling any longer," the Vizier sneered. "You were always a fool. Now you've proven it, coming here tonight without guards or allies."

In answer, the Baron drew a magnificent Great-Sword from the sheath at his waist. For one impossibly long moment, everyone froze, staring in wonder at the glittering diamond blade; it actually *glowed* with a soft blue light. "Now!" the Baron cried, then began swinging the Sword at the dark creatures who were about to harm him. With all eyes on the Baron, the little person he'd rescued was able to escape through the exit, the musician following after him quickly. And no one else but the Baron glimpsed the flutter of wings through the open window behind the Vizier.

Grinning tightly, knowing his plan had succeeded, the Baron focused his full attention on the fight.

With a dignified shout, he drove his Sword into the chest of a huge dragon-like beast coming at him from behind. There was a puff of yellow smoke, and the creature disappeared. Whirling, the Baron swung at two others, missing one, but catching a gray-furred man across one of his leathery wings. That creature puffed into smoke as well, banished from Overtwixt by the Baron's blade.

And then the Vizier was there, moving to block the Baron's Great-Sword with his own elegant saber. It shouldn't have worked. The Baron's diamond blade was supposedly capable of cutting through anything when wielded for the greater good—but it bounced right off the Vizier's saber in a small explosion of green sparks.

"Surprised?" the Vizier sneered.

"Perhaps yesterday, I would have been." The Baron didn't have a chance to say more, for the Vizier kicked him then, launching into a dizzying counterattack.

The duel raged back and forth across the stone floor of the Vizier's tower, the villain's dark minions diving out of the way now that their master had entered the fight personally. The two humans hurled insults as they swung their swords, and each scored small cuts on the other's clothing. But as the Baron told the Captain earlier, the outcome of this fight was never in doubt. The two magical blades were both powerful, but the Vizier was far more skilled wielding his. All too late, the Baron recognized a crucial truth: this matter never should have come to a fight at all. If only he had chosen a different Relic all those years before, he would have been quicker to see the Vizier for what he was. But the Baron had foregone Wisdom in favor of the Sword... and now his time in Overtwixt would be cut short by a sword.

Stepping into the Baron's very next attack, the Vizier used his saber to block a Sword thrust, then grabbed and *twisted* the Baron's wrist with his free hand. The Baron yelped and dropped his magnificent Diamond Sword. Within moments, he was being forced to his knees, dark creatures standing on either side to hold him in place.

The Vizier wiped a single trickle of sweat from his forehead and flicked it aside. He sheathed his saber before picking up the Baron's fallen Sword, inspecting it briefly, then shoving it through a loop in his own belt. The diamond blade's blue glow slowly faded.

"Now... what was I saying?" he asked the Baron with a cocky smile. "Ah, yes. You're a fool." His eyes shined victoriously as he stared down at the Baron. "But I *am* grateful to you—for all you've done over the years to advance my plans, *and* for your actions tonight. By delivering yourself into my hands, you've saved me a great deal of trouble."

The Baron shook his head. "I *was* a fool," he agreed. "But no longer."

The Vizier stroked the pointy black beard on his chin, studying his captive for a moment. Then he looked up, over the Baron's head. "You," he ordered one of his minions. "Fetch me a blank."

"Yes, my lord!" the creature cried, scurrying toward the laboratory.

The Vizier turned back to the Baron. "You mentioned my experiments. Well, before I eject you from my new empire, I think it only fitting that you be allowed to experience the harvesting process for yourself." He smiled. "From you... I will take your ability to inspire loyalty in others. It's the only worthwhile attribute you have, sadly."

"My lord Vizier!" the minion cried, returning to the room. "They're... they're gone!"

"*What's* gone?" the Vizier replied in annoyance.

"Your amulets—the blanks *and* the infused ones. They're gone, all of them!"

"What?!" the Vizier roared.

The Baron began to laugh quietly. "I believe you'll find your notebooks destroyed as well—everything you need to create new amulets, gone." The Baron felt like a great weight had been lifted from his shoulders. "This much, at least, I can do for the people of Overtwixt."

"But how?" the Vizier demanded. Then he whirled suddenly, looking straight at the open stained-glass window. He spun to face the Baron again.

"Who's the fool now?" the Baron asked quietly.

"All of you, out!" the Vizier shouted furiously. "Take to the skies. Chase down the traitor responsible for this disaster. Bring me back those amulets!" The various dark creatures moved to obey, flooding toward the open window, but the Vizier caught one of the dragon-like beasts by his huge arm. "Not you. *You* will fly to Huland. Destroy the final bridge."

"But what about this one?" the beast asked, indicating the Baron.

"Fear not. His story will come to an end long before you get there," the Vizier assured his minion. "Now go, and waste no time. Close the portal as soon as you arrive. Do this thing, and I will make you supreme commander over *all* my forces—I will name you *Warlord*."

The hulking, dragon-like creature smiled, revealing pointy teeth. "Yes, my master." And then he was squeezing through the window to fly after all the others. When he was gone, no one remained but the two humans and the lackeys who held the Baron's arms.

The Vizier turned back to the Baron, angry. "You think you've accomplished something here? One final act of heroism and sacrifice?" he spat. "This is just a temporary setback. I'm only annoyed that I cannot harvest your ability before you go."

The Baron smiled sadly. "For all your intelligence, that's the one thing you've never understood. We are more than our raw skills and abilities. We're defined by the *choices* we make, the *way* we use the talents we've been given."

The Vizier swept his cloak behind himself, freeing his sword arm and drawing his saber again. He raised the elegant blade high.

The Baron shook his head. "Even if you stole my leadership ability for yourself, you could never use it to its greatest potential. Because there is no love in your heart— only evil."

The Vizier ignored his words, smiling wickedly. "Enjoy being nobody again," he spat, then swung his blade in one smooth sweep.

The Baron lowered his balding head, an expression of peace and acceptance on his face as the sword struck him. In an instant, he was transported back where he came from all those decades before, leaving nothing behind except a small cloud of yellow smoke.

Part I
Questions

◇

The Children and their Guide

· one ·

(Cécilie)

Cécilie Ollivaros held on for dear life, afraid she might lose her balance and fall—which would be *very* embarrassing. She and her family were deep below the airport in Atlanta, Georgia, riding the underground train that carried travelers rapidly from one terminal to another. It was not a very smooth ride. Not for an 8-year-old, at least.

As she waited for the tense ride to end, she tried to distract herself by watching the people on the train around her. The nearest ones were all members of Cécilie's family:* Mom and Daddy, who seemed almost as nervous as she was, but probably because the family was late for its plane flight; her older brother Nachton, who had his nose in a book like always; her older sister Amélie, who was peering just as intently at the screen of her cell

---

* Find pronunciation clues in the Glossary on page 271. The names of the Ollivaros kids are pronounced:
  1. **NAWK-tuhn** (Nachton)
  2. **AWM-uh-lee** (Amélie)
  3. **SESS-ill-lee** (Cécilie)
  4. **YOO-wun** (Ewan)

phone; and finally, Cécilie's younger brother Ewan, who caught her looking and smiled back instantly.

Ewan was only 5, but as soon as he realized he had an audience, he cried, "Watch dis, Sessy!" Ripping his hand free of Mom's, he began stumbling toward Cécilie, pretending like he was walking on a balance beam at the playground— even though the train was bouncing and swaying. Cécilie giggled at his antics, but Daddy yelled at Ewan to "come back and hold Mommy's hand!" Then Daddy got upset at Cécilie just for laughing!

On the other side of Mom and Daddy was a family they didn't know, a mother and father with just *one* child, a girl around Cécilie's age. Cécilie wondered what it was like to be that girl. She was beautiful, with long blonde hair and bright blue eyes, and she didn't have to share her parents with three siblings. Cécilie supposed she didn't mind sharing; she loved her brothers and sister, even if they made her angry sometimes. But she would *die* to have blue eyes like that blonde girl.

Sighing, Cécilie turned the other direction and saw another girl, this one taller and older. She looked totally different from the first, with chocolate-colored skin and elaborate braids in her hair. This girl's eyes were almost green—no, what was the word for that color? *Hazel.* And she didn't have a single freckle on that beautiful skin...

"Cécilie!" Amélie hissed. "Stop staring!"

Cécilie stuck out her tongue. Even Amélie was beautiful, though she had the same straight brown hair and brown eyes as Cécilie. Cécilie's looks were just *boring*.

And this ride was taking forever. So Cécilie decided to pass the time by making jokes. At least *she* thought they were funny, even if they were meant to embarrass Nachton and Amélie, just a little. But her siblings ignored her, as usual, and she got in trouble with Daddy *again*. Then the whole family accused her of being a drama queen!

Cécilie folded her arms and huffed.

(Cécilie)

When Mom and Daddy finally finished lecturing her, Daddy tried to get everyone else's attention. "Listen up, kids. We're late for our next flight, so we'll need to run. As soon as the tram stops, we'll go straight out that door and up the escalator, then run all the way to Gate 3. You got it?"

Cécilie looked at her older brother and sister, but they were ignoring Daddy just like they ignored her, still focused on their book and phone.

"Cécilie!" Daddy said, "are you listening?"

She opened her mouth, but she wasn't sure what to say. Of *course* she was listening.

"This is important, Cécilie. I need you to listen when I talk. We cannot be late for this flight!"

Cécilie bit her lip to keep it from trembling. This was so unfair. She was the only kid who *was* listening. Nachton and Amélie certainly weren't, and Ewan's attention span didn't last longer than five words.

She didn't get a chance to say any of this, however, because that's when the train slowed to a stop and the door slid open. "Okay, let's go!" Daddy cried.

All six members of the Ollivaros family dashed from the train. Daddy took hold of Cécilie's hand as they began running up the escalator, and that made her feel a little better. It seemed like he was usually disappointed with her, for one reason or another, but Cécilie knew he loved her very much.

Then they reached the top of the escalator, and she didn't have time to do more thinking. They began to run *hard*, and even Nachton and Amélie focused on running instead of books or phones.

They passed airplane gates on both the left and the right, and Cécilie counted down the numbers as they ran: Gate 18... Gate 16... Gate 15... The even-numbered gates were on their right, the odd-numbered on their left. There was Gate 14, and... wow. They had to go all the way to Gate *3?*

"I don't think I can make it!" Cécilie gasped. "Go on without me!"

"C'mon, Cécilie, keep up!" Daddy said.   He was practically dragging her along. "You're slowing us down!"

"Yeah, *Cécilie*," Nachton added. "You don't wanna get left behind." He smiled at her in that way she didn't like, as if he was about to make fun of her. "If you're left behind, you'll probably be *kidnapped*—"

"Nachton!" Daddy said angrily.

"What?" Nachton asked innocently. "It's true!   They keep making announcements over the speakers. There are two kids missing in the airport, one of them since this morning, and I *bet* they got kidnap—"

"You're not helping, Nachton."

Nachton made a face, but of course no one saw it but Cécilie.

"Just a little bit farther, princess," Daddy told her. So she gritted her teeth and tried to run faster.

Gates 12 and 11... Gate 10... the Ollivaros family was getting there. Daddy released Cécilie's hand, and they all just focused on their running and breathing.   Gate 7, Gate 6...

Cécilie saw it! Gate 3—all the way at the very end of the terminal, near the back left corner. Why did it have to be at the very *end?*

There was an airline employee standing at the doorway to Gate 3, a man with a beard, wearing a blue uniform. Cécilie knew from their last flight that this was the person who would look at their tickets and decide whether they were allowed to get on the plane. As Cécilie's family got closer, the bearded gate agent noticed them running in his direction, and he smiled. He began waving urgently, and Cécilie put on a final burst of speed, grabbing Ewan's hand and running on ahead of the family with all her remaining strength.

The man in the uniform waved them through the open doorway, and Cécilie slowed to a fast walk as she entered a narrow hallway, breathing hard. The plane should be at the other end of this corridor, but she didn't want to slow down *too* much. Cécilie had learned that these hallways, which were called "jet bridges," were actually capable of moving— on *wheels*. If her family didn't keep going, she was afraid the jet bridge would be rolled away from the plane and they would miss their flight after all.

Cécilie turned a corner and almost ran into a red-headed boy a little older than Amélie. He looked dizzy, walking unsteadily towards her with one hand on the wall. Cécilie pulled Ewan out of the way and stepped around the boy... but Amélie didn't notice him in time.

Amélie's eyes were already glued to her phone screen again, and she walked right into the red-headed boy. They both yelled in surprise and fell to the floor—even as Nachton came around the corner, *his* attention already on his *book* again. *He* tripped and landed on top of the boy and Amélie. Their backpacks, book, and phone went flying in every direction.

"Quickly, quickly!" the bearded gate agent said, coming up behind them all, helping the kids to their feet. "It's almost too late!" Nachton and Amélie collected their stuff from the floor as fast as they could, and the red-headed boy kept going the other direction, toward the inside of the airport. The gate agent saw Cécilie watching and winked at her.

Cécilie smiled and turned to begin running again, Ewan's hand still clutched in hers.

She stopped almost immediately. There was something very strange going on here. For one thing, she could see the other end of the bridge now, but there was no plane parked there. Had they missed their flight after all? No, this bridge... that was the other strange thing. It didn't even *look* like a jet bridge anymore. The walls were gone, leaving nothing but *rope* as railings to keep the kids from tumbling over the sides. And the floor had changed from carpet to *wooden planks*.

"*Go*, Cécilie!" Nachton said angrily as he pushed her from behind. Meanwhile, Amélie sounded like she was on the verge of tears, complaining that her phone screen had gotten cracked when she ran into that strange boy.

Ewan tested one of the wooden planks, a delighted smile on his face. "Cool-awesome-neat!" he decided. "C'mon, Sessy!" Then he ripped his hand from her grip and started bouncing rapidly down the bridge away from her.

The entire bridge began swaying dangerously from side to side, causing Nachton and Amélie both to yell in alarm. Cécilie hurried after her little brother, even as Amélie called after them. "Ewan, Cécilie, wait!" She sounded scared— *really* scared—and Cécilie wondered if this was the first time she'd looked up from her phone long enough to see that their surroundings had changed.

Cécilie caught up with Ewan at the other end of the bridge, stepping off the last wooden plank and collapsing onto a blanket of soft grass beside her little brother—who was rolling around in that grass, squealing with delight. Chest heaving, Cécilie tried to catch her breath as she stared up at a majestic mountain towering over them. Behind that peak, the sky was solid white.

"What in the *world?*" Nachton breathed, dropping to his knees beside her. "There are no mountains in the Atlanta airport!"

Amélie joined them, eyes wide with fear. "Nachton?" she asked quietly. "Where are we? And... where are Mom and Dad?"

Cécilie heard the clip-clop of hooves on the rope bridge behind them—like the sound a horse makes when trotting—and everyone turned to look. There was no sign of Mom or Daddy, but the gate agent was stepping off the bridge behind them, and he looked very different now.

"Good morning, and welcome to Overtwixt!" the bearded man said... except he was no longer a *man* at all.

Cécilie still recognized him as the gate agent, but he wasn't wearing his blue uniform anymore; he was now a *horse*, with only the top half of a man's body coming out of the horse's neck where a horse head should have been! Cécilie stared in wonder, while her mind tried to understand. There was a word for this kind of creature. Her older brother had talked all about them when he studied Greek mythology in school. If only she could remember—

"You're a centaur!" Nachton blurted.

The tall man-horse nodded. "Now hurry, we don't have much time. Everyone back on your feet!"

The children just stared at him with wide eyes. Amélie tried to say something, but no sound came out. She ripped her gaze away from the strange creature and looked back down the rope bridge, but there was still no sign of Mom or Daddy, no sign of the airport at all. The bridge just faded to nothingness in the distance, like it was disappearing into a cloud. "We're going back, right?" Amélie asked finally, her voice as scared as Cécilie had ever heard it. "We need to find Mom and Dad—"

A terrible roar came from above, and everyone looked up—to see a *dragon* swooping out of the white sky!

Amélie stumbled away from the bridge, and Nachton fell over backwards in surprise. The half-man/half-horse turned as well, moving to place himself between the children and the flying creature, but the dragon didn't seem to notice any of them. Its attention was focused entirely on the bridge. It swooped down like it was going to land somewhere in the middle, but instead it grabbed hold of the ropes with both its muscular forearms. With another roar that sounded victorious, the dragon swept its powerful wings forwards, *heaving—*

And the ropes holding the rickety bridge together began to snap.

Just like that, before Cécilie could even scream, the bridge back to the airport—the bridge back to their *parents—* collapsed into the endless nothingness below. Leaving the children stranded here...

Wherever *here* was.

· two ·

(Nachton)

"Quickly," the centaur said, "get into the trees before you're spotted." His voice was strained as he watched the dragon, which wheeled around in midair to inspect its handiwork. "Quickly now!"

Nachton didn't need to be told a third time. Coming face to face with a centaur was one thing. Facing a *dragon* was something else entirely. Seizing hold of Ewan, he picked him up and *ran*. "C'mon!" he hissed. "Cécilie, Amélie, let's *go!*"

Amélie grabbed Cécilie's hand and followed as Nachton dashed for the trees at the base of the mountain. It was a good thing they didn't have far to run because Nachton was still tired from their race through the airport, and Ewan was a *heavy* little chunk.

Nachton ran several feet into the forest and dropped his brother behind a bush, then lay down quickly beside him. The girls joined them a moment later.

"What's going on?" Amélie demanded. She looked like she might start crying at any moment— and if *she* started crying, Cécilie definitely would too. "Was that a dragon? Where *are* we?"

"I don't know, okay?" Nachton hissed back at her. He was trying to see through the branches of the bush, to get a look at what was happening with the centaur and the dragon. "Now be quiet!"

Amélie wanted to argue—she *always* wanted to argue—but thank goodness, this time she didn't. Even

(Nachton)

Cécilie and Ewan stayed quiet, eyes wide with fear.

The centaur still stood on the grassy field between the forest and the chasm the bridge had fallen into. The half-man/half-horse cut a regal figure, chin held high, arms clasped calmly behind his human back... even though the dragon had landed and was now looming over him. The two fantasy creatures were talking, Nachton realized; it was too far away to hear what they were saying, but from the way the dragon was smiling and licking his long fangs, Nachton doubted it was a friendly chat.

They did not talk long. When they were done, the centaur nodded respectfully to the beast and turned to walk calmly toward where the children were hiding in the forest. The dragon flapped its powerful wings and leapt back into the sky. Nachton got his first good look at the creature and realized it wasn't a dragon at all, but... something else. Something more like a bat—a *huge* bat—but with muscular forearms and a long, sinuous tail, its whole body covered with midnight-black fur.

Nachton's siblings started jabbering questions almost immediately, but he shushed them. Bats had excellent hearing, and he guessed that any creature with a bat-like body would have sensitive ears too.

Nachton thought he had picked a good hiding place, but the centaur must have seen them anyway, because he walked straight towards them. "Quickly," he said again, his voice very soft. "Come with me. Speak not; make no noise at all." Without asking, he reached down and picked up both Cécilie and Ewan, one child in each of his thick human arms. Twisting at the waist, he set them down on his back, letting them ride like he was a normal horse. He said nothing further, just kept walking calmly, deeper and deeper into the forest.

"But—wait!" Amélie whispered furiously. "Where are we going? Who *are* you? We—we need to go back *that* way. We need to get back to our parents!"

"The bridge to your home is destroyed, young huwoman," the centaur said. He didn't stop moving, but he did glance over his shoulder and give her a sad smile.

"Can't we repair it?" she asked, and Nachton felt like rolling his eyes. As if it would be that simple.

The centaur stopped and offered Amélie a patient smile. "Take a good look back there, then tell me if you really want to return and begin a construction project today."

All four of the children turned and looked back through the trees, to find that the dragon-creature was no longer alone. It had been joined by dozens of... gargoyles? Hairy, gray man-shaped creatures with bat-like wings of their own, though Nachton was too far away to get a good look at them. The gray bat-men were swooping in circles above the site of the destroyed bridge, where they began to yell and whoop and *sing*. They were clearly celebrating, and yet the sound of their music—very soft, because of the distance—was enough to raise goose bumps on Nachton's arms.

Amélie swallowed so hard that Nachton was able to hear *that* too.

"They are quite excited about destroying your bridge," the centaur said quietly. "But that's nothing compared to what would happen if they saw *you*. You would be in chains before you knew it, then flown away to meet their dark master."

"But they let *you* get away," Amélie blurted.

"I am no threat to them, or so they think," the centaur said softly. "Just another citizen of Overtwixt. But you four are human, like their master—who has plotted for many years to make himself the *only* human in the land. Your arrival threatens to undermine all he has worked to achieve." The centaur cocked his head. "*Now* do you understand the danger you're in?"

Nachton and Amélie shared a look, and Amélie shivered visibly.

"Good," the centaur concluded. "Now please, for your own sakes, be silent until we put more distance between ourselves and those creatures of the night."

Amazingly, every one of the four children did exactly as the centaur asked.

· three ·

(Amélie)

mélie and Nachton followed the strange creature for so long it felt like hours, hurrying between trees and bushes and making as little noise as possible. Following him was the only choice they had, as far as Amélie could see. He was carrying Ewan and Cécilie, and besides, he at least *pretended* to be nice. Those flying creatures, on the other hand...

Amélie shivered again.

Almost everything about this place scared her. It was bad enough that the kids were lost in the woods without their parents, following a stranger who wasn't even human. She had no idea how they even *got* here; they definitely weren't in Atlanta anymore! What was worse, she had lost her cell phone and backpack somewhere along the way. She thought maybe she'd dropped them... until she discovered she wasn't even wearing the same *clothes* anymore. All four children were now wearing stiff woolen trousers and rough-spun tunics. The colors were about the same as their old clothes, but the style looked like something out of an old storybook. And Amélie's siblings had lost their backpacks too. Amélie began to wonder if *anything* from home had made it across the bridge aside from the four Ollivaros children themselves.

They had not traveled far through the trees before Amélie was breathing hard, only partly from fear. This was no easy stroll, like the walks her family sometimes took through their neighborhood. This was a *hike*. The farther they went, the higher they climbed up the forested slope of the mountain they had seen when they first arrived.

"Can we stop, please?" Amélie asked finally, and Nachton nodded eagerly.

The tall man-horse nodded. "There's a good place up ahead."

A few minutes later, they stepped out into a small clearing and the man-horse—the *centaur*, Nachton had called him—came to a halt. Cécilie immediately slid down from his back, but Ewan had somehow fallen asleep, face buried in the braided mane that grew from the centaur's human back. Nachton collapsed to the ground, trying to catch his breath, but Amélie faced off against the strange creature. "I think it's time we got some answers," she declared, voice wavering only slightly.

The centaur did not react at all to Amélie's challenging tone. He simply nodded his head, with the same polite respect he had showed the dragon earlier. "Very well. What would you like to know?"

Amélie licked her lips. "What did you call this place? Overtwick?"

"Overtwixt*," he corrected her gently. "The world of bridges, where all parallel universes intersect."

Nachton sat up, suddenly looking very interested. "We're in an alternate *dimension?*"

---

* See complete Glossary of Persons, Places, and Things on page 271.

"Not quite," the centaur said with a smile. "You're in a place where men and women *from* alternate dimensions can come together. *You* cannot travel to a parallel world any more than someone from that world can travel to yours. That is why Overtwixt exists—so you can meet in the middle."

Amélie felt dizzy just hearing all these words, none of which made sense to her. Nachton sucked in a breath to ask another question—something scientific, she was sure—but she spoke first. "Who cares? I want to know how and *why* we're here!"

"You passed through one of the portals in your real world," the centaur explained, "then crossed the human bridge into Overtwixt."

"We... *what?*" Amélie demanded. "We didn't pass through any portals. We were at the airport... we went through Gate 3, because that's where our plane was boarding."

"What is a gate, if not a portal from one place to another?" the centaur asked. "However... it was actually the Pi Gate you passed through, just *next* to Gate 3." He said this with a twinkle in his eye, a playful smile on his lips. "And so you find yourselves here, rather than on your plane."

(Amélie)

"Pie?" Ewan asked suddenly from the centaur's back. "*I* want pie!" Apparently, just hearing that word was enough to wake him from the deepest sleep.

"Oooh, I get it," Nachton said, ignoring his little brother. "*Pi*. Roughly equal to 3.14—that *would* be very close to Gate 3."

"*I* don't get it," Cécilie complained.

"You wouldn't," Nachton said with a cocky smile. "It's a math thing." At least *he* was acting like his normal self, even if nothing about this situation was normal.

"There no pie?" Ewan asked, getting upset now. "But I *hungy*—"

"Can we please get back to the point?" Amélie said impatiently, her voice cracking with emotion. Was *no one* else terrified that they were in this strange place with this strange creature?

The centaur's smile faded, and he nodded seriously. "Very well. You want to know why you're here? I invited you here, because Overtwixt needs you." He took a deep breath and seemed to grow even more serious. "You see, a great evil has overtaken this realm."

Amélie glanced at Nachton and found her own fear mirrored in his eyes. Cécilie hugged herself, like she was suddenly cold, and stepped closer to Amélie. Ewan...

Ewan had broken two sticks from a low-hanging tree branch. Completely ignoring the conversation around him, the 5-year-old was narrating an epic swordfight under his breath, banging the sticks violently against each other like they were held by enemy swordsmen.

The centaur went on with his explanation. "A man known as the Vizier has seized control of this realm, destroying all bridges back to reality and stranding every person left behind—forcing many of

(Ewan)

them into slavery. Your human bridge was only the most recent to be destroyed." He nodded towards Amélie. "You asked before about rebuilding your bridge, and that is exactly what must be done if you ever hope to return home. But the Vizier will never allow it, not while he rules in Overtwixt.

"Your mission, therefore—and the reason I brought you here—is to overthrow the Vizier," the centaur concluded. "That way, *all* the bridges can be rebuilt and *everyone* can go home, not just you."

There was a long silence following this pronouncement, and Amélie felt her fear growing. "Just to make sure I understand," she said with as much calm as possible, "you're saying that the bridge, the one the... dragon... destroyed"—she swallowed convulsively—"was the only way to get back to our parents."

The centaur nodded.

"And there are no other bridges?"

"There are no other bridges that go back to the real world, no," he confirmed.

"And if we try rebuilding our bridge"—not that Amélie had the first clue how to do such a thing, she was forced to admit—"we're gonna get arrested."

The centaur nodded again.

"By dragons and bat-people, who work for an evil tyrant."

"That is a fair summary of the situation, yes," the centaur said gravely. "Which is why you must first overthrow the Vizier and end his reign of terror."

Amélie sat down carefully on the ground, lowered her head, and hugged herself closely.

Nachton cleared his throat. "What exactly does that mean, overthrowing the Vizier?"

The centaur turned to face the oldest Ollivaros child. "Exactly what it sounds like. Only you four, working together, are capable of fighting back and defeating this villain."

Ewan gasped loudly enough that Amélie jumped to her feet, looking around for some new danger. But the little boy was just reacting to what the centaur said; of course the prospect of *fighting* sounded fun to him. He had dropped his sticks and was sitting up straight on the centaur's back now, listening very intently. At least Cécilie's reaction made more sense; she was staring at the centaur with her mouth hanging open.

"But... why *us?*" Amélie asked in a begging tone. "What's so special about *us?*"

The centaur smiled gently. "Everything... and nothing. Each one of you is special, no more or less than any other person from any world. However, the Vizier came from *your* world, which makes you four uniquely qualified to face him. You are exactly what Overtwixt needs in this time of peril."

"And why should we trust *you?*" Amélie demanded angrily. In truth, part of her wanted to trust him, but she didn't want to believe what he was saying. His words scared her... and Amélie often got angry when she was scared. "We don't even know you."

The centaur twisted at the waist and took Ewan from his back, setting him gently on the ground. Then the half-man/half-horse backed away several steps and knelt forward on his front horse legs, spreading his human arms to either side in an elaborate bow. "Allow me to introduce myself, then. I am the Guide," he said, "and I am genuinely delighted to make your acquaintance."

Ewan shrugged and started climbing a nearby tree, but Nachton and Cécilie turned to look at Amélie. She had taken the lead in asking the centaur all these questions, even though Nachton was the oldest. They wanted to see what she would say next.

"The *Guide?*" Amélie demanded. "Do you have a real name?"

"Many, in fact." The centaur cocked his head to the side. "But in this place, *what* you are matters more than the name people call you. And *what* I am, at this moment, is your Guide."

The sheer strangeness of this whole situation threatened to overwhelm her. "Our guide," Amélie repeated dumbly. "Like a tour guide?"

The half-man/half-horse chuckled. "If you wish, though my responsibilities are considerably more substantial than giving tours."

"I don't want a tour, and certainly not from a half-horse freak that can't possibly exist!" Amélie blurted. "I just want to go home!" And she buried her face in her hands.

Of course Nachton had to correct her again, as usual. "I told you before, Amélie. He's a *centaur*."

The centaur cleared his throat. "That's… not quite true, young human. Certainly, your world has legends of creatures who look like this, and you call them centaurs. But no such creature has ever set foot on your world. As I told you earlier, no man or woman can ever visit a parallel universe." He shook his head. "Many of your myths were inspired by tales brought back from Overtwixt by visitors such as yourselves. In *this* place, the very real people who look like me are called centmen and centwomen. Just as you four are called humen and huwomen."

Nachton gave the tall creature a strange look. "You mean human men and women," he corrected. "I've never heard anyone say *humen* or *huwomen*."

The centaur... or centman... or Guide—whoever or *whatever* he was—didn't respond to Nachton's correction. He only smiled.

Amélie tried to control her frustration and panic. First Nachton was concerned with scientific explanations; now he wanted to talk grammar or vocab or whatever? "We're not men *or* women," she interrupted. "We're just kids."

That made Nachton flush angrily. "Speak for yourself, you preteen brat. *I'm* already learning to drive a car—"

"Peace, young human," the Guide told Nachton, raising a hand. He was still half kneeling before the children; now he folded his back legs and settled the rest of the way to the ground, bringing himself much closer to Amélie's level. "You are wise not to trust strangers," he told her. "Caution is always warranted, especially in this place, during these difficult times. I suppose you will have to decide for yourself whether or not to trust me... or the things I'm about to tell you."

There was so much seriousness in the Guide's voice, Amélie felt her own eyes get even wider. It wasn't enough that the four kids were stranded in this strange place, separated from Mom and Dad, and tasked with overthrowing an evil ruler. Now this centman had *more* to tell them, and he thought it might be harder to believe than what he'd already told them!?

Whatever it was, it would have to wait... because Ewan chose that moment to start shouting from up in his tree.

· four ·

(Cécilie)

Cécilie climbed up next to Ewan in the tree, making room on the branch for Amélie too. Nachton climbed another tree nearby, and then everyone stared at the thing Ewan had seen.

"Is... is that... a *floating island?*" Cécilie asked in amazement.

"Are those *horseys* on the floaty island?" Ewan asked in excitement.

"Are *we* on a floating island too?" Amélie asked in horror.

The Guide laughed and smiled at their questions. "Yes, yes, and yes," he answered all three. "All of Overtwixt is made up of these floating islands," he explained, "which we call *nilands*.* And that's also why we call Overtwixt the world of bridges—because bridges are the only way to get around!" His smile was huge as he winked at Ewan. "And we don't call them horses here, young human. They may look like the horses from your world, but horses are just animals. These creatures—the

---

* See complete Glossary of Persons, Places, and Things on page 271.

ones you see galloping around on that niland over there—are eqmen. And they're people like you, capable of thinking and talking."

Cécilie couldn't believe her eyes. Apparently Nachton couldn't either. "When we crossed over that rope bridge earlier," he said slowly, "I thought we were just really high up. All the whiteness I saw below the bridge... I assumed it was the tops of clouds!" He shook his head and pointed at the floating island. "But this—it's impossible!"

Cécilie didn't know much about science, but she had to agree. Then again, she was looking at the proof, wasn't she? A big grassy field full of horses, with trees on one side and boulders on the other, and beyond that... *emptiness*, all around. It's like the grass and trees and boulders were on top of a big cliff, but there was nothing at the *bottom* of the cliff. It just... floated.

"Overtwixt need not obey the physical laws you are used to," the Guide explained. "This is not truly a physical place, after all; Overtwixt is a conceptual realm only."

Nachton could only keep staring, muttering the word "impossible" under his breath.

Cécilie looked back at the Guide again, and found him watching *her*. "It's known as Eqland," he said with a smile. "That floating island, I mean. We call it *Eq*-land because it's the port niland of the *eq*-men, those creatures that look like horses." The Guide stomped a hoof and pointed at the ground below them. "In much the same way, the niland we stand upon right now is called *Hu*-land, because it's the portland of you *hu*-men."

"What's that over there?" Amélie asked in an unsteady voice, pointing down the mountain the four kids were on, at a path running through the trees. Cécilie followed the path with her eyes, all the way to a big bridge.

"That," the Guide answered, "is the bridge linking Huland with Eqland."

And what a beautiful bridge it was, carved entirely from brown marble and lined with sculptures on top of the railings: human statues on one side, horse statues on the other. Unlike the bridge they'd crossed earlier, this bridge started halfway up the mountain, because the island it connected to floated higher in the air than *this* island did.

"I thought you said all the bridges were destroyed?" Amélie asked.

"All of the bridges back to the real worlds, yes," the Guide responded. "Fortunately, many of the bridges *between* nilands remain intact."

"What's *that?*" Amélie asked again, now pointing a different direction. "Buildings? Are there people there?"

Again, Cécilie looked where her sister was pointing. The island they were on—Huland—stretched away out of sight, too big to see all at once, but Cécilie could make out another mountain in the distance. In between that mountain and this one was a forest valley, and in the middle of the woods was a group of buildings, just like Amélie said.

"No," the Guide said apologetically, "there are no people there. If you'll recall what I told you before, there are no other humen in all of Overtwixt, save for yourselves and the Vizier." Amélie's excitement died. "But those buildings you see there," he added enthusiastically, "are the famed towers of the Grand Library of Huland."

The word *library* got Nachton's attention again.

"Oh yes," the Guide told him with a sly smile. "The Grand Library of Huland is the most complete repository of human knowledge in all the cosmos, either here *or* in your world. It was once rivaled by your Royal Library of Alexandria, but—"

Nachton's eyes got big. "The Library of Alexandria? It burned down two thousand years ago!"

The Guide nodded. "That was a great shame. So many priceless works of antiquity lost. Fortunately, most of that knowledge survives in the ancient texts stored here."

Nachton's eyes got even bigger. "Can we go there next? The Library?"

"I wanna see da horseys!" Ewan interrupted loudly.

"Are you *kidding me?!*" Amélie shrieked. "We're a million miles from Mom and Dad, *floating* on *islands* that could fall out of the sky at any moment, and you guys want to go *sightseeing?*" She was gripping the tree trunk so hard it made her fingers white. "Focus, guys, *please.*"

"There will be time for exploring Overtwixt soon," the Guide promised calmly, "but your sister is correct. There is a matter of great importance we must address first."

"Yeah," Amélie said. "Like how exactly a bunch of kids is supposed to overthrow this Vizier guy so we can go home." She even laughed as she said the words, but Cécilie knew her sister was on the verge of losing control... and that scared Cécilie more than anything that had happened so far.

The Guide did not answer Amélie's question, however. Instead, he got all official-sounding. "Humen and huwomen, visitors to Overtwixt," he intoned. "Before you proceed, you must each make a decision."

"*What* decision?" Amélie moaned.

"The same decision every visitor faces, the first time he or she sets foot in Overtwixt." The Guide looked around at each of them in turn. "Who will YOU choose to be?"

· five ·

(Nachton)

Nachton knew instinctively what the Guide meant, and he felt a powerful excitement in his belly. They got to choose what roles they would play here? This place was starting to sound exactly like an RPG, his favorite type of video game—the kind where he chose his character, picked out his clothes and gear, and led his squad into battle. Except this place was even better, because it was *real*. Amélie might be freaking out right now, but as far as Nachton was concerned, this trip through the Pi Gate might just be the best thing that ever happened to him.

Hopping out of his tree, Nachton helped the girls down from theirs. They were being very quiet, but Ewan seemed just as excited as Nachton. With no warning at all, the little boy flung himself out of the tree in a maneuver that would've broken both his legs if Nachton hadn't caught him in time.

The centman eyed each of the children in turn, stopping finally on the youngest. Ewan was literally jumping up and down, giggling.

"Ewan Ollivaros," the Guide intoned seriously. "Three paths stand before you. Will you be the Swashbuckler, the Knight, or the General?"

Ewan's excitement turned to confusion, and he looked at his older brother. "What a sosh— sosh—?" He struggled to pronounce the word.

Nachton traded a glance with the Guide. "A swashbuckler is kinda like a pirate."

Ewan got excited again. "And... um... da uvver one?"

"The other one? You mean the general? That's the person in charge of an army. He orders troops around, telling them who to fight."

"Do gen-rals get to fight too?"

Nachton glanced at the Guide once more, but the Guide didn't say anything. "Um... no," he told his brother. "Generals don't usually fight personally."

"But *knights* fight." Ewan looked from Nachton to the Guide with a mischievous smile on his lips. "And knights get horseys and armor and *swords*. Right? *Right?*"

The Guide chuckled. "Yes, young human. If you choose to become the Knight, one of the quests you undertake will be to earn a sword and armor—"

"*Shiny* armor?"

"Yes—"

"And do *soshbuckles* get shiny armor?"

"Well, no—"

"I wanna be da knight!" Ewan decided.

The Guide studied the little boy for a moment. "This is a momentous decision. Be sure you give it adequate thought before—"

"Da knight!" Ewan insisted. "I wanna be da knight!"

"Very well," the centman said solemnly, but Nachton could tell he was smiling on the inside. "I hereby recognize you as the Knight. Bear this responsibility wisely."

The Guide turned to Cécilie next. "Cécilie Ollivaros, three paths stand before you. Will you be the Princess—"

"The princess!" Cécilie blurted. "I want to be the princess. All I've *ever* wanted to be was a princess."

"But—"

"The princess," she said again, her voice firm and her eyes fiery—as if daring the centman to argue.

The Guide almost couldn't hide his smile this time. "Very well. Bear this responsibility wisely."

He turned to Amélie, and his expression grew serious again. "Amélie Ollivaros, three paths stand before you, and your choice will be difficult."

"I'm sorry," she interrupted, "but why does this matter? I just want to *go home.*"

"It matters," the Guide explained, "because who you choose to be will impact how you fight the Vizier."

Amélie wrestled with her emotions for a long moment, then took a deep breath and nodded jerkily.

"Three paths stand before you," the Guide repeated. "Will you be the Bard, or the Dancer..." He trailed off, giving her a chance to think about her first two options.

"What the heck is a *bard?*" she demanded.

"It's like a minstrel," Nachton explained. Thanks to all the books he had read, not to mention the *many* video games he had played, Nachton was familiar with the term. "They were both types of musicians, in medieval times."

Amélie seemed confused. "But... how could being a musician—or a dancer—help us defeat the Vizier? I mean, a knight can fight," she said, looking at Ewan. "And a princess probably has her own soldiers she can send into battle," she added, looking at Cécilie. "But... what good can a *bard* do?"

The Guide smiled gently. "A purveyor of the arts— whether musician, dancer, painter, writer, or something else—can accomplish things no Princess or Knight ever could. You see, artists have the power to bring joy to many, lifting their spirits. And in this time of darkness and despair, that is more valuable than ever."

Amélie nodded slowly, expression thoughtful but grim. "What's my third choice?"

The Guide met her eyes calmly. "The third path standing before you is that of Empress."

Nachton's eyes bugged out, and Cécilie gasped. "*Empress?*" Amélie asked weakly. "Like... I'd be in charge?"

"If you earned the loyalty of those peoples currently ruled by the Vizier... yes," the Guide agreed. "You have the gifting to be a great leader, if you choose to take that responsibility upon yourself."

Amélie thought this through for a long moment, before the Guide spoke into the silence.

"Please understand something. In normal times, Overtwixt would have no need for an Empress. Overtwixt already *has* a Sovereign, supreme ruler of all the infinite dimensions of the cosmos. But he is distant from the thoughts of most men and women, and some of the bridges the Vizier destroyed were the ones leading from this realm to the rest of Overtwixt—an act of rebellion, to keep the Sovereign's armies from returning to these nilands." The Guide glanced from child to child before returning his gaze to Amélie. "Indeed, the Vizier has named *himself* Emperor of this realm, though he's still just the Vizier. By accepting the mantle of Empress, you would make yourself his rival, someone for the peoples of this realm to rally behind.

"If it helps you make your choice," the centman went on, "the role of Empress is no more important than that of Bard or Dancer; you can do much good in any of these roles. But there is, perhaps, a greater need for an Empress right now than there is for an artist... if you are brave enough to face the greater danger."

Amélie swallowed hard, and Nachton could guess what she was thinking. Of the four Ollivaros children, Amélie was the one who lived most in fear—fear of something happening to herself or the people she loved, fear of what others thought of her. At times, she seemed to jump in fear at the slightest unexpected noise. It was hard to imagine *her* as a fearless Empress, facing down an evil Vizier. She was going to choose Dancer for sure, Nachton knew. She was already a ballet dancer, after all.

"I'll do it," Amélie whispered, to Nachton's absolute shock. "I'll be the Empress, if that's what's needed to get us back home safe."

The Guide nodded gravely and turned toward Nachton. "Nachton Ollivaros, three paths—"

"Wait," Cécilie interrupted. "You're not gonna ask *her* again and again if she's sure, like you did with me and Ewan? You're not gonna tell *her* to take her job seriously?"

The Guide's eyes flicked to Cécilie and back to Amélie, as if measuring her. "No." He turned again toward Nachton. "Nachton Ollivaros, three paths stand before you."

Nachton was almost jittery with anticipation. Hard as it was to believe, his sister was now *Empress* of this place, and the little kids were Princess and Knight. What would that make him? As the oldest and most responsible of the four Ollivaros children, he would have to play the most important role. But what could be more important than the ruler of everything? Some sort of superhero? A magician of awesome power?

The Guide was watching Nachton like he knew exactly what the teenager was thinking. "Nachton Ollivaros, will you choose to be the Medic?"

Nachton blinked. "What?"

"Or perhaps the Sage?"

"*What?*"

Amélie was confused too. "Like... the spice you use in cooking?"

"No!" Nachton turned on her. "Like a person who is very wise. But still—"

"Or will you choose to be the Loremaster?" the Guide concluded, offering Nachton his final option.

Nachton felt himself growing red in the face. "Are you kidding me? These options are garbage. *That* little squirt gets to be a knight in shining armor," he said angrily, pointing at his siblings in turn, "and *those* brats are *royalty*? But you want to shove me into some minor *support* role?"

The Guide held Nachton's gaze evenly, not even a hint of humor in his expression. "And what would you be instead, if you could pick any role you wanted?"

Nachton threw his hands in the air, frustrated. "I don't know! Some sort of mage or sorcerer?"

"Magic interests you," the Guide said, studying Nachton with a discerning gaze. "Magic... and power." He took a deep breath. "Those paths are dangerous. Great power should be wielded with great care, yet many who pursue the easy paths—to fame, riches, power—fall quickly. I would not see you make such mistakes, Nachton Ollivaros. Besides," he shook his head, "Overtwixt already has both a Sorcerer and a Mage, whether they still answer to those names or not. *They* pursued magic as an end instead of a means, and the example they set is not one I would wish you to follow."

Nachton was clenching his jaw so hard it hurt. "And if I choose one of those roles anyway?"

"That is not the choice you face." The Guide's expression seemed hard as stone. "Unlike what you were taught growing up, you cannot choose whatever you want to be in life. Rather, life presents you with specific opportunities based on who you are and what the world needs."

"Make me a ruler too, then. I could be King, or—"

"*You*, Nachton Ollivaros, do not have the gifting to be King or Ruler, and the world doesn't need another Sorcerer or Magician." The Guide took a deep breath, then spoke more gently. "But a Medic or Sage? A *Loremaster?* These are very real needs that *you* are equipped to meet. And you will find no greater satisfaction in life than when you're being who you were created to be—instead of trying to be someone you're not. That is a path to misery."

The centman finally stopped, and none of the four children were bold enough to interrupt the sudden silence.

Nachton turned away, hoping no one saw him blushing. "Fine," he muttered. "I'll be the Loremaster then." At least it had 'master' in the name. That had to earn him *some* respect, right?

The Guide nodded gravely. "So be it. I hereby recognize you as the Loremaster. Bear this responsibility wisely."

The centman stepped back to face all four children again. "Your paths have been chosen. I will say it one more time, for all of you: Bear wisely your chosen responsibilities." Abruptly, he smiled. "And know that I am proud of you all."

Amélie spoke hesitantly. "We made the right choices then? The right decisions to get us back home to Mom and Dad?"

"No."

Amélie blinked. "*No?*"

The Guide chuckled. "Not all choices are between right and wrong, or even between good and better. Sometimes, you demonstrate honor not in *what* you choose, but in how you follow through on whichever choice you make. I am proud of you because I know, in the end, you will perform your duties well."

"So now what?" Nachton asked, annoyed and impatient and much less excited about this adventure than he'd been a few minutes ago. "Take on this Vizier guy? Where do we find him, anyway?"

"Trust me when I say you are not yet ready to face him," the centman said. "There is much you must first do to prepare yourselves." He was looking at Nachton as he said this, a twinkle in his eye. "There are... quests... you must undertake."

Nachton perked up a little at this. Quests? Well... that didn't sound so bad.

"Sir Knight," the Guide said to Ewan, "there are three things a knight usually needs, as you already noted—armor to protect, a sword to defend, and a squire to help you bear the load."

"And a horsey!" Ewan blurted. "Knights need horseys!"

The Guide broke into a big smile. "Yes, precisely. Acquire these things and learn the use of them before your family seeks out the Vizier."

Ewan whooped with excitement and began running around like a crazy person, yelling battle cries.

"Princess," the Guide said to Cécilie. "You must win back the throne of Eqland... and you must discover for yourself a truth that no one else can teach you."

Cécilie took a deep breath and nodded, looking only a little confused as she raised her hand. "Eqland?" she asked. "So... I'm the leader of the horses?"

The Guide's eyes were definitely twinkling now. "The horses *and* the unicorns, yes." He tapped the center of his forehead. "Eqwomen grow beautiful horns, which is what gave rise to the legend of unicorns in your world."

Cécilie looked so excited about this that *she* started bouncing up and down on her toes. Ewan gave her a high-five in passing. "Horseys, horseys!" he chanted.

The Guide rested a hand on Amélie's shoulder. "Empress, your quest is both the simplest and the most difficult: you must build trust and loyalty among the peoples of Overtwixt, overcome prejudice, and unite the races beneath your banner. Before the Vizier can be overthrown, oaths must be sworn. But which oaths, and to whom? That is part of your quest to determine."

Amélie nodded, wide-eyed and visibly shaking.

"Finally, Master of Lore..." The Guide focused his gaze on Nachton. "Two things only must you seek: knowledge... and wisdom."

Nachton waited a long moment. "That's it?" he finally asked. "*They* get all sorts of guidance, and all I get is 'knowledge and wisdom'?"

"Yes."

"*Seriously?* That's not even two things. That's like *one* thing."

The Guide cocked his head. "Perhaps, once you've obtained both, you will understand the difference."

Nachton turned away angrily, throwing his hands into the air again.

"Above all," the Guide concluded, speaking now to all the children, "you four must be united in purpose, or your efforts against the Vizier will be in vain."

"Wait!" Amélie cried out suddenly. "Everyone, where's Ewan?"

It *had* been a little too quiet these last few moments. Nachton spun back, looking around quickly, but there was no sign of his little brother. Typical.

"He went that way!" Cécilie said, pointing toward the path they had seen earlier, the one leading down the side of the mountain.

"And you just let him?!" Amélie demanded.

"Way to go, Cécilie," Nachton said, disgusted. "You could've at least said something!"

"I *tried* to tell you—" Cécilie began, but Nachton ignored her, quickly climbing a tree with Amélie so they could search along the path with their eyes. Unfortunately, Ewan wasn't on the path. There *was*, however, a child-sized figure running across the brown marble bridge to Eqland, little legs churning for all they were worth.

"No!" Amélie cried. "Ewan!" she screamed. "Stop!" She whirled on Nachton, as if this was somehow *his* fault. "Where's he going?" she demanded.

"Isn't it obvious?" he shot back. "Eqland."

"But why!?"

"Well, let me think," Nachton said sarcastically. "The Guide practically told him to, remember? He's the *Knight*. He needs to get himself a *horse*."

Amélie scowled back at him. "He's only five, Nachton." She whirled again. "Cécilie, stay here with Nachton. Don't you move, either of you!" And with that, Amélie dropped out of the tree. Then *she* bolted down the path to the bridge, chasing after their little brother.

· six ·

(Ewan)

Ewan ran across the big brown bridge as fast as his little legs could carry him. Guide Guy said he could have a horsey of his own, and there was no time to waste.

He stared in surprise when he got to the other side, because the grass here was taller than he was! But Ewan didn't let that stop him. He picked a direction, and the grass let him through easy enough.

It wasn't long before he stumbled out of the tall grass next to a dark red horsey with black legs. "Good heavens!" it shrieked. Ewan tried to pet the horsey, but it reared up on its back legs. "Little man!" it screamed, then ran away.

Other voices began crying out in alarm all across the field of grass. Ewan didn't know much about horseys, but these horseys seemed to make very un-horsey noises. "Little man! Little man in the herd!" one voice screamed. "Run for your lives!" shouted another.

A unee-corn ran past. It was shaped just like a horsey, with a white body and long pink hair, except it had a *horn* of course. Where was Sessy? She would think this was *so* awesome-cool.

The unee-corn* saw Ewan, and its eyes got as big as dinner plates. "Ruuuun!" it screeched in a little girl voice. "He'll kill us all!"

Ewan chased her, but she disappeared into the tall grass too. All around, he heard horsey galloping sounds, but they got quieter and quieter. He tumbled out into a big area of trampled grass and looked around eagerly, but he was all alone. His lip began to tremble. Why had they all run away?

Something moved in the grass, and Ewan saw there was one horsey left, coming his way. It was *huuuuge*, all black with a white mark on its forehead. It stepped out of the tall grass and started pawing the ground with one big hoof, snorting loudly.

Ewan's lip stopped trembling, and he smiled. This horsey was *perfick*.

The big black horsey charged. Not knowing what else to do, Ewan charged right back. The two of them ran straight at each other, Ewan bellowing gleefully at the top of his lungs. At the last moment before they ran into each other, the horsey turned to the side, passing Ewan close enough to touch. So... Ewan reached out and grabbed the horsey's long tail with both hands.

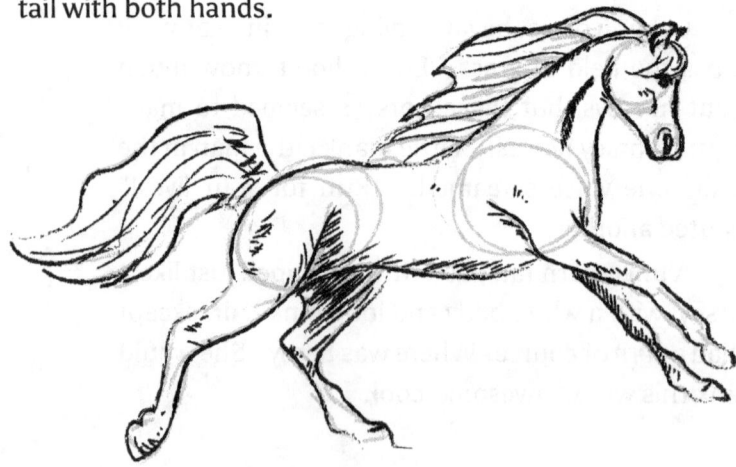

---

* Glossary on page 271 includes complete listing of "Ewanisms."

"Yow!" the horsey yelled, and Ewan was jerked off his feet. The horsey began to run even faster, dragging Ewan in midair behind him. "Let go, you silly creature!"

Ewan didn't listen.

The horsey stopped suddenly, turning and trying to *bite* him. But Ewan, hanging from that tail with all his strength, was always out of reach of the horsey's teeth.

The big black horsey screamed. "Let *go*." It talked with a fancy accent. "Do you have any idea how much that hurts?"

Shrugging, Ewan let go—then grabbed the long black hair coming from the horsey's head and tried climbing onto its back. Now the horsey *really* couldn't bite him. Ewan made it halfway up before the horsey screamed again and took off at full speed.

Ewan almost fell off, but he tangled his fingers in the horsey's long hair and held on for dear life. The horsey ran faster and faster, its hooves sounding like thunder on the ground. Ewan's arms started to hurt from all the bumping and bouncing.

"Slo-o-o-o-ow dow-ow-ow-ow-n," he tried to shout, his words interrupted by every bounce of the horsey's feet.

"Let goooo!" the horsey called back to him.

"Nev-ev-ev-ev-er!"

In the distance, Ewan thought he heard his sister Ommie screaming. She was telling him to let go too, but he was too busy taming a horsey to listen to *her* right now.

The big black horsey ran forever, but Ewan held on no matter what. Nock and Ommie might be older and smarter, having gone to school and learned stuff—like reading—but there was one thing Ewan and Sessy did better than either of them. They were *stubborn*.

The land began to change as the horsey left the grassy plain behind, going into a rocky area. Its running slowed down as they went uphill, and Ewan saw more and more boulders and cliffs coming out of the ground all around. Ewan was still hanging from the side of the horsey's neck, and suddenly, he saw what the horsey was planning: it was going to run next to one of the boulders and try to *scrape* Ewan off.

Ewan's arms were *really* hurting now, but with all of the strength he had left, he pulled up and jerked down hard on the horsey's hair.

"Ow!" the horsey cried, coming to a stop and rearing up on its back legs again. When the horsey landed, before it could start running again, Ewan saw his chance and took it. Using all of his jungle gym skills, he scrambled the rest of the way onto the horsey's back.

The horsey started shaking, but it didn't move. "How *dare* you?" it whispered, furious. "I am not some stupid animal to be ridden. I am a *person*."

Ewan didn't answer. He just tangled his hands more tightly in the horsey's mane, burying his face in the long hair and holding on tight. Then, taking a deep breath, he kicked with both feet. "Giddyup!"

"*What?*"

"Giddyup, horsey!"

The horsey lost all control and began bucking wildly. Fortunately, Ewan knew all about this; he'd watched a video about taming horses one time. When a man picked his horsey, he had to *break* it first. The horsey would jump around a lot, just like this, trying to throw off its rider. But after a while, the horsey got tired, and then the man and the horsey were best fwends.

So Ewan held on tight, even biting a mouthful of hair in his teeth, just in case.

Again, the wild ride took *forever*, but after a while—just like in the video—the big black horsey got tired. Finally, it stopped moving at all and lowered its head in defeat.

Smiling from ear to ear, Ewan let go of the horsey's hair and leaned back. His arms were *eggzawsted*, but he had won. He had a horsey of his own. Now all he needed was a sword and—

Screaming, the horsey bucked one last time—and Ewan, no longer holding on, went flying.

He flew right into a boulder, hitting so hard that he saw stars, then rolling down the big rock and landing on the ground below. A little puff of yellow smoke came out of his mouth.

The horsey stepped in front of him, spread its legs again, and lowered its head. It shoved its snout right into Ewan's face and bared its teeth like a dog.

"Why you do dat?" Ewan complained, fighting back tears.

"Why did I... *what?*" the horsey repeated, still talking in that fancy accent.

"What I ever do to you?" Ewan asked, shaking his head to clear it.

The horsey stared at him, confused, then backed up fast when Ewan stood up. It obviously didn't want to risk Ewan grabbing hold again.

"What was all dat stuff you were yelling 'bout?" Ewan asked.

The horsey blinked its big black eyes. "I... I said I'm a person. Even *gnomen* don't ride other gnomen."

Ewan stared back. "What's a no-man?"

The horsey cocked its head. "Why, I thought *you* were. But you're clearly young, and a gnoman your age should still have a beard. But if you're not a gnoman—"

"I'm a human!" Ewan said loudly. "*Duh.*"

"Yes! Yes, I see that now," the horsey said, suddenly very excited. "Forgive my confusion, young human. We eqmen hate gnomen, you see. It's a long story."

Ewan grinned suddenly. "No prob," he assured the horsey—the *eck*-man. "So... can I ride you now?"

The big black horsey tossed its head and blustered. "I don't know about *that.* Only the greatest of humen and dagmen are ever given the honor of riding an eqman."

"But I'm da Knight," Ewan said. "I *gots* to ride a horsey!"

The eck-man horsey guy didn't say anything for a second. Then it danced to one side, picking its feet up high as it moved. "You?" it asked him. "*You're* a Knight? Overtwixt hasn't had a Knight in millennia!"

"Minny-what?"

"Thousands of years!" the horsey blustered. "Really? You're a *Knight?*"

Ewan shrugged. "That's what Guide Guy said."

The big black horsey eck-guy shook his head and laughed. "You're certainly brave enough." He reared suddenly, neighing loudly with glee. "A *Knight.* Why didn't you say so?"

Ewan shrugged again.

"Did the Guide give you a mission?" the horsey asked.

"Yeah," Ewan began. "I gotta—"

"He gave *me* a mission too," the eck-horsey interrupted. "And *my* mission was to find the Knight."

This... actually confused Ewan a little. "Huh?"

"Don't you see?" the big black horsey demanded. "I'm your *Squire*, and it would be the greatest honor of my life to bear you into battle!"

· seven ·

(Cécilie)

S tanding next to her older brother, Cécilie watched as half her family sped away from her, running toward Eqland—which was supposed to be *her* niland, where she was going to be Princess.

Grabbing Nachton's hand, she tugged. "I want to go with them."

Nachton ripped his hand free. "Nothing's stopping you."

"But—but the Guide said to stick together." Or something like that.

Nachton looked around. "Maybe he did, but I don't see him around here anymore, making sure we obey. Do you?"

Surprised, Cécilie realized he was right. She and Nachton were the only ones left in the clearing. "But..." Cécilie's lip started trembling. "Amélie said to stay with you."

"And who's in charge, me or Amélie?"

"Um... Amélie?"

Nachton started getting angry; Cécilie could tell, because when Nachton got mad, he always narrowed his eyes into slits.

"It's what the Guide said!" Cécilie tried to explain. "He said Amélie was going to rule the world—"

"*No*," Nachton disagreed loudly, "he said she was going to rule Overtwixt, and only this little *part* of Overtwixt." He threw his hands into the air. "It doesn't matter what he thinks anyway! Who do *Mom and Dad* say is in charge, whenever they leave us alone at the house?"

"Um... usually Amélie—"

"Gah!" Nachton yelled, spinning around and stalking away.

"Wait!" Cécilie called. "Where are you going? Eqland is the other way!"

"Then you go that way, Cécilie."

Cécilie straightened to her full height and spoke in her most imperious tone. "Stop! I *command* you to take me to Eqland, you... you peasant!"

Nachton actually stopped. But then he turned and stared at her, shaking his head in disbelief. Ah well, it had been worth a try. That kind of thing never worked at home either, but now that Cécilie was really a Princess, she thought maybe... "But where are you going?" she asked when Nachton turned away again.

"I'm starting my quest, since there's nothing better to do." He kept muttering under his breath as he walked off. "Knowledge and wisdom... how obvious can you be?... It's not like there's a *library* lying around..."

Cécilie watched him go and tried not to cry. Finally, she turned around and started running after her sister, along the winding path down the side of the mountain.

By the time Cécilie reached the bridge, Amélie was most of the way across. Ewan was already running through the tall grass beyond, nothing but the top of his blond head visible; it almost looked like he was swimming in a bright-green sea.

Horses and unicorns were galloping away from him in every direction.

Cécilie stepped up onto the bridge, then stopped. The last bridge she used had been destroyed as soon as she got across. What if this one did the same thing?

Besides, she was supposed to be the Princess. Those horses over there, they were her subjects, and they were *amazing.* They had coats of all different colors, mostly blacks and browns and reds for the boy horses, but lots of whites and pinks and grays for the girl unicorns; some of the unicorns even had rainbow-colored hair! All together, they were the most beautiful thing she'd ever seen. How could *she* be *their* Princess?

Cécilie looked down at her clothes, which had magically changed when she got to Overtwixt: an itchy buttoned shirt and really-itchy pants. Why couldn't her clothes have changed to a princess dress instead?

Maybe she could find a princess dress somewhere? She closed her eyes and pictured the perfect pink dress with really big skirts. She tried to imagine herself wearing that dress, a tiara on her head and a wand in her hand, but it was no use. Even if she could find a dress like that, she would still be *her:* straight brown hair, plain brown eyes, pale skin and freckles. What good would a dress do? She was always gonna be boring, and nothing she did could ever change that.

But then she had an idea. There was magic in Overtwixt; Cécilie heard Nachton and the Guide talking about it earlier, though she wasn't paying much attention. Maybe... could Nachton help make her look like a real princess after all? Using magic? She *knew* she should have stayed with him!

Turning once more the way she had come, Cécilie started climbing the path back toward the clearing—and beyond, toward Nachton and the Grand Library of Huland.

· eight ·
(Amélie)

Amélie watched in dismay as Ewan grabbed a big black horse by the hair, then went galloping off in exactly the wrong direction—*away* from her. "Ewan!" she screamed, running into the sea of grass, which came up to her chest. "Ewan, let go!" She wasn't loud enough. "Ewan Ollivaros," she screeched, "you let go right this instant!"

He ignored her. Of course he ignored her. *All* of her siblings ignored her.

Amélie chased after her little brother anyway, but it was no use. He and the horse kept getting farther and farther away, until they climbed that hill in the distance and disappeared behind a group of tall boulders.

Breathing hard, Amélie stumbled to a halt. She turned slowly in a circle, feeling the usual fear threaten to overwhelm her. No, not the *usual* fear. She'd never found herself alone on an alien planet before, not to mention on an island floating in nothing. The very thought made her legs weak again, and she lowered herself to hands and knees—afraid the niland might tilt to the side at any moment, dumping her off. No, not the *usual* fear at all.

Amélie had never been in real danger before, and definitely not without Mom or Dad. She was supposed to be responsible for the others. Now she'd lost Ewan, who might be killed at any moment, and she'd left Cécilie behind with Nachton. *Nachton,* who wasn't responsible enough to turn off his video games when his screen time was up, much less watch out for his little sister.

But what was Amélie supposed to do? Turning back toward Nachton and Cécilie would mean abandoning Ewan, and she wasn't about to do *that.* She would just have to trust Nachton to do the right thing... for once.

Standing up again, shakily, Amélie looked around for ideas. *There.* Movement in the trees to her left, off the side of the grassy plain. That would be the other horses that ran away when Ewan came charging through—*talking* horses, according to the Guide. If she could convince one of them to give her a ride, she could catch up to Ewan.

Running again, trying to ignore the never-ending fear of the niland falling away beneath her, Amélie went straight toward the trees. That made her think of her family's arrival in Overtwixt, of trying to get away from the dragon creature, which only made her more terrified. But she pushed on, running as fast as she could.

As she got closer, she saw more movement, and changed direction toward it. There were definitely shadows moving through the forest, not too far away. "Hey!" she yelled. "Wait! Please!"

The shadows stopped moving, blending into the shade of the trees, and she lost track of them. But she hurried on as best she could. Passing between the first tree trunks, Amélie burst into the forest and ran toward the place she had last seen the shapes. "Please!" she yelled. "Help me! I need—"

Something shot out from the side, tangling around her legs and tripping her, sending her sprawling on the ground. Yelling in surprise and pain, Amélie rolled across the forest floor, her rough-spun shirt and pants catching on sticks and ripping. Mud and wet leaves slid across her face and got in her mouth and eyes.

Crying, she rolled to her knees and tried to clear her eyes, spitting mud. When she could finally see again, she looked up... and gulped.

Amélie was surrounded by four fierce creatures: centmen like the Guide, but not nearly as friendly-looking.

And each one held a long spear, pointed right at her heart.

· nine ·

(Nachton)

Finally, Nachton was alone. No Ewan to cart around like the heaviest backpack ever; no Cécilie to annoy him with non-stop noise; no Amélie to boss him around, or Mom to tell him he was being irresponsible, or Dad to give him disappointed looks.

No centman Guide to limit his potential.

No one at all—just Nachton and the Grand Library of Huland, which he had a feeling was going to be his new favorite place on Earth. Or, well, favorite place in Overtwixt, at least.

Of course, *no one* meant no librarians either, which could prove problematic. The Guide had made very clear that the Vizier was the only human left in Overtwixt, aside from Nachton's family. Still, if this library was made for humans—er, hu*men*—then Nachton should be able to figure it out for himself.

He wandered for a time, getting a feel for the place. At the very center of the complex was a squat building that seemed administrative in nature; it was here that the card catalog was housed, along with rooms stocked with materials for the creation and care of books. Knowing he would need such things on his quest, Nachton found a soft leather satchel and began filling it with various supplies: a stack of blank, leather-bound notebooks; several feathered quills; a couple vials of ink with cork stoppers. Just as important, Nachton found flasks of water and a cabinet with bread and dry meat, kinda like beef jerky.

Radiating out from the squat administrative building, like spokes on a wheel, every other building of the Library was devoted to a particular subject matter: Arts, Literature, Philosophy, Science, Magic, and History. The History section of the Library was by far the largest, comprising three whole pyramids all by itself. For a long time, Nachton walked down row after row of stacked books—rolled scrolls as well as bound volumes with pages that turned.

The Library was as much a museum as a place to store books, Nachton soon realized. The Arts building contained as many sculptures and paintings as written volumes. And the towers rising from the History pyramids were filled with displays—styles of clothing throughout history; replica skeletons and wax recreations of various Earth animals; 3D maps of Overtwixt from ages past. Nachton was amazed to see the differences in Overtwixt from map to map, as nilands grew, moved, and were created anew over time.

Once he'd figured out where everything was, he settled into a reading nook on the ground floor of the building dedicated to History of Overtwixt; then he picked a book off a bottom shelf and started reading. Before long, he was scribbling notes in the first of his blank notebooks. He was surprised just how hard it was, writing with quill and ink. He finally got the hang of inking the nib, using *lots* of ink so he didn't have to dip so frequently... but then he discovered that overly-inked writing didn't dry very fast. Instead, when he turned a page, the wet ink got all splotchy and made his handwriting hard to read.

Time passed, and Nachton sped through one book after another. He ate when he got hungry; he dozed when he got tired. He learned all sorts of things, developing an introductory knowledge of Overtwixt: the peoples and culture; the way nilands and bridges worked; and the fact that all written and spoken languages got translated magically, automatically, so that everyone could understand everyone else. (There were only two exceptions to that, which Nachton couldn't quite figure out.*) Nachton also read a *lot* about the rules this Sovereign character created long ago to control how things worked here.

The Five Fundamental Laws of Overtwixt were particularly interesting, even if they didn't make much sense—the Five Fundamental *Riddles* was more like it. The only one whose meaning seemed obvious was the first: *Every life is unique and precious.* That explained, at least, why the Guide wouldn't let him be Sorcerer or Mage; there was already one of each, and uniqueness was apparently enforced as some sort of natural law here.

More time passed—days, probably—but Nachton barely noticed. He'd always been capable of losing himself in books. He read and he read, and eventually, he decided he understood this Overtwixt place pretty well, if he said so himself. He had attained *wisdom.* So... what now? And where in the world were his brother and sisters? Was he going to have to take care of the Vizier problem all by himself?

"Knowledge and wisdom, knowledge and wisdom!" he finally yelled, as much to hear someone talking as any other reason. "You hear that, Mr. Guide? I've sought knowledge

---

* See Intro to the Ancient Languages of Overtwixt on page 283.

and wisdom, and I've found it. What the heck am I supposed to do now?"

"Based upon your newfound knowledge, what do you *think* you should do?" a voice answered unexpectedly. Nachton fell out of his seat, he was so surprised. Standing up and turning around quickly, he found the Guide behind him, leaning casually against a marble column with arms folded across his broad chest.

"How long have you been there?" Nachton demanded.

"Long enough." The centman nodded toward the stack of notebooks on Nachton's study table, one of them already full, a second partly used. "What have you learned?"

"Lots of things. Very little about the Vizier."

"Very little about the Vizier specifically, perhaps. But this Library still holds a great deal of knowledge that can be applied to your plans for overthrowing him." The Guide cocked his head. "Based on what you've learned, where do you think the Vizier gets his power?"

"From his magic. Every reference I *could* find about the Vizier said the same thing: he is an accomplished purveyor of magic."

"But what gives him his *power?*"

Nachton stared at the centman like he was crazy. "I just told you—his magic!"

"On the contrary, magic is just a tool, to be used for good or ill. It is merely a multiplier for the power a person already wields. So I ask you again: where does the Vizier get his *power?*"

"I don't know!" Nachton shot back.

"Does it come from within him," the Guide asked patiently, "or is it granted him by others?"

Nachton hesitated. "Both?" He thought about it a moment. "Some people—the creatures of darkness—follow him willingly. Others are just afraid of him."

"Very good!" the Guide said approvingly. "The people of Overtwixt cede great power to the Vizier because they fear him so greatly. And what power does the Vizier wield of his own?"

"I don't *know*."

"You will need to find out, if you hope to remove him from Overtwixt. This is *fundamental*, Nachton."

Nachton threw his hands in the air. The Guide clearly knew the answers to his own questions; why didn't he just *tell* Nachton what he needed to know?! Instead, frowning at Nachton's reaction, the Guide turned to go.

"Wait!" Nachton blurted. "At least tell me how to rob the Vizier of the power granted him by the people's fear."

The Guide eyed him for a long moment. Then, to Nachton's surprise, he actually answered. "Isn't it obvious? By giving the people a leader they don't *have* to fear." He raised an eyebrow. "Which is, I believe, the very quest I set before your sister the Empress."

Nachton summoned his courage. "Why can't it be me? Why can't *I* be that leader?"

"Because that is not the quest I set before you."

"But why not? Why *can't* I be the King... or the Chief Executive... or... or, I don't know, something? Something more important than *Loremaster*, at least!"

The Guide cocked his head, a small smile on his lips. "You think because you are the firstborn son, you are entitled to this kind of role? That you should be first in all things?"

Nachton shrugged and nodded. Wasn't it obvious?

"I don't expect you to know this yet," the Guide responded. "Many people never learn it in all their lives. But the responsibility of the first is not always to *be* first. And the best leaders aren't always the most important people." He cocked his head, then spoke cryptically. "The first must be last, you see—the servant of all."

Nachton somehow kept from rolling his eyes. His Dad liked to talk this way too, saying things that sounded wise but actually made no sense.

"Leave the leadership to your sisters," the Guide concluded, "and do not begrudge them the honor it brings. That is their calling, and their gifting, not yours."

"You clearly don't know my sisters very well," Nachton muttered. Before the Guide could respond to this, he quickly added: "So. I'm stuck being the Loremaster."

"Do not discount the value of *your* role either. No man or woman acting alone ever accomplishes anything of worth. Your sisters will have need of your wise counsel in the days to come, which is why I set before you the quest that I did." He paused. "And you *do* need to determine the source of the Vizier's own power, if you're to combat it effectively."

"Why do you keep pushing me away from magic?" Nachton demanded. "You wouldn't let me choose a magical role. Now you insist it's not magic itself that gives the Vizier his power, and I know it's because you don't want me researching magic!" He smiled victoriously, like he'd caught the Guide in a lie. "But you just said magic is only a *tool*, one that *could* be used for good. So..." he repeated, "why do you keep pushing me away from it?"

The Guide seemed to peer deep into Nachton's soul. Then he spoke slowly: "Because I do not believe you can resist the temptation to use it for evil."

Nachton gaped at the Guide's brutal honesty.

"At least not *yet*," the centman added. "In time, I think you would be wise to research magic, in the interest of defending your family. But only after you understand the *fundamentals* of Overtwixt." He eyed Nachton. "When that time comes, be sure it is not ambition or pride that motivates you, but only a desire to preserve and protect. I have encouraged you to seek out knowledge as a path to wisdom; but when it comes to magic, I think the wisdom should come first."

Still stunned by the Guide's lack of confidence in him, Nachton said nothing, and the Guide soon withdrew. The clip-clop of the centman's hooves faded to nothing, returning the Library to silence, but Nachton didn't move. He simply sat, thinking, weighing his options... and stewing over the conversation just ended. Finally, coming to a decision, the young human gathered his things and set off for a new section of the Library, one he had discovered in his explorations days ago:

The restricted section at the top of the tower devoted to Magic.

· ten ·
(Amélie)

"**I** was right!" one of the centmen cried. He had blond hair and fierce green eyes, and he looked very ready to use the spear he was pointing at Amélie's heart. "I *told* you it wasn't a gnoman!"

"But if it's not gnoman," one of the other centmen asked, "what else could it be?" Despite his uncertainty, he and the others kept their spears steady on Amélie too.

"It looks human," a third said, "but I've never seen one so small... or with so much hair."

"It appears to be a human *child*," the oldest of the four centmen finally spoke up. "It has been many years since Overtwixt beheld one such as this."

The blond centman snorted. "This is no human. There were only two humen left in Overtwixt when this day dawned, and now there's just one. This *thing* is either a creation of the Vizier, or..."

"Or it *is* the Vizier!" one of the others cried. "They say he can disguise his form using magic!"

"Exactly," the blond concluded. "So what are we waiting for? Let us dispatch this foul creature!"

It was all too clear to Amélie what the fierce-looking centman meant—he was talking about killing her!

Amélie was too afraid to talk. She was too afraid to even be insulted that he called her a foul creature.

But no one killed her. They seemed to be waiting on something, maybe orders from the oldest centman, who was obviously in charge. Like all his men, he was bristling with weaponry. In addition to the spear, each of them had a thick belt around his middle, with pouches and a curved sword strapped to it. But instead of a longbow slung over one shoulder, the leader had a crossbow hanging by a strap across his chest. He stood there calmly, studying Amélie.

"Captain?" the red-headed centman prompted. "The Baron is gone. The time for diplomacy is past."

"If we have the Vizier—or one of his minions—in our power," the blond said again, "we need to *strike*, while we have the chance!"

At last, Amélie managed to speak. "I'm not the Vizier!"

All of the centmen except for their leader, the Captain, tightened grips on spears and crowded closer.

"You—you think I'm some... old... ugly... *bad* guy?!" Amélie stammered. "I'm a *girl!*"

The Captain continued to hesitate, and the red-head spoke up. "I don't know, sir. Maybe she's telling the truth. I can't imagine the Vizier ever calling *himself* ugly."

That set the others to arguing again, back and forth, over whether to tie her up or just "strike now" and be done with it. No one seemed to consider the possibility of letting her go.

Summoning her courage, Amélie finally climbed to her feet. "I—I am—your *Empress*," she blurted. "And, uh, you *will* let me go!"

This caused the centmen to *laugh*. "Now that does sound like something the Vizier would say!"

"It's true!" she insisted, suddenly embarrassed—but could she blame them for laughing? She was wearing ripped peasant clothing, covered with mud and leaves. Even if she convinced them she wasn't a bad guy, she looked like nothing but a dirty child. "I'm serious! I'm the Empress and—"

All of a sudden, a black blur crashed through the woods from out of nowhere—and then a very small person was colliding with the Captain, wrestling with him, trying unsuccessfully to drag him to the ground.

It was Ewan.

The big black horse was with him. It pushed its way into the middle of the centmen, trotting in a tight circle to stand between Amélie and the two centmen on her other side. The horse—no, *eqman*—bared its teeth in a snarl, and the three centmen who weren't wrestling Ewan backed up warily.

Finally, the Captain managed to shake Ewan off, and the little boy hit the ground hard. He pushed himself to his feet, shook his head to clear it, then raised a crossbow—the *Captain's* crossbow—and aimed it at its owner's heart. "Get away from my sister," Ewan said through clenched teeth. Over his shoulder, he called, "You okay, Ommie?"

"I'm okay." She was still scared out of her mind, but having her brother back made her feel immediately better.

The Captain looked astonished at seeing his crossbow in the hands of the little boy.

"Captain?" one of the other centmen asked uncertainly. "Orders?"

"Stand down," the Captain growled.

"Sir? We won't have another shot at the Vizier."

"She's not the Vizier," the Captain said. "She's probably exactly what she appears to be."

"But—"

The Captain shook his head. "Standing before us now are *two* human children," he said, gesturing at Ewan, who still held the crossbow menacingly. "It grows difficult to believe this is some strange magic of the Vizier's when a simpler explanation exists: More humen have entered the realm. The Vizier is *not* the only one left." The Captain took a deep breath. "Besides, I know this eqman."

"Captain," the big black horse said softly, tossing his head in what appeared to be the eqman version of a nod.

"Squire," the Captain said, nodding back. "You vouch for these humen?"

"I vouch for the boy," the eqman said—in a British accent!—then hesitated. "He's claimed the mantle of the Knight."

All around the circle, the centmen straightened, surprised and excited.

"What about the girl?" the Captain asked.

"*I* vouch da girl," Ewan said, sounding very adult until he added, "Um... what do *vouch* mean?"

"It means you know me," Amélie said, her head spinning with the weirdness of this whole situation. "That you promise I can be trusted."

"Oh," Ewan said. "Yeah. I vouch her. She my sister."

"Captain?" a centman asked.

The Captain was starting to smile now, and Amélie was able to relax a little; he had a *nice* smile. "Stand down," he said again. "These humen may not be allies, but if the Squire vouches for them, they're no allies of the Vizier either."

Everyone else relaxed now too—except for Ewan, whose finger tightened on the trigger of the crossbow. "Horsey?" he called.

The big black eqman tossed his head and blustered. "I am your Squire, sir Knight," he said in that surprising accent of his. "Kindly do not call me horsey."

Now *all* the centmen were smiling and laughing.

"Well, Skire Horsey?" Ewan asked. "Do you... um... *vouch* dis guy?" He waved the crossbow at the Captain again.

"Yes, sir Knight. He is the Captain of the Baron's guard."

That couldn't possibly mean anything to Ewan, but the little boy lowered the crossbow anyway, then handed it back to its owner. Apparently he trusted this big black eqman he'd known for less than an hour.

"I am the Captain, yes," the lead centman said, "but no longer do I serve the Baron. He released us from his service, and..." The Captain turned away. "And I am sorry to report he no longer continues here in Overtwixt."

"No!" the Squire gasped.

"'Tis true," one of the others said. "The Vizier already sent out his Criers with the announcement. Fortunately we didn't run into any of the little spookmen ourselves, but we got the news secondhand on our way back from the Capital. The Baron was struck down by the Vizier himself."

"This is terrible!" the Squire said. "The Vizier... the rumors I've heard. *He* will lead the realm now?"

"With an iron hoof, no doubt," the Captain said. "Or an iron fist, I suppose. Seeing how he's human and has no hooves," he added unnecessarily.

The big black horse shuddered. "But what brings you to this side of Eqland? There are many more direct routes back to Centwick."

The Captain glanced at his fellow guardsmen. "With the Baron gone, the Vizier will want us in chains. Fearing pursuit, we took an indirect route home on purpose."

The horse nodded understanding, then seemed to notice Amélie again. "My lady," he said slowly. "I am the Squire, newly-sworn companion of your brother the Knight. Might I ask what role *you* are here to play?"

Amélie spoke with as much dignity as she could manage, considering her torn clothing and muddy face. "Well met, sir Squire," she said gravely, speaking like the queen from a movie she'd seen once. "I am the new Empress of this realm."

There was a long silence following these words. At least no one laughed this time.

"You spoke true, then?" the Captain asked finally. "The Guide named you Empress?"

Ewan nodded emphatically. "She gots *free* choices," he said, holding up three fingers. "She could be Empress or—"

Amélie elbowed her brother hard in the ribs. "Yes," she said simply. If these hardened soldiers found out her other options were Bard or Dancer, they'd *never* respect her. They probably wouldn't respect her anyway, but still.

Ewan scowled at Amélie and rubbed his side. "I just save you life," he complained.

"She's right, however," the Captain said, unexpectedly coming to her defense. "Each man or woman's choice belongs to him or her alone. That which *is* matters more than that which is *not*."

Ewan's forehead wrinkled in confusion at these words, but then he shrugged.

The Captain traded a look with the Squire and the other centmen, then all five of them knelt before Amélie... though the blond guy who'd wanted to kill her didn't look very happy about it. "Your majesty the Empress," the Captain said gravely. "Welcome to Overtwixt."

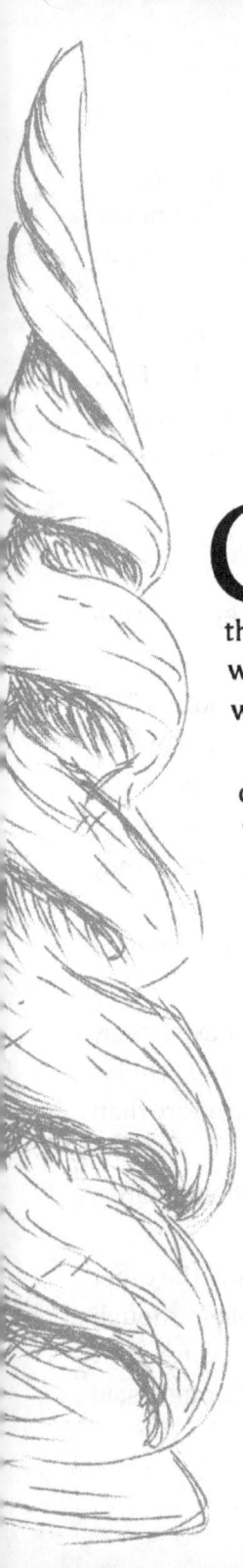

· eleven ·

(Cécilie)

Cécilie found the Grand Library of Huland easily enough. Even after she got down off the mountain, when she was walking through the thick forest, she could always see where she was going because the Library towers were taller than the trees all around her.

She walked inside the first building she came to and started calling for her brother. "Nachton! Nachton!" She cupped her hands around her mouth and called louder. "Nachton?"

No response.

Shrugging, she started to explore. Cécilie knew she should probably be scared, but she'd always liked libraries. She actually felt safe here.

Not everything here was books, which was good—because these books didn't have pictures and big writing like the ones she usually read. *These* books had tiny writing, and they made her sneeze when she opened them. So she ignored the books and started looking at all the animal statues.

Lions and tigers and bears... toucans, flamingos, and penguins... They were all animals from her world, and they looked so real! The higher she climbed up the stairs in this Library tower, the more animal statues she found, and she started seeing statues of extinct animals too, like dinosaurs. This *really* should have scared her, especially when she came around a corner and found herself standing under the open jaws of a T-rex. But it didn't scare her, not much anyway. Cécilie loved dinosaurs and knew a lot about them, and things were never as scary once you understood them better.

She started getting tired, so she found a place to lie down. Not on one of the benches made for people—those were wood and didn't look very comfortable. No, she lay down inside a dinosaur nest with a couple of triceratops eggs. They weren't real, of course; it was just part of the dinosaur display. But it was still cozy.

When she woke up, she wandered around hungry until she found some fruit in a bowl on a table, then she walked out onto a balcony while she munched an apple.

She was so high up! Cécilie hadn't realized how many stairs she climbed, but she was on the top floor of the tower now. From here, she could see across the forest to Eqland—and there, on the bridge, a group of people was coming this way. They looked tiny from here, but... Was that Amélie? And Ewan? And an eqman horse and a bunch of centmen like the Guide?

"Amélie!" she yelled at the top of her lungs, jumping up and down and waving. "Ewan!" They were too far away to hear, but that was okay. They would figure out where she and Nachton went, and they'd get here soon enough.

Cécilie turned around and realized she wasn't on a balcony at all. This was another *bridge*, leading from this tower to another one just like it, both of them coming out of the same building below. Eagerly, she ran across to the other tower, curious to see what statues she'd find *there*.

The statues in the next tower were more like mannequins, the kind of statues Cécilie saw in stores when she shopped with Mom. They were being used here to show off different styles of clothing—*old* styles, like people wore in the movies, not stuff people actually wore in the real world anymore.

Suddenly, Cécilie's heart was beating fast in her chest. Eyes wide, she ran along a line of statues... and there it was. *Exactly* as she imagined it, a bright pink dress fit for a princess. *Huge* skirts, layered with shimmering fabric and lace, every hem sewn with red ribbon. And it was her size.

She changed into the dress quickly, then pulled on a pair of long white gloves that came up past her elbow. There was even a pair of glittering red shoes. The only thing missing was a tiara and wand, but Cécilie didn't care. She went running again, this time to find a mirror.

The first mirror she located was taller than she was, and she stood in front of it a long time, turning this way and that, smiling so hard her face actually hurt. Then... her smile faded. It was a beautiful dress, and the gloves and shoes were perfect too. But *she* wasn't beautiful. She was just a boring little girl with pale skin and freckles.

Would some jewelry help? Could a pretty necklace or some earrings hide how boring she looked?

Turning away from the mirror, Cécilie went searching again. There wasn't anything on this floor, but she found an entire jewelry display just one floor down.

For a while, she forgot about the mirror as she tried on jewelry, necklaces and brooches and bracelets and earrings. Every piece was *stunning*—that was the word Mom used when she really liked the jewelry Daddy bought her. Of course, all the big glittering jewels here were probably fake, since this was a library, but it didn't matter. They *looked* real. Before long, Cécilie started feeling weighted down by all the jewelry she was wearing at the same time.

Then she saw *them*. Hanging from a mannequin in a corner, easy to miss, was a collection of *extra*-special-looking necklaces... and they called to her, somehow. Pulling off the other jewelry, Cécilie dropped it all on the floor and went to stare at these new necklaces.

They were simple, tasteful. Nothing more than a single glittering gemstone each, wrapped in a silver wire setting and hanging from a thick ribbon. The gemstones seemed to glow, faint green light throbbing within them, even though they were all different colors. Strangely reverent, unsure which one to try on first, Cécilie recited a rhyme under her breath:

"Cows go moo... while they chew... you look nice, so I pick *you*."

Slowly, Cécilie picked up the necklace her finger had landed on, then hung it around her neck. She'd been tired even after her nap in the dinosaur nest, but suddenly she felt good, *strong*. Eagerly, Cécilie pulled off the necklace and recited her rhyme again, picking another, and then another.

Suddenly desperate to see what she looked like wearing *these* necklaces, Cécilie grabbed as many as she could carry in both hands, then ran back upstairs to the mirror. Breathing hard, she stepped in front of the mirror—and gasped.

The person in the mirror, still wearing the pink princess dress... *she* was stunning now! Cécilie barely recognized herself. She looked older, more mature, more confident. And there wasn't a single freckle anywhere! Cécilie was now more beautiful than any lady she'd ever seen—an elegant young woman wearing an amethyst necklace, the purple gemstone hanging from a white ribbon.

A little afraid of what would happen, Cécilie took off the purple gemstone necklace... and sure enough, she went back to being plain, boring Cécilie. Swallowing, she tried on a different necklace, this one sapphire—a blue stone. Surprisingly, her hair turned blonde, and her eyes turned *blue*, even though the rest of her still looked the same as normal, pale and freckled.

Excitedly, Cécilie added the amethyst necklace, so she was wearing both the purple gem *and* the blue gem. She expected to look mature and beautiful *and* blonde-haired, blue-eyed, but... that didn't happen. Actually, nothing happened at all. She stayed blonde and blue-eyed until she took off that necklace; then the amethyst necklace started working again.

So. Only one at a time. She could live with that.

She tried on others, one necklace at a time. She eventually found another one that made her look different: it gave her rich bronze skin and midnight black hair, like a princess from the Middle East. But those were the only ones that changed her face. Another one made her shorter, and a different one made her clothes really tight all of a sudden. She tried the red ruby one again—the very first one—and it made her feel *awake*, just like before. But most of the necklaces didn't do anything at all.

Still, Cécilie trembled with excitement just holding these wonderful treasures. She needed to figure them out, all of these necklaces, and write down what they did. They all had different color gemstones, so once she learned them, she could remember which was which. She just needed some paper and a pen, and—

"Cécilie!" a voice yelled from downstairs. "Cécilie, are you up there?"

Eyes wide, Cécilie looked at herself in the mirror—she was wearing the amethyst necklace again. She looked mature and stunning... and she couldn't let her siblings see her like this, or they'd want the necklaces for themselves! Cécilie just *knew* Amélie would claim the purple one, and Cécilie couldn't let that happen. This needed to stay her secret.

Quickly, she took off the purple amethyst necklace and shoved it into a pocket of her princess dress, then stuffed in as many of the others as she could fit. Finally, she raised her voice to respond. "Coming!"

Then she started down the stairs to find her brothers and sister.

· twelve ·

(Nachton)

Nine people gathered around a large table in a Library conference room Nachton found: the four Ollivaros kids, the eqman named Squire, and the four centmen of the old Baron's guard.

"This is the Captain," Amélie nervously introduced the centmen's leader, who had silver running through the chestnut hair braided down his back. "Captain, this is my brother, the Loremaster."

The Captain seized his hand in a firm grip that Nachton tried to return. "Pleased to meet you," Nachton said.

"The honor is mine."

"And these are the Captain's men," Amélie continued, her voice unsteady even though she was clearly trying to act regal and adult. "The Ranger, the Scout, and the Operative." The other centmen looked pleased that she remembered them correctly... or at least two of the three did. "They've already sworn themselves to my service," she added in a whisper to Nachton.

Amazing. What was it about royalty, that people followed them automatically, even when they had *no* leadership ability? Of course, Amélie could get people to do whatever she wanted back home too, including Mom and Dad. Maybe she *was* the perfect Empress.

Then again, she wasn't ordering everyone around at the moment. With everything that had happened, she was scared, off-balance—not quite ready to step into her role as Empress. It wouldn't last, but as long as it did, it gave Nachton an opportunity to lead this group himself. Which was good, because his latest research had given him a good idea what needed to be done.

Everyone quieted and began looking toward Amélie expectantly. Licking her lips, she opened her mouth—

And Nachton took charge. "Now that we're all here," he said with a glare at Cécilie, who had been last to arrive, wearing that ridiculous pink dress, "let's get started." He spoke confidently, as an adult, seeking to impress the non-humen and bring them onto his side. "This is a council of war to plan the defeat of the Vizier and the liberation of Overtwixt."

The centmen all reacted favorably to this, one of them stomping a hoof repeatedly, another thumping his chest with a fist. The eqman Squire tossed his mane and blustered. "Hear, hear!"

Amélie cleared her throat. "I was going to say... Shouldn't we, um, wait for the Guide?"

"*Him?*" the Squire snorted.

The Captain frowned slightly. "Have you spoken with him, your majesty? Is he even aware we're meeting?"

Amélie shrugged uncomfortably. "Well, no. It's just... he was the one who gave us the mission of overthrowing the Vizier. Seems like he should be here."

The Captain shook his head. "All due respect, Empress. That's what the Guide does: travel the length and breadth of the portlands, greeting new arrivals, presenting their choices and handing out missions."

"You'll be lucky if you ever see him again," the centman named Scout said dismissively; the hair on his head and back was bright blond. "He's already done his job where you're concerned. He doesn't actually *care*."

The Squire tossed his head in agreement, and Nachton found himself liking these guys a little more. He wasn't sure he agreed with them—the Guide seemed to care all too much how the Ollivaros kids fulfilled their roles—but Nachton didn't want to delay the meeting longer, and certainly not for the Guide. "Okay," he said. "So we can get going then?"

Amélie clearly didn't like it, but she nodded.

"I'm hungry," Ewan said.

Nachton ignored him. "Let's recap. Our overall mission is to defeat the Vizier and rebuild the bridges. Specifically—"

"I'm *huuuuuungy*," Ewan bellowed. "Hungy, hungy, hungy, hungy."

"I know where there's some food!" Cécilie announced to everyone, even though only Ewan cared. She glanced at Amélie, who nodded. "C'mon, Ewan, I'll show you." And with that, the two little kids bounced out of the room.

Nachton stared at Amélie. "You made us wait for her to get started, and now you let her leave?" he demanded. "Way to lead, Empress." Disgusted, he took a deep breath. "Whatever. Each of us has a different quest to fulfill in support of the overall mission. Ewan—"

"Forgive me," the Captain interrupted, "but the Loremaster makes a good point. I believe the Empress *should* be leading this strategy session."

Nachton ground his teeth. That was *not* the point he'd been trying to make.

Everyone looked at Amélie, who seemed to shrink under their combined attention. With Cécilie and Ewan out of the room, she was suddenly the youngest and smallest person here, and she knew it. "It's, um... that's all right, Captain," Amélie squeaked. "I..." She swallowed. "I give the Loremaster my leave to speak, and to lead this meeting. I hereby recognize him as my, um, chief advisor."

The Captain frowned, seeming disappointed in her.

"*Thank you*," Nachton growled. "Now, as I was saying, Ewan's quest is to secure armor, a sword, and a squire—part of which he's already accomplished," Nachton added with a gesture toward the eqman. "Cécilie is supposed to win back the throne of Eqland and discover some sort of truth about herself." He waved his hand again, dismissively this time. "Whatever that last part is about, it sounds personal; no need to discuss here. *Amélie* needs to convince all the peoples of Overtwixt to follow *her* instead of the Vizier."

There was more shuffling and hoof-stomping at this.

"And I," Nachton concluded, with a hand on his chest, "was tasked with attaining knowledge and wisdom. Which I've done." He smiled, feeling very self-satisfied. "And based on those insights, which I've gleaned from my research, I know exactly what each of us needs to do next."

The Captain snorted softly.

Amélie summoned the courage to speak. "You're saying... you figured out everything we need to be doing... after just one afternoon in the Library?"

Nachton lifted an eyebrow at his sister. "Amélie, I've been here researching for weeks. Almost the entire time we've been in Overtwixt."

Amélie stared at him like he was crazy. "Nachton, we just got to Overtwixt *today*. We've only been separated a couple of hours."

"It was longer than *that*," Cécilie said from the doorway. She and Ewan were walking back inside, chewing on fruit. "I been here alone for *days*." She offered the Squire an apple, and he accepted eagerly, allowing the Princess to pat his muzzle while he munched.

The Captain cleared his throat. "If I may, your majesty..." He looked to Amélie and she nodded quickly. "Time passes strangely in Overtwixt," he explained. "Sometimes faster than the real world, sometimes slower... sometimes different on one niland than another. And time *always* passes more quickly in libraries."

That actually made sense, Nachton realized. It was consistent with one of those Five Fundamental Laws he'd read about—not that he wanted to derail this meeting by talking about it right now. He stared pointedly at Amélie.

The inconsistency of time clearly didn't make sense to her, but she took an unsteady breath and let it out slowly. "Um... okay. So. You've been researching for weeks now. Um, very well, Loremaster," she said deliberately, "what do you recommend?"

Nachton smiled and jumped right into it. "I suggest a three-prong strategy. Let's start with Ewan. He needs armor and a sword, but not just *any* armor or sword. Since our ultimate goal is to take out the Vizier, he'll need the best available—*magic* armor and sword."

The Ranger let out a gasp. "You mean... Sovereign's Relics?" he asked with reverence.

"That's right."

"Wait, what?" Amélie interrupted. "Sovereign's *what*?"

"Sovereign's Relics are special magical artifacts of enormous power," Nachton explained.

The Captain spoke up. "Legend holds that, in the beginning of Overtwixt, the Sovereign gifted four holy Diamond Relics to each and every race. *Powerful* Relics, as the Loremaster says, but only when used by the pure of heart, for the greater good." He hesitated, toying with the strap that hung around his chest. "I know of a few of them. For many years, the old Baron wielded one of the four human Relics, the mighty Diamond Great-Sword."

"The Vizier has the Sword now," the Scout said sourly.

"True, but he cannot wield it as the Baron did," the Captain explained. "Again, Sovereign's Relics cannot be used except for the greater good. Even so, the Vizier will certainly keep the Sword—and well protected—to ensure no one else can wield it either."

"We will need the Sword eventually," Nachton said, taking control again. "But I agree; it's out of our reach at the moment. Right now, I want to recover two of the *other* human Relics. For Ewan, that means—"

"The impervious Diamond Armor," the Ranger supplied, a gleam in his eye. "Plate-Armor, to be precise, a full suit designed to cover the wearer from head to toe."

"I thought the human Armor was lost long ago," the Operative put in. "When the ancient Knight—the *last* human to wear it—fell to the lugman horde."

"You're both right," Nachton said with a smug smile. "But I've discovered something in my reading. It seems that the lugmen, after defeating the ancient Knight in battle, built a shrine to honor his bravery and sacrifice."

"And you think this shrine holds the Armor?" the Captain mused. "Even after all this time?"

"I'm certain of it. I read a book that says so." Nachton grinned. "So that's the first prong of my strategy: Ewan and Cécilie set out for Lugard to recover the Diamond Armor, and the old Knight's sword too. It won't be as good as the *Diamond* Sword, but it should still be a decent weapon. The Squire will accompany Ewan, of course—" Nachton glanced at the Captain. "—and maybe Cécilie could be escorted by one of your centmen?"

"I'll go!" the Ranger volunteered.

The Captain looked toward Amélie. "If the Empress allows it. We are sworn to her now."

"Wait," Amélie said. "You want us to split up?"

"Exactly," Nachton said. "Our arrival won't remain a secret forever. The more we can accomplish before the Vizier finds out, the better."

"The Guide said we should stick together," Cécilie said around a mouthful of banana.

Nachton ignored her. "Obtaining the Armor is critical. Not only will it make Ewan indestructible, it will make him *look* more believable as the Knight. And let's face it; we need that. Because right now, he's somewhat... uninspiring."

All eyes turned to Ewan, and the little boy looked back with surprise, one finger still shoved up his nose. "What? Why you staring at me?"

Nachton went on. "Only with that Armor—and the legitimacy it grants—does Cécilie have a hope of claiming the throne of Eqland. Wouldn't you agree, Squire?"

The big black eqman nodded slowly. "My people will not like the idea of a child *hu*woman on the throne, not at first. But if she looks the part... and more importantly, if she's accompanied by a *Knight* that looks the part... they will come around." The horse bowed his head quickly to Cécilie. "No offense intended, your highness."

Cécilie didn't seem upset about waiting a little longer for her throne. "It's okay," she said brightly.

"There's no rush in any event," the eqman continued. "No one *else* is eager to take the throne. Not after what the Vizier did to the *last* Prince."

Cécilie's smile vanished. "What happened to the last Prince?"

"So that's the first prong," Nachton said quickly. Cécilie could be a real drama queen sometimes, and if she found out the kind of danger she would be in as Princess, there'd be no living with her. "The *second* prong of my strategy involves Amélie doing what Amélie does best." He smirked. "Talking."

"Nachton—" Amélie began.

"I'm not kidding, Amélie. You're going to start your tour of Overtwixt, meeting with the leaders of each race, convincing them to side with us against the Vizier."

"I don't like the idea of splitting up."

"Yeah," Cécilie said again, "the Guide told us to stick together."

"The Guide *also* said Amélie's task will be the toughest," Nachton argued, "and I believe him. It's certainly going to take the longest. The travel time alone, visiting the nilands of all the major factions of Overtwixt... Let's just say, the sooner you start, the better off we'll be." He turned to face the Captain. "Considering our need for secrecy, who would you suggest visiting first?"

"My own people," the centman said immediately. "Centwick is easily accessible by way of Hucentia. After that..." He looked thoughtful. "The old Mystic of Shanagrailia. He holds no official power, not since he abdicated, but convincing *him* of the Empress's claim would go a long way toward bringing the little peoples onto our side.

Many of them are already outraged over rumors that the Vizier is kidnapping gnomen and using them for slave labor in the Shadowlands." He shrugged. "Shanagrailia is just three bridges from Centwick. And we can trust the Mystic not to betray us, no matter what he thinks of the Empress." The Captain nodded definitively. "From Shanagrailia we could take the aqueducts to Delphyrd and on to Caymerdelphia—"

"Good, good," Nachton interrupted. "Sounds like we're in agreement about the second prong, then."

Amélie stared at him, her mouth hanging open a little, as if she didn't agree at all. But finally, she asked, "What's the third prong?"

"The third prong is *me*, continuing my research here," Nachton said. "I've found a promising lead on another human Relic: the Diamond Lens of Discernment. According to my sources, it's actually hidden right here, in this very Library." He smiled slowly. "I don't want to say anything more at this time, but I believe that securing the Diamond Lens will do more to help me fulfill my own quest than anything else I could do."

"Isn't there a way to do all this while staying together?" Amélie asked uncomfortably. "I really don't want us to split up."

"The Guide *said* we should stick together," Cécilie repeated one more time.

"*No*," Nachton retorted finally, "he said we should be united in *purpose*. There's a difference." He glanced at the Captain. "What say you?"

The Captain took a deep breath and gave Amélie an apologetic look. "I think it makes wise tactical sense to split up—divide and conquer, as they say. Surely the Guide would agree."

Nachton clapped his hands together victoriously. "That settles it, then."

The Captain glared at Nachton. "Do not forget your place, Master of Lore. The Empress has named you advisor. You may advise, as will we all. But the final decision must rest with *her*, always."

Yet again, all eyes fell on Amélie, and she trembled under the weight of that attention. Then she met the Captain's gaze... and she seemed to take courage from his confidence in her. "Very well," she said after a short pause. "I approve of Nachton's three-prong plan. Ewan and Cécilie will head to Lugland—"

"Lugard," Nachton corrected.

Amélie squeezed her eyes shut briefly, taking a deep breath. "Ewan and Cécilie will head to Lu*gard*, after which they'll return here, rejoining Nachton in the Library. I think—" She stopped herself and stood a little straighter. "No, I *command* that the three of you then *remain* here, until I return." She nodded to herself. "Together, we will ride for Eqland to claim Cécilie's throne. But only after I've won the support of the other leaders of Overtwixt. Cécilie will be the last of those leaders—and as soon as she's crowned, we'll launch our campaign against the Vizier."

Until now, Nachton had been pleased by the way the centmen and eqman responded to his plans. That was nothing compared to the reaction Amélie received. All four of her guardsmen stomped their hooves and thumped their chests, cheering loudly in support, while the Squire neighed loudly, "Hear, hear!" The Captain's eyes were glittering brightly. He looked proud of Amélie and inspired by her, all at once.

The little kids got into the cheering too. Cécilie started beating her hands on the table, and Ewan was yelling, "For

Overchix! For Overchix!" Nachton forced himself to smile, but inside he was seething.

Amélie looked relieved at this overwhelming display of support. "Great," she said, more confident than earlier. "Now, Captain... Ranger, Scout, Operative... Squire," she named them all again, "if you will excuse us, I want to spend a few minutes alone with my family before we go our separate ways."

"As you command, your majesty." All four centmen thumped fists to chest in a salute, then bowed low.

Ewan was *still* shouting at the top of his lungs as the non-humen filed from the room. "For Overchix! For Empess Ommie and Overchix!"

The End of
Part I

Part II
Quests

◇

The Five Fundamental Laws
of Overtwixt

Huh??

Law of Life / Uniqueness:
Every Life is Unique and Precious

~~Law of Equality:~~
No one Race is Greater than any other

Law of the Balance of Power!

Law of TIME:
Time marches Forward
independent of constraint

Law of _____:
All must Choose one Master

Law of DEATH ?
Once only may any man Live,
and after, to know Reality

It's the key!

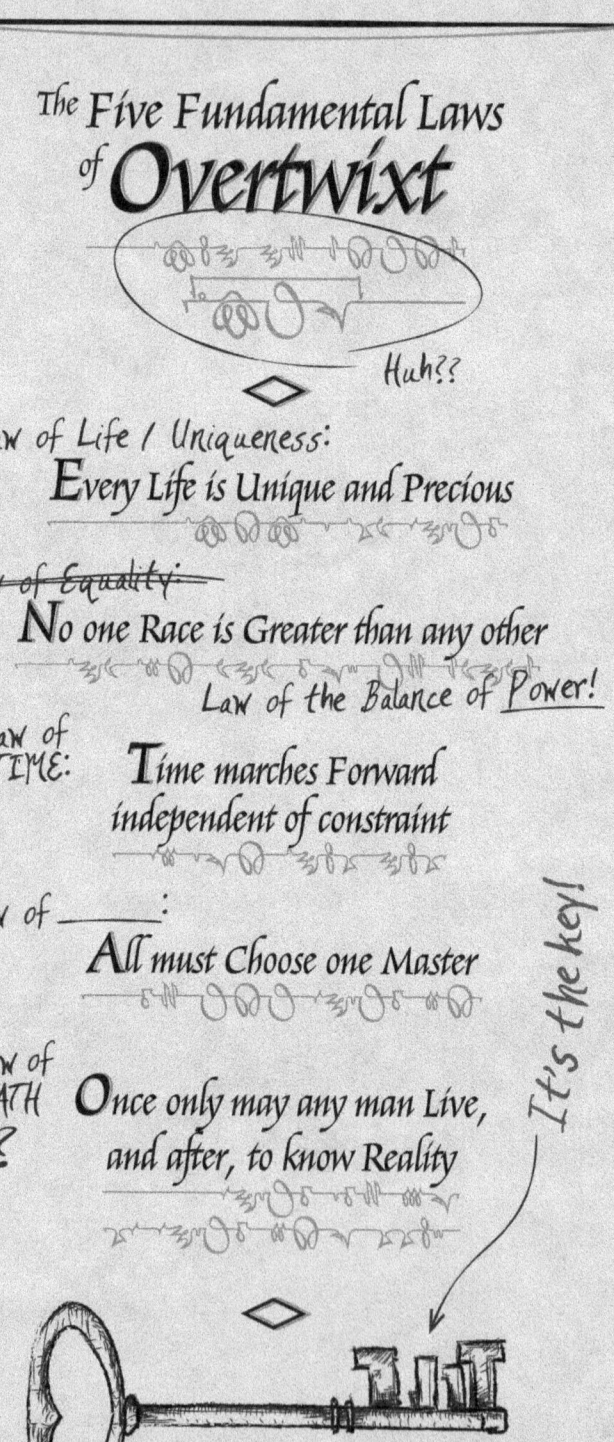

· thirteen ·

(Cécilie)

The sun was shining brightly as Cécilie, Ewan, and their two escorts got close to the mountain at the north end of Huland. The mountain was short and ugly, covered with strange dark spots. Cécilie squinted and asked the Ranger what they were.

"Caves," he answered. "The mountain is full of them, and tunnels too. The whole thing is one big maze on the inside."

"Why?" Cécilie asked. She was wearing her normal clothes again, riding on the Ranger's back like she'd ridden the Guide that first day in Overtwixt.

The Squire sniffed. "Because no one really wants a mob of uncivilized *lugmen* escaping Lugard to invade the other nilands."

"Huland is the only niland that still has a bridge to Lugard," the Ranger explained. "And after that business with the ancient Knight so long ago, the humen hired the gnomen to build a maze *around* the bridge—"

"*Gnomen*," the Squire snorted disdainfully. He seemed to like them even less than he liked lugmen.

"—so no one can get through without a map," the Ranger finished. "The lugmen especially."

"How *we* gonna get there?" Ewan asked. He was riding on Squire's back.

The Ranger held up a roll of parchment and smiled. "*We* have the map. Your brother the Loremaster found a copy in the Grand Library map room."

A little while later, the four companions entered one of the caves and everything went black... until Cécilie's eyes got used to the darkness and she noticed little amber points of light on the walls. "What are those?"

"Glowstones," the Ranger explained as they walked deeper and deeper into the cave. "The gnomen use them for light, and as signs for travelers." He stopped at a place where the cave split into two different tunnels. There was a really big glowstone on the wall here, and the Ranger read the symbols on it, checking them against his map. "The gnomen's entire niland—Gnobury—is a network of underground tunnels just like this. Anyway... I think we need to go *this* way."

Cécilie quickly got bored as they traveled through the tunnels. The glowstones were cool, but every tunnel looked exactly the same. She tried talking to Ewan, but he fell asleep on Squire's back. Squire and the Ranger were talking, but that was mostly boring adult talk. So she started playing with her necklaces. She still wanted to keep them a secret, but it was dark enough that she didn't think the Ranger or Squire would notice.

She put on the amethyst necklace first, and even though she didn't have a mirror, she *felt* more beautiful. She stared into the purple gemstone for a long time, cupping her hands to hide its dim green glow from the others. But eventually she took it off and quietly recited another rhyme to choose the next one, and the one after that:

"Batter you lick... could make you sick... you look fine, so *you're* my pick!"

Just like before, most of the necklaces didn't seem to do anything. They were just pretty, which Cécilie guessed was okay. Then something really strange happened when she put on the topaz necklace.

The Ranger's talking got very, *very* slow. And besides that, his voice got really deep too. Frowning, Cécilie pulled off the yellow-colored gemstone—and suddenly the Ranger's voice sped up to normal.

"Whoa," Cécilie whispered.

"—and that's how I became a member of the Baron's guard," the Ranger was saying. Cécilie put the necklace back on again. "Thhhhuhhhh Cawwwwppppptuhhhhnnnn awwwwllwayyyyzzzz ssssehhhhdd—" She took it off again. "—that I was the most gifted tracker he ever met. And..."

Cécilie ignored the rest of what he had to say. This was *cool*. The topaz necklace made other people slow down!

Eagerly, she went back through her other necklaces again. But... nothing. Aside from the ones she'd already figured out, the other necklaces still didn't do anything. With a sigh, she gave up, stuffing them back in her pocket, but leaving the useless obsidian one around her neck. She liked the way its chiseled facets reflected the light from the glowstones. "Are we there yet?" she asked in a whiny voice.

The Ranger chuckled. "Be glad you didn't go with your sister. She has an even longer journey ahead of her."

"Where is Amélie going again? Centwick and... Sha, um... Sha-nuh-something?"

The Squire broke into a gale of horsey laughter. "Shanagrailia, yes," he said, with that fancy accent of his.

Cécilie folded her arms and huffed.

Squire saw it and stopped laughing immediately. "Forgive me, your highness. I meant no offense."

"It's okay," Cécilie forced herself to say, but inside she was embarrassed and discouraged. So far, she knew only one of her future subjects, and he thought she was just a silly child.

Everyone fell silent for a while. Then—

"Who iss *Ammm*élie?" a creepy voice asked in the darkness. "And why iss she going to Shhana*graillll*ia?"

Cécilie sat up straight. "What? Who is that?"

The Ranger froze, sensing her alarm. "Who is what?"

"That voice! That creepy voice!"

"What voice?"

"I don't hear a voice," Squire said, though he sounded alarmed too. Both the Ranger and the Squire were turning in circles, trying to look everywhere at once.

"It's *here*," Cécilie hissed. "In the tunnel with us!"

"Whichh tunnel?" the creepy voice asked. "Gnnnoburry?"

Cécilie swallowed hard. "There it is again."

The Ranger and the Squire searched all around, but they never found anything—and they never heard the voice for themselves. Maybe that was because the voice never said anything else. Cécilie didn't either; she was too terrified to talk anymore.

Of course, Ewan slept through the whole thing.

Eventually, the centman and eqman gave up searching, and they continued on their journey. But everyone—except Ewan—was feeling nervous now.

After a while, Cécilie thought of something, and she looked down. She was still wearing that obsidian gemstone, of course. She hadn't noticed before, but the black gem didn't glow green like the others—instead, it seemed to suck green light *into* it. With a shiver, Cécilie took off the necklace and shoved it in her pocket with the others. She promised herself she'd never wear *that* one again... just in case it had anything to do with the creepy voice. Either way, she no longer thought the obsidian necklace looked quite so pretty!

At long last, the four companions came out of a tunnel onto a ledge at the top of a huge cavern. They started down a set of steps carved into the wall, twisting around like a funnel, the cavern getting smaller the lower they went. It came almost to a point at the bottom, connecting to an old metal spiral staircase that poked out of a hole in the cavern floor.

Cécilie felt a breeze as soon as they went through that hole. Fresh air, for the first time in hours! And all around her, she saw rolling hills—with *red* grass. Suddenly, the creepy voice didn't seem so creepy. She was outside again, and everything was okay.

"Welcome to Lugard," the Ranger said softly, when they reached the bottom of the spiral staircase and stepped out onto the red grass. The sky wasn't as bright as before— Cécilie guessed it was almost nighttime now—but she could see okay. The red hills went for miles, no mountains anywhere. Then she looked up, back the way they'd come, and gasped. There was a mountain above her, except it was upside-down, getting bigger the higher it went until it disappeared into the whiteness overhead. It was the *maze* mountain, Cécilie realized, part of Huland that stretched down to almost touch Lugard.

And the spiral staircase was the bridge.

"Look out!" the Squire hissed suddenly. "Lugman!"

The Ranger spun around, Cécilie still on his back, and Cécilie looked where the eqman was pointing. A huge person stood on a nearby hill, looking the other direction. He was shaped kinda like a human, with thick hair all across his shoulders and chest, and really—*really*—big muscles. His head was like a horse's, but with a horn on his nose that made him look more like a rhinoceros.

"Sir Knight," the Squire hissed over his shoulder. "Sir Knight! 'Tis a foe! What should we do?"

Ewan continued snoring.

Cécilie had a bright idea. No one was looking; the Ranger and Squire were focused on the lugman. So Cécilie pulled out the ruby necklace—the one that made her feel awake—and leaned over to put it around Ewan's neck.

Instantly, Ewan sat up straight on Squire's back, eyes wide. "What happing?" he demanded.

"A *foe*, sir Knight!" the eqman repeated.

Ewan saw the lugman, and somehow, his eyes opened bigger. With a scream of "Giddyup, Skire Horsey!" he kicked the eqman hard in the side—

And went charging off toward his first battle.

· fourteen ·
(Amélie)

The first day of Amélie's journey was drawing to a close by the time she and her centmen saw the Castle of Hucentia on the horizon. They had made good time, the centmen moving at a steady trot on the road from the Grand Library to the Hucentia bridge. Crossing that bridge had been a terrifying experience, now that she realized there was literally nothing beneath those weathered wooden planks. But she had squeezed her eyes shut and wrapped her arms tightly around the Captain's chest; and before too long, he had carried her safely across onto Hucentia.

Unlike Huland or Centwick, which were "portlands" (nilands linking Overtwixt to a real world), Hucentia was a "hubland" (a niland linking two or more portlands). This one was named *Hu-cent-ia* because it linked *Hu*-land and *Cent*-wick, the portlands of the humen and centmen. Or so the Captain had explained.

"This Castle was the seat of the old Baron's power," he said now, turning to glance at Amélie, still riding on his back. "Back before the Vizier showed up spouting all that nonsense about unification, and we moved to the Citadel on Twixt."

"So this was your old home?" Amélie asked, staring at the tall gray walls of the Castle in the distance.

The Captain nodded. "Long abandoned now. We'll camp there tonight."

"Camp? You mean, that's not where we're going?"

The Scout grunted, but the Operative smiled. "No, your majesty. The leaders of our people hold council on our own niland of Centwick. We are but partway there."

Amélie nodded. Stopping soon made sense anyway, what with night approaching. "Wait a sec," she said, frowning. "Overtwixt isn't a real world. It's not a planet that rotates, so... how can there be day and night here?"

"Excellent question, your majesty." The Captain pointed at the sun... which was somehow still high in the sky, even though it was almost dark. "That is what we call a Sky Light, and *it* rotates on an axis. One side is bright like a sun, the other side dim like a moon." He shrugged. "So whenever our Sky Light shows its bright side, that's day—"

"And we see the dim side at night," Amélie finished, understanding. That way, things at least *seemed* normal here, even though they were totally different. "Do you ever miss the real world?" she asked quietly, staring up at the slowly turning Sky Light.

"Never," the Scout said immediately. "I don't ever want to go back."

"I do," the Operative disagreed. "Overtwixt was never meant to be our home forever. Someday I want to go back, get married, have kids." He looked wistful as he added, "There was this girl..."

He trailed off and Amélie smiled. She missed her own loved ones for sure, and she'd only been here a day. Most of all, she missed Mom and Dad, her aunts and uncles, and her cousins Ivory and Ivan. The thought of never seeing them again—being trapped here forever—made her heart begin to thump painfully in her chest.

There was silence for a time, then the Captain spoke quietly. "I barely remember the real world anymore. I've been here so long..." He frowned thoughtfully. "But now that I can't go back, I find that I miss it too. How odd..."

"We'll get back there someday," Amélie promised. They *had* to. "We'll overthrow the Vizier and rebuild the bridges so everyone can go home."

The Captain and the Operative thumped fists to chest in agreement.

Night fell more quickly than Amélie was used to, even though the shadows stayed in the same place and never got long. They were nearly to the Castle when daylight ended, the Sky Light now giving off a soft silver light like the moon. And suddenly, the sky was full of twinkling stars.

"What—?" Amélie gasped.

"All the other Sky Lights," the Operative said with a smile. "There aren't as many Sky Lights as nilands, but still more than you could ever count. Infinite."

And just like that, Amélie felt safer and more at-home than she had since getting here. She had always loved the night sky, and this... this felt familiar.

Amélie and her guardsmen passed through the gates into the Castle, still able to see by the nighttime glow of the Sky Light. Inside the tall stone walls, they stopped in the outer court and started pitching tents. There were buildings all around, but the Captain doubted there were any human beds left inside; best to camp here, all together.

Naturally, the centmen wouldn't let Amélie help, but the Captain didn't want her exploring on her own either. So she seated herself on one of the stone steps leading to the Castle's feast hall, then tilted her head back to admire the night sky again. All those beautiful, white and yellow twinkling Sky Lights, so distant they looked just like stars.

Then she noticed a pair of *red* stars sitting very low on the horizon. Amélie squinted, confused. She could clearly see the top edge of the Castle wall by silver Sky Light, and these two red stars were below that. They weren't stars at all. Whatever she was seeing, it was *inside* the Castle walls.

"Captain—" she started to say.

"Hush now," he whispered, surprising her by how close he was. He was still fiddling with a tent pole, one-handed... but his other hand was pulling back the catch on his crossbow. Suddenly, he dropped the pole and turned in one smooth motion, firing the crossbow with a *thwack*.

The crossbow bolt shot across the outer court in an instant, and the two red stars disappeared in a puff of yellow smoke, the bolt clattering as it hit the stone wall behind. There was a moment of silence, then Amélie heard the flutter of wings.

"There's another!" the Operative yelled, already pulling the longbow from his shoulder and nocking an arrow. Amélie caught a glimpse of movement in the sky above, and she looked up just in time to see the shape of a bat flying overhead. Then the Operative released his arrow, and the bat disappeared in a second puff of smoke.

Amélie was standing now, the three centmen surrounding her with weapons drawn, eyes on the sky. They stood that way a long time, looking and listening.

"I guess that's it, then," the Operative finally said.

"Amateurs," the Scout spat. "I can't believe he exposed himself, flying across the sky like that. He should've stayed put."

The Captain snorted. "Be glad they *weren't* more experienced. If they'd reported to the Vizier about us..."

Amélie's head was spinning. "I don't understand. You just shot two bats, right? Animals?"

The Captain shook his head gruffly as he returned to setting up the tent. "No, your majesty. There are no animals here in Overtwixt. Just people."

"But—"

"Those creatures may have *looked* like bats from your world, but they were spookmen," the Operative explained. "Spooks, we call them—the eyes and ears of the Vizier."

Amélie swallowed. "And... you killed them. *People.*"

"I wish," the Scout muttered.

"None of that, now," the Captain growled. "Taking a life is no small thing." He turned to Amélie. "No, your majesty, we didn't kill them. One cannot be killed in Overtwixt... though if you get hurt badly enough, you *will* be ejected—returned in an instant to your real world."

"We call it 'getting smoked'," the Operative put in. "Since there's no blood here, just yellow smoke. Still, it's pretty serious. If that's the way you leave Overtwixt, you can never come back again."

"Hence the Fifth Fundamental Law," the Captain intoned. "*Once only may any man live in Overtwixt, and after, to know reality.* Men and women are meant to pass in and out of Overtwixt as often as they desire, but if they 'die' here... well, that's why the Vizier 'executed' so many during his purges. To ensure they could never come back."

"But don't worry," the Operative told Amélie with a reassuring smile. "Those two poor fools we just shot are still quite alive. They're waking up in their real world this very moment, with a *really* bad headache."

"Are they, though?" the Scout interrupted.

The Captain looked surprised. "What do you mean?"

"Do we really know for sure that those spooks are back in their real world now? What the Vizier did, destroying the bridges... what if it changed everything?"

Amélie felt a chill. The Guide *had* said that getting back to the real world was impossible now. But then, where else would people go when they got 'smoked'?

"I... don't know," the Captain admitted, but almost that quickly, he shook his head definitively. "No. I cannot believe that even the Vizier is capable of thwarting the Fundamental Laws of Overtwixt so completely." When the centman noticed the fear on Amélie's face, he added, "But even if things *have* changed, I can tell you one thing that hasn't: I will still do everything in my power to avoid getting smoked, and to save you from that fate too, majesty."

The other centmen nodded firmly, and Amélie hugged herself more tightly, agreeing wholeheartedly. No matter how badly she wanted to get home, she wouldn't want to go that way—even if she knew that it *would* take her home, which she wasn't so sure of.

The Captain waved a hand, putting an end to the discussion. "Enough talk for one night. Let us finish with these tents and turn in. We depart before daybreak."

This time when Amélie tried to help, no one stopped her. Within minutes, she was lying on her bedroll, staring up at the inside of her tent.

Wondering if she would ever find sleep.

· fifteen ·

(Ewan)

"**F**or Overchix!" Ewan bellowed. "For Empess Ommie and Overchix!" He kicked his horsey hard in the side again. "Faster, Skire Horsey! Faster-faster-faster-faster—"

"I say, sir Knight. Kindly do not kick me!" The horsey sounded out of breath, running and talking at the same time. "I am not some dumb animal. You may simply *tell* me what you wish, and I will—"

"Go *faster*, Horsey!"

Skire Horsey sighed, but he ran a little faster.

Ahead, on the next hill over, the lugman finally noticed them. He had two legs like Ewan, but his head looked like it came from a rhino-saurus... or... whatever those things were called. And he was *huuuuge*.

Surprised, Rhino Guy cocked his head at the sight of a little human kid—about as tall as his knee—charging him on the back of an eck-man horsey.

"Attack!" Ewan bellowed.

This made Rhino Guy smile, and he pulled out a sword, which was *also* huuuuge.

"You do realize," Skire Horsey asked Ewan, "that *you* don't have a sword yet. Right?"

"I take *his* sword."

"His sword is bigger than you."

"So?"

The horsey sighed, still galloping. "I just feel I should be the voice of reason here. The plan was to sneak *around* the lugmen—to *steal* the ancient Knight's Armor and sword. Only then would we start fighting people."

They were almost to the lugman now. "You wanna run away?" Ewan asked, confused.

Skire Horsey snorted. "No, not really."

"Then *attack!*"

The horsey ran straight at Rhino Guy, and Ewan got his feet under him, so he was crouching on Skire Horsey's back. When they got close enough, he *jumped*—and landed on the lugman's chest, where he grabbed fistfuls of thick hair so he wouldn't fall off.

"Owhh!" Rhino Guy yelled. His voice was so deep that Ewan *felt* him yelling.

"For Empress Ommie and Overchix!" Ewan yelled, then yanked the longer hair coming from the lugman's horsey head. Without a sword, what else was he gonna do?

"Owwhhh!" Rhino Guy yelled again. And with one big hand, he grabbed Ewan by the neck and threw him on the ground.

"Ooof," Ewan gasped, a little puff of yellow smoke coming out his mouth. He had to shake his head to clear it. When he looked up, Rhino Guy was standing over him, raising his big sword. Ewan couldn't possibly get away in time—

The lugman suddenly howled and dropped the sword, grabbing his hand, which had an *arrow* sticking out of it. He yelped again—and now there were *two* arrows. That would be Ranger Guy; Ewan had noticed before that he carried a bow and arrows.

The lugman ripped out the arrows and picked up his sword, but then something started zipping around him, moving so fast it was a blur. Ewan woulda thought it was a bug or something, except the blur was as big as Ewan!

With the thing buzzing around him, Rhino Guy forgot all about Ewan. "What that?" he said. "Stop that! Go way!" He swung his big sword at the blur, then swatted with his other hand. It did no good. The blur was too fast!

Then Skire Horsey was there, rearing up on his back legs and kicking the lugman's hand with both front legs.

"Owwhh-ughh!" the lugman bellowed—and dropped his big sword again, right next to Ewan's head this time.

Eyes wide, Ewan stood up quickly and got a grip on the sword's handle. It *was* bigger than he was. He tried picking it up... and had no trouble at all. Smiling like a fool, Ewan swung the sword hard as he could, accidentally hitting Rhino Guy with the flat side instead of the sharp part. It sent the lugman flying through the air.

"Gaaa-aah-aah!" the lugman screamed, his voice getting quieter as he tumbled to the bottom of the hill.

"Wow!" Ewan said in surprise. "This. Sword. Is. *Awesome!*" And with another bellow, he chased after Rhino Guy.

The big dude was getting to his feet, shaking his head. "Ow!" he complained. "That hurt." He grabbed another weapon that was hanging from his belt, a really big stick.

"For Ommie and—" Ewan started to say.

The lugman hit Ewan with the really big stick, sending *him* flying. This time when Ewan hit the ground, a bigger puff of yellow smoke came out. He felt like he might throw up.

He stood up again as Rhino Guy walked over. Where was the sword? Ewan had lost the sword!

The blur started zipping around Rhino Guy once more, but the lugman ignored it, getting ready to swing the big stick. Ewan *really* didn't want to get hit again, but he didn't know what else to do—so he grabbed the big dude's leg.

"Gah!" the lugman cried, as Ewan pulled him off his feet.

"Wow!" Ewan said. "*I* awesome!" With a big smile, Ewan flipped the lugman over his own head to crash into the ground on his other side. "I. Got. Awesome. *Muscles!*" And he started flipping Rhino Guy back and forth, from side to side, holding onto the lugman's ankles the whole time. "Cool-awesome-neat-neat-neat!"

"Mercy!" the lugman yelled. "I yield!"

"Let him go!" Skire Horsey called from up the hill. "Sir Knight, he yields to you!"

Ewan let go of the lugman's ankle, then climbed on top of his chest. The big dude was breathing really hard, and it prolly didn't help having a human—even a little human—*standing* on him, but... it seemed the right thing to do. Ewan put his hands on his hips, victorious.

The blur stopped zipping in circles and Cécilie appeared next to Ewan. She was pulling off a necklace and putting it in her pocket. "Wow, Ewan, that was amazing!"

"You 'mazing too, Sessy!" Ewan said back.

She was staring at Ewan's chest, and he looked down. He was wearing a necklace too, except his had a big red ruby. How did *that* get there? He started to take it off—

"No!" Sessy said quickly. "You keep it, Ewan. Um, knights should always carry something from a lady. For good luck."

Ewan shrugged. "Okay."

"You... you a Knight?" the lugman asked. And again, Ewan *felt* the big dude's words, this time through his feet.

"Yep!"

"You fight? Lots of fight?"

Ewan smiled really big. "Yep! I wanna!"

Skire Horsey caught up with them again, still short of breath. "At this rate," he mumbled, "we will likely fight every person we encounter, friend *or* foe."

"Good!" Rhino Guy said. "Take me! I want fight, lots of fight. You best fighter I ever know! I follow you, call you big boss, promise!"

"Okey dokey!" Ewan said excitedly.

Ranger Guy trotted down the hill with his bow and arrow, staring at Ewan on Rhino Guy's chest. "What—? How did you—?"

"You didn't see?" Ewan asked in disappointment.

"He's the *Knight*," Skire Horsey told Ranger Guy proudly, "that's how. And this lugman he defeated has just asked to join our party. Can you believe it?" Skire turned back to the big guy. "Now, what shall we call *you*?"

"Rhino Guy!" Ewan suggested, hopping off so the big dude could stand up.

"What?" Rhino Guy rumbled. "No. I am Berserker."

Ewan sounded that out. "Ba-zoo-ka."

"No, *Berserker*."

"That what I said!" Ewan repeated. "Bazooka."

The lugman looked at the horsey, who looked at Ranger Guy, who looked at Cécilie. Cécilie shrugged.

"What now?" Bazooka asked.

"Now we raid da shrine of da— um—" Ewan got a little frustrated. "We go steal da old Knight's stuff!" he announced finally.

Cécilie looked uncomfortable. "But... what if we have to fight other lugmen?" She glanced at Bazooka and blushed.

Ranger Guy nodded. "Good question. Will that be a problem, Berserker? Fighting others of your kind?"

Bazooka started laughing so loud, it sounded like booms. "Problem? No! Is what we do!"

"What you do?" Cécilie repeated, confused.

"Yes! You people—eqman, human, little man. You say, 'Hi! Hello!' and you shake hand. We lugman, we hit. Is what we do. Is okay." And he boomed more laughter.

Ewan was smiling very, very big now. He was really gonna like these lugmen Rhino Guys.

"Come, come!" Bazooka said. "I take you to shrine of ancient Knight! And we hit things, together!"

The
GRAND LIBRARY
of HULAND
782 HE
circulation 263 million

History

Arts

Magic

Admin

Literature

to Lugard via
Mazemount

to Eqland
& Hucentia

Philosophy

Science

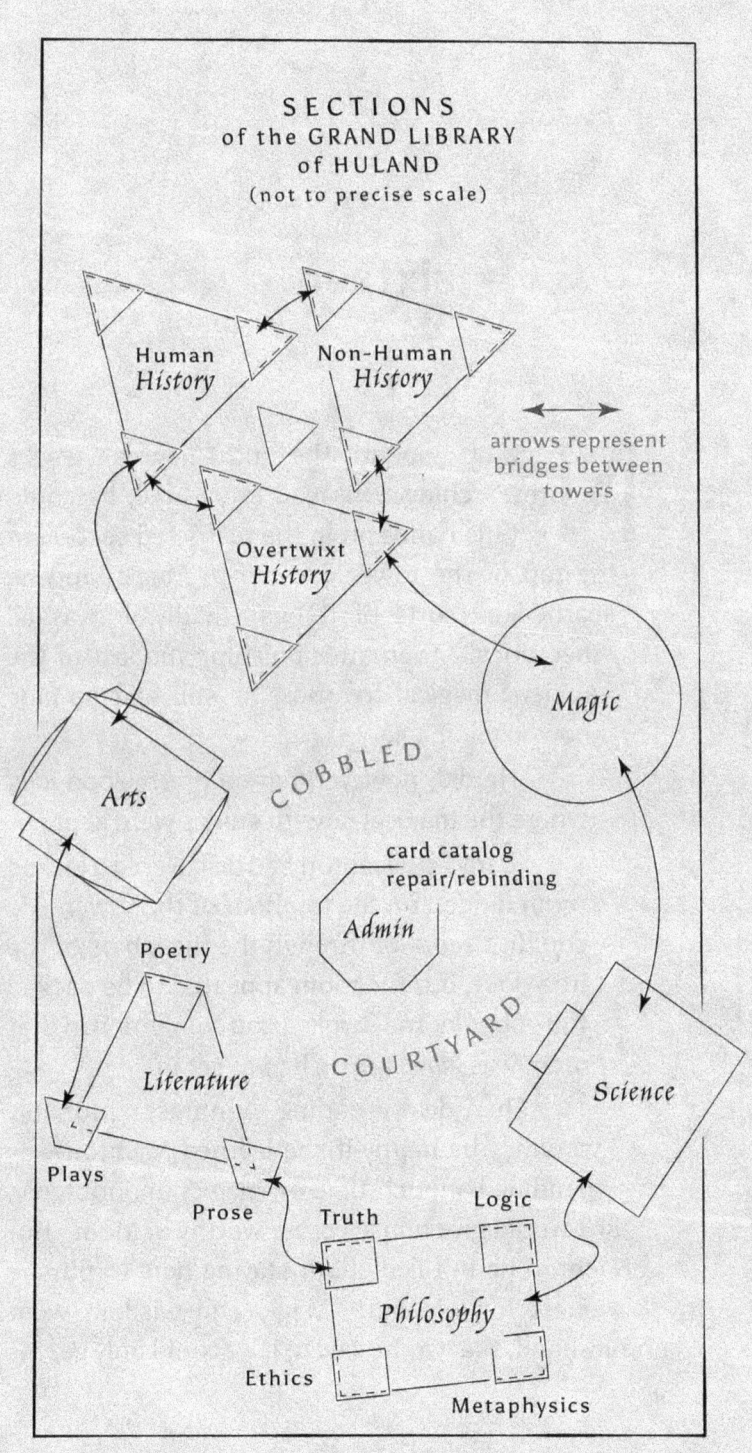

SECTIONS
of the GRAND LIBRARY
of HULAND
(not to precise scale)

Human *History*

Non-Human *History*

arrows represent bridges between towers

Overtwixt *History*

Magic

COBBLED

Arts

card catalog
repair/rebinding

Admin

Poetry

Literature

COURTYARD

Science

Plays

Prose

Truth

Logic

Philosophy

Ethics

Metaphysics

· sixteen ·

(Nachton)

Nachton spent the next three weeks researching. He read every book he could get his hands on in the restricted section at the top of the tower devoted to Magic, and he learned all sorts of things. Sadly, it was all theoretical. Even after finishing the last of the ancient magical treatises, he still had no clue how to *use* magic.

He did, however, have a pretty good idea where the magical how-to guides were kept.

Early on, Nachton had discovered a locked room hidden on the top floor of the tower. He couldn't see a lot through the thick bars of the iron door, but the room appeared to be packed full of books and scrolls. And something in that room was *glowing*. He had to get in.

The dear, darling Empress probably wouldn't be happy if she learned Nachton was spending so much time on magic; undoubtedly, she would give him a lecture worthy of Mom. But Nachton hadn't lied about staying here to pursue his quest for wisdom. Magic and wisdom went hand-in-hand, the way he saw it; if he could only get his hands on the Diamond Lens of Discernment—one of Sovereign's magical Relics—he would acquire *vast* wisdom.

And the more he studied magic, the closer he got to finding the Lens... until a note in one of his books pointed him right at its hiding place. And then Nachton felt plain silly, because the Relic's location was so obvious. Of course the Diamond Lens of Discernment was kept with all the other powerful stuff—in that same locked room!

Now he *really* had to get in.

What he needed was to find the key to that room. So, Nachton started working his way back down the tower of Magic. By now it had been a month (in library time) since his siblings left on their quests, and in that month, he'd only read the unlocked books on the top floor. There wasn't time in the rest of his life to read all the books on the lower levels, so he started skimming instead, looking for any hint about that key's location.

Two floors down from the top, midway through his second month, he found something in an old book that made the hair stand up on the back of his neck. It was a riddle, and it went like this:

> *Who seekest great Wisdom,*
> *first must seek small*
> *For from the five factums,*
> *comes the key to it all*

The key to finding wisdom? This sounded like exactly the lead he was looking for.

According to the riddle, if he wanted *great* wisdom, he first needed *small* wisdom. Well... that made sense, he supposed. Great wisdom probably built on top of smaller, common-sense wisdom.

What was this about factums, though? That was just another word for facts, right? Facts were information, knowledge. Well, duh. Naturally wisdom would come from knowledge. Suddenly, this stupid riddle reminded Nachton of his conversations with the Guide.

Fine, so he had to seek knowledge in order to find the key to the hidden room. You sought knowledge by reading books, which suggested that the key was hidden in one of the books here in the Library. Again, not a surprise. But *which* book? *Which* facts should Nachton be seeking!?

It wasn't until a day later—after hours of racking his brain to figure out the riddle—that Nachton realized what the phrase "five factums" must refer to. The wisdom he was supposed to seek first wasn't *simple*-small; it was *basic*-small. Profound, foundational... *fundamental*.

Of course. The key to the locked room would be found in the Five Fundamental Laws of Overtwixt.

Duh again.

Pulling out his notebook, Nachton found the right page and reviewed the Five Fundamental Laws once more. First on the list was the one he'd dubbed the Law of Life: *Every life is unique and precious.* After that came: *No one race is greater than any other;* he called that one the Law of Equality because it made him think of the civil rights movement, and Martin Luther King, Jr. The Third Fundamental Law, the Law of Time, read: *Time marches forward independent of constraint.* So far so good. These first three laws made sense to Nachton... but the last two were more cryptic. He wasn't even sure what to call the Fourth Law, which said: *All must choose one master.* And while he dubbed the Fifth Fundamental Law the Law of Death, that one left him scratching his head too: *Once only may any man live, and after, to know reality.*

Over the weeks that followed, Nachton immersed himself in the Five Fundamental Laws, more than he had before. Beyond the meaning they held at face value, he discovered that each one held a clue—and each clue was the next stage of an elaborate scavenger hunt that led Nachton to every corner of the Grand Library.*

Honestly, he didn't spend much time actually *reading* the books he encountered on his quest; he just skimmed or flipped pages as quickly as possible, focused entirely on the prize. Time and again, a misunderstood clue led him on a wild goose chase that wasted days or weeks. Slowly but surely, however, he found the pieces of the key he sought—actual pieces of a physical key that could be reassembled to unlock that door at the top of the tower of Magic. First he found the body of the key, which had notched slots in the shaft where square teeth could be inserted. Then he found those missing teeth, one by one.

Until only one puzzle remained: the Fourth Fundamental Law, which he'd already skipped once.

All must choose one master. What did that even mean? That all people had to choose which master they would serve? That all people had to choose the *same* master? So far as Nachton was concerned, he had no master but himself—at least while he was here in Overtwixt, away from Mom and Dad! Unfortunately, if he couldn't figure out the meaning of that Law, he would never find the last piece of the key.

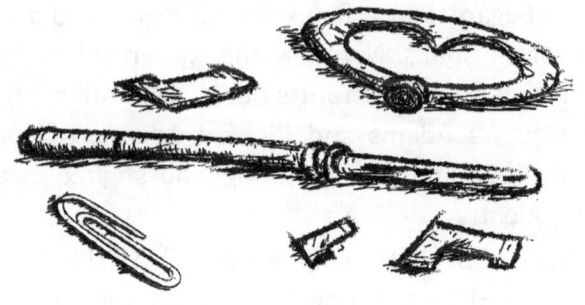

---

* The complete tale of Nachton's adventure finding clues in the Grand Library is documented in the novella *Scavenger Hunt*.

Unless he could find the piece *without* solving the puzzle? Most of the previous pieces of the key had been hidden inside a book, usually tucked inside a small envelope. Nachton had found each piece in a different section of the Library—Philosophy, History, Science, and Arts. Since the locked room itself was in Magic, he assumed that meant the last piece of the key was in the tower of Literature. So... knowing what he knew about how and where the last piece was hidden, could Nachton take a brute force approach and *bypass* the final puzzle?

That's exactly what he tried to do. Setting up shop in the Literature section, he started opening *every* book, one at a time, looking for an envelope.

It was terribly boring. Open book, look for envelope, close and reshelve book. Repeat. Open, look, close, reshelve... on and on forever. After a while, his brain turned off. Sometimes he would reach the end of a row and realize he couldn't remember the last fifteen minutes, which made him wonder if he'd passed the envelope without noticing. More than once, he had to start over on a particular shelf.

By the end of the first day of this—or at least, by the time he chose to take a break for a nap—Nachton had only made it to the 'Ab's. He still had a *long* way to go.

The next day, he started taking breaks more frequently. Anytime he began to lose focus, he sat down and actually read some of the books. Naturally, this was great fun. Unlike Science or even Magic, Literature books were full of stories. He read Douglas Adams and Richard Adams, of course. Aesop and Albee and Albom, though he steered clear of Louisa May Alcott.

By the end of that week, he was only to the 'Am's. A whole week, and he was only halfway through the books written by authors whose name started with 'A'? At this rate, it would take two weeks per letter and *fifty*-two weeks total.

That was an entire year! Even if time *did* pass more slowly outside the Library, Nachton's siblings would be back long before he finished.

Maybe a brute force approach wasn't the best use of his time after all.

Then again, there was more than one way to brute force this problem. Abandoning his fruitless search, Nachton returned to the top of the Magic tower. For the first time, he inserted his mostly-complete key into the keyhole in the iron door, and he could feel that it really did fit, almost. It *wanted* to turn in the hole, if only it wasn't missing that last tooth!

Determined to complete his quest, by any means necessary, Nachton started trying to recreate the missing tooth. Using paperclips and pliers retrieved from the supply rooms, he worked painstakingly for two *more* weeks. It took a lot of trial and error, a great deal of yelling and screaming, and even saying some words that would have gotten him grounded for sure, but Nachton eventually zeroed in on the correct height and shape of the missing tooth. Even then, when the key finally turned in the lock, there was no satisfying click. It *screeched* as the mangled paperclip scraped against the tumbler and caught.

But the door swung open.

Nachton was now inside the locked room at the top of the tower of Magic.

He went straight to the source of the faint blue glow: a small leather box sitting about chest high on a bookshelf, blue light showing in the cracks beneath the lid. Barely daring to breathe, Nachton opened the box and gasped. Inside was—

A pair of eyeglasses.

They were cool eyeglasses to be sure, really old and handmade-looking, with thin wire earpieces that wrapped entirely around the ears. But they were still just... Oh. Of course. This was the Diamond Lens of Discernment—or rather, Lens*es*. As in, eyeglass lenses.

Nachton picked them up reverently and put them on. The blue glow slowly faded as Nachton grabbed a book at random, reading the words within. The Lenses were crystal clear, and somehow, he knew they would never scratch or need to be polished.

He had done it! It had taken him *ten weeks* of research and effort since his siblings left on their own quests, but Nachton had obtained discernment, literally. He had seized hold of wisdom, kicking and screaming.

Feeling a sense of accomplishment, Nachton reshelved the book he had grabbed. Now that his quest was completed, Nachton could focus entirely on researching magic. With luck, he would clear up the Vizier problem all by himself, without the hassle of working with his siblings. In fact...

Nachton frowned. With the eyeglasses no longer glowing, he became aware of a second, lesser glow in the room, an eerie *green* glow. He soon identified the source: a small, black leather book lying on a nearby pedestal.

He walked over and stared down at it. There was a sizable emerald set into its cover—that was the source of the green glow—and the book's simple title was stamped in gold foil across the top in two languages:

CONJURING

With an eager smile, Nachton pushed his new eyeglasses up his nose and opened the book to the first page.

· seventeen ·

(Cécilie)

The lugman shrine to the ancient Knight was pretty cool, Cécilie had to admit. It was basically a tall hut covered in hairy brown animal skins, bones sticking out on all sides. Two giant tusks curled around the front entrance.

"It looks like they killed a wooly mammoth to build that place!" Cécilie said in awe. Dinosaurs were her favorite, but since wooly mammoths were also extinct, she liked them too.

"What a mammuff?" Ewan asked.

"A really big elephant with brown hair. But wait a sec." Cécilie frowned and looked at the Ranger. "You have wooly mammoths in Overtwixt?"

The Ranger laughed softly. "Actually, no. We don't have *any* animals in Overtwixt."

"Then... how did..." Cécilie stared again at the shrine in the distance.

"Those bones and skins are fake, replicas," the Squire spoke up. "Stolen long ago from a display in your human Library.

According to the stories, it was one of the provocations that brought the ancient Knight to battle the lugmen in the first place."

"Is true," Berserker said with a grunt.

Cécilie, Ewan, and their three companions fell silent as they studied the shrine... and the small valley that separated them from it.

A valley full of lugmen fighting each other.

There were no armies or battle lines, just a massive free-for-all—every lugman hitting, kicking, or biting any other lugman within reach. The only weapons Cécilie saw were big sticks, though, no swords; and whenever someone got knocked down, the winner moved on to a new opponent. So... they weren't actually trying to kill each other, just *hurt* each other. Really badly.

"Do we *have* to fight them?" Cécilie asked. There had to be a hundred of them down there.

"Some," Berserker rumbled.

"We could sneak around," the Ranger suggested. "Avoid the bulk of the fighting."

"No!" the lugman said angrily. "No sneak. *Fight.* Is what we do."

"I don't wanna fight *some* them," Ewan complained.

The Berserker looked horrified. "Must fight," he insisted. "Lots of fight, you promise!"

"Don't wanna fight some," Ewan shot back. "Wanna fight *all!*"

The lugman paused. "Oh." Then he smiled real big, and Cécilie noticed he was missing several teeth. "Okay."

"Now, we're going to need a plan—" the Ranger began, but Ewan was done waiting.

"You ready, Skire Horsey?"

The fussy eqman sighed. "I suppose."

Ewan stood up on Squire's back. "Hey you guys!" he screamed at the top of his lungs. "Uggy Rhino Dudes!"

None of them heard or looked.

"Hey you—"

"Bah-le-le-le-leeeee-i-oo-uuuu," Berserker bellowed, and every one of the lugmen in the field below turned to stare. "Is new Knight!" he yelled, pointing at Ewan. "Wants ancient Knight stuff. Wants fight—*lots* of fight!"

"Bah-le-le-le-leeeee-i-oo-uuuu," the other lugmen started shouting back, beating their chests. Their previous duels forgotten, they started crowding toward Ewan and his friends with big smiles.

Berserker smiled too. "Okay," he said. "Now we fight *all* 'em."

Ewan grinned back. "Awesome-cool!" And he kicked Squire in the side again. "Giddyup, horsey!"

Squire sighed, but he leapt into motion, Ewan sitting down to ride normal. The lugman Berserker ran down the hill with them, his long legs letting him keep up with the horse.

The Ranger sighed too. "He can't keep doing this! I know he's just a child, but he has to learn to *think* before attacking."

Cécilie didn't say anything. She was too worried for her little brother, watching him charge down the hill screaming. Her hand was already in her pocket, fidgeting with the necklaces.

The centman turned at the waist and pulled Cécilie from his back, setting her on the ground. "I'll do what I can, same as before, your highness. But this time, please remain *here*, where it's safe!" He didn't wait for a response, just pulled out his bow and arrows and charged after the others.

Cécilie took the topaz necklace out of her pocket and put it on—and instantly, everyone else got really, really slow. The Ranger was practically floating in the air, suspended mid-gallop. She ran forward, quickly passing him, then Berserker and Squire. She glanced at Ewan as she went by, to make sure he was still wearing his ruby necklace, and he was. Good.

But not good *enough*. She had thought the ruby necklace gave its wearer awakeness, but now she realized it gave strength; the awakeness was just a side effect. Ewan was about to fight a hundred guys, and he needed that strength to help him hit people harder, but it wouldn't protect him from getting hit or hurt himself. Cécilie wished she could give Ewan her topaz necklace too, so he could have strength *and* speed, but you couldn't wear two necklaces at the same time. So *she* would have to keep wearing the topaz, and find a way to help again.

But what could she do? It's not like she could distract a hundred people at once, the way she'd done with Berserker.

Cécilie stared at the horde of excited lugmen slowly charging toward her friends. Every single one of them was taller than the Ranger, with huge muscles on their bare arms and chests. The only clothes they wore were dirty pants or kilts, with thick belts around their waists and lots of weapons hanging from those belts.

She got an idea suddenly, and it made her giggle.

Running up to one of the lugmen, she took a dagger out of its sheath on his belt—then sawed *through* the big guy's belt. The weight of the weapons on his belt made his pants start falling down immediately, even in slow motion. Moving on to the next big lugman, Cécilie cut through his belt too, and then the next guy's, on and on. She didn't cut every belt, just the ones in a straight line between Ewan and the shrine.

By the time Cécilie reached the shrine and looked back, Ewan and the others were already colliding with the first wave of lugmen. She had a really good view of it, since the shrine was on a tall red hill. Lugman fists and sticks were swinging in slow motion, and Squire was rearing up on his back legs, kicking equally slowly. Ewan was already on the ground, hands around a lugman's ankle.

But the *next* wave of lugmen all had wide eyes, mouths open in comical expressions of surprise—as they slowly tried to keep their pants from falling off.

Giggling, Cécilie took off her necklace, and time went back to normal.

All throughout the enemy horde, lugmen were shrieking in embarrassment. Some were hopping up and down, others tripping and falling. They were wearing underwear, of course—loincloths, ew!—but it was still horrifying to lose your pants unexpectedly. Especially if you were a big manly man in the middle of a big manly battle.

Suddenly, lugman bodies started flying left and right. That would be Ewan. With all his enemies bent over, embarrassed, there was nothing to stop the little boy from knocking them aside. Cécilie heard him bellow, and then she glimpsed him charging forward full speed.

Ewan was like a bowling ball going through the crowd of lugmen, knocking them over like bowling pins. And all the way across the field to where Cécilie stood, he cackled gleefully. "I. Am. *Awesome!*"

Soon, Ewan was standing next to her again, a huge smile on his face. The Squire, Berserker, and Ranger joined them moments later, the centman looking at Cécilie with surprise and suspicion. "How did you...?"

Cécilie gave him her most innocent smile. "I snuck around the back, just like you suggested."

"But—"

The lugmen were staring up at Ewan in awe. Berserker raised his hands overhead. "Best Knight ever!"

"Bah-le-le-le-leeeee-i-oo-uuuu!" the others agreed loudly. "Bah-le-le-le-leeeee-i-*oo-uuuu*!"

Berserker grinned at Ewan. "Come," he rumbled. "Get ancient Knight stuff. Yours now."

Everyone filed into the shrine, which was very dark inside. It took Cécilie's eyes a long time to get used to it. When she could finally see again, she was surprised.

A wooden table stood in the middle of the hut. Ewan rushed forward and picked up a sword, holding it up to the light with a gleam in his eye. Meanwhile, the Squire inspected everything else lying on the table: a saddle, a folded blanket thing, and a set of saddle bags.

There was nothing else in the room.

"Where's the Armor?" the Ranger demanded.

"Armor?" Berserker replied. "There no armor."

"But... but the Loremaster said..."

A tiny little man stepped into the shrine behind them. "The *Armor*?" he asked in a nasally voice that sounded just like Cécilie's Aunt Judy from New Jersey. "You came here for the ancient Knight's Diamond *Armor*?"

"Yes—" the Ranger started to reply.

"You came to *Lugard* to find a *human* Relic of Sovereign?" the little guy repeated, as if he couldn't believe his ears.

"Yes! That's—"

"That's the most ridiculous thing I've ever heard!" the little man declared, and he burst into gales of honking laughter.

· eighteen ·

(Ewan)

Ewan liked to talk. He liked talking about things that happened to him, things he watched during screen time at home, and things he made up. He liked talking to his parents, his friends, his brother and sisters, or no one at all. Even when he talked to someone, it was *like* talking to no one, because everyone mostly ignored him. That was okay. He liked to talk anyway.

But the little guy they met at the shrine of the ancient Knight? That guy really, *really* liked to talk.

"I'm the Weaponsmaster!" he introduced himself for the third time as Ewan and his friends walked back toward the bridge to Huland. "Expert in various and sundry forms of combat, including but not limited to swordplay and hand-to-hand fighting, though I draw the line at bows and arrows—ranged combat is for lily-livered layabouts." He didn't just like to talk; he liked to talk *fast*.

"What *are* you?" Cécilie asked.

"I'm a shaman, doll, a shaman. Was my distinguished appearance not clue enough to my heritage?" He looked kinda like a dolphin, with flipper-arms ending in fingers, but hairy legs and clawed feet; and for clothes, he wore a pair of flowery swimming trunks, a poncho, and a funny round hat. Best of all, he was the exact same height as Ewan.

"But what you doing on—" Ewan started to ask.

"On Lugard? My job, kid, my job. I'm the *Weaponsmaster*. I train fighters, champs. Unfortunately, the Baron is way too good at *his* job, 'cause all we got these days is peace. Peace! My services being less in demand, I took myself away to the one place where *everyone* is always fighting: Lugard." He shrugged. "'Course, then I got stuck here."

"You mean—" Cécilie began.

"Yes, yes, that convoluted maze," the shaman said, waving his hand. "I didn't plan to stay long, just a couple weeks, but my map got destroyed. Been here years now. Let me just say how happy I am to finally be rescued from those uncivilized brutes."

Ranger Guy stopped walking suddenly, and Skire Horsey actually tripped. Both of them looked at Bazooka, like they thought he might get mad or something. "What?" the lugman asked. "Shaman right. Brutes—is what we are!"

Everyone started walking again.

"What I'd like to know," Ranger Guy said, before the shaman could talk again, "is why you think the Diamond Armor is on Huland."

"It's a magical Relic, isn't it?"

"That's ri—"

"Part of the cultural heritage of the humen, yes?"

"Yes, but—"

"Last borne into battle by the ancient Knight, who was slain wearing it?"

Ranger Guy waited to make sure the shaman was done talking this time. "So say the stor—"

"Then it's obvious, isn't it? When a person is slain in Overtwixt, he and any magical Relic he's carrying return home—him to his real world, the Relic to *its* home. The Armor is a human Relic, ergo, the Armor's on Huland."

"Oh," Ranger Guy said.

"'Sides," the shaman added, "I saw where the Diamond Armor was hidden last time I passed through Huland."

"You *what?*"

Everyone stopped walking again and stared at the little shaman, who stared back. "Well, *yeah*," he said. "I was under contract to locate said Relic on behalf of a private collector. Acquisition of rare gear is one of the services I offer as Weaponsmaster, you see, in between training gigs." Ranger Guy started to ask a question, but the shaman went right on talking. "No, don't ask me who the collector was; I'm bound by strictest confidentiality. In any event, I did my research and found the Armor, only I never got a chance to *tell* my client, on account of my getting stuck down here."

"So where is it?" Skire Horsey demanded.

They'd gotten back to the staircase and the upside-down mountain now, and the shaman just lifted an arm and pointed straight up. "In one of the caves above. On the back side of the mountain, outside the maze. I'll take you there, if you want."

Skire Horsey neighed. "Why? Why would you help us?"

"Why do you think, horse-face? In payment for services rendered. For rescuing me from the likes of this one." He jabbed a finger at Bazooka.

"But what about your contract?" Ranger Guy asked suspiciously. "The private collector?"

"*That* guy?" the shaman snorted. "He can eat rocks for all I care. Never liked him. I agreed to confidentiality, but there was no guarantee of delivery. And he wasn't gonna pay until then, so I owe him nothing."

"And just how much *was* the Vizier planning to pay for the location of the Armor?" Ranger Guy asked casually.

"I'm afraid I can't say. That was another confidential detail of our—" He blinked. "Did you just ask how much the *Vizier* was planning on paying me?"

Ranger Guy smirked.

"But... how could you know I was working for the Vizier?"

Ranger Guy shrugged. "The Armor is a human Relic. So your client had to be human if he hoped to wear the Armor himself. That meant the Baron or the Vizier... and you said yourself, you didn't like the fellow." Ranger Guy suddenly looked sad. "Everybody liked the Baron."

The shaman's mouth twisted like he was sucking a lemon. "I really should learn to keep my mouth shut."

Skire Horsey snorted. "Good luck with that."

"Wait just a momento," the little shaman said suddenly. "You said everyone *liked* the Baron. They don't like him anymore?"

Ranger Guy took a deep breath. "The Baron is gone. The Vizier slew him, right before destroying the last of the bridges back to the real worlds. Now he claims to rule all the nilands in the realm."

The shaman's eyes got big. Then, to Ewan's surprise, he smiled. "There's to be war, then? Rebellion? *Combat?*"

"Yes, but—"

"What about you, kid?" he turned to Ewan. "You gonna fight?"

"I'm the Knight!" Ewan announced proudly, happy to get a chance to talk again. It had been way too long.

"A *Knight!?* Why didn't you say so before? I'll train you, of course. Teach you the way of the sword, show you how to use that shiny new Armor of yours."

"Now hold on—" Ranger Guy began.

"What I call you?" Ewan asked the little man, ignoring everyone else.

"Me?" the shaman replied. "I'm the *Weaponsmaster,*" he said again. Ewan didn't know how many times that was; he couldn't count bigger than five.

"Weppamadda?" Ewan complained. "I can't say dat. I call you... *Fight Guy.*"

The little shaman just stared at Ewan for a while, then shrugged. "Yeah whatever, kid. You and me, we're gonna do big things. Big things, I tell ya."

Ewan smiled.

Fight Guy turned really fast and stared at Ranger Guy. "Now what are we waiting for? Let's get the kid his Armor already."

Ewan and Cécilie and their friends—*four* friends now—climbed the stairs back into the upside-down mountain. They climbed all around the inside wall of the really big cave room, then went through lots and lots of tunnels before going back outside again. And Ewan and Fight Guy talked *the whole way.* Ewan could already tell they were gonna be great friends.

Fight Guy led them around to the back of the mountain, and right to the opening of a dark cave. "There it is, kid. The hiding place of the ancient Knight's Armor."

Ranger Guy started leading the way into the cave.

"Whoa-whoa-whoa!" Fight Guy said, jumping in front of the cent-dude. "Where d'you think *you're* going?"

Ranger Guy frowned down at him. "To check the cave for danger."

"Oh no you're not," the shaman said. "This is part of the kid's rite of passage. Believe me, I'm the *Weaponsmaster.* I know all about this stuff. It's important for the kid's self-esteem and confidence and all that mumbo jumbo. He needs to do this by himself." Fight Guy shrugged. "'Sides, he'll be perfectly safe in there." He paused, then gripped Ewan's shoulders with his flippered hands. "Still, kid, be careful and come back to me, you got it? I *like* you. You're the only human I ever met who didn't look down on me."

Ewan grinned. "Okay!"

With a sigh, Ranger Guy stepped out of the way so Ewan could go through. "Just... be careful, sir Knight," he said. "And if you encounter anything unexpected, please *think* for once before acting."

Ewan rolled his eyes. "*Okay.*"

And then Ewan was running into the dark mouth of the cave. He ran until he almost couldn't see anything at all, then he ran some more. The cave wasn't just dark; it was quiet, too. Really quiet, after spending half a day with Fight Guy.

Ewan ran right into a wall he couldn't see. But he was able to *feel,* so he used his hands to figure out where to go from there, following the tunnel around to the left. And slowly, he started seeing things again. There was a blue glow coming from up ahead. He came around a corner and saw a big stone table in the middle of a big room. And lying on that table—

Armor. Glittering *Diamond Armor*, a separate piece for every part of Ewan's body.

He started hopping up and down excitedly.

"Who are *you?*" a raspy voice asked.

Ewan was so surprised he jumped in the air. Staring into a corner of the room, he saw two little red eyes glowing in the darkness up near the ceiling. Ewan thought the stranger must be really tall, until he realized the guy was actually hanging upside down from the ceiling!

With a flutter of wings, the little creature flapped down and landed right-side up on the table. "Who *are* you?" it asked again. It didn't look like anyone else Ewan had met since coming here.

"I'm da Knight!" Ewan said proudly.

Very, very slowly, the little guy smiled, showing off pointy fangs. "Excellent. And tell me, sir Knight. Would you like someone to help you put on your new Armor?"

Actually, Ewan had been thinking of attacking the little creature. The thing had red eyes, fangs, and claws, and Ewan was pretty sure that made it a monster. But for once, he decided to actually *think* before acting—just like Ranger Guy said.

"Okay, thanks!" he told the little bat-guy. "I don't dink I can get dis big piece on by myself anyways." He cocked his head. "Hey, what *your* name?"

· nineteen ·

(Nachton)

The green fireball struck the book straight on, consuming it in an instant. And just like that, the Grand Library of Huland lost its last remaining copy of a book by Louisa May Alcott.

Nachton grabbed another book off the stack to his side: all the worthless girly books he'd collected from the Prose tower of the Literature section, books that didn't deserve to be *called* literature. He glanced at the spine briefly—*Anne of Green Gables*—then threw it across the room as hard as he could.

Before the book could hit the opposite wall, Nachton waved his hands in a complicated manner, then flicked his wrist to shoot out a glowing green whip. The green tendril wrapped around the book and jerked it back toward him at roughly the same speed. Releasing the whip, which immediately disappeared, Nachton waved his hands in a different pattern. This time, creepy green light condensed all around him in the form of green *mist*, which he flung toward the flying book with another gesture. The book practically froze in midair, still flying toward him, but now moving so

slowly Nachton could have flossed all his teeth before it arrived. Instead, he waved his hands in the last of the basic magical patterns, producing one more green fireball to vaporize the book.

Briefly removing his spectacles—the Diamond Lenses of Discernment—Nachton mopped sweat from his brow. Combat magic was a lot of fun, but it was also a serious workout. He'd been surprised to learn there were no magic words to memorize, no phrases or spells to recite. You just had to know what you wanted to do, and you had to *really* want to do it, and then you made the proper hand and arm gestures. It was kinda like sign language, or conducting an orchestra. The more you threw your whole body into it, the better it worked.

It also helped to really hate whatever it was you were trying to destroy.

Nachton glanced sidelong at the stack of books. The temptation was almost overwhelming... he would need more books to practice with later, but... oh, why not? With a complicated gesture followed by a casual flip of one hand, he lobbed one last green fireball onto the stack.

"Ho there!" a distant voice called urgently. "Anyone here? I say, ho!"

Nachton leapt to his feet. Someone was finally back. He really *had* been toying with the idea of going after the Vizier on his own—though in his wisdom, he had so far resisted the temptation.

"Ho, anyone?"

"I'm coming!" Nachton yelled.

There was a clatter of hooves from somewhere down below. "Lord Squire?" the voice called.

Nachton reached the ground floor of the tower of Magic, where he was surprised to discover a delegation of eqmen. Not Amélie and her centmen; not Ewan and Cécilie and their two friends; but three horses Nachton had never seen before.

One of them gasped at Nachton's appearance. "It's true! There *are* other humen in Overtwixt."

"I told you!" the second eqman said. "I was there; I saw a human chase down the Squire."

The third eqman—no, eq*woman*, judging by her unicorn horn—snorted. "That was no human. That was a gnoman. Humen are taller." She hesitated. "Like this one."

Nachton cleared his throat. "Can I, um, help you?" He had encouraged his siblings to keep their presence in Overtwixt a secret, so it would be a surprise to the Vizier when they finally confronted him. He wasn't sure how he felt about these eqmen learning the truth. True, they were Cécilie's future subjects, but... could they be trusted?

"Can you help us?" the first horse repeated. "Yes, you can help us! Yes, please!"

The eqwoman tossed her head impatiently. "We need our champion—we need the *Squire*. And he was last seen crossing the bridge to Huland in the company of four centmen and two gnomen." She snorted. "Though I can't imagine how he managed to withstand the stench of the filthy little creatures."

"Because they weren't gnomen," the second horse insisted. "They were little *hu*men."

"I'm afraid the Squire isn't here right now," Nachton said slowly, not sure what else to say.

"Then where is he?" the eqwoman demanded. "We've been all over Huland looking for him."

"He's not on Huland anymore," Nachton said, "but he'll come back here to the Library eventually. Can I, um, take a message?"

The eqwoman stared at him. "I don't think you understand the gravity of the situation. We've been overrun!"

Something about the way she said the words sent a chill up Nachton's back. At the very same moment, he felt an excitement begin to bubble up within him. "Overrun? What do you mean?"

"I mean the Vizier has seized control of Eqland," she explained.

"He came out of nowhere," the first eqman took up the tale. "With drachmen—two of them!—and so many impmen their forms darkened the sky. We didn't stand a chance. Pastoral City fell in under an hour, and now he's clapped our people in chains. He has us hauling carts and delivering supplies."

"So you see," the eqwoman concluded, looking Nachton in the eye, her whole body trembling with emotion. "We need our champion. We need hope. We need any help we can get freeing our people and liberating Eqland from the forces of darkness!"

· twenty ·
(Amélie)

Two days after leaving the Castle of Hucentia, Amélie and her companions arrived at the Grove of the centmen on the niland of Centwick. After the way everyone talked about secrecy, she expected to slip into the Grove in the dead of night, meet with the leaders quickly and quietly, then be gone before daybreak.

Instead, Amélie was greeted warmly by almost every centman in Overtwixt—and told the morrow would hold an entire day of feasting, in her honor.

"My people are above reproach," the Captain explained when she asked. "No centman would ever side with the Vizier or the forces of darkness."

"But what about spies?" Amélie whispered. "What about those spookman bat creatures?" As she spoke, she was shaking the hand of yet another centman lining the path into the Grove, this one a woman covered with glorious brunette tresses from shoulders to haunches.

"We need not fear spookmen here," the Captain replied, and he pointed back at the pair of guards who'd let them into the Grove.

"The Grove is protected all around by sentries with sharp eyes and quick reflexes," the Operative explained, patting his bow lovingly. "And the canopy is too tightly woven for even the smallest of spooks to get through."

Amélie glanced up, noticing for the first time that the branches overhead formed a kind of basket that blocked even sunlight. That explained why everyone here used torches, even during the day.

"Rest easy, Empress," the Captain concluded. "So long as you're here, you're safe."

Amélie had grown to trust the Captain over the last several days, so she took his advice. And on the day of feasting that followed, she even enjoyed herself. It wasn't the kind of food she normally considered feast food—centmen were vegetarians, after all—but the cornucopia of edible plants was just marvelous: tables stacked high with multi-tiered serving platters, each level holding a different kind of leafy vegetable, interspersed with the most succulent bulb-shaped peppers she'd ever seen. And the dipping sauces! Sweet and tangy enough to make her eyes water today, and her mouth water for days afterwards.

None of it was *real*, of course. She understood Overtwixt well enough by now to realize that living plants didn't grow here; people didn't really need to eat in Overtwixt, any more than they needed to sleep. But eating and sleeping were familiar patterns for most people, and so

Overtwixt provided for those needs magically, as it had for Nachton and Cécilie in the Library. Here in the Grove, the desire for food was met with traditional centman fare.

Between meals, Amélie talked with the centmen. There were only about fifty in Overtwixt at any given time, and she spoke at length with most of the ones trapped here by the Vizier—even the Grove's sentries, since they rotated frequently on and off duty. She found herself impressed. The centmen were both passionate and self-controlled, and Amélie realized they would not rebel against the Vizier before the time was right. Well, she just had to convince them the time *was* right. So she put on her sweetest disposition and spoke respectfully with everyone, even finding ways of complimenting the centmen whenever possible.

Eventually the feasting ended, and the real talking began: Amélie's audience with the Council, the four wisest centmen and -women in the Grove. All the others were invited to listen, but the Captain explained that only the leaders would be allowed to speak. And they would speak for *all* centmen when they made their decision.

Everyone fell silent, and the Councilmembers gestured for Amélie to begin.

She took a deep breath, expecting to be nervous... but she wasn't. Her guardsmen had been treating her with deference for days now, and she was finally starting to *feel* like an Empress. "Men and women of Centwick," she began, "a great evil has overtaken this realm." She was quoting—as best she could remember—what the Guide had told her that first day, knowing his words would have the maximum impact. "A human called the Vizier has conquered all the nilands of Overtwixt, destroying the bridges back to reality and stranding all of us here. We cannot let him get away with this."

She went on from there, talking about her mission to unite everyone and overthrow the Vizier. She told them about her three siblings, and how they would contribute by fulfilling their own quests. She spoke passionately, knowing that none of the centmen needed to be convinced of the Vizier's evil nature. And for the first time since arriving in Overtwixt, Amélie cared about completing her mission for the sake of everyone affected, not just herself. She still wasn't clear what terrible plans the Vizier had for the people of Overtwixt, but *no one* deserved to be stranded or ruled over by a tyrant.

"And so I ask that the centmen join me in fighting the Vizier," Amélie concluded in the end. "With the support of all the peoples of Overtwixt, rallying behind me—your Empress—we can overthrow the tyrant and return Overtwixt to the way it should be." She was short of breath when she finished, flushed with excitement.

After the way everyone responded to her speech days ago in the Library, Amélie expected people to cheer, but they didn't. Instead, the four leaders of the centmen studied her calmly, expressionless. Finally, one of them repeated her last words: "The way Overtwixt should be?"

Amélie blinked. "Uh, yes. With the Vizier gone, Overtwixt will return to the way it should be."

"If you defeat the Vizier," a different Councilmember said, "wouldn't that leave us exactly where we already are? Except with you on the throne instead?"

"What?" Amélie objected. "No, I—"

"A human on the throne, ruling over everyone else," the third leader said thoughtfully. "Funny how a human would think *that* is 'the way things should be'..."

"You misunderstand," Amélie finally managed to say. "I have no desire to rule you. Not forever, at least."

"Forgive us if we don't take the word of a human for that." The words seemed harsh, but they were spoken as calmly as everything else the Council said.

Amélie swallowed hard. "I don't understand," she complained, trying not to sound whiny. "Of all people, I thought you centmen would be the most ready to support me." She glanced at the Captain, who seemed as bewildered as she was, though he obeyed Council rules and stayed silent. "Weren't the centmen ruled by a long line of human Barons?"

"Yes," one of the leaders admitted quietly. "And look where that got us."

There was another lengthy silence. Then the last of the Councilmembers stirred. He was the only one who hadn't said anything yet, a *very* old centman with a brilliant diamond pendant on his forehead, hanging from a circlet. "She does not know," he said in an aged voice. "Tell her, so she understands."

One of the other leaders nodded and began to speak. "Yes, we once followed a human Baron willingly. We have long enjoyed fellowship with the humen, a special relationship built upon shared knowledge and experience. The niland of Hucentia was itself born of that relationship, though it was originally called by another name, back when centmen ruled. We eventually ceded control to the humen, because they desire to lead and are often talented at it. But no Baron ever held absolute power, not even over us."

"Then came the Vizier," another Councilmember took up the tale, "and he was crafty. Wise, yes—something we greatly respected at first—but in a manner we later recognized as devious. We realize now that he started scheming his very first day in Overtwixt." The leader shook her head sadly. "The Vizier knew that everyone would be suspicious if he sought power for himself, especially so soon after coming to Overtwixt. So instead, he became an advisor to the five current rulers of this realm: the Underlord of Caymerdelphia, the Kaiser of the Shadowlands, the Mystic of Shanagrailia, the old Prince of Eqland... and the Baron of Hucentia, of course."

"And over time," said the ancient centman with the diamond pendant, "the Vizier began talking of unification. A new Golden Age of Overtwixt like existed long ago, in which all peoples became *one* people, united under a single monarch. Not some distant Sovereign most of us will never meet, but a single ruler *right here*."

"The idea took hold," the first Councilmember continued. "Our Baron was already popular, for he was a good man—not *perfect*, and not as wise as the Vizier, unfortunately, but a good man. When the Underlord of Caymerdelphia gave up his throne, the Baron resisted for a time, but he soon allowed himself to be named ruler of the aquatic peoples. The Mystic of Shanagrailia was next to abdicate, withdrawing into seclusion, and the little peoples voted to follow the Baron instead." The centman leader looked down at the ground, and Amélie realized he was blushing. "Even I was pleased to see the Baron assume greater power. It brought greater honor upon my people, for we enjoyed a closer relationship with the Baron than anyone. Woe upon me for my pride."

There was a moment of silence, then another leader spoke. "The Prince of Eqland was not so quick to step aside. Neither was the Kaiser of the Shadowlands, the leader of the creatures of darkness. And that would have been the end of all this unification talk... except the Vizier manipulated everyone masterfully." The story began to speed up, the leaders speaking one after another to weave the tale of the Vizier's rise to power.

"Visiting the Baron in his throne room one day, the Vizier produced a series of messages the Kaiser and the Prince supposedly sent each other, in which they plotted to eject the Baron from Overtwixt. This caused an uproar among those loyal to the Baron, and the Vizier acted quickly. Rounding up the Kaiser and the Prince and the other supposed ringleaders, he executed them—ejecting *them* from Overtwixt forevermore, with no hope of return."

"Mind you, the Vizier had no authority to execute anybody. Legally, only a ruler may take such terrible responsibility upon himself, to order another person's banishment. But in that time of uncertainty, the Baron proved disastrously indecisive. Instead of exercising strong leadership, he allowed the Vizier to act for him."

"With the Kaiser out of the way, many of the spooks and imps swore themselves to the Vizier personally. The spookmen he used as secret police and spies, the impmen as soldiers and workers, to start building walls around Capital City. We believe the Vizier's followers were also the ones who began destroying bridges and kidnapping people from the Capital, but they blamed these crimes on anyone who still opposed unification—giving the Vizier an excuse to execute those people too. This continued until all who remained here lived in fear... and this realm became isolated from the rest of Overtwixt, cut off from our real worlds as well."

"Of course, none of us *knew* that the Vizier was behind it all. There were rumors, but no evidence. Not until the Baron placed his own spy in the Vizier's inner circle and learned he was dabbling in forbidden magics. The Captain tells us this happened during the Baron's final week in Overtwixt. By then, it was too late, but the Baron confronted the Vizier anyway. He sacrificed himself as a distraction, to give his loyal subjects time to flee Capital City—and so the Captain and his men could escape to bring us this evidence.

Now we know for sure what we long suspected: that the Vizier is evil, to his very core."

The story came to a sudden, ragged stop. "That," the ancient centman concluded, "is how the Vizier came to rule this realm." He cocked his head. "Now do you understand?"

Amélie took a deep breath. "No," she said hoarsely. "I mean, yes, I understand how he came to power. But I don't understand why you won't support *me*. I want to *end* the Vizier's evil reign!"

"Truly," one of the Councilwomen said apologetically, "You seem to be a sweet, genuine person. But so did the Vizier at first."

"So you'll forgive us if we're not so quick to follow another human overlord," one of the other leaders added.

Amélie racked her brain for any argument she could use to sway them. "But the Guide!" she blurted. "The Vizier was never meant to rule. Viziers are advisors, right? Ruling Overtwixt was not the mission the Guide gave him. But it *is* the mission the Guide gave *me!* To unite all of Overtwixt beneath my banner."

The ancient centman's brow furrowed thoughtfully under that diamond pendant, but he didn't say anything.

The others did. "The Guide?" one scoffed. "Don't be naïve. That fellow holds no real authority."

"The Guide gives *all* men and women missions when they come to Overtwixt," another snorted. "Do not think yourself special just because he says so."

"But I *am* special!" Amélie retorted, too upset to think before she spoke. "I'm the Empress. You're supposed to follow me!"

The leaders of the centmen just shook their heads sadly. "This meeting of the Council of Centwick is concluded," the first said formally.

"No!" Amélie objected angrily. Her eyes fell again on the ancient centman leader with the diamond pendant, and she finally realized why that pendant kept grabbing her attention—because it was glowing with a very soft blue light. "You!" she cried, pointing at him. "You're wearing one of Sovereign's Relics, aren't you?"

The centman touched the gem on his forehead. "Yes," he said quietly. "The Diamond Coronet of Perception, gifted to my people by the Sovereign in ages past."

"It grants you wisdom, doesn't it?" Amélie insisted. "Tell them, then!" She waved her hands at the other centmen. "Tell them to follow me! Tell them it's the right thing to do. The Guide gave me the mission to unite all peoples beneath my banner, so we can overthrow the Vizier and rebuild the bridges. After that, I promise I will step down from the throne and leave Overtwixt." Amélie's eyes were fiery as she pronounced, "I don't want to rule! I just want to go home."

The ancient centman studied her for a long time. Every single person in the Grove waited on his next words. "I believe you," he whispered finally.

Amélie's breath rushed out. "Thank you—"

"However," the wise centman added, shattering Amélie's sense of relief. "I do not believe *you* fully understand the mission you've been given." He shook his head slowly, sadly. "No, I don't believe you understand it at all. And until you do, the centman people cannot help you."

Then he, and all the other centman leaders, turned their backs on her.

· twenty-one ·

(Cécilie)

The journey back to the Grand Library of Huland went faster than Cécilie expected. She spent most of that time staring at her little brother—who looked *glorious* in his new Diamond Armor.

It covered him from head to toe, every piece glittering in the daylight. Ewan said it was even glowing when he found it, though that stopped when he put it on. Even so, Cécilie finally understood why Nachton wanted to recover the Armor before Ewan accompanied Cécilie to Eqland. It was easy to forget Ewan was just a little kid when he was wearing that Armor.

Cécilie still wasn't sure how the little boy managed to *put on* the Armor by himself. He'd already been wearing it when he came out of the cave, all alone. For that matter, Cécilie wasn't sure how the Armor even fit him. But the Weaponsmaster claimed that was part of the magic of Overtwixt, that clothes and armor always fit perfectly, no matter who wore them.

They had made camp for the night, just outside the cave. The Weaponsmaster spent the evening teaching Ewan how to fight with a sword—how to *really* fight, not just swing the sword like a stick. Cécilie was amazed to see Ewan listening and obeying the shaman's instructions. Maybe it was a boy thing. Ignore anything an adult told you, unless it was how to *fight* better.

Now, the next day, Ewan sat proudly in an actual saddle on Squire's back, the sword hanging from his belt. Even Squire was prancing proudly, wearing a blue-and-white cape across his back, beneath the saddle. (The Weaponsmaster called it a *caparison*, but Cécilie couldn't pronounce that.) All of it—except the Armor itself—had come from the shrine on Lugard. All of it—*including* the Armor—had last belonged to the ancient Knight. And now Ewan wore it.

Ewan had completed his quest, acquiring Armor, sword, and Squire. He was now, truly, the Knight.

Cécilie realized she was smiling really big. Ewan saw her staring, and he flipped open the faceplate of his helmet. Inside, he was smiling just as big.

The six adventurers reached the Grand Library just after midday. Moving among the buildings together, Cécilie, Ewan, Squire, Ranger, Berserker, and Weaponsmaster searched for Nachton. To Cécilie's surprise, he wasn't in any of the History pyramids, so they checked the tower of Magic next.

They found her big brother leaning over a table, nine different books open in front of him. Nachton was so focused on his reading that he didn't even notice them come in, not until they stopped in a line in front of him. Then his head jerked up and he stared at them.

His eyes went first to Berserker, who towered over the rest of them. Then he stared at the little Weaponsmaster, half the size of an adult human, even though the shaman *was* an adult. And finally, Nachton's eyes stopped at Ewan in his glittering Armor, sword at his side, seated on top of a beautiful saddle and blue-and-white cape on Squire's back.

"Whoa," Nachton whispered. "Ewan..." He glanced again at the lugman and the shaman, then back at Ewan. "You've done well. I'm proud of you, squirt."

Cécilie folded her arms and huffed. Nachton never even looked at *her*.

The shaman Weaponsmaster was squinting at Nachton like he wasn't impressed. "So this is him? The *Loremaster* who thought you'd find the Armor on *Lugard?*"

Nachton looked surprised. "It wasn't there?"

The shaman laughed that honking laugh of his. "*Please.* It was on Huland, of course, the only place it could have gone after its bearer got smoked. Any Loremaster worth his salt would understand the magical behaviors of Relics."

"But... but I read it in a book..." Nachton insisted.

The Ranger frowned. "Perhaps one shouldn't believe everything one reads."

Weaponsmaster snorted. "If this *Loremaster* doesn't know that, I question how good a *Loremaster* he'll be."

Nachton pulled himself up to his full height, and he looked angry. "I don't believe we've been introduced."

The shaman snorted. "I'm the Weaponsmaster! Expert in various and sundry forms of combat—"

"And I am *not* the Loremaster," Nachton interrupted. "I have chosen a different path, that of Conjurer."

The scorn disappeared from the shaman's face, and he suddenly looked very interested. "Here now, is this true? You can conjure?"

In response, Nachton waved his hands in the air, and a glowing green tendril whipped from his fingers to grab a book from a nearby shelf. He pulled it back to himself and caught it, then offered it to the shaman with a smirk.

"Here now. Here now indeed! Color me impressed, perhaps even *green* with envy!" The Weaponsmaster honked another laugh. He did seem impressed with Nachton now. "A Conjurer! *And* a Knight! Why, with both at our disposal, we could take quite the battle to the Vizier." He stepped forward eagerly, peering at the books on the table to see what Nachton was reading. "Have you given any thought to our campaign? Where would we start?"

Nachton casually shut his notebook and slipped it into his satchel. "Funny you should ask that, as we've had a delegation from Eqland."

This made Cécilie blink, but it was the Squire who spoke up. "What's this?" he asked. "My people came here?"

"That's right," Nachton said, closing the covers of the other books on his table. "They came galloping up just days ago. It seems Pastoral City—the main eqman city—has fallen. All the eqmen who live there are now enslaved."

"No!" Squire gasped.

"The delegation is still here, over in the tower of the Arts. We've been awaiting your return so we can discuss our counterstrike."

The Squire was already galloping out the door to find his people, Ewan whooping excitedly from his back.

Cécilie was horrified. She was wearing normal clothes, and no amulets. This couldn't be the way the eqmen met their Princess for the first time. She started backing out of the group. She had to get over to that one tower in the History section, where all the dresses were. She had to change quickly, before Squire returned with his friends!

"Don't you think we should wait for the Empress before discussing this counterstrike?" the Ranger asked as Cécilie slipped away.

"No," Nachton said.

"But the Empress was explicit. We were not to reveal ourselves to the Vizier until the four of you are reunited."

Cécilie almost spoke up to agree. Plus, the Guide *had* said they should stick together.

Nachton snorted. "Think about it, Ranger. This is an opportunity we can't miss! The Vizier's forces are stretched thin, his imps divided between Capital City and Eqland. The eqmen in the outlying villages are still free, and they want to fight before it's too late. *And* we've got a Conjurer and a Knight, each one bearing one of Sovereign's Relics."

"Plus you've got a Weaponsmaster!" the little shaman said quickly. "An expert in tactics and strategy."

"And... um... um... *me*," Berserker boomed.

By now, Cécilie was at the door, and she glanced back one more time. No one noticed her leaving. "Best of all," Nachton told the centman, "the Vizier himself is on Eqland. If we attack now, we never have to march an army to Twixt and fight all his minions in the Capital. The Vizier is *exposed*."

The Ranger was still uncertain. "Yes, but—"

Cécilie slipped out the door. Running as fast as she could, she reached the human History building and barged inside. She ran all the way to the top of the stairs, puffing by the time she got there. She ripped off her boring clothes and yanked on the shimmering pink princess dress, pulling at the skirts until they hung right, then tied the red ribbon laces, jammed her hands into the long white gloves, and stuck her feet into the glittering red shoes. Only then did she pause.

Reaching slowly into the pockets of her old clothes, she pulled out all of her necklaces, carefully hiding them inside her dress. Then, taking a deep breath, she put on the amethyst necklace—the purple one that made her look older and beautiful. Her brothers were so oblivious, they probably wouldn't even notice the difference; but she was determined to make a good first impression on her new subjects.

Minutes later, she stepped back through the entrance to the tower of Magic. The Squire and Ewan had gotten back already, accompanied by three other eqmen—one of them a *unicorn*. The eqwoman was clearly older, dappled gray and white with a gray mane.

The Ranger was still arguing with Nachton, but Cécilie could tell immediately that the centman was the *only* one arguing. "—must wait on the Empress," he was saying. "The Vizier is more powerful than you can possibly imagine."

With one finger, Nachton tapped the spectacles he wore, an ordinary pair of glasses as far as Cécilie could tell. But wait... Nachton had never needed glasses before, had he? "Need I remind you," he asked, "that I bear one of Sovereign's Relics? The one that grants wisdom beyond compare?"

"Even so. Surely you don't think yourself the Vizier's equal, not after so short a time in Overtwixt."

"On the contrary," Nachton smirked. "These glasses revealed to me a secret message embedded within the Second Fundamental Law. I am *more* than capable of defeating the Vizier, even in single combat."

"But what if you're mistaken—"

"I'm not," Nachton said firmly, in a tone that ended the argument for good. "Wearing the Lens of Discernment, I am better prepared to see the wisdom of this situation than anyone. And in light of all the facts, the path forward is clear to me. We *must* attack, and we must attack *now*."

All four of the eqmen cheered at this. "Hear, hear!"

At that moment, the Squire caught sight of Cécilie standing in the entrance—and the horse's eyes almost bugged out of his face. "I nearly forgot!" he gasped, turning to the other eqmen. "Matron, Archivist, Scholar, please allow me to present another of the humen, sister to the Knight and the Lore—um, Conjurer. The lady standing before you is our new Princess of Eqland."

Everyone stared at Cécilie in awe— Nachton most of all, she was surprised to see. The eqmen knelt forward on their front knees, and even the Ranger did the same, blinking in surprise at the sight of her. The lugman Berserker suddenly seemed shy, and Ewan blurted, "You bootiful, Sessy!" The shaman grinned a needle-toothed smile and agreed, "That you are, doll, that you are."

Cécilie blushed with pleasure.

Nachton recovered first and turned to the Ranger. "Besides, who needs the Empress when we have the Princess of Eqland herself? The eqman villagers will rally to our cause. By this time next week, the Vizier will be defeated, and Overtwixt will be liberated."

"Hear, hear!" the eqmen cheered again. "Hear, hear!"

And feeling more confident than she ever had in all her life, Cécilie stepped forward to greet her new subjects.

The End of
Part II

Part III
Quarries & Quarrels

◇

Crystal City
of Caymerdelphia

· twenty-two ·
(Amélie)

Amélie rode out of the Grove in silence, the morning after her audience with the Council. Though many of the centmen bowed or lifted hands in farewell, she avoided their eyes. She was too ashamed, too angry.

"Should we return to Huland?" the Captain asked.

Amélie cringed at the thought. Face her siblings and admit her failure? Never. "We ride on. Who was next on our tour?"

The Captain nodded, obviously pleased that she wasn't giving up so easily. "Next is Shanagrailia, to meet with the old Mystic. The best route is via Eqland, across the great white arch south of Pastoral City."

"Whatever," Amélie said. She was in a funk at the moment, and the details didn't interest her. "How long?"

The Captain looked to the Scout, who shrugged. "We'll camp on Eqland tonight. Cross the white arch tomorrow, Shaland the day after. I'd say... four days to Shanagrailia, give or take."

Amélie nodded, and they rode forth in silence.

It was afternoon by the time they reached the covered bridge from Centwick to Eqland. Trotting out of the trees and into the open, they were halfway to the bridge when two figures appeared from its shadow.

"Halt!" the first one cried.

It was an imp. They were *both* imps. Similar to gargoyles with bat-heads and furry gray chests, they had bat-like wings furled under their armpits and wore nothing but ratty trousers.

"Halt in the name of the Vizier!" the second added.

The first imp scowled at his friend. "He's not the *Vizier* anymore, you fool! He's the *Emperor* now!"

"Well sure, *I* know that," the second gargoyle growled. "But how are *they* supposed to know that? If we just start saying *Emperor*, no traveler this side of Overtwixt will have a clue who we's talking about!"

"So?" the first answered sarcastically. "I say if they don't figure it out quick, we show 'em the inside of a cell!"

Both the impmen chortled at this as they turned to face Amélie's party again. "Wait!" the first said, laughter ending abruptly. "That ain't no gnowoman! That's a—"

The Captain's crossbow bolt took the imp in the chest, and he erupted in a billow of yellow smoke. It took the Operative slightly longer to draw back and fire his longbow. The second imp was flapping his arms, rising into the air, before he puffed to yellow too.

"What now?" the Operative asked. He glanced at Amélie, but he was really asking the Captain. "Do we still risk crossing, or—"

"Alarm!" a voice cried in the distance. "Raise the alarm!" Two more imp shapes flapped into the air from behind the covered bridge on the Eqland side of the divide. They immediately flew *away* from Amélie and her guards, toward the interior of Eqland.

"Not good," the Captain muttered under his breath.

"Can't you shoot them?" Amélie asked fearfully.

"They're out of range," the Scout growled.

"Besides," the Captain put in. "A squad of imps here, protecting just one bridge into Eqland? That's unlikely. They must've established a garrison, putting guards on *all* the bridges." He glanced at the Operative, who nodded agreement. "Eqland's been occupied."

Amélie's eyes went wide. "But my family—"

"They'll be safe on Huland. As long as they stay hidden in the Library, all will be well."

"We should go back to them—" Amélie began.

"No!" the Captain said sharply. "That's the *worst* thing you can do for them. We've already been spotted. You would be leading the enemy straight to them."

"Where then?" Amélie demanded. If Huland was out of the question, Hucentia was too, for it lay in the same direction. Eqland clearly wasn't an option...

The Captain and Operative shared another look. "Gnocentia," they said together, and the Captain explained. "It's another hubland, this one between Gnobury and Centwick."

"Where?"

"Back the other way," the Operative said with a grimace, tossing his head to indicate the road they'd just traveled, back toward the Grove.

"We ride!" the Captain yelled. "Quickly, we ride!"

Amélie and her guardsmen spent the rest of the day re-crossing Centwick, but this time at a gallop. At some point, their new route turned east, and Amélie stopped recognizing the landmarks they passed. Even so, they were still far from Gnocentia when dark specks appeared above the horizon behind them.

"More impmen?" Amélie asked. She was short of breath, but mostly from fear. The centmen were all panting heavily from the effort of maintaining their pace.

The Scout glanced back long enough to squint into the distance. "No," he said. "Not imps. Bigger."

The Captain grunted, but Amélie could sense his sudden unease. "Drachmen then," he said. "Or phomen."

Somehow, the three centmen increased their pace, and they didn't let up the rest of the way.

The Sky Light was showing its night side before they reached their destination, another covered bridge leading to the niland of Gnocentia. Amélie glanced back just as the centmen thundered onto the bridge, their hooves echoing loudly in the enclosed wooden space—and what she saw *terrified* her. Two flying horses, black as night, suspended in air by skeletal wings. She caught only the barest glimpse of them as they screamed at her, disappearing from sight as Amélie and her friends entered the enclosed bridge, the black horses swooping away to the left and right of it.

"Horses!" she gasped. "With wings!"

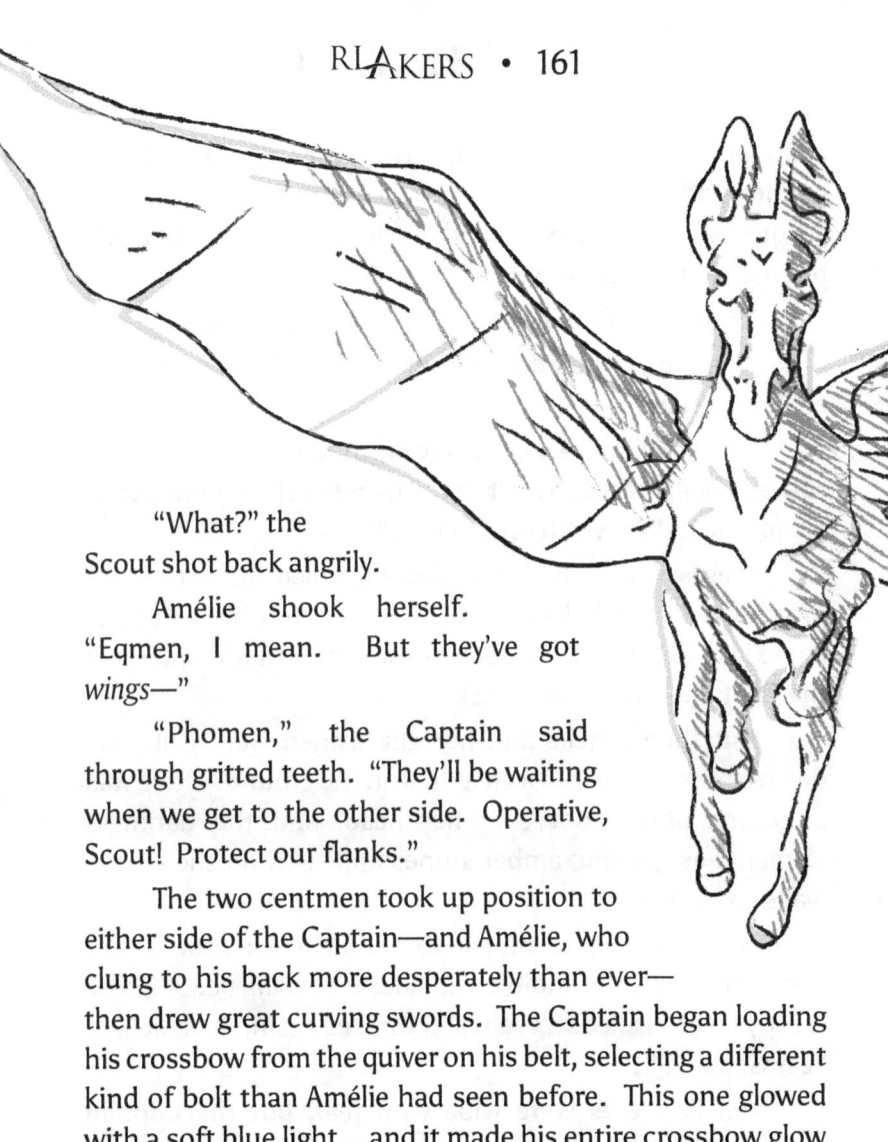

"What?" the Scout shot back angrily.

Amélie shook herself. "Eqmen, I mean. But they've got *wings*—"

"Phomen," the Captain said through gritted teeth. "They'll be waiting when we get to the other side. Operative, Scout! Protect our flanks."

The two centmen took up position to either side of the Captain—and Amélie, who clung to his back more desperately than ever—then drew great curving swords. The Captain began loading his crossbow from the quiver on his belt, selecting a different kind of bolt than Amélie had seen before. This one glowed with a soft blue light... and it made his entire crossbow glow when he loaded it.

Amélie's party was nearing the end of the bridge when the phomen landed on the rocky surface of Gnocentia before them. "Hhalt!" the first phoman hissed, flashing white fangs and glowing red eyes. "Hhalt, hhuwomann, in the nnname of the Emmmperor!"

The Captain fired without hesitation, the crossbow bolt shooting through the gloom like a blue streak of lightning. Both phomen shrieked in terror, diving to either side as the centmen thundered through. The Operative and Scout slashed with their swords as they passed, but there were no eruptions of yellow smoke, and Amélie lost sight of the black phomen in the darkness.

"Ride!" the Captain yelled. "We're almost there!"

Then Amélie heard something that made her blood run cold. Her *name*.

"*Ammm*élie..." a creepy voice drifted down to her from above. "*Ammm*élie... Hhalt in the name of the Emmmperor, *Ammm*élie... We wishh only to talk."

"Yesss, only talk," the second voice agreed. "We promisssse." And they began to laugh, terrible wheezing chuckles. She heard no trace of the terror they'd shown at the Captain's crossbow attack.

But then Amélie and her guardsmen were galloping down a rocky ramp into a great hole in the ground. There was a natural stone roof over her head, and the darkness retreated as glowing amber stones appeared on the cavern walls around her.

The centmen stumbled to a halt, even though the phomen were still audible outside. "*Ammm*élie..." those creepy voices called. "We will mmmeet again, *Ammm*élie... Yessss, we will..."

Amélie's eyes were wide with fear, but the Captain reassured her. "They will not follow us in here."

"They fear enclosed spaces," the Operative explained. "It negates the advantage of those wings. And since there are only two of them, *we* would hold the advantage if they were trapped on the ground."

"But there could be more of them!" Amélie began. "For all we know, there are dozens—"

"No," the Captain said firmly, gripping her shoulder to calm her. "There are only two phomen—only two in all of

Overtwixt, thanks to the Vizier's purges." He hesitated. "But they are formidable enemies even so. The Inquisitor and the Enforcer, perhaps the most rabid and loyal of the Vizier's minions."

Amélie swallowed hard. "So what now?" she squeaked. "Can we still make it to Shanagrailia?"

The Captain hesitated. "Yes, but I do not think that would be wise at this point. The phomen... they knew your name, Empress."

Amélie hugged herself to keep from shivering.

"How they learned your name, I cannot guess." The Captain looked very troubled. "But we cannot assume it is the only thing they have learned. If we continue on to Shanagrailia, I fear they'll be waiting for us somewhere along the way."

Amélie nodded jerkily. "Then we go somewhere else. *Anywhere* else." She licked her lips. "But where?"

The Captain took a deep breath. "Caymerdelphia."

· twenty-three ·

(Ewan)

E wan pouted at Nock. First he had to wear this scratchy blanket over his Armor, so it wouldn't glitter. Now they were *hiding*, all 'cause of a bunch of bad guys? That was the whole reason they were going to Eckwind, to fight bad guys, so Sessy could get her Pincess throne.

"Let me *go*," he whined at his brother, who gripped his leg tightly. "Skire Horsey, let's *fight* dem!"

Skire shifted on his feet, but he didn't charge. Nock shushed Ewan and kept watching the dark specks moving across the sky—which were shaped like tiny flying *horseys*.

Okay, so Ewan prolly couldn't fight *them*, way up in the sky. But there were four perfickly good enemies down *here*. Two on this side of the big brown bridge to Eckwind, two on the other side. Ranger Guy called them wimpmen—or was it impmen?—and they kinda looked like Ewan's friend from the cave; except these guys were bigger, with human arms and legs. These were the *bad* kind of bat-thing, though all of his friends seemed to hate all bat-guys the same. That's why his new bat friend from the cave didn't want Ewan telling anyone about him.

But *these* man-bat-guys—the wimpmen near the bridge to Eckwind—were *definitely* bad guys, and Ewan *knew* he could take 'em. He had a sword and a horsey and the best Armor in all Overchix. He kicked Skire in the side—

Skire Horsey didn't budge.

"But we can *defeat* dem!" Ewan told his big brother, starting to get mad.

"No, you couldn't," Nock said calmly. "Maybe the ones on this side. But you wouldn't make it halfway across the bridge before the ones on the other side saw you coming. They'd fly off and raise the alarm, and we'd lose the element of surprise."

Ranger Guy ran his hands over his bow and arrow. "I could make that shot... maybe." He didn't look very sure.

"No," Nock said again. "Even if you managed it, what happens when the next patrol comes by? If they find this bridge unguarded, they'd raise the alarm anyway."

"So whaddya propose?" Fight Guy asked. "Do you know some way of sneaking all ten of us across the bridge without these bozos seeing?"

Their group *was* getting big. In addition to Ewan, Nock, and Sessy, there was Ranger Guy, Fight Guy, Bazooka, Skire Horsey, and the other three horseys. That had to be at *least* five people—way too many to sneak across without being noticed. Especially since they'd have to walk right past all four of the uggy wimpy guys.

But Nock smirked anyway. "Actually, yeah. I know just the thing." He checked the sky again, making sure the two flying horseys were finally gone. Then he looked at the wimp-bat-things and waved his arms in the air. Green light started glowing around him, turning into green mist. One of the man-bat-things started turning this direction. Good. Maybe he would see them, and Ewan would actually get to fight someone.

Nock flung his arms out. The mist blew away from him, clouding around the two wimpmen at this end of the bridge before going across to the other side. The bad guy who was starting to turn this direction froze in place.

"Okay," Nock clapped his hands. "*Now* we can go."

Ewan didn't have to be told twice. Kicking Skire Horsey in the side, he drew his sword and followed Nock toward the bridge. Nock stopped right in front of the first wimpy guy and waved a hand in its face. The wimpman didn't even blink. Nock smiled at Ewan. "Frozen in time!" he said. "Or very nearly." He saw Ewan's drawn sword and scowled. "Put that away, squirt. The point is to get across without leaving any evidence we were here." He glanced at the wimp dudes again. "Let's go, quickly now! I'm not sure how long this will hold."

Ewan's other friends ran or galloped up, staring at the frozen bad guys as they went by. Everyone was amazed about Nock's green mist powers, and Fight Guy was smiling like it was the coolest-neato thing he'd ever seen. Nock got on one of the other horseys' backs, then everyone crossed the bridge onto Eckwind. Ewan made as much noise as possible riding past the bad guys on the other side, but they didn't wake up either. That *really* made Ewan mad. He never even got to use his new sword!

When they got far enough into the trees on Eckwind, everyone started talking again. Sessy was riding the gray unee-corn, and they were the only two girls, so they just talked to each other. Everyone else crowded around Nock, telling him how awesome he was. Fight Guy couldn't stop talking about the "applications" of Nock's powers in "the battle to come," and Bazooka asked if Nock would "make bad guys slow so I can hit 'em harder." Even Ranger Guy looked impressed by the green mist thing, which was crazy, 'cause Ewan thought *that* guy disagreed with Nock about *everything.*

Skire Horsey and the other two boy horseys insisted on riding at the front of the group, since they knew where they were going, but that was the last place Ewan wanted to be. "Let me down," he whined. "Skire Horsey, let me *down.*"

"As you wish, sir Knight." The big horsey stopped long enough for Ewan to get off. "Make sure you keep up. Call my name if you start falling behind!"

"'Kay, whatever," Ewan said with a really big pout, but Skire Horsey was already trotting to the front of the group again, declaring loudly that Eckwind was "all but liberated already."

Ewan kicked a stone in frustration. It didn't budge, and it couldn't possibly hurt him inside his awesome-neat Armor, but it *did* make him trip and fall on his face. "Graw-buh-fumba-dubba!" Ewan said, almost yelling. Nobody turned around to check on him.

He got up and pulled off the scratchy blanket; at least it made a satisfying ripping sound when it caught on his Armor. Annoyed at *evveybodies,* Ewan almost tore off the red ruby necklace Sessy gave him too, but he stopped himself and tucked it back inside his breastplate. With his Armor glittering in the sunlight again, Ewan started feeling better. Then he saw everyone crowding around Nock again, and his nose wrinkled.

"I agree," a raspy voice said.

Ewan was so surprised he jumped in the air again. Staring into the woods, he finally saw a little bat-guy hanging upside down from a nearby tree branch. Not a *man*-bat-thing like those wimpy guys; an *actual* bat-guy, like his friend from the cave. "Oh!" he said, realizing it actually *was* his friend from the cave. "Hi, Shark!"

"Sir Knight," the bat-guy acknowledged, nodding upside-down as a way of saying hello. Shark wasn't his real name, just the closest Ewan could get to saying it.

"So you agree with me?" Ewan repeated. "Um... 'bout what?"

Shark dropped from the tree with a flutter of wings as Ewan passed, flapping ahead to land in another tree. No one saw him except Ewan. No one else was even looking. "I agree that your brother stinks," the little guy said.

This made Ewan smile really big. He loved Nock, of course; Nock was his hero. But *Ewan* was supposed to be fighting all the battles, not Nock. Guide Guy *said* so.

Shark saw Ewan smiling and smiled too. His little fangs glittered in the sunlight almost as much as Ewan's Armor. "I meant that literally. Your brother actually stinks. There's an odor about him..." The bat's red eyes shifted to follow Nock again. "I don't like the smell of his magic."

"Oh." Ewan didn't really know what that meant, but he decided it didn't matter. He was feeling a *lot* better now that Shark was here, talking to him.

Shark dropped from his new branch and fluttered to another tree again—his way of keeping up as Ewan walked along the path. "Hey!" Ewan asked, "you wanna meet him? Nock? And my uvver fwends too?"

The little guy didn't say anything for a long time, and Ewan thought he was going to say yes. "No," Shark rasped finally. "Thank you."

"But—"

"They wouldn't trust me," Shark said. "The centman might even shoot me." He looked at Ewan. "You can't tell them about me."

"But you my fwend!"

The bat-thing smiled a toothy smile. He really did look like a little monster, with those fangs and red eyes. "Yes, I *am* your friend. And you are mine. But..." he glanced back up the path again, and his smile disappeared. "*They* would not be so quick to offer their friendship. No." He shook his head. "Tell no one of me." He sighed, dropping out of the tree, but flapping his wings to stay in place above ground. "I must go."

"What?" Ewan said. "You just got here!"

"On the contrary, I've been here since I left the cave. It is *you* who only just arrived." Shark jerked his head to the right. "I need to go scout the Palace in Pastoral City, see about the Vizier's distribution of forces. I just wanted to check on you first."

"Oh," Ewan said. Only part of what the bat-guy was saying made any sense to him.

"Can you whistle?" Shark asked.

Ewan shrugged and tried to whistle. It came out more like a high-pitched hissing hum. Ranger Guy *did* turn around when he heard it, but he relaxed when he saw Ewan was okay. He didn't notice Shark.

"That... was terrible," Shark said with a shudder. "But distinctive. Do that again if you ever need me. If I hear and I'm able, I'll come quickly." He glanced at Ewan's friends. "I'd better go. Your destination is just ahead."

"Really?!" Ewan sped up. He knew they were going to Skire Horsey's village first. "We here awready?"

Shark didn't answer. Ewan turned back, but there was no sign of the little bat-guy. He was already gone.

· twenty-four ·

(Cécilie)

Cécilie did her best to sit up straight on Matron's back for the ride to Squire's village. The Matron spent much of the journey lecturing her, after all, on the proper "comportment" of a lady. "A lady always uses good posture, whether sitting or standing. A lady lifts her chin, just slightly—proud, but not too proud. A lady is quiet and dignified at all times; if she must speak, she forces others to quiet themselves in order to hear her." The Matron even taught Cécilie to ride *sideways*, both legs dangling off the same side of the eqwoman, so that she didn't show anyone the inside of her skirts. (This was called riding "sidesaddle," all one word.)

The eqwoman's instruction had done almost as much to build Cécilie's confidence as the amethyst necklace she still wore. Cécilie *was* the Princess. She didn't need to convince anyone else of that. If anything, her subjects needed to prove themselves to *her*.

Eqland was beautiful, and Cécilie quickly fell in love with it. When Matron wasn't lecturing (and even when she was), Cécilie admired the niland's rolling hills, tall swaying grass, and majestic forest trees. The Guide even joined them for a time, walking and talking with her and Matron, though no one else seemed to notice. But that was just how Cécilie's brothers were, never paying *any* attention to the world around them.

Squire's village looked exactly like human villages back home on Earth. Not that Cécilie had ever been to one, but she'd seen pictures. There was a water well at the center, surrounded by huts with straw roofs. None of the doorways had *doors*, though, so Cécilie was able to look inside as she passed. Each hut had two or three rooms with straw on the floor, but no furniture. She guessed that made sense for horses, except—

"How are eqmen able to build houses?" she blurted.

The Matron laughed politely. "Since we have no hands, you mean?"

Cécilie blushed, realizing how rude her question was. But she forced herself to nod, very lady-like.

"We have our ways," the eqwoman said simply.

"Oh! You mean *magic?*"

Matron laughed genuinely at this. "I suppose it might look like magic to you, if you saw it. But no. To us it is simply science, the same techniques we use for building homes in our real world." And she would say no more on the subject.

Cécilie and her friends reached the center of the village, and Squire began introducing them to his neighbors. Everyone knew the Matron and the other two eqmen already, so he skipped them. He started with the Berserker, then the Weaponsmaster, then the Ranger and Nachton, whom he presented as the Conjurer. Squire got a bit flustered when he couldn't find Ewan; but then the Knight came running out of the woods, Armored legs churning wildly. All the villagers *oohed* and *aahed* at the sight of him in his glittery Armor, and they didn't seem to care he was acting like a little kid.

Then the Squire came to Cécilie. "Last but not least...
most important, in fact... it is my great honor and pleasure to
introduce the Princess—our new Princess of Eqland!"

Eyes widened and gasps left eqman throats. Everyone
stared at her.

Cécilie remembered her training from the Matron. She
didn't need to prove herself to these people, except to show
that she cared about them. She lifted her chin, but she also
smiled, just a little. "It is my pleasure to meet you all," she
said slowly, her voice soft. "I look forward to learning your
names."

"All hail the Princess!" someone cried. "Come to save
us from the Vizier!"

"All hail the Princess!" the others agreed, and all the
horses and unicorns—eqmen and eqwomen—bowed,
kneeling forward on their front legs. Then they were
crowding around Cécilie, every one of them wanting to nuzzle
her hand. Her heart thumped hard in her chest, but it was a
good thump.

Eventually, the villagers settled down, spreading out
again after they'd met Cécilie. "Now that *that's* over with,"
Nachton said, "it's time to start planning our attack."

"This way, lord Conjurer," Squire said, leading Nachton
to a large building nearby. Ranger, Weaponsmaster, and
Berserker followed, and Squire called to a couple other
eqmen. "Mayor, Steward, join us please."

Cécilie swung down from Matron's back and started to
follow, but a small eqwoman appeared suddenly in front of
her. She was tiny, even smaller than most of the other
unicorns—barely an adult, if Cécilie had to guess—with a
pure white body and long pink hair for mane and tail.

The little unicorn coughed politely. "Your highness,"
she said, dipping her knees in a curtsy. "May it please you,

um..." She kept shuffling her feet, and she wouldn't look Cécilie in the eye. She was nervous!

"I really like what you've done with your hair," Cécilie blurted. She immediately wished she'd thought of something more mature to say.

But the little unicorn seemed to appreciate the compliment. Tossing her mane and nickering softly, she finally met Cécilie's eye. "Thank you, your highness."

"What's your name?"

"I... I'm the Handmaiden," she squeaked. Then she took a deep breath and summoned her courage. "And, if it please you, your highness... I would like to join your retinue."

Cécilie looked at the Matron, confused.

"She wants to be one of your ladies-in-waiting," the older eqwoman whispered. "A servant, but also a friend."

"Oh!" Cécilie said.

"Forgive me, your highness!" the Handmaiden gushed. "I did not mean to be too forward. If you already have ladies to serve you—"

"No, it's okay," Cécilie told her, beaming a big smile. "I would be *delighted* to have you."

"You would?!" the little unicorn squeaked, prancing.

"Yes!" Cécilie assured her.

"Oh, I'm so happy! What would my new mistress ask of me first? I'm not very good at braiding hair, but—"

"Let's go for a ride," Cécilie blurted, then felt ashamed. That wasn't the sort of thing a princess *or* a lady would get excited about, was it? But when she looked at the Matron, she saw the older unicorn smiling broadly. She even *winked.*

"Yes!" the Handmaiden gushed. "It would be the greatest honor of my life!" And she lowered herself on all four knees, to make it easy for Cécilie to climb on her back.

The Princess of Eqland hesitated only a moment before mounting the unicorn the normal way, a leg on each side. She shrugged, apologizing to the Matron. "I wanna ride *fast*."

"I'll run like the wind!" the Handmaiden promised, leaping to her feet and prancing excitedly again. The tiny eqwoman was the perfect size for Cécilie to ride, considering Cécilie herself was still just a kid. It was like they were made for each other.

"Be safe!" the Matron called after them as they galloped from the village. "Stick to the trees around the village, and be back by nightfall! Above all, have fun!"

· twenty-five ·

(Nachton)

"This is the southern half of Eqland," the Mayor said, drawing in the dirt with one hoof. That was apparently why the floor of the villagers' meeting hut was covered in such fine sand. "Pastoral City is here, where the impmen are garrisoned inside the Palace. And this is the quarry, to the east."

Nachton regarded the silver eqman, the leader of Pastoral City. "You say this quarry is new?"

The Mayor nodded his long head. "The Vizier brought in gnoman slaves to carve out great blocks of stone."

Squire neighed in disgust. "Gnomen."

"Believe me," a voice said from the door, "we don't want to be here either." Everyone turned to see a little man walking into the meeting hut to join them.

"Ah," Mayor said, "this is the Crafter. He's one of several gnomen that escaped the quarry." The older horse gave Squire a warning look. "Remember who our true enemy is. Whether we like it or not, eqmen and gnomen have become allies in the fight against the Vizier."

Nachton studied Crafter. He understood now why his younger siblings were confused for gnomen their first day in Overtwixt. Except for the fact that Crafter's legs ended in hairy clawed feet, the gnoman could have been a human child... well, a really *ugly* human child, with big ears and a really big nose.

"Why open a quarry?" the Weaponsmaster asked. "Is the Vizier building something, to need so much stone?"

"Yes," the Mayor scowled. "He started fortifying Capital City about a year ago, supposedly to protect the Baron. Now he's accelerating those plans, and building even taller walls around the capitol building itself, turning it into a fortress—a Citadel."

"But why?"

The Mayor shrugged. "I don't know. In case the Sovereign sends armies to end his rebellion, perhaps?"

"But why quarry the stone *here?*" the Ranger asked. "Why put so many imps on Eqland when eqmen can't even help with the mining? He could have left the gnomen chipping away at stone in their home niland of Gnobury."

Crafter shook his head. "Wrong kind of stone. Geologically, Gnobury is mostly made up of porous limestone—easy enough to carve tunnels through if you're careful, but not a very good building material." He hesitated. "But Eqland... much as the stench of its inhabitants makes me ill, the niland itself is rich with beautiful veins of granite."

"*And,*" the Mayor added, "Eqland is just one bridge away from Twixt, where Capital City lies."

"Which is important," Crafter said tiredly. "My family and I, we were kidnapped a year ago to work the Vizier's secret mines on Pholand. But that's a long way to transport stone." He scratched his big nose and sighed. "Now that the Baron is out of the way, the Vizier doesn't need to keep this secret anymore. So he opened up this new quarry here, and pressed more of my people into work crews. We're able to produce more stone more quickly, and we're much closer."

"Which is why he's enslaved my people now too," the Mayor added angrily. "They're actually hitching noble eqmen to *carts*. Carts! To haul stone to Twixt!"

Nachton nodded slowly. He was finally seeing the bigger picture involving the Vizier's many plots. "Why garrison the imps in the Palace at Pastoral City?"

"Because it's defensible," the Steward spoke up. "Tall walls and a locking gate. At night, they lock themselves inside, along with their new slaves, all chained together. That way they don't have to worry about people like us attacking or mounting a rescue while they're asleep."

Nachton eyed the Steward. "You were in charge of taking care of the Palace, weren't you? Is there a way to sneak inside so we *could* attack while they're asleep?"

The Steward whinnied. "I wish it were so, but the Palace has no secret passages. Without the key to the front gate—which the Warlord ripped from my neck after Pastoral City fell—there's no way in. Unless you can fly."

Nachton frowned. "Warlord? Who's this Warlord?"

"Exactly the question I was gonna ask," the Weaponsmaster put in. "His *name* sounds impressive, but I've never heard of the guy, so he can't be all that special."

The Mayor cleared his throat. "He's a drachman. Previously the Commander of the forces of darkness. Served under the old Kaiser, before the Kaiser was banished from Overtwixt, after which he swore himself to the Vizier."

"Oh," the Weaponsmaster said quietly. "Him." And he said nothing further.

"Exactly," the Mayor agreed. "The Vizier only just renamed him Warlord, but I can already tell you, this new name suits him. He's a fearsome warrior even with his bare hands, much less wielding that staff of his. And that's saying nothing of the army he commands."

"You called him a drachman?" Nachton asked. He was sure he'd studied this at some point in the Library, but there was truly an infinite number of races in Overtwixt, far more than the sixteen peoples currently stranded in this small realm. "What exactly is a drachman?"

"Big," the Berserker rumbled for the first time since the meeting started, lifting muscular arms over his head. "Is bigger than me. With wings, and fangs, and tail."

"Oh," Nachton said, eyes widening. "One of those bat-dragon things." He'd seen one the day he entered Overtwixt, he realized. The creature that destroyed Nachton's bridge home must have been a drachman.

The meeting hut was quiet for a time, everyone studying the rough map drawn in the sand. It was *too* quiet, come to think of it. Nachton looked around quickly for Ewan, then relaxed when he saw him through the window. The little Knight was just outside, hacking at a wooden post with his new sword.

The Weaponsmaster saw where Nachton was looking and smiled fondly. "The kid's doing great with his training. He took to the sword like a natural! Gimme a few more weeks with him and—"

"You've got one day," Nachton said, coming to a decision.

The shaman honked a laugh, clearly thinking this was a joke.

"I'm serious. We attack tomorrow. There are still a lot of other details to work out, but as far as timing goes… it has to be tomorrow."

"That's madness!"

"We can't afford to wait longer," Nachton explained, "or our secret *will* get out. Then we lose the advantage of surprise."

"But how will we get inside the Palace?" the Steward asked.

"Are we sure that attacking the Palace is even the right move?" the Mayor replied. "If we attack elsewhere—the quarry, for instance—maybe we can draw off some of the Vizier's troops without facing the Vizier himself."

"I honestly don't care where the battle takes place," Nachton said, "so long as the Vizier *is* there."

That shocked everyone into silence for a moment.

"Wouldn't it be better if we fought the Vizier's army *without* the Vizier there?" the Ranger asked cautiously.

"Preferably without the Warlord either," the Weaponsmaster muttered under his breath.

"Consider our objective," the Ranger went on. "We want to liberate Eqland. If we can free the slaves, retake the Palace, and defeat enough of the Vizier's impmen, it won't matter if the Vizier survives the battle. Eqland will be ours, and he won't be able to retake it immediately—not singlehandedly. But he *can* singlehandedly turn the tide of this first battle, if he's there to rally his troops."

"Consider our objective?" Nachton repeated, getting annoyed at the centman for disagreeing with him yet again.

"The Vizier *is* our objective. What good does it do to liberate Eqland if he still rules the rest of Overtwixt?"

The Ranger frowned. "It is foolishness to face the Vizier *and* the Warlord *and* all those impmen, all at the same time. Not if there's an alternative."

"That's what I have you people for," Nachton said. "To distract the imps while I face the Vizier."

"What about the Warlord?" the Mayor asked.

"Leave him to Ewan," Nachton said with a shrug.

"No!" the Weaponsmaster objected. "The Knight's not ready to face that monster, not even if he had *months* of training under his belt. Drachmen have nearly indestructible skin—"

"And so does Ewan, with that Diamond Armor," Nachton pointed out. "Remember, he doesn't have to *defeat* the drachman, just distract him until *I* defeat the *Vizier*. The Vizier is their leader, their figurehead. Once he's out of the picture, the others will retreat or surrender. Even this Warlord, don't you think?"

"I don't know—" the Ranger began.

Nachton pointedly tapped the spectacles perched on his nose. "*You* may not know, but I do," he said firmly. "You speak of foolishness, but I'm the one wearing Sovereign's Relic of Wisdom!"

The Mayor's eyes widened, and the Steward gaped too. This was all the convincing *they* needed, at least.

Not so with the Ranger, of course. "And you're sure you can handle the Vizier?" the centman pressed.

"I can," Nachton said confidently.

"But he's so powerful," the Ranger argued. "He's been here for decades, amassing more power with each passing year. Even the Baron couldn't defeat him."

"And where do you think the Vizier gets his power?" Nachton asked, just as the Guide had once asked him.

"His magic, of course," the Ranger answered. Just as Nachton had once answered the Guide.

"On the contrary," Nachton replied with a superior smile. "Magic is merely a multiplier for the power a person already wields. So I ask you again: where does the Vizier get his *power?*" The Ranger clearly had no idea, so Nachton went on: "The truth lies buried in the Second Fundamental Law," he said, like a master lecturing pupils.

The centman eyed him. "You told us before that you found a secret meaning to the Second Law. You're finally going to explain that?"

Nachton nodded. "*No one race is greater than any other.* You may think that means all peoples of Overtwixt are equally valuable to the Sovereign. But the Second Law actually defines the balance of power in Overtwixt."

The Ranger blinked.

"That's right," Nachton smirked. "When the Sovereign created Overtwixt, he made it so that every race is allocated an equal amount of power here."

The Weaponsmaster's eyes widened. "That way, no one race could ever subjugate another race simply because they outnumbered them!"

"Exactly," Nachton continued. "The total magical potential of any one race would always equal that of any other race, regardless of numbers. Of course, that means the magical potential of each *individual* would always depend on how many members of his race were present in Overtwixt at any given moment."

The Ranger groaned, finally catching on. "And the Vizier perverted that. As he's perverted so many things."

Nachton nodded. "He tried to become the *only* member of his race in Overtwixt. As the only human, he—all by himself—would wield power equal to any other entire race. Which would make him *immensely* powerful."

"I had no idea such a thing was possible!" the Squire exclaimed.

"But... how does this make *you* more powerful than *he* is?" the Ranger asked Nachton. "You're both human. According to everything you just said, wouldn't you wield equal power?"

"You're forgetting the multiplying effect of magic—" Nachton began.

"That would only make *him* more powerful, since he's been practicing magic longer!"

"Except *I* bear a magical Relic," Nachton said, tapping his glasses. "The greatest kind of multiplier."

"And you don't think the Vizier has relics of his own?" the Ranger asked.

"He has the Diamond Sword!" the Squire put in. "He took it from the Baron before smoking him."

"Yes, but he can't *use* the Diamond Sword," Nachton said with great satisfaction. "Remember, Sovereign's Relics can only be used for the greater good. The Sword will never act as a multiplier for the Vizier so long as he pursues his own agenda. But *my* goal is the liberation of Overtwixt, so the Diamond Lenses *will* multiply *my* power. Ergo, I am more powerful than the Vizier."

"It can't be this simple," Ranger said, dismayed.

"It is," Nachton assured him.

"But the Vizier is so confident—"

"He's *over*confident, precisely because he doesn't know about *me* yet." Nachton cocked his head. "Now do you understand why surprise is so important to my plans?"

Everyone nodded—even the Ranger, though he still seemed troubled.

"Good." Nachton took a deep breath. "Now. I don't care where we fight this battle, but we do want to retake the Palace eventually—and that's almost certainly where the Vizier is staying—so let's brainstorm some more. Are we sure there's no way of sneaking someone inside to unlock the gate, so we can attack the bad guys there?"

Everyone was silent for a moment.

The Squire spoke up, his lip curling a little. "Maybe the runaway gnomen could tunnel under the wall?"

Crafter rolled his eyes. "Wrong kind of stone, remember?"

"Or the gnomen could make ladders and go *over* the wall?" the Steward suggested hopefully. "The little men are really good with their hands."

Crafter whirled to face Steward angrily. "Why do all these ideas involve putting *gnomen* at risk? If we try marching up to the Palace with a *ladder*, the guards on the walls would see us coming from a mile away!"

Everyone was silent again.

"Is too bad all fly guys work for Vizier," Berserker rumbled.

The Weaponsmaster honked a laugh. "That's true. If we had an ally with wings, he wouldn't have to tunnel *or* climb; he could just *fly* over the wall, quick and quiet-like."

From the entrance to the meeting hut, a small voice spoke up. "I got a fwend who can do it."

All eyes turned to Ewan, the Knight, who stood resplendent in his glittering Diamond Armor.

"I got a fwend who can fly," the little boy said. And then he smiled really big.

twenty-six

(Amélie)

G nocentia was both the smallest and strangest niland Amélie had visited so far. Created long ago as a hubland between Gnobury and Centwick, it mostly served as a way to get between the two nilands, since Gnobury floated *below* Centwick.

The surface of Gnocentia was almost nonexistent, and considering how Amélie had been in a hurry to escape the phomen, she'd missed it entirely. She had a pretty good view of the interior, however: a single open shaft from top to bottom, with a downward-sloping ramp carved into the sides. Peering over the edge of that ramp, she saw that it looped around the shaft at least a dozen times before disappearing into darkness. "We're going all the way to the bottom?" she asked, knees wobbling as she stumbled back from the ledge. "That'll take forever!"

The Operative grinned in the amber light of the glowstones all around. "Fortunately, gnomen are not just stonemasons, but cunning engineers as well." The Captain nodded agreement, reaching for a pulley mounted on the wall nearby. It was clear from the centmen's expressions that they didn't share the same disgust for gnomen that Squire and the other eqmen had demonstrated.

The Captain pulled the thick cable of the pulley, and Amélie forgot all about eqman prejudices. Gears clicked and whirred somewhere out of sight, and for the first time, she noticed four more black cables hanging down the inside of the shaft. They were now trembling with motion.

"No..." Amélie whispered in amazement. With a clatter, a mesh-walled square platform rose into view and stopped before her. "It's an elevator!"

"You might say all of Gnocentia is the elevator," the Operative replied, still grinning. Then he noticed her wide eyes. "Oh, there's nothing to fear, your majesty. Gnoman engineering is second to none." And he trotted onto the elevator platform, hopping up and down a few times. To Amélie's surprise, the rickety-looking contraption didn't sway in the least.

"Can we get on with it?" the Scout asked sourly.

The ride down was surprisingly smooth. The Operative and Scout operated the pulleys from within the elevator car, but the ingenious gnoman design meant the centmen never bore the platform's full weight; all they really did was keep the car moving downwards.

They reached the bottom quickly, passing briefly through open air before entering a new hole in the ground and coming to a halt. The Operative grinned at Amélie again. "And that was Gnocentia. Hope you didn't blink!"

"You mean—"

"We've reached Gnobury," the Captain confirmed. "Now be silent, all of you—even your majesty, if you'll forgive my directness. Allow me to negotiate with the gnomen for passage through their warrens." The four of them stepped out of the elevator and into another tunnel lit by amber glowstones, but... it was an empty hallway.

"There should be guards," the Captain muttered.

They waited several minutes and even called out, but none of Gnobury's inhabitants appeared.

"Enough," the Captain eventually growled. "Our path lies this way." And he led the foursome to the left.

At each intersection they came to, the Captain chose a branch without hesitation, only occasionally consulting the symbols engraved in the larger glowstones. It was clear he'd spent time in Gnobury before.

Amélie continued walking instead of riding, since the tunnels were a bit cramped—obviously carved for the convenience of smaller peoples than humen or centmen. After an hour or so, she moved up next to the Captain. "Why aren't there any gnomen?"

The Captain didn't speak for a long moment. "Gnobury is an endless warren of passages and caverns. The lack of guards at the entrance is concerning, but it's not so odd to find these tunnels empty. They're just roads used by travelers. I'm sure we'll meet some gnomen when we reach the next settlement."

"Unless the rumors are true," the Scout said darkly.

Amélie glanced between them. "Which rumors?"

"About a year ago," the Operative explained slowly, "the Vizier started building a wall around Capital City on Twixt. The Baron didn't like it—said we didn't *need* a wall—but the Vizier insisted it was for the protection of the city's citizens."

"A number of little people had gone missing from Capital City in the months before that," Scout added. "No one knew what became of them, but the Vizier blamed the Baron's enemies—the opponents of unification. He said a wall would keep those enemies from sneaking into Capital City and kidnapping more of the Baron's subjects." The centman scowled. "But *rumor* said the Vizier himself was behind the kidnappings. That his minions were stealing gnomen and nagmen to work as slaves, mining the very stone the Vizier was using to build the wall."

"The Vizier claimed the stone was mined by impmen on Pholand," the Operative concluded, "but everyone knows imps aren't that good with their hands."

Amélie nodded slowly. This wasn't the first time she'd heard them speak of the Vizier's wall around Capital City, or about the missing little people.

The Captain sighed. "It's been hard enough accepting that the Vizier deceived us for so long—deceived *me*. But to think he was abducting citizens right under my nose? I certainly don't want to believe *that*."

The Scout snorted. "Whether or not it was the Vizier, we can't deny that someone was kidnapping little people... and that they got to the ones here too. Look." They had just stepped out of a tunnel into a large open space. It wasn't a cave or cavern; more like the inside of a building carved out of the rock, with square doorways spaced along the walls at even intervals. And it had a definite air of abandonment.

The Captain grimaced. "It's late. I was planning to stay the night here anyway. No reason we still can't."

"What is this place?" Amélie asked.

"A den, the gnoman equivalent of a town or village. There's a traveler's lodge just ahead, with stalls for centmen. No human-sized beds, probably, but you're not much taller than a gnoman, Empress."

"A bed would be wonderful, thank you." She'd been sleeping on the ground ever since coming to Overtwixt... a week ago now? Longer? Still, comfortable bed or not, she couldn't help feeling uneasy in this forgotten place.

The Captain woke Amélie some time later, claiming it was morning—though *she* couldn't see any way of distinguishing day from night in the amber-lit tunnels. She and her guardsmen enjoyed a hot meal prepared over a gnoman stove, then they continued on their journey.

The next five days were much the same, with stops to sleep and eat at dens the Captain knew along the route to Caymerdelphia. And never once did they see a single living soul, aside from themselves. If any gnomen remained in Gnobury, they were doing an excellent job of hiding.

By the time Amélie's party reached the north side of the niland (where another elevator descended to Caymerdelphia) she was quite ready to leave the tunnels and glowstones behind. She missed fresh air and sunshine most of all. Or whatever kind of light their Sky Light put out.

Like their passage through Gnocentia, this elevator ride was perfectly uneventful. Soon enough, Amélie was stepping onto Caymerdelphia for the first time—into a mountain pass so chilly, she almost regretted wanting fresh air so badly. Her discomfort was only momentary, however, for the Captain offered her a warm cloak, encouraging her to keep the hood up so no one would recognize her as human. Then the centmen led her along the pass, rounding the peak of a snowcapped mountain to stand at the top of an icy waterfall. And there, spread out below them in all its glory, was the niland of Caymerdelphia.

Vast lakes glittered in the sunlight, separated only by narrow isthmuses, with ridges running along the outside of the niland to keep the water in. The niland was *mostly* water, aside from these mountains; the Captain had already explained that Caymerdelphia was a hubland where four aquatic species lived together in harmony.

At the very center of the niland, a colossal crystalline structure erupted from the water and reached for the sky, sparkling as if made from water itself. It was too big to be a single building, but it was obviously all connected—a *city*, with countless delicate towers, tallest at the center and shorter near the perimeter. The network of clear buildings even spilled onto dry ground in places.

And everywhere, creatures splashed playfully in the water. They were too far away to make out clearly, but even so, the sight of their carefree antics brought a smile to Amélie's lips. This place was the complete opposite of Gnobury in every way.

"Oy!" someone called over the roar of the waterfall. "Lookie 'ere!"

Amélie spun to see two bizarre creatures climbing up the mountain pass behind her. They were roughly human-shaped and human-sized, but with webbed fingers and toes, and fins on their heads, elbows, and the backs of their knees. Her guardsmen stood straighter, but they didn't seem alarmed at the sight of the creatures.

"She's 'uman!" one of them exclaimed—and only then did Amélie realize her hood had slipped.

The Captain groaned.

"'Ere now, I fink you're right!" the second strange creature replied.

Amélie tugged her hood back up. Then, feeling awkward, she said, "Um... you have a beautiful city."

The creatures' bug eyes bugged out even more. "Wha's this? Y'ain't ne'er been t' Caymerdelphia 'fore?"

Amélie could only shrug and shake her head.

"We have business with the Committee," the Captain started to explain—

"That lot?" the first creature said with a laugh. "Good luck peelin' 'em away from the 'ssembly!"

The Captain groaned again. "The full Assembly is in session?" He massaged his temples, then began muttering. "Not good. It could be days before they're able to see us privately. But—that's not your problem." He focused on the strange creatures again. "Listen, friends, we would be immensely grateful if you agree to keep our presence here a secret." The two creatures looked confused. "Beyond that... would you mind pointing us to the safest road down the mountain?"

"Safest?" one of the finned men objected.

"*Road?*" the other seemed equally horrified.

"No, no, no," the first continued. "Tha's no way to travel t' Caymerdelphia fer the very firs' time!"

"No indeed. It lacks style; it lacks *flair*."

"And it's not very ex-citin'!" The two creatures were practically finishing each other's sentences now.

"Nevertheless—" the Captain began.

"C'mon," one of the locals said, grabbing hold of Amélie's upper arm in a webbed hand. "We'll show you the *fun* way down." And before she or her guardsmen could object, the creatures leapt off the side of the mountain and into the waterfall.

Dragging Amélie screaming after them.

· twenty-seven ·

(Ewan)

Ewan found a good spot in the woods outside the village: an awesome-cool twisted stump in the middle of a clearing with no other trees. It had lots of little branches Shark could hang from, so it was *perfick*.

Jumping down from Skire Horsey's saddle, he sent his friend back to get the others. "Just Nock and Ranger Guy!" he reminded him. "Nobodies else."

The horsey complained, of course. "Are you sure about this, sir Knight? There *are* no flying people except those who serve the Vizier. Not in this part of Overtwixt."

"He a *good guy*, Skire."

"Yes, but—"

"Would you *pease* go get my bwudder?"

The horsey snorted, but he trotted back toward the village, his hooves crunching on dried leaves. Ewan waited until he couldn't see or hear Skire Horsey anymore, then he whistled at the top of his lungs.

Shark appeared almost instantly, swooping out of the sky and landing upside down in the tree stump.

"You was watching?" Ewan asked in surprise.

"I'm never far," Shark said. "What's going on? You sent the eqman back for someone?"

"My bwudder. He wants to meet you."

"What?! You promised not to tell anyone about me!"

"I *had* to," Ewan said. "We gotta have a guy with *wings*."

Shark scowled and got ready to fly away. He *really* didn't want to meet Ewan's other friends. Gently, the young Knight put a hand on his chest.

"We need you, Shark. To get in da Palace."

Shark opened his mouth to respond, but he was cut off by shouts of alarm. Ranger Guy was galloping into the clearing, next to Nock riding Skire Horsey. "Spook!" Ranger Guy cried, while Nock yelled, "Get away from my brother, you monster!" Ranger Guy already had his bow and arrow out, and before Ewan could say anything, he shot an arrow right at Shark's heart.

"No!" Ewan screamed. Moving really fast, he drew his sword—and chopped the arrow out of the air, right before it woulda hurt Shark!

Everyone stared at him, and even Ewan was surprised. Fight Guy had been teaching him how to use his sword better, and he *had* practiced chopping arrows, but... WOW.

Shark recovered first. Dropping out of the branches, he flew away as fast as he could. "Get him!" Nock cried, and Ranger Guy shot another arrow, but this one missed.

"Stop it!" Ewan screamed, but Nock was waving his arms now, shooting a glowing green whip at Shark. The little guy dodged out of the way, barely. He was going to make it!

Nock waved his arms again, this time blowing a cloud of green mist after Shark. The little creature dodged again, but the mist still touched one wing, and that wing froze instantly. Shrieking, Shark tumbled out of the sky, even though his other wing was still flapping hard.

Ewan ran towards him, but Skire Horsey galloped between them; Nock hopped down and grabbed Shark's tiny body in both hands. The bat-guy's wing was already unfreezing, and he started flapping madly, but he couldn't escape Nock's hands.

"Stop it!" Ewan screamed again, running to get around Skire Horsey and face Nock. "He my fwend!"

Nock stared at him. "You said your friend *wasn't* a bad guy!"

"He not!"

Ranger Guy frowned. "Young Knight, this is a spook." He shook his head. "Every one of the spooks swore themselves to the Vizier. They're his eyes and ears—Spies, Thieves, Messengers, and Criers."

Ewan shook his head stubbornly.

Nock elbowed him to get his attention. "Don't you get it, squirt? *All* spooks are bad guys."

"Well, *he* not!" Ewan insisted.

"I'm not!" Shark agreed.

"See?" Ewan asked.

Nock just shook his head. "Ewan, you can't just trust people because they *say* they're good guys!"

"I don't," Ewan said stubbornly. "I tust him 'cause he my *fwend*. Now LET HIM GO."

But Nock just ignored Ewan and started shaking little Shark, hard. "Tell us what you know, spook. Has the Vizier learned of our arrival yet? Did *you* tell him?"

"I... don't... know," Shark tried to say as Nock kept shaking him.

"Stop it!" Ewan screamed *again*. "You hurting him!"

Ranger Guy rested a hand on Nock's arm, and Nock scowled, but he stopped shaking the little creature. "Well?" he demanded.

"I don't know!" Shark repeated. "I haven't seen the Vizier in a week. Not since before I met the Knight."

"What else do you know, then?" Nock asked. "Tell me about the Palace. Defenses? How many imps? How many of *your* kind?"

Shark scowled. "Too many for you to defeat. Not unless you can get inside, and you can't."

"Yes we can!" Ewan interrupted hopefully. "That why we need you. To unlock da Palace."

Nock got *really* mad. "Would you SHUT UP, Ewan?" He was squeezing Shark so tight now that the little spook started coughing.

"*You* shut up, Nock! You hurting him!"

"Of course I'm hurting him!" Nock screamed back. "I'm *interrogating* him!"

Shark coughed miserably. "I... would have told you... what you wanted to know... anyway. I am no friend to the Vizier," he rasped.

Skire Horsey spoke up for the first time. "Lies! Spookmen serve evil—all of them, always."

"I was a friend to the old Baron!" Shark snarled.

The horsey neighed a laugh at this, but Ranger Guy looked surprised. "Wait... lord Conjurer, stop squeezing so hard!" He licked his lips, thinking. "The old Baron *did* have a friend among the spooks." He shook his head. "But I never saw the spook for myself. The Baron always sent me and the other guards out of the throne room first."

Nock stared really hard at Shark. "You're telling us *you* are this friend?"

"Yes!"

Nock frowned. "Anyone could make that claim."

Ranger Guy slowly shook his head. "I doubt very many knew. No spook who was friendly with the Baron would have been popular with others of his kind. This was a pretty big secret."

"The centman is right!" Shark insisted. "I spied on the Vizier for the Baron. No one knew, but I was a true friend of the Baron's."

Nock didn't look convinced, and he didn't let the spook go, but he *did* finally ease his grip.

Shark took a deep breath and relaxed a little. "Is what the boy says true?" he asked. "You want me to fly in and unlock the Palace gate, so you can attack?"

Nock and Ranger Guy looked at each other.

Shark was suddenly excited. "You've already raised an army then? What's your strength? We should attack immediately. Believe me, the time to attack is *now*."

Nock studied the little spook again. "I don't trust you. Why would you help us?"

"Aren't you listening? I was the Baron's friend! I want the Vizier defeated as much as you do!"

"Then why didn't you come to us and say so in the first place?" Nock demanded.

"Because I knew you'd shoot me out of the sky—which is exactly what you tried to do! I revealed myself to the boy because he's too young to have any prejudice."

This made Ewan angry. "Yes I do! I gots *pred-joo*... um..." He looked at Skire Horsey, then at Ranger Guy. "What *pred-joo-dust*?"

Skire Horsey laughed, and even Ranger Guy smiled a little before explaining. "Prejudice is disliking or distrusting someone for no good reason, maybe just because they look different from you. Even if you don't actually know them."

Ranger Guy glanced at Shark and then away again, a little ashamed. "What do you think, lord Conjurer? What if this little spook *is* the old Baron's friend, and our ally in the fight against the Vizier?"

Nock stared at the spook for another long moment. "No," he said finally. "We'll find another way. If need be, we can attack the quarry instead, drawing the Vizier to us."

"But Nock—" Ewan began.

"I said no!" Nock repeated. "It's too big a risk. I don't trust this little rat-with-wings, and I'm not letting him out of my sight until after the battle, if then. I'm certainly not sending him into the Palace to warn our enemies that we're coming!"

Ewan's brother handed the little spook to the Ranger, then started waving his magic. Another whip of green light suddenly wrapped around Shark's stubby little legs. Nock held onto the other end of the whip like a leash.

"C'mon," Nock said, "let's get back to the village. There's still an attack to plan, and we've wasted too much time on this creature already."

· twenty-eight ·
(Amélie)

Amélie screamed in terror until the moment she actually entered the waterfall, and then she gasped and nearly choked. The water was frigid, soaking her to the bone in an instant!

On either side of her, the aquatic man-shaped creatures continued whooping and hollering as they fell. They acted like tourists at a water amusement park.

Suddenly, Amélie felt something at her back— the slick, smooth face of the cliff behind her. She had just enough time to realize she was going to die... and then the face of the cliff curved up underneath her like a giant slide. Amélie shot forward and off to the left, momentarily airborne before plopping onto another smooth stretch of rock, water gushing all around her. Now she was going even faster than before, but moving forward almost as fast as she was falling.

One of the fin-men zipped in front of her on his belly, *face-first*, arms tucked at his sides to make himself more aerodynamic. He whooped again, and Amélie heard his friend answer from behind her.

Ahead of them, the rock banked on the left, and Amélie watched as the first thrill-seeker slipped around the curve and shot off to the right. Then she

was following, whether she wanted to or not. The rock banked again, and she shot back left, with only a momentary glimpse of the vast lakes below. The huge crystalline city was *much* closer than before.

By now, Amélie's wild ride had lasted long enough for her brain to start working again. She forced herself to stop screaming as she realized this actually *was* a giant slide—but carved from rock, not made out of fiberglass like at the water parks she'd visited before. Coughing, she sucked in a breath to yell a question at the moron who'd pulled her over the cliff, then suddenly she was airborne once more.

And for a final terrifying moment, she found herself hurtling toward the surface of a lake. She belly-flopped *hard*, then got her limbs tangled in her heavy cloak before she could rip it free and splash to the surface. Coughing, she forced herself to tread water until she could breathe again.

Then she launched into an angry tirade at the bizarre human-shaped creatures as soon as they surfaced beside her. "How could you do that to me!?" she screamed.

"Oy, you're welcome!" one of them said with a grin.

"I wasn't *thanking* you!" Amélie blurted, flustered.

"I ne'er gone 'at fast afore!" the second said to the first. "Fancy anutha go?" he asked Amélie.

"How *dare* you!?" Amélie blubbered. "I could've been *killed*."

The two guys stared at her, almost looking hurt. "So..." the second one said. "You *don't* fancy anutha go?"

Amélie only splashed her hands hard into the water and screamed in frustration. She had no idea where she was, she was separated from her friends, *and* she was soaking wet. Just about the only positive she could see in the situation was that the water here was warmer.

The two thrill-seekers shrugged and dove beneath the surface, reappearing moments later as dark underwater shapes darting toward shore—much faster than she would have expected.

"That's dagmen for you," an exasperated voice said.

Amélie spun in the water, surprised to see a small crowd gathered around her. Five or six dolphins, and three *women*. Who'd have thought the sight of other humans would be more surprising than finding herself in the company of dolphins?

"How'd you get up there, anyway?" the closest woman asked. "They carry you, I guess?"

Huh? "I... walked," Amélie said slowly.

This set off a flurry of conversation among the dolphins and women. A younger woman, not much older than Amélie, ducked underwater suddenly. A moment later, she came back up shrieking, "She's got no tail! She's got no tail!"

"What!?" the first woman gasped.

"She's got *legs!*"

At this, *everyone* dropped underwater, Amélie included. Beneath the surface, she was able to see the others fully. The dolphins looked like normal dolphins, but the women were only human from the waist up! Beneath that, *they* had dolphin tails *too!*

Amélie surfaced. "You're mermaids!" she blurted when the others rejoined her.

"I beg your pardon!" the first woman said, clearly offended. She swam closer and gave Amélie a clear view of the ring she wore on one finger. "I'm no *maiden*. I'm a happily married woman, thank you very much."

"What? No, I just mean... You're a mer-, um..."

"Merwoman?"

"Uh, yeah. I guess." Amélie blushed, realizing what a fool she was making of herself.

"And you're a *hu*woman," the younger merwoman said excitedly. "I've never seen your type before!" Then she and several of the dolphins were ducking beneath the water again—presumably to stare at Amélie's legs some more. Amélie blushed even deeper. "How are you able to swim without a tail?" the girl asked when she returned.

"Um... with my arms and legs?"

"So *weird*." The mermaid girl started to duck underwater again, but the older woman caught her arm.

"Don't stare, daughter. It's rude. And swimming with arms and legs isn't *that* unusual. Dagmen do it."

"Well, dagmen are weird too!"

"That's enough," the merwoman told her daughter. "Come along, it's time for dinner." And without another word to Amélie, she turned a cold shoulder and swam away, in company with her daughter and the third merwoman.

"Merwomen," one of the dolphins said, speaking with that same combination of affection and scorn Amélie had heard earlier. All the other dolphins erupted in clicking laughter. "Welcome to Caymerdelphia," the dolphin said to Amélie. "I rather suspect I'm the first to say so, at least."

"Yes, actually," Amélie admitted.

The dolphin bobbed a nod. "In that case, may I offer you any assistance? Is this your first visit to the niland?"

"That's right," Amélie said. "I'm supposed to speak with your leaders..."

"The Committee?"

"Um, I guess." That was what the Captain had said.

"Well, the Committee's meeting with the Assembly," the dolphin answered, "on account of the Vizier naming himself Emperor. I doubt they'll be seeing you anytime soon—unless that's the matter you've come to discuss, and you're willing to appear before the full Assembly?"

"How big is the Assembly?" Amélie asked, a feeling of dread in the pit of her stomach.

"Oh, could be a hundred or a thousand, depending on the urgency of the issue. Any citizen of Caymerdelphia is welcome to attend, you see." The dolphin click-chuckled. "The issue of the Vizier... I'd plan on a pretty big audience."

In other words, if Amélie wanted to appear before the leadership of Caymerdelphia, there'd be no chance of keeping her presence in Overtwixt a secret. Then again, those dagmen had already seen her, and the three merwomen, and all these dolphin-creatures. And the phomen who'd chased her across Centwick had known all about her anyway. Was her arrival even a secret anymore?

Amélie realized she was getting ahead of herself. "I arrived here with an escort," she said, "but we got separated. Three centmen—"

"Well, no centman is going to come down the same way you did!" the dolphin joked, setting off another round of clicking laughter. "Not even a cent*woman* is that brave."

"I really need to find them again."

"Have no fear," the dolphin said. "If they know your business is with the Committee, they'll look for you at the Amphitheater, where the Assembly meets. I can take you."

It was the first good news Amélie had heard since falling into that waterfall. "Thank you!" she gushed.

"You lot!" the dolphin called to her friends. "Hurry on ahead and inform the Assembly we have a human visitor."

She turned to Amélie. "Here, grab hold of my fin. Unlike those backwater merwomen, I *have* met my share of humen. You may be capable swimmers, but you're also slow. Come, come, don't be shy. Grab hold!"

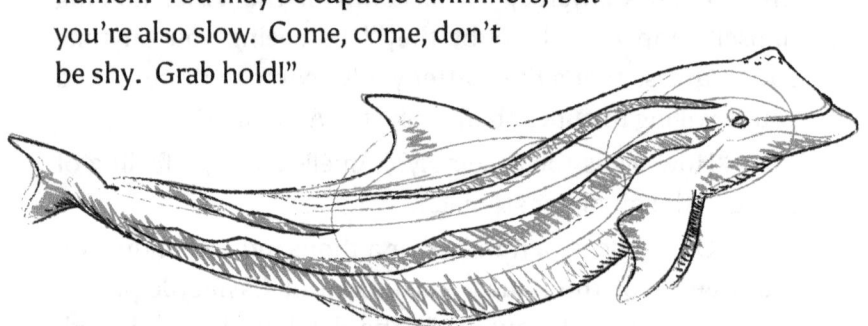

Amélie did as instructed, taking a firm grip on the dolphin's dorsal fin, and they were off!

The ride was like nothing Amélie had experienced before—in some ways, just as thrilling as the water slide she had ridden down the mountain, but nowhere near as terrifying. And, much to Amélie's relief, her new friend came up for air often.

Dolphins were mammals too, of course; just like humen, they had lungs and breathed air. So far as Amélie had seen thus far, *all* the races of Overtwixt were air-breathing mammals, dagmen included. Still, she suspected it was primarily for Amélie's benefit that her new friend surfaced so frequently.

They chatted each time they stopped. Amélie was not surprised to learn that the dolphins weren't actually called dolphins in Overtwixt; they were *delph*men, or in the case of her new friend, delph*women*. This particular delphwoman was the Hostess, and one of the most pleasant women Amélie had ever met.

The warm saltwater of Caymerdelphia's lakes was crystal clear, and it didn't hurt to open her eyes underwater, so Amélie gaped at every amazing sight as she and Hostess rocketed past. The water wasn't terribly deep, and she could easily see to the sandy bottom; she was amazed to discover glass structures even this far out from the niland's center, though they were short and squat, no more than two stories tall and completely underwater. *Homes.* Here and there, Amélie saw the citizens of Caymerdelphia going about their daily chores, cleaning house or preparing meals. Some were even sleeping! Apparently they were all capable of holding their breath longer than she was, even for hours at a time.

Hostess explained that all the structures were the handiwork of the merpeople, who were the most renowned glass blowers in all of Overtwixt. The niland of Merpool (the portland of the merpeople) boasted many miles of sandy beaches, and sand was the primary component in glassmaking. To hear Hostess tell it, most merwomen liked nothing better than to sun themselves on the beach for an afternoon, working on jewelry or glassware for use around the house, while the mermen did the structural glasswork. But it didn't have to be that way, and sometimes the opposite was true.

Amélie definitely saw more dolphins and merpeople on her ride to the Amphitheater than anything else, though she glimpsed a dagman here or there. The Hostess said *they* preferred to spend their days having fun; thrill-seeking was such a big part of their culture that the bridge from Caymerdelphia to Dagmoor was itself the most elaborate water slide ever created.

The last of the four aquatic species was the caymen, who reminded Amélie of Earth's manatees, except with the head of a sea horse. They looked cumbersome at first, but they were actually pretty nimble. In fact, the more she saw of them, the more Amélie began to think of them as aquatic eqmen. The Hostess had only good things to say about them, though she warned Amélie never to get trapped in an argument with a cayman, even about the most trivial matter.

The closer they got to the center of Caymerdelphia, the higher the glass structures rose from the sandy bottom, until they began cresting the surface all around. Soon, Amélie and Hostess were swimming—at a slower pace—down narrow avenues between towers. Even then, it took another quarter hour to reach the Amphitheater.

One of Caymerdelphia's isthmuses ran right alongside the Amphitheater... and to Amélie's relief, that's where she found her three centman friends, anxiously awaiting her.

"Sovereign be praised!" the Operative said, extending a hand to Amélie, then hoisting her from the water.

"We heard word you were on your way," the Captain said. "There'll be no containing the news that a huwoman was seen in Caymerdelphia. Still," he grinned, "I'm just happy to see you unharmed."

"No thanks to those dagmen," Amélie said, then laughed and gestured to the Hostess. "But many, *many* thanks to my new friend here."

"Think nothing of it," the delphwoman replied. "I hope we have a chance to speak again soon."

"Me too!" Amélie turned back to the Captain. "I guess we should go ahead and present ourselves to the full Assembly?"

The Captain nodded gravely. "That would be my counsel."

Amélie nodded too. This was hardly ideal, and not at all what she'd been expecting when they stepped out of the elevator from Gnobury this morning. But she might as well make the best of it, right? "Okay, I'm ready," she said with as much confidence as she could muster.

And to her surprise, she realized that she actually was.

· twenty-nine ·

(Cécilie)

The Vizier's quarry on Eqland wasn't at all what Cécilie expected. She had pictured some dwarves swinging pickaxes in a little cave, whistling while they worked. Instead, the quarry was a big hole in the ground, with big ledge-ramps on all sides going down to the deepest point in the very middle. The Crafter explained that the ledges came from when the gnomen carved stone blocks out of the ground. Every day, the hole got bigger and deeper.

Gnomen *did* look a little like dwarves, except only the youngest ones had beards. They definitely weren't whistling, though. They sweated silently as they swung their axes, chipping away at the stone, sometimes tripping over the ankle chains that tied them all together.

The eqmen down in the hole didn't look any happier. *They* were chained to two-wheel carts, which they used to move the stone blocks after the gnomen cut them free. The blocks were so big, only one fit on each cart; but even *one* block must have been heavy, because the eqmen seemed to struggle hauling them uphill and out of the quarry, one painful step at a time.

Above it all flew the imps: gray-furred bat-winged creatures who laughed and joked, sometimes swooping down and cracking a whip at a gnoman or eqman who wasn't working fast enough. It made Cécilie want to cry, seeing people treated this way—especially *her* people.

Beside her, Handmaiden made a sound of anguish. "Don't worry," Cécilie said. "We'll rescue them." That was what they were here to do. After lots more arguing yesterday, Nachton and the other leaders finally agreed that attacking at the quarry made the most sense.

"I know," the little eqwoman said. "But we've lost so many already. My best friend..."

Cécilie nodded. The Handmaiden had already told her about the Debutante. Although the Vizier's goal was to enslave everyone, some eqmen had gotten hurt in the fighting the night the Vizier and Warlord attacked Eqland. Now those people—including Handmaiden's friend Debutante—were gone from Overtwixt forever.

The Princess and her unicorn were hiding behind some trees and boulders on a hill near the quarry, just high enough to look down into the quarry. With them were the Ranger and Steward, plus Nachton holding Ewan's little friend Shark prisoner on a tight green leash. Squire, Weaponsmaster, and Berserker were keeping Ewan distracted farther back in the forest, because no one wanted him "accidentally" charging into battle again. There were more than a hundred other eqmen back there too, villagers ready to fight for the liberation of their niland, along with Crafter and three other escaped gnoman slaves. Cécilie could hear all of them talking quietly.

Here on the hill, where they could see the quarry, no one was in a talking mood. Only the Ranger was actually doing anything. He had shot so many spookman Spies on their journey here that he was almost out of arrows; so, while they waited, he used a pair of knives to make new arrows from tree branches.

When the Sky Light started dimming, Cécilie knew it was afternoon, almost time for the attack. Nachton took his prisoner to a nearby tree and tied him up tightly with ropes, the little spook hissing and spitting angrily the whole time. Then Nachton walked over to talk with Cécilie. "You remember what you're supposed to do?" he asked.

"Yes," she said with confidence, the way Matron taught her... even though her belly was doing backflips.

"Good. Remember that I have to stay hidden until the Vizier arrives. If he knows I'm here, he may not come."

"What about Ewan and me?"

Nachton shrugged. "I'm not worried about you guys. You're such little squirts, the bad guys will assume you're gnomen." Cécilie's brother smiled at her, and it was one of his nice smiles. Then his eyes fell on the amethyst hanging around her neck, glowing green like always, even though it was purple. Cécilie tried to cover it, but she was too late.

"It took me a few days to figure it out," Nachton said slowly, "but now I understand why you seem so grown up all of a sudden." He pulled her hand away gently, then touched the gemstone... and shivered.

"I don't know what you're—" she started to lie.

"It's okay. I'm proud of you, Cécilie. You're doing what needs to be done for your people."

Just like that, Cécilie was smiling so hard it hurt. *Nachton* was proud of *her*? And he knew about the necklaces, but he didn't want to take them away?

"Where did you find it?" he asked.

"In the Library. The History section."

Nachton nodded. "It's magic, you know. A more subtle form than what I've been using, but..." He trailed off when he saw Mayor trotting up the hill to join them. "Let's talk about it more later. For now," he flashed her a grin, "let's go win back your throne."

The Mayor bowed low to Cécilie when he arrived. "Your highness." He turned to Nachton. "Lord Conjurer, everything is ready down below."

"Excellent," Nachton said. He looked excited. "The gnomen have finished setting their traps?"

"Yes, lord Conjurer."

"And you're sure all the eqmen know what to do?" The silver eqman nodded, so Nachton called to the Ranger. "What about you? Done making arrows? Good. Just don't shoot *too* many of the bad guys. Remember, we want at least some of them getting away, to lure the Vizier back here."

The Ranger squeezed his eyes shut and took a deep, steadying breath. "Right. We *want* the Vizier here." He opened his eyes again, then looked out over the countless imps and spooks flying in circles above the quarry. "Well, you needn't worry. There's not much chance we'll defeat *all* of the Vizier's minions this day."

Nachton smirked. "As long as they bring the Vizier to me, it won't matter. Once I've defeated *him*, Overtwixt will be free no matter how many imps remain."

The woods fell silent for a long moment as everyone prepared mentally for the attack. Then Nachton turned to face the army of eqmen. He raised a fist high in the air, then brought it down fast. "Charge!"

The eqmen didn't have to be told twice. Bellowing in excitement and rage, all of the horses and unicorns charged straight over the hill and down toward the quarry. "Freedom!" they screamed. "Freedom for Eqland!" Ewan tried to run after them, but Berserker held him tightly. He would get his chance to fight, but for now, it was important the bad guys see no one except the eqmen.

Down in the quarry, *everyone* stared at the charging army in shock... but then the impman taskmasters started laughing. After all, the Vizier's minions could all *fly*. They assumed these eqmen would never lay a hoof on them.

The army charged ahead anyway. But they were only halfway to the quarry when the impmen started shooting arrows at them. Cécilie hugged herself tightly when she saw the first puff of yellow smoke, then she and Handmaiden hugged each other when two *more* eqmen disappeared in yellow puffs. The eqman army started to panic, or at least they *pretended* to panic. Slowing down, they neighed in horror, then turned and fled back up the hill towards Cécilie and her friends.

"Cécilie?" Nachton called. "It's almost time."

Cécilie climbed onto Handmaiden's back. No one was looking at her, so she quickly took off her amethyst necklace and got the topaz necklace ready.

The panicky eqmen reached the top of the hill and started disappearing into the trees again... and the impmen finally took the bait. "After them, fools!" one of the bad guys screamed. "That's more slaves getting away!" Every single one of them started flying toward the woods.

Cécilie looped the topaz necklace ribbon around her hand, then draped the rest of it around the Handmaiden's neck—and somehow, the ribbon was long enough. Everyone slowed down like before, except this time both she *and* Handmaiden were excluded.

"Your highness?" the little unicorn squeaked. "What's happening?"

Cécilie smiled really big. It was working, just like she hoped! "Don't worry about it. Charge!"

Handmaiden did as ordered, darting forward with Cécilie on her back. The little unicorn dodged easily between all the horses running the opposite direction, since those other eqmen were moving in slow motion. She charged right over the hill and down the ramp into the quarry. Cécilie waited until she and Handmaiden were in the middle of a bunch of slow-motion slaves, then she swapped necklaces and dismounted.

"Eek!" a gnoman cried. "Where did *you* come from?!"

Cécilie was greeted by surprised neighs and whinnies from the eqmen too. Pulling a small hacksaw from her pocket, she started sawing at a big padlock that tied the slaves' chains together.

"What is the meaning of this?" an eqman voice demanded. "Who is this gnoman?"

"She's no gnoman!" a gnoman answered.

"She's the new Princess of Eqland!" the Handmaiden announced as loudly and excitedly as she dared. "And she's here to rescue you!"

With a clank, the padlock fell to the ground, and Cécilie began pulling the chain out of the loops on all the collars and ankle manacles. The freed slaves stared at Cécilie in awe.

"All hail the Princess!" Handmaiden cried softly.

"All hail the Princess!" the others repeated.

Cécilie was smiling almost as big as when Nachton said he was proud of her. "Now," she asked her new subjects. "Who wants to go kick some bad guy butt?"

· thirty ·

(Ewan)

Back in the woods, Ewan was still trying to get free. He wanted to go fight! And there was something else he needed to do, too. But Bazooka held him too tightly. "Let. Me. GO," Ewan begged.

Fight Guy and Skire Horsey looked at each other and nodded. "Fine, fine," Fight Guy said, "but you need to stay here, kid. *This* is where we'll fight the bad guys. The eqmen are gonna be bringing 'em over that hill any minute now!"

Ewan shrugged but stopped struggling, so Bazooka released him. Immediately, Ewan drew his sword and went charging up the hill.

"No!" Skire cried. "Sir Knight, you must wait *here!*"

Ewan ignored him. Running as fast as his little legs could carry him, he reached the top of the hill—and stopped next to the tree where Shark was tied up. He got ready to swing his sword.

Skire Horsey galloped up next to him. He looked surprised that *this* was why Ewan ran up the hill. "Are you sure about this?" the horsey asked him quietly. After all, Nock was still standing nearby. If he turned around...

Ewan nodded big. "He a good guy. He my *fwend.*"

Skire sighed. "I don't like it, but..."

Ewan chopped at the ropes, careful not to hit Shark himself. Soon enough, the little spook was free, flapping hard to get his wings working again. "Thank you!"

"Get away, Shark. I don't want you get hurt."

Skire Horsey puffed out a breath. "Get *far* away. No one here can tell you apart from the other spooks. They wouldn't care even if they could."

Shark looked at Ewan with his beady red eyes. "*You* are a true friend and good guy. Thank you, thank you!" He glanced at Skire. "You're not too bad yourself, four-legs." And then he escaped into the sky.

By now, the horsey army was coming back over the hill. "Let's go," Skire Horsey said, letting Ewan climb into his saddle, then joining the other horseys running into the woods. Ewan saw Nock get on Ranger Guy's back and follow too.

Then wimpy guys and spooky bats were flying over the hill behind them, down low between the trees. The wimp dudes started shooting arrows, and horseys started screaming.

"Crafter!" Nock shouted. "Now! Now!"

Ewan heard a *snap*, and when he looked back again, there were suddenly big nets stretching between the trees. Some of the bad guys avoided the trap, but lots flew right into the nets, hard. A couple dudes even went *poof* with yellow smoke, but most of them fell down on the ground.

"Shift configuration!" someone yelled, and Ewan looked up in the trees to see Arts-and-Crafts Dude. He and the other no-mans were running on branches, dragging the nets and retying them diff'rent. When they were done, the knocked-down bad guys were trapped on the ground by a net roof over their heads. And there were bunches of big boulder-rocks all around them too, keeping them from getting away that way either. That was why Nock picked this side of the quarry for his trap.

The wimp dudes started getting up, holding their heads and complaining. "Attack!" Nock yelled.

Finally. Ewan pulled on Skire Horsey's hair to make him turn back. "Attack!" he repeated. He stood up on Skire's back and pointed with his sword, like a gen-ral. "For Pincess Sessy and Eckwind, *attack!*"

All the horseys started neighing. They stopped running away and charged past Ewan, running right under the nets and trampling the wimpy guys who couldn't fly away. Every time a bad guy got trapped under their hooves, he puffed into a cloud of yellow smoke.

Ewan and his friends were still outside the nets, and all the bad guys who missed the net traps started swooping down to attack them. Ewan drew his sword and chopped at one, but missed him when Skire Horsey lunged forward to pummel a different one with his front hooves. A bat-dude shrieked and dove at Ewan's face with his claws, but Bazooka swatted him out of the sky—the same way Ewan would swat a bug. "Thanks, 'Zooka!" Ewan said excitedly.

Suddenly, more people were screaming battle cries. "Freedom for Eqland!" and "Long live the Princess!" It was the slaves, galloping into the battle from the other direction. Some of the little no-mans were actually *riding* on some of the horseys, even though they hated each other. Sessy had freed them already? Man, she was FAST!

Sessy herself rode on her little unee-corn, screaming, "Get 'em, get 'em!" while the unee-corn speared wimpy guys on its horn. Yellow puffs were everywhere. The wimp dudes weren't fighting back very well.

Then Ewan realized he was staring instead of fighting. "Attack, Skire Horsey!"

Ewan swung his sword left and right, the way Fight Guy taught him. Skire Horsey struck at more wimpmen with his front hooves. Soon there was a really big yellow cloud all around them. "Knight! It's a Knight!" the wimp dudes started screaming, pointing at Ewan's Diamond Armor.

Now the wimpy guys outside the nets were flying *away* from Ewan. He couldn't hit them with his sword anymore, no matter how hard he tried. Some of them grabbed handfuls of gravel from the ground and threw little rocks at him. That wasn't fair!

Nearby, Bazooka was holding two wimpy guys by the ankles, one in each hand, using them like weapons to hit *other* wimpy guys. "Hey, Bazooka!" Ewan called. "Lemme borrow you big stick fing!"

Bazooka squeezed both fists really hard, and both of his wimpmen disappeared in yellow smoke. Then he pulled the cudgel thing off his belt and tossed it. Ewan jumped off Skire's back and picked up the big stick, then ran up to a big boulder-rock. He swung the cudgel thing, shattering the rock into a bazillion pieces. He was so strong in Overchix! "I. LOVE. THIS. PLACE!" he bellowed joyfully.

Grabbing a piece of rock bigger than his head, Ewan threw it at one of the bad guys who was pelting him with pebbles. It turned the guy to yellow smoke instantly. Smiling even bigger, Ewan dropped the big stick and started throwing rocks with both arms, smoking more and more wimp dudes out of the sky.

Bazooka chopped down a tree with three swings of his big sword. The tree fell over, squashing three wimpy guys and a spooky-bat, then the lugman tried to pick it up. It musta been really heavy, 'cause it was too heavy even for the lugman.

"Lemme try!" Ewan cried. He ran up and grabbed the tree by its end. He *heaved*—and lifted it! That didn't mean he could control the thing. Bad guys flew away screaming as Ewan swung the tree back into the air, catching like *five* of the wimp dudes in its branches. Then he lost his grip and the tree crashed back down, smushing the stuck bad guys into yellow smoke. It was a good thing most of the good guys were still under the net, fighting the bad dudes there, else Ewan mighta hurt his friends too.

Between Ewan and Skire Horsey, the horseys under the net trap, Bazooka and Sessy and Sessy's unee-corn, there was yellow smoke everywhere. Ranger Guy was shooting his bow and arrow, Fight Guy was swinging a little stick-and-chain thing, and Arts-and-Crafts Dude was firing a slingshot. Even more yellow smoke! But there were *so many bad guys*. This was gonna take forever.

"Hey 'Zooka, chop down a *wittle* twee dis time—" Ewan started to tell his friend, but then the ground shook with a big thump. Ewan spun around to see a HUGE scary MONSTER landing on top of a big boulder-rock nearby.

A *DWAGON*.

"What is the meaning of this?" the dwagon roared. Reaching out with one massive arm, he grabbed the net trap in his sharp talons and ripped it out of the trees—just like that, all by himself!

Suddenly, everything changed. Horseys started running away and wimpmen flew back into the air. They attacked gleefully now, suddenly brave again. *Ewan* didn't feel brave anymore. He knew Nock wanted him to fight this dwagon-guy; but seeing him up close, he really, *really* didn't want to. Eyes wide with fear, Ewan started backing away from the huge monster, hoping the dwagon wouldn't notice him.

Unfortunately, Ewan was wearing glittery Armor.

"You there!" the dwagon demanded. "Human?"

Ewan turned and fled, all thought of battle and fun gone. He had no idea where he was going or what he would do when he got there. He just wanted to *run*. In that moment, he was nothing but a scared little kid, and he desperately needed his Mommy.

Then Nock stepped out of the trees right in front of him, his robes swirling. He caught Ewan and held him in a fierce hug for a long moment. "It's okay, buddy. Shh, shh, it's okay."

"I'm scared, Nock."

Nock smiled. "That's nothing to be ashamed of. I love you, and I'm still proud of you, squirt." He cocked his head. "Do you think you can go back and fight some of the smaller bad guys for me?"

Ewan took a deep breath and swiped at his eyes. "Yeah, okay."

Nock nodded and looked around the forest. "No sign of the Vizier yet anyway." He looked back at the dwagon. "Yeah. You can leave the big scary monster to me." And he started walking toward the dwagon.

· thirty-one ·

(Nachton)

"**H**umen *here?*" the drachman growled, his barbed tail coiling and undulating constantly. He dropped off the boulder and prowled forward with deadly grace, his shiny midnight fur reflecting the afternoon light. "How is this possible?" he demanded.

"We slipped through right before you destroyed our bridge," Nachton smirked. "You must be blinder than a bat if you didn't see us," he added, mocking the big monster.

The drachman ground his fangs audibly. "The Vizier won't like that, but he'll forgive me—when I bring the lot of you to him in chains!" he roared.

"Ha!" Nachton laughed. "You're welcome to try."

With the nets destroyed, the battle spilled out in all directions, imps and spooks clashing with eqmen and gnomen. But even as they fought, everyone was making space for the showdown between Nachton and the drachman.

The dragon-like creature snarled and leapt into the sky, wings sweeping so forcefully that they buffeted Nachton like gusts of wind. For the first time, Nachton noticed the drachman's long staff, which confirmed this *was* the Warlord. Though the staff was longer than Nachton was tall, the beast wielded it easily in one hand.

Sinuous and graceful despite his size, the Warlord darted between two trees and jabbed at Nachton with the staff. Nachton dove aside, but the staff's sharpened end came close enough to tear a hole through his cloak. Rolling out of the way and shucking the garment from his shoulders, Nachton forced himself to laugh at the nightmare creature. "You missed, you big clumsy—*woof!*"

While Nachton was distracted by the staff, the Warlord's long tail had whipped around, catching him in the chest and driving the air out of his lungs. Now the Warlord swung his tail back the other way, through Nachton's legs, knocking the human onto his backside on the forest floor. Only then did the Warlord brandish his staff again, raising it high and spearing down with it.

Nachton wove both hands desperately, producing a cloud of green mist that froze the staff's tip mere inches from his chest. The Warlord cursed, trying without luck to push or pull the staff that had somehow gotten stuck in midair. Nachton made another complicated gesture, this time hitting the drachman with a pair of green fireballs: one in the chest, another in the face.

The Warlord yowled in surprise and pain, sweeping his huge wings forward to push himself backwards. He collided with a tree but righted himself, turning and sinking his talons into the bark to climb *around* the tree, halfway up its trunk. Throwing himself back into the sky, he whirled to face Nachton again, staff at the ready. But Nachton was already pressing the attack, weaving his magic to send two whip-like green tendrils after the big creature. Each tendril caught one of the drachman's muscular forearms.

"How?" the Warlord bellowed, still blinking rapidly in the aftermath of the fireball attack. "How can this be?"

"Behold, fiend," Nachton responded. "I am the Conjurer. It is a master of magic you meet on the field of battle this day." And he jerked down on both green whips, with the intent of pulling the Warlord to the ground.

The Warlord growled and pulled the other direction— and since the drachman outweighed Nachton's entire family put together, *his* pull sent *Nachton* flying instead. With a yelp, Nachton released the glowing green tendrils and raised arms to protect his face as he hurtled through the air. Moments later, he collided with a pile of shattered rocks that used to be a boulder.

Okay, maybe that sort of magic wasn't the best to use against a drachman.

Rolling to his feet, Nachton tried the freezing magic again, sending a great billow of green mist at his flying enemy. It caught and froze exactly *half* of the Warlord—his right arm and wing—sending the creature tumbling to the ground. The drachman just snarled, grabbing another tree with his good arm and pivoting around to swing his barbed tail again.

Nachton scrambled out of the way, came up on one knee, and sent another cloud to freeze the Warlord's other side. It worked, but not before the first cloud wore off. The Warlord was just too big for Nachton to use the freezing magic effectively, and he was starting to get tired. The motions necessary for weaving magic were exhausting.

Best to stick to his fireballs, then.

Weaving as fast and hard as his growing exhaustion would allow, Nachton began peppering the great beast with smaller balls of green flame. Arm, chest, face, arm, and face again. One after another, he shot his fireballs at the Warlord, and they clearly caused the drachman great pain. But somehow, impossibly, they didn't penetrate the creature's thick skin. The Warlord snarled as each fireball hit, but he never let off even a wisp of yellow smoke.

Finally, with a growl of fury, the Warlord leapt high in the air, flapping hard with those powerful wings to buy altitude. Soon, he was level with the tops of the trees, high enough to dodge Nachton's attacks. Nachton grudgingly stopped firing, and he risked a quick look around the forest to take stock of the battle, the exact same thing the drachman was doing.

To Nachton's pleasant surprise, the good guys were winning. There were still imps and spooks beyond count, but the mob of them had thinned since earlier.

With another frustrated growl, the Warlord demanded the attention of his troops. "Fall back!" he cried. "Fall back to the Palace!" The drachman spun in midair, repeating his orders the other direction, and light glinted off something hanging from his neck.

A big brass key.

"Back to the Palace!" the Warlord repeated—just as Nachton got a bright idea, shooting another tendril of magic to wrap around the Warlord's neck. Snorting contemptuously, the drachman jerked free, not even realizing that the tendril had gotten tangled in the brass key too. He sneered at Nachton. "After the last time you tried that, I would've thought you learned your lesson."

Nachton just smiled, hurrying forward to pick up the big brass key from where it had fallen on the forest floor. Holding it up for all to see, he cried, "The Palace is ours!"

Eqmen cheered, and the Warlord's eyes almost popped out of his head. For a long moment, Nachton thought the drachman might come back down and fight him for the key. Then the Warlord looked west, and Nachton knew he was thinking about going back to the Palace anyway; considering they were able to fly, these creatures of darkness hardly needed a key to come and go. But *without* that key, they would never feel safe in their beds at night, knowing their enemy could walk back through the front door anytime they wished.

The moment passed. The Warlord threw back his head and howled. In that sound, Nachton heard all the frustration and shame of defeat, as well as a healthy measure of fear for how the Vizier might punish him. Still, the drachman gave the inevitable order. "Back to Capital City! Retreat to the Citadel." And with one final, murderous look at Nachton, the Warlord and his soldiers flew off toward the southeast— where the massive niland of Twixt, the Vizier's seat of government, bordered Eqland.

Speaking of the Vizier...

Nachton frowned, looking around. Everywhere he turned, eqmen and gnomen were cheering, some of them even *hugging* each other. Ewan's squad was lifting the little Knight onto Berserker's shoulders for a victory lap, and none of them—Ewan included—seemed to recall the little boy's momentary lapse of courage at the Warlord's arrival. Meanwhile, a group of rescued slaves crowded around Cécilie with worshipful expressions, chanting "All hail the Princess! Long live the Princess!" Considering the way everyone celebrated, they clearly thought the attack a complete success. But this was *wrong*. Nachton's primary objective remained incomplete.

The Ranger trotted past, and Nachton grabbed his shoulder. "What about the Vizier?" he demanded. "Has anyone seen the Vizier?"

A spook flapped down out of nowhere, and Nachton almost roasted the creature in midair. Then he saw the knotted end of a rope trailing from its foot, and he realized this was Ewan's little friend. Only Nachton's love for his brother held him back from firing, and then only barely.

"How'd you get free?" Nachton demanded, then shook his head. "Never mind that. Where's the Vizier?"

"Not here, obviously," the spook replied. "How else do you think you won?"

Fury bubbled within Nachton. "I didn't ask where the Vizier *wasn't*," he snarled. "I asked where he *was*."

The spook landed on a tree limb and bit his lip, like he didn't want to answer. "The Archives," he finally said, grudgingly.

"Where?"

"The Archives." This time it was the Ranger who responded. "That makes sense. It's Eqland's version of your Library, but not so extensive."

"He's been there since the day he conquered Eqland," the spook put in, leaping into the air again. The disgusting creature started zipping in and around trees, like he realized Nachton might try to shoot him at any moment. "At least, that's what my brethren said the other day, when I was fishing around for info. As soon as Pastoral City fell, the Vizier withdrew to the Archives, demanding privacy."

Nachton's fury started to surge. "And you're only telling me *now?*" he raged.

"Why do you think I told you to attack immediately? So you could win this victory before the Vizier returned!"

"But—" Nachton began.

"Maybe if you hadn't been so quick to *torture* me, I would've had a chance to explain!" the spook went on.

"Defeating the Vizier was the whole point of attacking!" Nachton practically shouted.

"You fool," the spook spat, flying closer than he had before, beady little eyes glaring at Nachton. "You only barely fought the Warlord to a standstill. You honestly think you could have bested him *and* the Vizier?"

"You bet I could!" Nachton yelled back at him, not realizing he was massaging his exhausted arms even as he spoke. "Where are these Archives?" he demanded.

"You *are* a fool!" the spook exclaimed. "You should be licking your wounds, not rushing off to earn more!"

"The spook has a point—" the Ranger began.

"No!" Nachton disagreed, spinning to face the centman. "Don't you get it? The Vizier is even more exposed than we originally thought! You think me incapable of facing both him and the Warlord? Fine. But the Warlord is gone now, fled with all his army. If this spook speaks true, the Vizier is *alone*—still within reach and still unaware of my arrival in Overtwixt. I'll gladly bring you and Ewan and all the others along to face him with me, but *we cannot miss this opportunity.*"

"I don't know..." the Ranger started to say, then his eyes flicked to Nachton's spectacles. "Do we at least know *why* he's at the Archives?"

Nachton waved a dismissive hand. "No doubt studying some new spell to use against the peoples of Overtwixt."

"What did he tell his minions of his purpose?" the Ranger asked, turning back to Ewan's spook friend.

The spook was climbing for the sky, high in the trees already. "If you're so determined to face him," he yelled over his shoulder, "I'm outta here. I want no part of it."

"So much for being our ally in the fight against the Vizier," Nachton sneered. "Was that a lie, or are you just scared?"

"Oh, I'm just scared," the spook shot back. "And you'd be wise to fear the Vizier a little more yourself." With those final words, the little bat broke through the tree tops and disappeared, flying north.

Nachton watched the creature worriedly for a moment. "Um, which way to the Archives?"

"Southwest," the Ranger answered promptly.

The human relaxed a little. At least the filthy creature wasn't flying straight to the Vizier to warn him. Then again, there was nothing stopping the beast from circling around. There was nothing stopping *any* of the bad guys from doing exactly that if the idea occurred to them.

Nachton started pushing his way through the crowd of eqmen and gnomen, toward Cécilie. "C'mon, we really can't waste another moment."

· thirty-two ·
(Cécilie)

"Long live the Princess!" the eqmen shouted, and more than a few of the little gnomen joined in. Despite all her attempts to be ladylike, Cécilie knew she had a silly grin on her face.

She was still riding Handmaiden, surrounded on all sides by the largest crowd of horses she'd ever seen. The Steward spoke up. "We will perform a proper coronation once we return to the Palace. For now... Your highness, please climb up where everyone can see you."

The Handmaiden pranced over to a boulder, then held still while Cécilie climbed off and turned to face the crowd. Everyone hushed expectantly.

"Your highness," the Steward continued, in a serious tone. "Will you solemnly promise to govern the people of Eqland with mercy and justice?"

Cécilie swallowed. "Yes."

"Will you swear to maintain the law, and to uphold the Sovereign as the true high ruler of all Overtwixt?"

"Yes."

The Steward knelt then, bowing his face to the forest floor, and all the other eqmen followed. Even the non-eqmen dropped to one knee, watching in awe. "Thus therefore may you rule, Princess of Eqland, mistress of the eqmen! May the Sovereign grant you wisdom as you restore Eqland to its former glory."

Everyone stood again, and the Steward turned to the crowd. For a long moment, Cécilie didn't know what was happening. Then she saw that the horses and unicorns were passing something from the back of the group up to the throne. A bunch of beautiful little flowers, woven together in a circle about the size of her head.

"As tiaras go, it's not too impressive—" Steward began.

"Hey, I made that!" the Crafter said.

"—but this tiara *is* a symbol of the love and devotion you earned today from eqmen and gnomen alike," the Steward finished. Then he took the flower circlet reverently in his mouth and carried it the rest of the way to Cécilie.

The Princess reached down and accepted the tiara, then placed it gingerly on her own head. It fit nicely.

The Steward backed away. "All hail the Princess!"

"Long live the Princess!" everyone answered.

"May she rule with wisdom!" the Squire shouted.

"Long live the Princess!" everyone answered again.

"May she restore Eqland to its rightful place!" the Mayor bellowed.

"Long live the Princess!" the crowd shouted, the loudest yet. Then they broke down into individual cheering.

Looking out on those excited, grateful faces—the faces of people she had rescued, people who trusted her now—Cécilie felt her confidence grow more than ever. These people loved her, and from the look of things, they would follow her anywhere.

Of course, she *was* wearing the amethyst necklace again. She suddenly felt overwhelmed with doubt, despite the great victory they had just won. *Would* her people still love and follow her if she wasn't wearing this necklace? Better that they never find out who she really was. From now on, she would never take it off.

As the cheering died back down, several non-eqmen pushed their way to the front of the crowd—Nachton and Ewan and the rest of her friends who'd been with her since Huland. Nachton grinned. "Congrats, sis."

"Thanks, Nachton!" she blurted, hopping down from the boulder. Then she made her voice more ladylike. "Thank you for all you did to assist in the liberation of Eqland, lord Conjurer. You too, sir Knight."

Ewan whooped, and Nachton smiled even more deeply. "Now," he said, "I fear I must slip away. And I must take all of these with me," he added, indicating all her friends— Ewan, Squire, Berserker, Weaponsmaster, and Ranger.

"What?" Cécilie cried. "But, where are you going?"

"To the Archives, the eqman library," Nachton said, without any explanation.

Nachton was always running off to libraries, so that didn't really surprise her, but... Cécilie turned to the Steward. "*You* have a library?"

"Of course," the horse replied, sounding offended. "Just because we don't have hands, you think we're incapable of recording knowledge for future generations?" He tossed his head. "Books are not the only format for such things, your highness, and *hands* are overrated."

Cécilie decided not to press the matter. She turned back to Nachton. "You really have to go now? Steward says we're about to have a party."

"As soon as we get back to Pastoral City!" the Steward agreed. "A celebration such as you've never known, with feasting to rival—"

"Yes, we really must go," Nachton interrupted, "and quickly."

The Ranger stepped forward suddenly. "Your highness, I would ask a boon as well. I request that you release me from your service, that I might return to the Empress and my fellow centmen."

"What?" Cécilie and Nachton said at the same time. "You're not coming with us to the Archives?" Nachton added.

"I must bear the news of this victory to the Empress," the Ranger said. "Truly, it is the Empress I have served all along, only attending to the Princess at her majesty's request. And it has been an honor to serve you!" he added quickly, bobbing his head apologetically at Cécilie. "But you are now surrounded by more loyal subjects than you can count, and I've been separated from my brothers-in-arms for too long."

Cécilie felt a tightness in her throat, but she forced herself to nod like a lady. "Very well, friend centman, I release you. Thank you for your service. I... I'll miss you."

The Ranger's face softened. "And I will miss you as well, highness, though I hope we will all be reunited soon. Know that I will always count you a friend, even though it is the Empress I serve."

Cécilie managed a smile at that. Then the Ranger turned and left.

Nachton stepped close and pulled Cécilie into a hug. Half a moment later, Ewan collided with them too. "I love you both," Cécilie told them, her voice muffled by Nachton's chest. Why did it suddenly seem so important to say that?

Ewan grinned. "It okay, Sessy! We just going to da libary!"

Nachton chuckled. "That's right, we're just going to the library. But if all goes as planned, I think I'll have some very good news to report when you wake in the morning..."

· thirty-three ·

(Amélie)

The Amphitheater of the Assembly of Caymerdelphia was an immense, perfectly circular pool of crystal-clear water, surrounded on all sides by towering glass. But unlike the theaters Amélie had known back home, this one had no rows of seats; the hundreds of aquatic creatures in attendance simply listened from wherever they floated in that great pool.

The water was divided only by a narrow, grassy peninsula, which entered the Amphitheater from one side and ran to the exact middle, where the Committee of Eleven congregated and directed proceedings. *They* had seats, at least—a circle of semi-submerged glass chairs, with a single empty glass throne standing on dry ground at their center. Amélie and her centmen walked along the narrow strip of land to reach them.

Her arrival created a stir, attracting the immediate attention of the eleven Committee members, though it was clear they knew she was coming. Since they were already discussing the matter of the Vizier, the Committee invited Amélie to speak at once.

Amélie gave much the same presentation as before, when she'd appeared before the Council of Centwick; and somehow, the unique acoustics of the watery

Amphitheater carried her voice to everyone in attendance. She spoke passionately, but she also prepared herself to be challenged. She couldn't take it personally if the aquatic peoples expressed doubts. She could *not* afford to embarrass herself the way she had with the Council of Centwick, losing control of her emotions.

To Amélie's relief, neither the Committee nor the Assembly rejected her request for support out of hand. When she claimed to be Overtwixt's new Empress, they accepted it at face value, as they did her mission to unite all the peoples of the realm. They seemed delighted at the idea that the Vizier had a rival, and not a single one of them challenged anything she said.

In fact, when Amélie was done talking, the Caymerdelphians didn't speak to her again at all.

Instead, they proceeded to ignore her entirely, incorporating the new information she'd provided into the discussion they were already having about "the Problem of the Vizier." In the hours that followed, her name actually came up frequently, as the members of the four aquatic races discussed the merits of her proposal. But always they mentioned "the Empress" in the same way they referred to "the Vizier," as if she were some distant person and not standing right there with them.

And when the Sky Light set that night, the Assembly was no closer to making a decision than when she first made her presentation.

A pair of young merpeople—a mermaid and a merlad, a *boy* merman—guided Amélie and her escort back out of the Amphitheater. Swimming alongside the narrow strip of land, they led the non-aquatics to a hotel three blocks away, a homey glass tower overflowing with colorful flowering vines. Within, the dagman Innkeeper had some fun at their expense, offering them several underwater rooms before finally leading them to the penthouse on the seventeenth floor.

It was a beautiful suite of rooms, with a huge four-poster bed clearly reserved for visiting dignitaries. Amélie collapsed onto the mattress almost immediately (it was a water bed, of course) and fell asleep within moments.

The golden rays of the daytime Sky Light woke her late the next morning, and Amélie stretched happily. She had not felt so safe, rested, or relaxed since her last morning back home in the real world; and for a long moment, she simply luxuriated in the warm sunlight. Then she opened her eyes all the way and realized for the first time where she was.

In a glass bed.

In a glass room.

At the top of a glass tower.

In the middle of a glass city.

And all of that glass was very, *very* clear. She'd barely noticed in the dark, but now that morning had come, she could hardly ignore it. All around her in the Crystal City of Caymerdelphia, countless aquatic individuals moved about their everyday lives, in full view of each other.

In full view of Amélie as well—which meant *she* was in full view of *them*. Even as she watched, various citizens of the city stared at her from the streets below, through her nearly-invisible floor. And those streets were way, *way* below, with seemingly nothing to keep her suspended where she was.

"Captain!" she squeaked. "Captain?!"

The centman answered her call at once. Thanks to the glass walls, she saw him leave a room on the other side of the tower, trot up the hall, then enter her room. "Majesty?"

"It's glass!" she gasped, waving a hand at the room around her. "It's *all* glass!" The words sounded stupid even to her, but she was too horrified to care.

"Yes, your majesty," he said, trying to hide a smile.

"I can't live like this! How can *anyone* live like this!?" she demanded.

"It's said there are no secrets in Caymerdelphia," he answered. "The aquatics pride themselves on their openness and, well, transparency." He seemed to think it was the lack of privacy that offended her worst, though her fear of heights had an equally firm grip on her heart at the moment.

"Just—just *fix* this," she ordered irrationally, though she had no idea how he might accomplish such a thing.

Nevertheless, the Captain ordered his men into the room. Thanks to the glass walls, Amélie saw *them* coming too: the Operative with a studiously neutral expression, but the Scout with a smirk on his face. They quickly unpacked the tents and blankets from their supply bags and spread them across the floor and walls of Amélie's room, until she could finally breathe normally again. Then the Operative bowed, coughed into his fist—like he was embarrassed or something—and left without a word.

"What?" Amélie asked.

"Your hair," Scout said with another smirk, then *he* left.

To her renewed horror, Amélie realized her hair was sticking out stiffly in every direction, a knotted, tousled mess. This was more than just bedhead. This was a result of her swim through saltwater yesterday, then failing to use shampoo and conditioner before falling asleep.

And all of Caymerdelphia had just seen her like this.

"Get out!" she screeched, throwing a pillow at the Captain, the only other person left in her room.

Amélie did the best she could to fix her appearance, but it wasn't until the Innkeeper brought up warm water and soap—at the Captain's request—that she made any real progress. When she was finally presentable again, she invited her friends back inside to share the breakfast the Innkeeper had also brought: seaweed for the centmen, various shellfish for Amélie. Her room was plenty large enough to accommodate all of them, and the alternative was to join them in the penthouse common room, giving up the privacy granted by her tents and blankets.

When they were done eating, they settled in to await the Committee's summons to return. According to the Captain, the Assembly would invite them back once it came to a decision, or if it had further questions for her. The worst thing she could do now was demonstrate any sort of impatience; the caymen in particular prized self-control and careful consideration above all other character qualities, and she would not help her case if she tried to hurry them along.

Amélie impressed even herself by listening to the Captain's counsel. When the waiting stretched longer than expected, she allowed Operative to distract her with tales of old Overtwixt: the legend of Caymerlot, the niland kingdom that preceded Caymerdelphia; and of Jacques, who climbed a beanstalk bridge to Orqland and stole one of Sovereign's Relics, inciting a war. She let Scout teach her games from his real world, and she taught him checkers and I-Spy. She even managed not to worry that the Vizier would send minions to Caymerdelphia to attack or capture her, which seemed a very real risk as the days passed (after all, the whole city knew she was here). Instead, she trusted the Captain when he told her there was no place for spook Spies to hide amongst all this glass. Amélie grudgingly agreed there was *some* advantage to transparency.

Stories, games, meals, and more—it all became a blur as Amélie did everything in her power to wait patiently. She waited more patiently than anyone had a right to expect. But in the end, she couldn't wait any longer for the summons she was increasingly sure wasn't coming.

After nine days, Amélie decided she'd had enough.

· thirty-four ·

(Nachton)

The trek to the Archives took several hours, mostly because night soon fell. Nachton's strike team had to navigate the forest southwest of the quarry by the light of a thousand twinkling Sky Lights.

Every member of the team felt a nervous energy—they were going to face the *Vizier*—but also confidence. They had just defeated the Warlord and his army, and that seemed a lot scarier on the surface than fighting some mere human, all by himself, no matter how powerful he might be. Overall, the strike team's mood was festive.

"You see me?" Berserker asked, reenacting part of the battle they'd just fought. "I beat up impman *with* impman!" He boomed a laugh.

"And I. Was. *Awesome!*" Ewan added, flexing his muscles inside his Armor. "I knock bad guys outta da sky!"

"That you did, sir Knight," the Squire agreed. "I must say, your strength and courage continue to impress me."

A flicker of a smile crossed Nachton's face. It seemed no one remembered how Ewan turned and fled at the sight of the Warlord. Well, Nachton was okay with that.

"I've lost three stars!" the Weaponsmaster complained, counting the throwing stars in the pouch at his belt.

Squire eyed the rest of the arsenal hanging from that belt. "Looks like you've still got plenty of weapons."

"Well, I *am* the Weaponsmaster."

"What is all dat?" Ewan asked.

The shaman tapped the pouch with the throwing stars. "Shuriken." Then he rested hands on a set of little sticks connected by chain. "Nunchucks." He continued around his belt. "Battle axe, short sword, dagger. This is a bolas," he added, indicating a rope with little weighted balls at the ends. "You can throw it to tangle up your enemy's legs."

Even Nachton stared. The shaman had been adding weapons to his belt ever since joining their group. "Yeah," he agreed, "I think you've got enough."

"Wait," Squire objected. "A bolas? I thought you said ranged combat was for layabouts and cowards!"

There was a long pause in the darkness. "Yes, well," the shaman said finally. "Close quarters is my preference, but I'm a *well-rounded* Weaponsmaster." He cleared his throat. "So what's the plan for taking out the Vizier?"

"More than likely, the contest will be decided by magic," Nachton said, "so I'll take the lead. He doesn't know we're coming, so I'll make use of surprise, attack without warning. The rest of you hang back. Be ready, in case I need support, but don't get in the way."

"But—" the Berserker began.

"All of you are close-combat fighters," Nachton explained, "well, except for the Weaponsmaster." Squire chuckled at this, and the shaman *humphed*. "My point is, you have to get close to the Vizier to fight him, and I don't want to hit you with my magic by accident." He turned to the little shaman. "I won't complain if you decide to fire off a few of those throwing stars, though."

"Yeah," the Weaponsmaster said. "I think I will."

Ewan looked disappointed. "You sure, Nock?"

"I'm sure. Remember, when I'm wearing these spectacles"—he tapped Sovereign's Relic of Wisdom—"I more than match the Vizier in power." Nachton smiled confidently. "The Vizier's reign of terror ends tonight."

All three of Ewan's non-human friends cheered at this. "He won't know what hit him!" Weaponsmaster said.

"And he can't flee like the Warlord!" Squire added.

"He be trapped!" Berserker agreed. "In Archives!"

"Bah-le-le-le-leeeee-i-oo-uuuu," Ewan cheered from Squire's back, in an admirable imitation of a lugman.

"Good," Nachton said, looking over his strike team with a smile. "Now, we go the rest of the way quietly. We don't want him to hear us coming."

The Archives consisted of one big building on a cliff at the very edge of the niland. None of the outside torches were lit, but an eerie green glow came from inside. Nachton put a finger to his lips, reminding everyone to be quiet, then they crept forward and entered the building through the open doorway.

It was like a big warehouse, all one floor, with row after row of shelves. But instead of books, the shelves were filled with *seashells*. Conch shells, clamshells, scallops, sundials, and helmets... Nachton even saw a nautilus and a murex. These were just like the shells he'd seen in the Arts section of the Library of Huland, except *these* shells were larger and more elaborate. Frowning, he picked one up—and it started talking! *"In the words of the 372nd-era Philosopher, the unexamined life is not worth—"*

"Shh!" everyone insisted, and Nachton shoved the conch shell under his robes to muffle it.

"No, no!" Squire hissed. "Put it back!"

Nachton hurriedly returned the shell to its place, and it fell silent again. "What the *heck?*"

"It's how we store knowledge," Squire whispered. "We trade for the shells from—"

"Never mind!" Nachton whispered back. "Forget I asked!" He led the team deeper into the Archives, toward the dim green glow. They began to hear a voice from up ahead, similar to the one from Nachton's shell. Another archive recording? Something the *Vizier* was listening to? Considering they hadn't heard it before now, it seemed a safe bet the Vizier hadn't heard the one Nachton activated either. That was a relief.

The strike team was somewhere near the middle of the warehouse when the other voice stopped talking—and the green glow winked out. Suddenly wrapped in complete darkness, Nachton froze in place and listened.

For a long moment, there was nothing... and then footsteps, ever so softly approaching. The footsteps got closer... and closer... and then they stopped as well.

"What a pleasure to finally make your acquaintance," a deep voice said. The sound came from everywhere at once.

Nachton cleared his throat. "Vizier?" So much for the element of surprise.

"Once was I called that," the voice agreed. "But no more. Now I am crowned Emperor of these United Lands."

The room was still dark, and Nachton could feel his friends getting nervous around him. He forced himself to laugh. "Emperor? Please. You're just a pretender." He started weaving magic to light the room.

"Ah, yes," the Vizier chuckled. "I've heard all about your plans to put an Empress on my throne. Amélie, is it?"

Nachton fumbled his weave. The Vizier already knew? Even Amélie's *name*?

"There are four of you, are there not?" the Vizier whispered. He sounded close, very close, and Nachton took an involuntary step backwards. "An Empress, a Princess, a Knight, and... something else."

"How?" Nachton asked, his voice hoarse. "How could you know?"

The Vizier laughed out loud, the sound low and villainous in the darkness. "My spookmen make effective Spies, do they not?"

"I *knew* it!" Nachton hissed. Ewan's disgusting little friend had betrayed them after all. Of all the spooks they'd encountered before today's battle, he was the only one they hadn't shot on sight. That meant he was the only one who could have reported back to the Vizier about Nachton's family!

"Nock," Ewan whispered, tugging at his sleeve. "Nock, I want to go. *Pease*." He sounded terrified.

"It's okay," Nachton whispered back. "I'll protect you."

He heard Ewan take a deep breath. "Okay," the boy said, and he sounded less scared. He trusted his big brother.

Nachton was suddenly very angry. They'd been betrayed, lost the element of surprise. So be it. Nachton was still more powerful than this fraud. The Vizier was using scare tactics against them—the darkness, the deep voice, acting like he was in complete control. "Enough of this," Nachton growled. And he wove his magic, throwing fireworks into the air, bathing the interior of the warehouse in a bright green light.

The Vizier was standing *right there*, so close Nachton could reach out and touch him. A tall figure cloaked entirely in black, head down so that even now, Nachton couldn't see his face. And he didn't move a muscle.

Everyone *else* moved, jumping backwards with cries of alarm. The Berserker ran right into a bookshelf, knocking it over and starting a domino effect. Bookcases toppled one after another, their seashells crashing to the floor, each and every one of them speaking in the voice of an ancient eqman as it tumbled from its shelf.

The Vizier looked up, his features finally visible in the green light. He was *not* a handsome man. His face was long with a pointy black beard, and his lip curled in disgust. "You fool!" he spat at the lugman. "That knowledge is priceless!"

"Enough!" Nachton snarled again, and began weaving another spell. With a shout, he hurled his biggest fireball ever, straight at the Vizier's chest.

With a gesture of contempt, the Vizier raised one hand and swatted the fireball away. It got even bigger as it bounced off—and hurtled toward the Berserker instead.

"Bazooka!" Ewan cried. "Look out!"

The fireball slammed into the lugman, knocking him off his feet. Before Berserker could even hit the ground, he was gone, nothing remaining but a cloud of yellow smoke.

"No!" Ewan screeched. And with a bellow, he drew his sword and charged the Vizier.

"Ewan, don't!" Nachton cried, but his little brother didn't listen. Afraid any fireball he threw would harm the little boy, Nachton flung a pair of green tendrils instead, like he'd done with the Warlord. It hadn't worked so well then, but the Vizier wasn't nearly so big as the drachman.

As intended, the tendrils wrapped around the villain's arms, trapping them. Nachton crossed his own arms and pulled, forcing the Vizier's arms together, just as Ewan came at the man with sword held high.

The Vizier stepped sideways, whirling in a circle and ducking beneath Nachton's magic tendrils with hands overhead so that the strands tangled around each other. Then he threw his hands forward, creating a loop in the tangled lines, wrapping the loop around Ewan's sword. Jerking backwards again, he pulled the tendrils tight—and ripped the sword out of Ewan's hands. Raising one booted foot, he kicked Ewan solidly in the chest, sending him flying.

"Ewan!" Nachton yelled, but the little boy landed without injury. Of course, he was still wearing his impervious Diamond Armor. He couldn't *be* hurt.

The Weaponsmaster was hurling those little throwing stars, but even with wrists and arms trapped, the Vizier wove magic with his *fingers*. He produced little green sparks that consumed each shuriken before it got close.

With an angry growl, Nachton pulled hard on the green tendrils, jerking the Vizier off-balance so he couldn't weave his magic. The Vizier simply rolled with the movement, coming up again on one knee just as the Squire attacked him with raised hooves. There was so much slack in Nachton's magic green tendrils now that the Vizier easily wrapped them around the Squire's legs, tripping the horse. "Gah!" the Squire bellowed, landing painfully on his side. Then the Vizier was pulling the tendrils free of the horse's legs and wrapping them around the horse's *neck*.

Immediately, Nachton released the magic, for fear of hurting the Squire further. With a smile, the Vizier rose to his full height once more—and in half the time it took Nachton to form his next fireball, the Vizier formed a fireball in *each* hand, shooting them straight down at the fallen eqman. He didn't even look as the Squire screeched and disappeared in a puff of yellow. Instead, the Vizier held Nachton's gaze with that cold smile.

"You're not impressing me so far," he said as he stepped out of the billowing yellow cloud. "What is it you call yourself again?"

"I am the Conjurer," Nachton growled, already weaving his next spell.

The Vizier began to laugh again, low and dangerous. He sounded genuinely amused.

The Weaponsmaster attacked the Vizier with impressive speed, battle axe in one hand, nunchucks spinning in the other. Nachton finished his spell at the same moment, pushing a freezing cloud at the Vizier.

The Vizier sighed, as if disappointed. With a casual gesture, he redirected the cloud toward the shaman instead. The Weaponsmaster froze in midair, only his nunchucks still moving, now very slowly.

"Such fascinating creatures, shamen," the Vizier said musingly. "And this one is especially talented. I think I'll add him to my collection, if I ever recover it. Until then..." The villain clenched his fist suddenly, and the green cloud seemed to collapse on itself, crushing the shaman into a ball. One moment the Weaponsmaster was there, the next he was gone, like he'd been sucked into a black hole. Yellow smoke mingled with green mist as his weapons clanged to the floor, all around where he'd been frozen.

Nachton gaped, overawed. For the first time, he began to doubt himself. The Vizier had resisted all of his attacks easily, even redirecting some of them. Every bit of offensive magic Nachton had learned, the Vizier was able to use it to greater effect—*and* the Vizier knew tricks Nachton hadn't learned yet. Just that quickly, Nachton and Ewan were the only ones left in the room with the villain.

Bellowing an agonized battle cry—"Bah-le-le-le-leeeee-i-oo-uuuu!"—Ewan charged the Vizier again, holding the Berserker's massive cudgel high overhead. He ran straight at the villain... and right through that lingering cloud of green.

It didn't quite freeze him, as there wasn't enough of the cloud left for that, but it *did* slow the little boy considerably.

"Is he wearing the Diamond Plate-Armor?" the Vizier said with a gasp. It was the first time he'd actually sounded surprised since the encounter began. "One of Sovereign's Relics?"

Nachton took courage from the other man's shock. "That's right!"

"So the Weaponsmaster *did* find it," the Vizier mused. "But he gave it to my enemies instead of to me. I shall have to punish him for that."

"I think the Weaponsmaster would tell you to eat rocks," Nachton said.

The Vizier shook his head in amazement and sadness. "It's too bad, really. I would have liked to recover the Armor, as I did the Great-Sword..." There were *two* swords sheathed at his belt, Nachton noticed suddenly, for the Vizier had begun caressing one of the hilts. "Alas, I haven't the time," the Vizier concluded, drawing forth one of the two blades, an elegant saber.

"You fool," Nachton spat. "You can't hurt my brother while he's wearing that Armor. It's Sovereign's Relic of Protection for the human race. So long as its bearer is pure of heart, using the Relic for the greater good, he is safe!"

The Vizier only laughed. "I am not the fool here." And he swung his saber right through Ewan.

Ewan himself disappeared first, replaced by a vibrant cloud of yellow that oozed from every joint in the Diamond Armor. The Armor remained suspended a moment longer, then *it* pulsed with a sudden blue glow and winked out of sight too. The Vizier waved away the lingering green and yellow cloud, and with a clatter, the cudgel Ewan was holding dropped to the floor—alongside something else.

A *necklace*. A red ruby pendant attached to a wide silver ribbon.

"What's this?" the Vizier gasped, surprised for only the second time.

"Ewan..." Nachton whispered in horror. How could this be? Their entire strike team, defeated in minutes. His *brother* defeated, despite the Armor. "Ewan, *no*..." he whispered, his throat thick with emotion.

"It *is* you!" the Vizier said in wonder, but he wasn't talking to Nachton. He was talking to the necklace lying on the floor, the necklace Ewan had apparently been wearing beneath his Armor. "Oh, how I've missed you," the villain said with a trembling voice. "Come back to me now." He reached out a hand. "Come *home*." And the necklace leapt into the air, shooting straight into that outstretched hand.

With a sob, Nachton turned and fled.

Running as fast as he could in his robes, the sole survivor of this disaster fled the Archives, pursued by the exhilarated laughter of the Vizier. He stumbled over shelves and broken seashells and out the front entrance. Racing across the front lawn, he was halfway to the trees when his legs suddenly stopped working. Staring down, Nachton saw a small cloud of green had frozen him mid-stride. Then a green tendril wrapped itself around his waist, jerking him around in a half-circle so he was facing the Archives again.

"Now, now," the Vizier said calmly, gliding out of the Archives to stand at the top of the steps. "You needn't be so upset. You'll be reunited with your brother shortly." And he began weaving, very slowly, intentionally giving Nachton's terror plenty of time to grow.

"Help!" Nachton screeched. "Someone, help me! Amélie, Cécilie!" he blubbered. "Ranger? Captain!" Who else did he know that hadn't just gotten smoked? Who else besides Cécilie was even here on Eqland right now? "Guide!" he blurted. "Guide, help me, *please!*"

With a thunder of galloping hooves, the centman Guide exploded out of the trees, diving between Nachton and the Vizier just as the Vizier released a great ball of fire. The fireball struck a direct blow on the centman's haunches, but he shrugged it off like it was nothing. Rearing up on his back legs, the Guide whirled around and came to a stop between the two humen once more.

With his back to the Vizier.

"Take my hand," he told Nachton, extending his arm.

Wide-eyed, Nachton did as he was told, reaching as far as his frozen legs would allow—and the moment he grasped the Guide's hand, the green magic around his legs disappeared. Nachton stumbled forward, then took a running jump as the Guide pulled him up onto his back.

The Guide turned one last circle, staring back at the Vizier with infinite sadness—a look the Vizier returned with undisguised hatred. Then the centman galloped into the woods once more, Nachton clutching at his back and sobbing into his braided mane.

· thirty-five ·

(Amélie)

Amélie swept through the entrance to the Amphitheater with a determined step. She was closely followed by her three centmen, a dagman, and a merman who swam alongside. Both of the Caymerdelphians were warning her urgently that she couldn't just barge in, that she needed to wait until she was summoned.

"What is the meaning of this?" a merman Committee member demanded as Amélie approached the ring of seats at the center of the Amphitheater.

"I've come for your decision," Amélie announced.

This caused a stir, a combination of anger and frustration. "We have not yet *made* a decision—" the merman began.

"Then do it now," Amélie interrupted. "You've been talking *for ten days*. What's left to discuss?"

"Such impatience!" a caywoman exclaimed.

Amélie ground her teeth but forced herself to speak calmly. "Will you support my claim as Empress? Or will you support the reign of the false Emperor, the Vizier, a schemer and murderer?" She spoke loudly so everyone else in the Assembly could hear.

"It is not a question of you or the Vizier!" a delphman Committee member objected. "It is a question of action vs. inaction. None here wish to support the Vizier. The question is whether we can afford to support *you*."

"You can't just stay on the sidelines!" Amélie argued. "If you do nothing, that *does* help the Vizier!"

"We mustn't be hasty—" a cayman began.

"Sometimes haste is needed!" Amélie shot back, causing the Captain to cringe. "The longer you delay in supporting me, the more opportunity the Vizier has to solidify his rule."

"What's it t' us if some gnomen get 'emselves nicked?" a dagman shouted. "The Vizier leaves *us* 'lone."

"He's left you alone *so far*," Amélie corrected the man. "Every day you sit here doing nothing is a day the Vizier doesn't have to worry about you—another day for his impmen to enslave the other races of Overtwixt, and not just the little people. But that won't last. When he's got the others in chains, he'll come for you, too." Heads started to nod; she was getting through to them. "*Now* is the time to resist, united with all of the other peoples of Overtwixt, because you're stronger together. Don't leave them to fight alone, or you'll be alone in the end, too. Help me form a coalition *now*."

"The Empress," a cayman Committee member said grudgingly, "speaks wisdom."

"That doesn't mean she's qualified to *lead* this coalition," a merwoman called out. The way she said the words, it sounded like this was something the Assembly had already argued back and forth about.

"What coalition?" a merman asked. "Has anyone else sworn themselves to your cause yet, Empress?"

Amélie hesitated. The Captain and his guardsmen had sworn themselves, of course, but that's not what the merman was asking. The aquatics wanted to know what other *races* of Overtwixt already supported her claim, and the answer was... well, none of them. "I can't answer that question," she said carefully. "At this time, I, uh, need to keep the support of the other races secret, so they don't get in trouble with the Vizier. When the coalition is complete, we will go public together—"

This set off a flurry of individual arguments and discussions, drowning out Amélie's feeble response.

"Even if we support your claim," the merwoman Committee member persisted, "what evidence do you offer that you can defeat the Vizier?"

Amélie didn't have a clue what to say to this. Fortunately, a distraction at the entrance to the Amphitheater saved her from having to answer. Someone new, a centman, was forcing his way past the dagman guard.

"Is that the Ranger!?" Amélie exclaimed.

"It is," the Captain answered, equally surprised, and obviously concerned.

The Ranger broke free of the dagman and trotted up to Amélie and the other guardsmen, a broad smile on his face. "Empress, I bring great tidings!" he announced, his excitement causing him to speak loudly. "Your brothers and sister have led Eqland in revolt against the Vizier! The Warlord brought a great army of impmen to enslave the eqmen, but we fought them back, and the Princess has taken her throne. The eqmen and gnomen have all sworn themselves to our cause!"

A stunned silence fell over the Amphitheater. This was *it*—the evidence Amélie needed to convince the Assembly, the proof that this coalition *could* defeat the Vizier. The timing of the Ranger's arrival couldn't be more perfect.

And yet, the Ranger's report angered Amélie as much as it excited her. "My siblings did *what?*" she demanded without thinking.

The Ranger blinked at her reaction.

"I told them to wait for me before attacking!" she said furiously. "Whose idea was this? Nachton's? Of course. When I get back there, so help me..." She forced herself under control, turning to face the Assembly again.

Only then did she realize the opportunity she had just squandered. For the Caymerdelphians were now staring back at her with more uncertainty than ever.

"You speak of unity," a cayman said slowly, "but even within your own family, you are not united."

"If you cannot lead *them*," the merwoman asked, "how can you lead anyone else?"

Amélie took a deep breath. "I'm sorry you had to see that. We... we had a misunderstanding, that's all. But as you just heard, we've won a great victory. The eqmen and gnomen now support me—publicly!—and we've proven the Vizier can be defied." The people were muttering, and from the sound of it, she was losing them. "Please," she cried, "you must make a decision about supporting me. Do not delay any longer!"

"Very well," the cayman Committee member said. "I call the vote." His colleagues seemed surprised by this, but no one objected. So the Committee of Eleven voted.

And the vote was unanimous.

"Caymerdelphia chooses *not* to support your claim at this time," the cayman announced formally.

"But," a delphwoman added, "I hope you can convince us otherwise in the near future."

Amélie ground her teeth. "If you're not already convinced, I'm not sure what else I can say."

The merman Committee member barked a laugh. "Don't you get it? We don't want you to convince us with your *words*. We want you to convince us with your *actions*. Show us a true coalition, its leadership united in purpose, and maybe then you'll have our support."

"Until then," the delphman spoke up, "I think it's time you left us. We've spent more than enough time on this issue already, and we still have other matters to discuss."

Trembling with emotion, Amélie pulled herself onto the Captain's back, then urged him to a gallop. She didn't want to stay here a moment longer than necessary.

"Where to now?" the Captain asked quietly, once they had exited the Amphitheater.

"Eqland," Amélie said sourly. "As fast as we can possibly get there."

· thirty-six ·

(Nachton)

The Guide maintained a full gallop for a time, until they'd left the Archives far behind—and Nachton wept the whole way. Every time he thought he could stop crying, he would remember the sight of Ewan disappearing in a puff of yellow smoke, and the tears erupted once more. Finally, the centman slowed to a trot.

"He's gone," Nachton moaned. "Ewan's *gone*... The Vizier killed him, and... and..."

The Guide turned at the waist to look Nachton in the eye. Taking a deep breath, he said, "You should know—"

"Oh, I know, I know!" Nachton interrupted. "Ewan wasn't actually *killed*." He took an unsteady breath but forced himself to keep talking. "The Fifth Fundamental Law: after being ejected, you return to the real world. Ewan's probably back with Mom and Dad already, telling them all about how I let him fight with a real sword. They're gonna ground me for sure." Nachton tried to take courage from the reminder that Ewan really was okay, somewhere.

But almost immediately, he felt himself losing control again. "It's just... he's not *here* anymore, and he can never come back! The greatest adventure of our lives, and he'll miss out on the rest of it. I don't even know when I'll see him again!" And Nachton's tears resumed their flood down his cheeks. He knew he was making a fool of himself, but he just couldn't stop it. Ewan...

The Guide looked like he might say something more— some stupid platitude, probably, about how sorry he was— but Nachton barreled on before the centman could speak.

"It wasn't my fault!" he growled, though no one had said it was. "It was that lying spook! He was a Spy after all!" Snot and tears mixed with the spit flying from Nachton's mouth as he raged. "That filthy creature warned the Vizier we were coming. Or— or— he told the Vizier about us, and the Vizier had him lure us to the Archives! The Vizier *knew* we were coming, otherwise he never could've stood against me!"

The Guide was silent for a long moment. Then he asked gently, "Are you so sure of that?"

Nachton had said the words by reflex, but inside, he *wasn't* so sure anymore. Still, what other explanation could there be? "I've studied. All I've done since coming here is study, starting with the Five Fundamental Laws, just like you told me to. I'm pretty sure I understand the workings of power in Overtwixt!" he concluded with a sarcastic confidence he didn't really feel.

"Then you know all, now? Is it not possible you... misunderstood something? Or that magic works differently from how you think? From how you want to believe?"

This made Nachton doubt all the more, but he waved a hand impatiently. Who was this centman to question *him*, anyway? The Guide was a glorified doorman, and not all that good at his job either. He hadn't even guided Nachton to his proper calling; he'd tried to guide him *away* from magic!

But Nachton took another deep breath, forcing himself to choose his words carefully. "Look," he said finally. "Thank you for... for your assistance back there." Assistance, that's all it was, not a *rescue*. More like a buddy giving him a ride home from school because Mom got caught in traffic. "But," Nachton continued firmly, "let *me* worry about questions of magic and power."

The Guide nodded humbly. "Very well."

Nachton took another steadying breath, on the verge of losing control yet again. Ewan... oh, Ewan. *I will get revenge on the person responsible for this,* he promised his brother. *When I get my hands on the Vizier and that spook...* He looked around then, suddenly aware of his surroundings. "Where are we?" he asked the Guide. "Where have you brought me?"

"We're nearly to Pastoral City, and your sister's new Palace," the centman responded. "I assumed you and the Princess would want to be together during this difficult time."

Nachton gritted his teeth but forced out another polite response. "Thank you."

"What will you do next?"

"I... I don't know." The loss of Ewan left him feeling adrift. In a very real sense, both Ewan and Cécilie had succeeded in their quests, and even Amélie was off building her coalition. But what had Nachton accomplished? What even *was* his quest now? Taking on the role of the Conjurer, he'd been sure he could defeat the Vizier. But whatever the reason, no matter whose fault it was, Nachton had failed to do that. Spectacularly.

"If I may suggest," the Guide began hesitantly, "stay at the Palace for a time, with the Princess. If I understand correctly, the Empress will return here soon. Her efforts have not been as fruitful as she hoped. She and the Princess will both need your support in the days to come, and... minus one of the four of you, it'll be more important than ever that the rest of you are united."

Nachton wasn't so sure—he wasn't ever sure of anything the Guide said—but he nodded anyway. Better to just agree than give the annoying centman the impression that Nachton needed convincing. "Fine," he said.

The Guide stopped moving. "Then this is where we part ways."

"What?" Nachton said in surprise. He stared into the darkness, and realized he could see lights. They were nearly to the outskirts. "You're not taking me all the way?"

"I am not welcome there," the Guide said simply.

"The eqmen?"

The Guide nodded. "Among others."

Nachton was suddenly fearful again. Notwithstanding his brave words about the Vizier, he found himself asking, "What if the Vizier attacks?"

"He will not. Not tonight, at least." The Guide turned, staring off into the distance. "The Vizier is already making haste to the Shadowlands, thoughts consumed by his many schemes—and the amulet your brother returned to him. He will not pass this way."

"Amulet... you mean that necklace? Cécilie has one too. What *are* they, exactly?"

"Magical artifacts of the same sort as Sovereign's Relics. The Vizier thinks them his own creation, but their magic is far older—and far more evil—than even he knows."

"The Vizier can make relics too?" Nachton said in surprise. "And they're more powerful than Sovereign's?"

"No," the Guide answered with a sharp, confident shake of his head. "For that to be so, the Vizier himself would have to be more powerful than the Sovereign. And none is more powerful than the Sovereign, not even the Adversary."

"Then how could the Vizier defeat the Diamond Armor so completely?" Nachton demanded. "He cut through Ewan's Armor like it wasn't even there!"

The Guide gave Nachton a penetrating look. "The Diamond Armor could not protect your brother, for the same reason the Diamond Lens could not grant you wisdom."

Nachton refused to be baited. "*Why?*" he repeated.

The centman gazed at the human for a long moment. "If you've studied magic as much as you say you have, then you already know the answer to that question. But you can't acknowledge the truth because you've deceived yourself— *about* yourself." He shook his head. "Until you recognize just how wrong you are, you'll be incapable of seeing the truth about Ewan or the Vizier either."

Nachton stared back at the Guide, a dozen new questions flitting through his mind. But he refused to give the infuriating centman the satisfaction of asking. He slipped off the Guide's back and stepped away. "Fine then," he said in a level tone.

The Guide looked sad. "Be well, Master of Lore. And bear your responsibility wisely." He said nothing more, whirling instead and galloping back into the woods.

Nachton walked the rest of the way to the outskirts of Pastoral City. Then he stopped, feeling more alone than ever, even though there were eqmen dancing and singing in the streets all around him. Some of them noticed Nachton and stared, regarding him with awe.

Could Nachton return to Cécilie? Could he bear to look her in the eye and tell her Ewan was gone? Hardly—and he certainly wasn't ready to endure *Amélie's* scathing disapproval. Before he submitted himself for judgment, he wanted to have a plan to offer, a way for the three remaining siblings to recover from this mess. And even before that, he needed to figure out how the Vizier defeated Nachton's team so quickly. Obviously, that filthy spook's warning gave the Vizier time to prepare, but that still didn't explain everything. Nachton needed to understand *how* the Vizier had bested him, then determine what to do next.

Still, he couldn't just leave his sisters hanging. They deserved to know the truth about Ewan.

Nachton tore a sheet of paper out of a notebook from his satchel, then beckoned one of the eqmen in the street. "I need you to get a message to the Princess. Can you do that?"

"Oh yes, wise one!"

Nachton nodded. And feeling like slime for doing this in a letter, he scribbled his note with ink and quill. When he was done, he rolled the paper and sealed it with wax, then winced when the eqman took it gently in his teeth.

"Um, try not to drool on that too much."

"Uh cose, why one," the eqman tried to say.

But Nachton had already walked away, turning his back to Cécilie and the Palace—directing his steps toward the Archives once more, now that he knew the Vizier was gone.

He *would* reunite with his sisters soon enough, as the Guide suggested. But first, he needed answers, and the Archives seemed a good enough place to start looking. Nachton would figure out how the Vizier had defeated him, and he would figure out how to defeat the evil tyrant in turn.

Then Nachton, Amélie, and Cécilie would take their revenge on the Vizier.

The End of
Part III

· epilogue ·

The Vizier flew through the sky, perched atop the broad, dark-furred shoulders of his drachwoman protector. Blackguard, he called her, though she used to go by another name. The Vizier always renamed his minions when they swore allegiance to him... though now, he considered renaming the woman again.

"Coward?" he mused under his breath, loud enough for her to hear. "No, that's too harsh. Maybe... Slacker?" He snapped his fingers. "Deserter! That's it."

"Master?" the dragon-like woman asked in her mewling, subservient voice. "What do you speak of?"

"Your new name, dear girl. What I'm thinking of calling you from now on." He often called her "dear girl," but out of condescension, never affection. Nothing was truly dear to him except power—and the relics and monuments he'd created to magnify or demonstrate that power.

"Your majesty!" the Blackguard objected fearfully. "What have I done to offend you?"

"Oh, well, let's see." He began counting off points on his fingers. "You allowed a team of well-armed assailants to sneak up on me without warning. You left me to fight off these assailants all by myself. And you were so far away when all this happened, that even if I'd called for help, you never would have made it back in time!" He snorted. "Some protector you are."

"But master," she whined. "You always say I stifle you, that I should give you more space. Besides, you *did* fight them all off."

"Of course I did!" the Vizier snarled. He had to suppress a shiver, though. What if they'd taken him by surprise? What if he'd been *unable* to defeat them? "Just don't let it happen again!" he growled.

"Yes, highness. Of course, highness!" She bobbed her ugly, big-eared head submissively, though of course she couldn't look back at him while he was perched on her shoulders.

The Vizier raised a hand to shade his eyes. They were nearing Caymerdelphia now, the wind of their passage fluttering under Blackguard's leathery wings—but the worlds of water were not his destination. Not yet. For now, he was content to let the aquatics squabble among themselves while he conquered everyone else. The Vizier dug his heels into the drachwoman's sides, and she tucked her wings and dove *beneath* Caymerdelphia.

The bulk of the massive hubland suddenly blocked the yellow glare of the Sky Light, and the Vizier dropped his hand, instantly feeling better. He'd never liked bright light, even in the real world. Just like the imps and spooks who now served him, he was a creature of darkness, and that was okay with him. It was why he enjoyed the indoors, libraries especially; but he wouldn't be content until everyone else wallowed in the dark as well. Someday soon, he would inflict eternal night on all the people living in Capital City, the seat of his rule. And what a gloriously gloomy day that would be! He couldn't wait for the culmination of all his dreams and dastardly designs.

But until that day came, it was good to return *here*, to the Shadowlands in the darkest depths of Overtwixt—the nilands that floated in the perpetual shade cast by Caymerdelphia and all the other nilands above.

The Vizier almost smiled as the steaming lava pools of Drachölm came into sight below them. Then the Blackguard unfurled her wings with a snap and banked left, turning toward the north. Together, the drachwoman and her passenger glided across the desolate wasteland of Pholand until the murky forest of Spookwood appeared before them in the distance. As usual, the gloomy scenery of the Shadowlands improved the Vizier's mood even more, though none of these nilands was his destination either.

No, his destination this day was Gaoland, a hubland at the very center of the Shadowlands—*his* hubland, the niland he and he alone had brought into existence. A place with a very special purpose that was close to the Vizier's own heart.

Gaoland was a prison and torture facility. An entire niland—a small one, to be sure, but still a whole niland— covered by a single sprawling dungeon. The prison structure was roughly square, with tall stone walls rising from the very edges of the niland, and an open courtyard at the exact center. It was there, on that patchy lawn, that the Blackguard finally landed. Without a word of thanks, the Vizier dropped from her back and stalked inside. A half- dozen impmen fell in around him as an honor guard, with the drachwoman bringing up the rear. She was quickly joined by another of her kind, the Jailer, both of the dragons hunching low to squeeze through the prison's stone corridors.

Yes, the Vizier was quite proud of his Gaoland. He had completed construction of the facility itself months ago, though he'd waited to apply the finishing magical touches until he was crowned Emperor—the day *after* he expelled the Baron from Overtwixt. Of course, at the time, he had thought the Baron was the final person he needed to expel from the world of bridges. He should have known the Guide would have a backup plan.

Just that quickly, the Vizier's mood soured again. Now, instead of just *one* other human in Overtwixt, he had *four* to deal with—and children, no less!

In a sudden rage, he punched the stone wall of the hallway he walked along. One of his imp escorts failed to get out of the way, and the fool burst into yellow smoke amid a shower of stone chips and grit. When the dust settled, the Vizier examined the deep furrow he had gouged in the wall, and he felt immediately better again.

The Baron and his traitorous ally—the Vizier *still* didn't know who that was—had stolen the Vizier's precious amulets and hidden them somewhere, which really threw his plans into chaos. But now, unexpectedly, one of those amulets had returned to him. He lifted the ruby pendant, which hung from his neck by its wide silver ribbon... and he smiled. Then he kicked savagely, and the already damaged wall collapsed entirely. Unfortunately, it had been an outside wall, and its big stone blocks went tumbling over the edge of the niland to disappear into the empty abyss below.

"Someone fix that before it causes a problem," he growled, nudging another stone over the edge with his toe.

The imps leapt to obey, gathering the loose stones and stacking them haphazardly atop one another.

"Not *you*, you imbeciles!" the Vizier snarled. "Get some of the gnomen. It's what they're good for."

And with that, he stalked away again. He entered the south wing of the dungeon and slowed to inspect his prized collection of prisoners. First were his low-value convicts, like raimen and nags and those slimy, good-for-nothing dagmen. Next came the eqman cells, and the Vizier was pleased to see many more convicts stuffed into those cages than the last time he'd been here. He would put them to work as carthorses on Twixt, along with the gnomen—who had also multiplied!—in the high security cells that followed. Those ugly, half-sized creatures were the Vizier's favorite, the preferred labor force on his many building projects.

The magic he had woven into the foreboding walls of this prison was truly impressive, if he said so himself. It automatically sorted new arrivals into cells designed for members of their race. The enclosures for the little peoples were smaller than those of the eqmen and centmen, for instance; and gnomen were so good with their hands that *their* cell doors employed more sophisticated hinges and locking mechanisms. The Vizier had accounted for every possibility, including mesh-lined cages for the spooks who currently served as his Spies, just in case they ever turned on him. The empty spook cells were in the next ward, in the east wing of the prison—

He stopped short as he rounded that corner. The spook cages were now teeming with new arrivals, as were the imp cells. For every new horse or gnome the Vizier had noted in the cells he just passed, there must be five or more of his own minions now trapped in this prison. He passed cell after cell stuffed full of them, all unconscious, and his disgust built with every step—disgust for these dull tools he was forced to use, but also disgust for the *children* who had caused this.

After all, these imps and spooks were the Soldiers and Spies who'd been smoked by the children and their allies, at the quarry battle on Eqland. Now these sad fools would need a week or more to recover before he put them back to work.

But they *would* go back to work, even after "dying" in Overtwixt. Because the Vizier really was that powerful. Even now, this reminder of his own magical ingenuity brought a smug smile to his lips. While the Vizier couldn't entirely break the Fundamental Laws of Overtwixt, he could certainly *bend* them. So maybe he wasn't as mighty as the distant Sovereign (may he ever *remain* distant!), but he was obviously in the same league. And as more people were smoked in the days to come, automatically ending up in a cell here—instead of their real world, as they expected—they too would learn how powerful he'd become. Then everyone, minions and enemies alike, would fear the Vizier more than ever before.

Just as it should be.

Frowning, the Vizier stopped in front of a cell containing two imps who were clearly in better shape than the rest. Fully conscious, they picked their noses and ears and bickered with each other... which meant they had been smoked long before the battle on Eqland. "You two," he barked. "Identify yourselves."

The first one snapped to attention and saluted sloppily. "Stooge here, your Vizier-ness. That there is the Flunky."

The second gargoyle ignored the Vizier and slapped the Stooge across the face. "You fool, I keep tryin' to tell ya: the big boss ain't called *Vizier* no more. He's the Emperor now!" Only then did he eye the Vizier up and down, sneering. "Besides, this ain't the big boss."

"Sure it is!" Stooge insisted.

"Nah," Flunky disagreed. "You never *has* been able to tell one human from another. But the Vizier—erm, the *Emperor*—he's much taller."

"Silence!" the Vizier boomed finally. Then he removed his newly-recovered ruby amulet, feeling that impossible strength drain from his body. Stuffing it into his coat pocket, he retrieved another amulet—the emerald, the one he'd been wearing when all the others were stolen—and hung it around his neck instead. He shivered at the uncomfortable sensation as his body... changed.

Flunky's eyes widened as he craned his neck, looking up at the suddenly-taller Vizier. "Oh," he said stupidly.

"Now," the Vizier said with strained patience. "Explain how you both came to be here."

Flunky quickly spoke up again, eager to make up for insulting his master. "Well, it was all Stooge's fault. See, we was tasked with protectorin' the bridge from Centwick to Eqland. But ole Stooge here let a squad of centmen get into bow-and-arrow range before raisin' the alarm!"

"It ain't *my* fault!" Stooge blurted. "I was all distracted by who them centmen was with." He turned to the Vizier. "Get this—they was 'companied by a *hu*woman." He waggled his wrinkly eyebrows. "I was gettin' ready to take her into custardy, but then Flunky got us smoked—"

"Silence!" the Vizier demanded again, his patience spent. He rubbed his forehead. Dull instruments indeed. It was a good thing he'd already learned of the four children from... other sources... because Stooge and Flunky's report was way too late to do him any good now. He supposed these idiots weren't entirely useless, however. "I'm putting you back to work guarding bridges." He waved a hand, and the big Jailer slithered up quickly, selecting the right key from a huge keyring and jamming it into the lock.

Stooge saluted again. "As you wish, your most majestic Emperor-ness. We'll fly back to Eqland at once—"

"Not there," the Vizier said through clenched teeth. "Eqland has been lost. I want you at Shanagrailia." He thought for a moment. "At the bridge coming from Shaland. Yes, that's the little Empress's most likely route, so we need as many guards there as we can get." He clenched his teeth and glared. "And this time, if you see a huwoman—or *any* human, aside from me—shoot first and ask questions later, got it?"

The wide-eyed gargoyles nodded emphatically.

"Good!" The Vizier spun on his heel.

He strode purposely through the rest of the east wing, ignoring countless more of his minions lying unconscious in their cells. Tension mounting, he turned the next corner, passing several oversized enclosures (currently empty) before reaching the most secure wing of the prison. Waving away his escort dismissively, the Vizier entered alone.

And breathed a sigh of relief. The dungeon's newest arrivals were here, right where they should be. He walked slowly between the cells reserved for high-value prisoners, perusing his newest victims, who were also still unconscious:

The big black eqman. There were stories about this one's exploits. The Vizier had wondered months ago if he needed to worry about the muscular warhorse, but he'd ultimately decided the horse was no threat. The eqman had never showed much initiative before now... so what had changed?

The fast-talking shaman. The Vizier felt his anger kindle again. Truly, there *were* traitors everywhere. He had hired this dolphin-faced fool to recover the Diamond Armor for *him*, and instead the pipsqueak had turned coat and joined his enemies, leading them to the Relic instead. Well, the rodent would pay for that mistake.

And the hulking lugman, an actual *lugman*. Few lugs were ever seen off their niland, and for good reason. The Vizier had considered using them as his Soldiers, but they were too hard to control. No, dull and weak as the imps were, he'd been right to choose them, leaving the lugmen trapped on Lugard. So how had this one escaped?

All in all, these three made an unlikely band of allies. He never would have thought to see their like fighting *together*.

A groan sounded, and the Vizier turned to inspect the last of his newest prisoners.

The little human boy.

As surprising as the others were, this one troubled him most of all. There weren't supposed to be other humen in Overtwixt! It upset all of the Vizier's carefully laid plans, dividing into *fifths* the power allotted to the human race, instead of granting all of it to the Vizier.

Well, at least one of the four children was now dealt with, trapped for all time in this prison, unable to escape Overtwixt. And so long as he was here, his share of the power belonged to the Vizier. The black-clad villain just needed to bring the boy's three siblings here also, to join their brother in jail for eternity.

Then nothing would stand between the Vizier and ultimate power... and a never-ending life of riches, rule, and *darkness* here in Overtwixt.

The fight against the Vizier concludes in...

ESCAPE FROM
OVERTWIXT ™

Or continue the adventures of Nachton, Amélie, Cécilie, and Ewan with these tie-in stories, one for each of the children:

The Knight and His Friends • picture book

The Princess and Her Throne • chapter book

Perilous Flight • novella
(bridges the gap between Overtwixt
and Escape from Overtwixt*)*

Scavenger Hunt • novella

glossary
of persons, places & things
(with pronunciation clues in **bold gray**)

Note: *[Ew.]* indicates a "Ewanism," unique pronunciation or slang used by Ewan Ollivaros for words he cannot pronounce.

Alabaster (AL-uh-bass-tur) **City** – major metropolitan area on Shanagrailia

Amélie (AWM-uh-lee), *huwoman* – 12-year-old human girl, second of the Ollivaros children; see Empress

Amphitheater (AM-fuh-thee-uh-tur) – main meeting hall of the Assembly of Caymerdelphia, a circular open-air pool of water capable of "seating" more than a thousand people

aquatics – general term referring to the cayman, dagman, delphman, and merman races

Archives (AR-kyvz) – the main eqman repository of knowledge on Eqland

Archivist, *eqman* – administrator of the Archives

Arts-and-Crafts Dude *[Ew.]* – see Crafter

Assembly – the voting population of Caymerdelphia, comprised of any aquatic with an interest in making his or her voice heard in current affairs

Baron, *human* – former ruler of the humen and centmen, who reigned from the Castle; later ruled all the United Lands from Capital City, until overthrown by the Vizier

bat-dudes/guys *[Ew.]* – see spookmen

"Batter you lick…" – one of many counting rhymes created by Cécilie; full rhyme goes: "Batter you lick could make you sick; you look fine so you're my pick!"

Bazooka *[Ew.]* – see Berserker

Berserker (bur-ZUR-kur), *lugman* – huge companion of Ewan who loves to fight

Blackguard, *drachwoman* – sworn bodyguard and secret admirer of the Vizier

bwudder *[Ew.]* – brother

Cap Dude/Guy *[Ew.]* – see Captain

Capital City – major metropolitan area on Twixt, and foremost city of the United Lands

capitol complex – see Citadel

Captain, *centman* – companion and leader of the guardsmen sworn to protect Amélie; formerly served the Baron in the same capacity

Cartographer, *shaman* – expert mapmaker who surveyed and plotted the nilands of the United Lands

Castle – former seat of the Baron's rule on Hucentia

caymen, *race* – see Nachton's Reference Book

Caymerdelphia (cay-mur-DELF-ee-uh), *niland* – hubland joining Caypool, Merpool, and Delphyrd originally; bridges were later built to join Dagmoor as well

Caymerlot (CAY-mur-laht) – ancient name for Caymerdelphia

Caypool, *niland* – portland of the caymen

Cécilie (SESS-ill-lee), *huwoman* – 8-year-old human girl, third of the Ollivaros children; see Princess

cent-dudes/guys *[Ew.]* – see centmen

centmen (SINT-min), *race* – see Nachton's Reference Book

Centwick (SINT-wik), *niland* – portland of the centmen

Citadel (SIT-uh-dell) – seat of the Vizier's rule in Capital City; formerly the capitol complex, under the Baron's rule

Committee – ruling body of Caymerdelphia; historically responsible for voting on motions put forth from the Assembly and acting as intermediary between the Assembly and the Underlord; comprised of eleven members elected from all four of the aquatic races

Conjurer (KON-jur-ur) – title assumed by Nachton Ollivaros for a time

Council – ruling body of Centwick; comprised of two centmen and two centwomen

Councilmember – member of the Council of Centwick

"Cows go moo..." – one of many counting rhymes created by Cécilie; full rhyme goes: "Cows go moo while they chew; you look nice so I pick you!"

Crafter, *gnoman* – companion of Nachton who is talented at fabricating needed items

creatures of darkness – general term referring to the drachman, impman, phoman, and spookman races; see Shadowlands, or forces of darkness

Criers (KRY-urz), *spooks* – any of several spooks renamed by the Vizier to pronounce his decrees throughout the United Lands

Crystal City – major metropolitan area on Caymerdelphia

dagmen, *race* – see Nachton's Reference Book

Dagmoor, *niland* – portland of the dagmen

Debutante (DEB-yoo-tawnt), *eqwoman* – friend of the Handmaiden who was smoked during the Vizier's conquest of Eqland

delphmen (DELF-min), *race* – see Nachton's Reference Book

Delphyrd (DELF-urd), *niland* – portland of the delphmen

dink *[Ew.]* – think

drachmen (DRAWK-min), *race* – see Nachton's Reference Book

Drachölm (DRAWK-holm), *niland* – portland of the drachmen

dwagons *[Ew.]* – see drachmen

eck-dudes/guys/mans *[Ew.]* – see eqmen

Eckwind *[Ew.]* – see Eqland

Emperor – title assumed by the Vizier after overthrowing the Baron and taking control of the United Lands

Empess *[Ew.]* – see Empress

Empress – future ruler over all sixteen races of the United Lands, and rival to the Vizier; role chosen by Amélie Ollivaros upon entrance to Overtwixt

Enforcer, *phoman* – the Vizier's minion primarily responsible for imposing punishments throughout the United Lands

epoch (EP-uhk *or* EE-pok) – any period of time during which a race inhabited Overtwixt, marked before and after by periods of non-habitation; for example, the 782nd Human Epoch refers to the 782nd period during which humen visited Overtwixt; also known as eras by some races

Eqland (EK-luhnd), *niland* – portland of the eqmen

eqmen (EK-min), *race* – see Nachton's Reference Book

era (AIR-uh *or* EER-uh) – see epoch

Ewan (YOO-wun), *human* – 5-year-old human boy, youngest of the Ollivaros children; see Knight

Fight Guy *[Ew.]* – see Weaponsmaster

Five Fundamental Laws – basic rules governing the innerworkings of Overtwixt, as established by the Sovereign when Overtwixt came into being; listed on page 92

Flunky, *imp* – one of the Vizier's minions responsible for guarding niland bridges; also see Stooge

forces of darkness – general term referring to the Vizier's minions; see creatures of darkness

fwend *[Ew.]* – friend

Gaoland (JAIL-luhnd), *niland* – mysterious hubland joining Impstead, Pholand, and Spookwood

glowstone – stone mined on Gnobury that gives off a natural amber (yellow-orange) light; used by the gnomen to provide illumination and act as signposts

Gnobury (NO-bur-ree), *niland* – portland of the gnomen

Gnocentia (no-SINCH-yuh), *niland* – hubland joining Gnobury and Centwick

gnomen (NO-min), *race* – see Nachton's Reference Book

Grand Library – the main human repository of knowledge on Huland

Grove – primary settlement of centmen on Centwick

Guide, *centman* – the first person to greet every new visitor to Overtwixt; responsible for presenting newcomers with three paths to choose from; otherwise provides assistance and guidance as requested by the visitor

Handmaiden, *eqwoman* – adolescent companion of Cécilie who serves as her primary lady-in-waiting

horseys *[Ew.]* – see eqmen

Hostess, *delphwoman* – friend of Amélie who first welcomes her to Caymerdelphia

hubland – a hub niland, any new niland created by the inhabitants of Overtwixt when two or more peoples desire to come together for mutual benefit

Hucentia (hyoo-SINCH-yuh), *niland* – hubland joining Huland and Centwick

Huland (HYOO-luhnd), *niland* – portland of the humen

humen, *race* – see Nachton's Reference Book

hungy *[Ew.]* – hungry

imp – slang for any impman or impwoman

impmen, *race* – see Nachton's Reference Book

Impstead (IMP-sted), *niland* – portland of the impmen

Innkeeper, *dagman* – owner/operator of a glass tower hotel in Crystal City near the Amphitheater

Inquisitor (in-QUIZ-it-ur), *phoman* – the Vizier's minion primarily responsible for interrogating the Vizier's enemies

Ivan (EYE-vuhn), *human* – cousin of the Ollivaros children

Ivory (EYE-vur-ee), *huwoman* – cousin of the Ollivaros children

Jacques (JAWK), *unknown race* – historical figure who inspired the fairy tale Jack and the Beanstalk

Jailer, *drachman* – minion of the Vizier responsible for imprisoning the Vizier's enemies

Kaiser (KY-zur), *drachman* – former ruler of the Shadowlands who reigned from the Fastness, until the Vizier fabricated evidence to have him banished from Overtwixt

Knight, *human* – primary defender of a ruler's honor; role chosen by Ewan Ollivaros upon entrance to Overtwixt, after which he served his sisters the Empress and Princess; also a historical figure

little peoples – general term referring to the gnoman, nagman, raiman, and shaman races

Loremaster, *human* – chief advisor to the Empress, responsible for researching issues and uncovering lost knowledge in libraries, then rendering judgment or providing counsel; role chosen by Nachton Ollivaros upon entrance to Overtwixt

Lugard (LOO-gard), *niland* – portland of the lugmen

lugmen, *race* – see Nachton's Reference Book

man-bat-dudes/guys *[Ew.]* – see impmen

Matron (MAY-truhn), *eqwoman* – friend and advisor of Cécilie who trains her in the proper "comportment" of a lady

Mayor (MAY-ur), *eqman* – leader of Pastoral City

mermen, *race* – see Nachton's Reference Book

Merpool, *niland* – portland of the mermen

Messengers, *spooks* – any of several spooks renamed by the Vizier to carry messages to and from his allies throughout the United Lands

Mystic (MISS-tik), *raiman* – former leader of the little peoples who ruled from Alabaster City before abdicating in favor of the Baron

Nachton (NAWK-tuhn), *human* – 15-year-old human boy, oldest of the Ollivaros children; see Loremaster and Conjurer

Nagland, *niland* – portland of the nagmen

nagmen, *race* – see Nachton's Reference Book

niland (NY-luhnd) – an island landmass floating in nothingness

no-dudes/guys/mans *[Ew.]* – see gnomen

Nock *[Ew.]* – see Nachton

Ollivaros (awl-iv-VAIR-os) – last name of Nachton, Amélie, Cécilie, and Ewan

Ommie *[Ew.]* – see Amélie

Opera Dude *[Ew.]* – see Operative

Operative, *centman* – one of the Captain's guardsmen, sworn to protect Amélie; formerly served the Baron in the same capacity

Orqland (ORK-luhnd) – niland currently inaccessible from the United Lands

Overchix *[Ew.]* – see Overtwixt

Overtwixt – the world of bridges, where all parallel universes (or alternate dimensions) intersect

Palace – seat of the Prince/Princess's rule in Pastoral City

Pastoral (pass-TOR-uhl) **City** – rustic major population center on Eqland

pease *[Ew.]* – please

perfick *[Ew.]* – perfect

Pholand (FO-luhnd), *niland* – portland of the phomen

phomen (FO-min), *race* – see Nachton's Reference Book

Pincess *[Ew.]* – see Princess

portland – a port niland, any landmass that exists where a real world intersects with (bridges into) Overtwixt

pred-joo-dust *[Ew.]* – prejudice

Prince, *eqman* – former ruler of the eqmen who reigned from the Palace, until the Vizier fabricated evidence to have him banished from Overtwixt

Princess, *huwoman* – future ruler of the eqmen; role chosen by Cécilie Ollivaros upon entrance to Overtwixt

prolly *[Ew.]* – probably

Raibourne (RAY-burn), *niland* – portland of the raimen

raimen (RAY-min), *race* – see Nachton's Reference Book

Ranger, *centman* – one of Captain's guardsmen, sworn to protect Amélie; formerly served the Baron in the same capacity; also a companion of Cécilie for a time

ray-dudes/guys *[Ew.]* – see raimen

relic – any magical artifact

rhino dudes/guys *[Ew.]* – see lugmen

Scholar (SKAWL-ur), *eqman* – intellectual and academic, often a companion of the Archivist

Scout, *centman* – one of the Captain's guardsmen, sworn to protect Amélie; formerly served the Baron in the same capacity

Sessy *[Ew.]* – see Cécilie

Shadowlands – general term referring to any of the nilands of the drachman, impman, phoman, or spookman (and occasionally dagman) races, which are generally overshadowed by the nilands above; see creatures of darkness

Shaland (SHAW-luhnd), *niland* – portland of the shamen

shamen (SHAW-min), *race* – see Nachton's Reference Book

Shanagrailia (shaw-nuh-GRAIL-yuh), *niland* – hubland joining Shaland, Nagland, and Raibourne originally; tunnel bridges were later engineered to join Gnobury as well

Shark *[Ew.]*, *spook* – controversial friend of Ewan

Skire *[Ew.]* – see Squire

Sky Light – one of countless celestial artifacts put in place by the Sovereign to provide illumination to the nilands of Overtwixt; bright like a sun one side and dim like a moon on the other, it rotates on its axis to simulate daytime and nighttime

smoke, *verb* – to hurt a person badly enough to eject him or her from Overtwixt; example: "The Kaiser got smoked," meaning the Vizier executed him; see yellow smoke, and the Five Fundamental Laws

Soldiers, *imps* – any of several impmen renamed by the Vizier to serve in his armies throughout the United Lands

Sovereign (SAWV-rin), *unknown race* – distant supreme ruler of all the infinite dimensions of the cosmos

Sovereign's Relics – special magical artifacts of enormous power that can only be used by the pure of heart for the greater good, of which four were gifted by the Sovereign to each and every race when Overtwixt came into being

Spies, *spooks* – any of several spooks renamed by the Vizier to move quietly throughout the United Lands, spying on the populace and gathering information

spook – slang for any spookman or spookwoman

spookmen, *race* – see Nachton's Reference Book

Spookwood, *niland* – portland of the spookmen

spooky-bats *[Ew.]* – see spookmen

Squire, *eqman* – primary companion of Ewan who carries him into battle

Steward, *eqman* – individual responsible for the day-to-day operation of the Palace

stick-and-chain thing *[Ew.]* – nunchucks

Stooge – one of the Vizier's minions responsible for guarding niland bridges; also see Flunky

Thieves, *spooks* – any of several spooks renamed by the Vizier to steal items of interest to him throughout the United Lands

Twixt, *niland* – hubland joining Caymerdelphia, Shanagrailia, Hucentia, Eqland, and Drachölm

uggy *[Ew.]* – ugly

Underlord, *merman* – former ruler of the aquatics who reigned from Crystal City before abdicating in favor of the Baron; left Overtwixt immediately thereafter

unee-corns *[Ew.]* – see eqwomen

United Lands – the realm of Overtwixt united and ruled by the Baron, later isolated and ruled by the Vizier

uvver *[Ew.]* – other

Vizier (viz-ZEER), *human* – the villain who schemed and plotted to unite the realm beneath the Baron, then overthrew the Baron to assume control himself, destroying bridges and building walls to secure his reign

Vizier's tower – the tallest tower of the Citadel, which houses the Vizier's residential chambers and preferred audience chamber

Warlord, *drachman* – supreme commander of the Vizier's forces of darkness; formerly served the Kaiser in the same capacity

Weaponsmaster, *shaman* – companion of Ewan who trains him to be a swordfighter

wimpmen *[Ew.]* – see impmen

wimpy-bats/dudes/guys *[Ew.]* – see impmen

yellow smoke – the emission that appears when a person is hurt badly enough to be ejected from Overtwixt

yug-dudes/guys *[Ew.]* – see lugmen

'Zooka *[Ew.]* – see Berserker (abbreviated form of Bazooka)

introduction to the
ancient languages of
Overtwixt

(condensed from a primer
by the Ancient Wizard of Merlyn)

Observant visitors to Overtwixt (in any age or epoch) will soon notice that they can easily understand the speech of other races, even though each people speaks one or more languages unique to its own dimension. This is one of the passive magical functions of Overtwixt, to facilitate communication and understanding.

The written word is translated automatically in much the same way. Any book a person reads (in one of the many libraries or elsewhere) will appear to be inscribed in the reader's own language.

With just two exceptions.

The oldest treatises are written in one of the two ancient languages that originated within Overtwixt itself. The first is **High Epitopian**, a graceful script that was used during the First Age in Epitopia, the earliest society in the world of bridges. The Epitopian language relies on simple, easy to remember rules of grammar and spelling, and the words for many concepts are spelled symmetrically. However, these many rules are rigid and unyielding, such as the requirement that Epitopian always be inscribed from right to left. It also has a limited lexicon, and many concepts simply cannot be expressed in Epitopian.

Example *(right-to-left):*

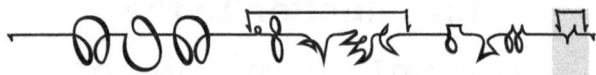

!rule (of (Human race, *lit. The Stubborn Ones*)) Doom [is] *[FUT]* ←

The other ancient language is **Unterstygian**, which was developed in the ages after the Schism as a proposed improvement on Epitopian. It employs a boxier, utilitarian script, and is much more flexible in its use. Unlike Epitopian, Unterstygian can be inscribed in any direction: right-to-left or left-to-right, top-to-bottom or bottom-to-top, or even some combination of the above, with lines of text changing direction as needed. Unterstygian's only unbreakable rule is that words are *never* spelled symmetrically.

Example *(left-to-right):*

→ *[FUT]* [is] Destiny (of (Human race, *lit. The Proud Ones*)) rulership!

Interestingly, vocabulary and pronunciation are both highly similar between these two languages, since again, Unterstygian evolved from Epitopian. However, varying connotations and subtle gradations of meaning between the two can result in significantly different interpretations.

As one might expect, many of the oldest tomes written on the subject of Sovereign or the blue magic are inscribed in High Epitopian, while the morally flexible green magic is typically documented only using Unterstygian.

OVERTWIXT
Reference Book

Prepared by Nachton Ollivaros,
782nd Human Epoch

INDEX

The Peoples of Overtwixt

Warning ~ This document deals with topics that are perhaps less interesting to younger readers.

Introduction ~ Having been in this place called Overtwixt for a few weeks now, I will now endeavor to document my observations. Overtwixt is not a "world" or "planet" as we would normally define such things. It is a conceptual realm where all real worlds intersect, and where the people of those worlds can interact. Even though it's NOT a physical place, our minds still visualize it that way, because the physical world is most familiar to us. That's why we find ourselves walking on land (or swimming through water, in the case of the aquatics). I also think that our non-physical link to this place accounts for the irregular and relative passage of time, much as we experience when dreaming.

About Nilands ~ Overtwixt has no core structure, and it only obeys the laws of physics when it feels like it. It appears to consist of unending white nothingness, with an infinite number of "nilands" floating inside. (Just as an "island" is land floating in water, a "niland" is land floating in nil, or nothing.)

Portlands - For each real world that intersects Overtwixt, a single port niland—or "portland"—occurs naturally. (Huland, for example, is the portland linking Overtwixt to the human real world.) Portlands are then linked to each other by bridges of all sorts.

Hublands - New nilands can be created by the inhabitants of Overtwixt if two or more peoples want to come together for mutual benefit. These hublands must be "planted," at the intersection of two or more bridges, by bringing together soil from

2

each of the linked portlands. The new niland is then "cultivated" through inhabitation. The more people come to live on the burgeoning niland, the greater the landmass (or body of water) will become as it grows to accommodate its population.

About Flora and Fauna ~ As a conceptual realm, Overtwixt has no naturally occurring species of animal life. Each niland DOES feature plant life reminiscent of its linked real world(s), but these plants are not truly alive. They are simply mental constructs created by the niland's inhabitants—the mind's way of surrounding itself with the familiar.

About the Peoples of Overtwixt ~ Since no true flora or fauna exist, the only real life in Overtwixt is INTELLIGENT life. That's why Overtwixt exists, after all—to bring together every people from every dimension of reality, for a "meeting of the minds."

Each race represented in Overtwixt (as far as I know) has both males and females, and they are referred to as men and women (or boys and girls), just like in OUR real world. It isn't two arms and two legs which makes someone a man or woman. Instead, it is the state of personhood—the existence of a personality and a soul. It's taken some getting used to, but I've come to recognize (for example) that a merman is just as much a "man" as I am.

The rest of this notebook represents my initial attempts to study and document just sixteen of the infinite races present in Overtwixt—the peoples of this realm who have been trapped by the Vizier.

3

About the Ollivarian system of classification ~

The longer you study the peoples of Overtwixt, the more clearly a pattern emerges: every race is essentially a hybrid of two other races (and each of THOSE races is a hybrid of the first and yet another, and so on and so forth).

Examples ~ Humen and eqmen (physically identical to horses from our real world) are distinct races sharing no physical attributes. However, centmen and lugmen might both be described as a cross between humen and eqmen. To be extremely simplistic, a centman (like a centaur from our mythology) is essentially the top half of a human and the bottom half of an eqman (horse). The lugman (like a minotaur) is the same mix in reverse: the top half of an eqman (horse) and the bottom half of a human.

As I've noted, this methodology of describing all races as hybrids of each other is simplistic. But it's not far from the truth. For my system of classification, I think of the contributing "halves" in terms of dominant and secondary, as follows:

- DOMINANT ~ upper body features, including circulatory, respiratory, and (usually) integumentary systems (body covering like skin, fur, hair, scales, feathers, etc.)

- SECONDARY ~ lower body appendages and overall stature

4

Notation - All peoples, therefore, can be classified as having one dominant half and one secondary half. For example, using the races discussed above:

- Humen - Hu>hu
- Centmen - Hu>eq
- Lugmen - Eq>hu
- Eqmen - Eq>eq

Base races - The "halves" used in this notation (whether dominant or secondary) always reference what I call "base races." Base races are those races I've identified as being physically identical to organisms from Earth. (I acknowledge this is a very hu-centric way of thinking. No offense toward non-humen is intended by this.) Base races include:

- Hu - humen
- Eq - eqmen - horses
- Del - delphmen - dolphins
- Spu - spookmen - bats
- ... and many others, undoubtedly

~~This system of classification is not without its flaws and exceptions. For example, not all hybrids with dominant delphman attributes are aquatic, therefore their respiratory system must come from their secondary half~~

Correction: I'm an idiot. Delphmen (like dolphins) are mammals; even though they are aquatic, they must surface to breathe air, which they process through lungs. The pattern holds—and the Ollivarian system of classification works.

Human

Ollivarian classification: Hu>hu

Traditional liege lord: Baron of Hucentia
(historically a human)

Nilands occupied: **Huland**, Hucentia

Anatomy: Your garden variety human being, as
originating from Planet Earth; two arms, two legs, so
forth and so on

6

Culture: As best I can tell, there has seldom existed any great population of humen in Overtwixt; at many times in history, Overtwixt has gone a long time without any humen at all, hence our method of recording human history within Overtwixt as occurring during human epochs. (My own visit to Overtwixt marks the 782nd Human Epoch—the 782nd time humans have come here.) From what I have read, the only epoch that lasted long enough to establish a true human society was Epoch 394, when travel between Overtwixt and Ancient Greece was almost commonplace. Not surprisingly, much of Classical Greek mythology was influenced by events taking place here during that time... Perhaps MORE surprisingly, that era of Overtwixt's history bled back into our real world AGAIN much later, in the form of legends regarding King Arthur and Camelot. I fully intend to study/document more about the ancient human Knight and ~~his~~ involvement with the utopian niland kingdom of Caymerlot as soon as I get the chance.

7

Centmen

Ollivarian classification: **Hu>eq**

Mythological cognate: **Centaurs**

Traditional liege lord: Baron of Hucentia
(historically a human)

Nilands occupied: **Centwick**, Hucentia, Gnocentia

Culture: Centmen prize loyalty and wisdom above all
other character qualities, and are famous for
demonstrating those same qualities themselves. A
person cannot ask for a better bodyguard or advisor
than a centman, or so most people believe. In the
absence of a ruling Baron, the centmen in Overtwixt
are led by a Council of four elders (two men and two
women) identified as the wisest among their people.

Anatomy: The upper body of a human attached at the
waist to the four-legged lower body of a horse,
covered in its entirety by a pattern of skin and
hair; the hair grows especially long down the back of
the human upper body (much like a horse's mane) and
in thick tufts along the equine back haunches,
forming patterns similar to zebra stripes; the
females of the species, which are generally more
slender, grow an even shaggier pelt below the
shoulders to protect their modesty, while the males
are known to braid the hair down their backs.

9

Eqmen

Ollivarian classification: **Eq > ea**

Base Race cognate: **Horses** (male)

Mythological cognate: **Unicorns** (female)

Traditional liege lord: Prince of Eqland (historically an eqman)

Nilands occupied: **Eqland**

Anatomy: Identical to the Arabian stallions of Earth; the males of the species exhibit the same variety of coat colors normal on Earth (browns, blacks); females tend to be markedly smaller and display more whimsical colors (including white, pink, and red coats, with even more vibrant and varied manes and tails); the eqwoman's forehead horn is undoubtedly what gave rise to the human legends of unicorns.

Culture: Eqmen are sometimes considered primitive by the other races, partly because they lack fingers or opposable thumbs (even though they've developed their own forms of technology which seem magical by comparison with our own), but also because of their overwhelming interest in simple pursuits: running, eating, and talking. Nevertheless, eqmen are renowned deep thinkers, and their Archives (essentially a library of philosophical audio recordings) rivals that of many other races.

Eqmen are also very adventurous. At times in the past, they established trade with other races, both for the construction of their settlements and for the acquisition of the seashells they use at the Archives.

11

Lugmen

Ollivarian classification: Eq >hu

Mythological cognate: the Minotaur

Traditional liege lord: none

Nilands occupied: Lugard

Culture: Lugmen have little culture to speak of, at least not in the traditional sense. They are isolationist with respect to other races and warlike amongst themselves, constantly fighting with little need for provocation. They fight most viciously with close friends and family members, though they always stop short of doing serious harm. Family reunions and other gatherings typically consist of a feast followed by a free-for-all with blunted weapons.

Anatomy: Bipedal thanks to secondary human traits, but immense, with a horsey head and face; males and females both feature a single thick horn sprouting from the end of the muzzle; despite this similarity in appearance to a rhinoceros (or the fact that lugman facial features are equine, not bovine), I am convinced the lugman is the inspiration for our human myth of the Minotaur. Lugmen of both genders grow great shaggy pelts over the upper chest, similar to a buffalo; their upper arms end in hooves like a horse, but articulated into three fingers and an opposable thumb. Most lugmen wear trousers or kilts but otherwise hate clothing.

13

Gnomen

Ollivarian classification: **Hu>spu**

Mythological cognate: **Gnomes**

Traditional liege lord: Mystic of Shanagrailia

Nilands occupied: **Gnobury**, Gnocentia, Shanagrailia

Culture: The gnomen are a people most comfortable
   underground. As such, their portland looks like
   nothing more than an un-navigable chunk of stone
   from the outside. On the INSIDE, Gnobury is
   riddled with warrens and tunnels, hence its name
   (equivalent to Gno-burrow). Gnomen are incredibly
   crafty, very creative, and quick with their hands,
   and this area of Overtwixt knows
      no better stone masons
      or sculptors.

14

Anatomy: Short of stature, like all races with secondary spookman attributes (those races generally called "little peoples"); at a glance, gnomen are easily confused for small humen, or young humen not yet fully grown, primarily because of their dominant human traits and their propensity for wearing clothes; on closer inspection, gnomen prove to be extremely bowlegged, with the same padded and clawed feet as bats; young gnomen of both genders typically grow thick, peach-fuzzy beards, but the hair falls out by the time the gnoman reaches middle age.

15

Nagmen

Ollivarian classification: **Eq>spu**

Mythological cognate: none

Traditional liege lord: Mystic of Shanagrailia

Nilands occupied: **Nagland**, Shanagrailia

Culture: Nagmen are cliff dwellers, but there is nothing primitive about their habitats, which they carve meticulously from sheer cliffs in geometrically-precise shapes. Known as peacemakers and lovers of harmony, nagmen have been compared favorably to the hippies of Earth's 1960s. Nagmen play a wide variety of musical instruments unique to their real world (many of which they have recreated in Overtwixt) and are famous for producing more talented musicians per capita than almost any other race.

Anatomy: One of the so-called "little peoples" (short-statured, thanks to secondary spookman attributes), nagmen are capable of walking naturally on all fours or on back legs only, as humen do; reminiscent of nothing so much as Earth's Shetland ponies, though much smaller; like lugmen, their front hooves have articulated "fingers" (three, plus an opposable thumb); nagman hair grows uniformly across the entire body, thick and shaggy, though a recent fad among younger nagmen involves shaving that coat in places in order to wear gnoman clothing.

Raimen

Ollivarian classification:	**Delzea**
Mythological cognate:	none
Traditional liege lord:	Mystic of Shanagrailia
Nilands occupied:	**Raibourne**, Shanagrailia

Culture: Raimen enjoy a strange reputation among the other peoples. Known as wise and insightful, they are also mocked for their tendency to speak in riddles (and for their physical appearance too, of course!).

Many a pilgrim has sought answers to some great question in the Alabaster City of Shanagrailia, only to turn away confused at the end. This has given rise to the saying, "A raiman would set you straight, if only you could get a straight answer." The raimen lost significant political clout when the current Mystic (a raiman) was forced to abdicate as a result of the Baron's campaign of unification (which led to the Vizier's eventual seizure of power). The raiman portland of Raibourne is one of the most isolated nilands in this part of Overtwixt.

Anatomy: The same hybrid mix as a cayman, but in reverse—the head of a dolphin affixed to the body of a miniature horse—the entire body covered with smooth gray skin; raimen tend to be rotund, with stubby little legs barely long enough to keep their bellies from scraping the ground; raiman heads feature a unique growth of cartilage running like a fringe from just above the eyes to the back of the head, and this ridge contains olfactory and secondary breathing apparatus (operating much like a human nose or dolphin blowhole).

Shamen

Ollivarian classification: **Del>spu**

Mythological cognate: none

Traditional liege lord: Mystic of Shanagrailia

Nilands occupied: **Shaland**, Shanagrailia

Culture: Shamen are the most outgoing and widely traveled of the "little peoples" who come together in Shanagrailia. By some quirk of their real world culture, adult shamen devote their lives to a single field of study, within which they seek to become an unparalleled expert. That is why shamen often attach themselves to prominent individuals of other races, to serve as coaches, trainers, or advisors.

Anatomy: The upper body of a dolphin attached at the waist to the lower body of a bat, including upper appendages that seem a cross between the dolphin's fins and the bat's winged arms; the shaman's arms are broad and flat, ending in extremely dexterous articulated fingers; vestigial webbing grows from the armpit to the elbow, but does not grant the ability to fly; shamen have sharp, carnivorous teeth; they often wear pants and shoes, and sometimes bowler-style hats with ponchos (especially for the shawomen), but their underarm webbing makes it impossible for them to wear actual shirts or tunics.

21

Caymen

Ollivarian classification: **Eq>del**

Mythological cognate: **Hippocamps**

Traditional liege lord: Underlord of Caymerdelphia

Nilands occupied: **Caypool**, Caymerdelphia

Culture: Caymen are essentially the eqmen of the sea, though more sedate and individualistic. They have the same propensity for lengthy philosophical discourse, and are favored speakers at the Amphitheater in Caymerdelphia. More so than any of the other aquatic peoples, caymen prefer to remain in their underwater environs, ignoring groundwalkers and surfacing only for air—or to debate their aquatic brethren about some topic or another.

Anatomy: A cross between a horse and a dolphin, they look more like a mix of sea horse and manatee; they are physically ponderous, even if they ARE known to be quick-witted.

23

Dagmen

Ollivarian classification: Del>hu

Mythological cognate: various

Traditional liege lord: none

Nilands occupied: **Dagmoor**, Caymerdelphia

Culture: Dagmen are renowned pranksters and thrill-
seekers. One of Overtwixt's most versatile species,
dagmen are comfortable on land or in water (though
they must rehydrate their skin at regular intervals
while out of the water). Dagmen are nomadic,
sometimes banding together with like-minded associates
rather than members of their birth families. Outside
of Dagmoor and Caymerdelphia,
roving bands of dagmen
have historically
provided entertainment
for the other races,
by putting on
carnivals or building
amusement parks.

24

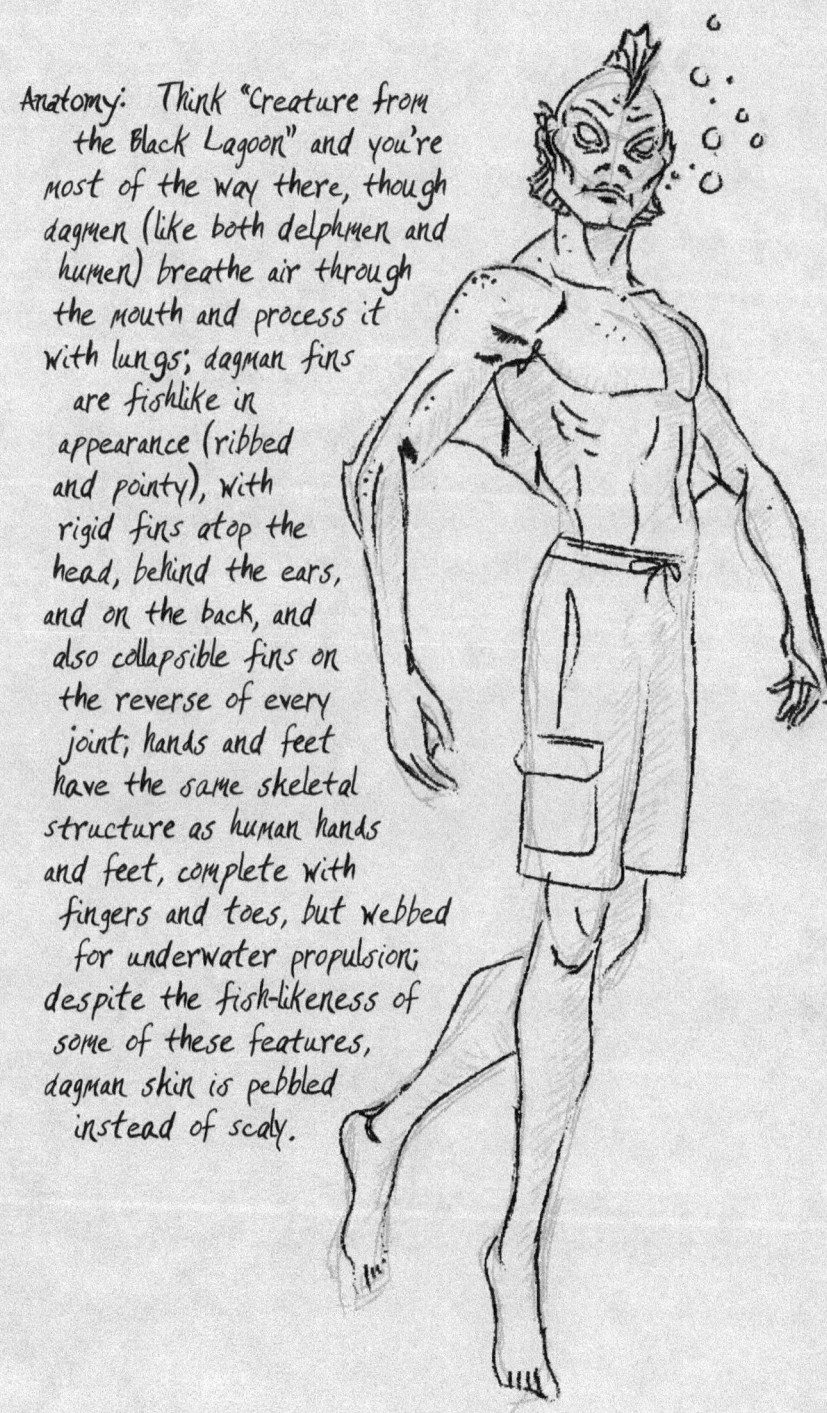

Anatomy: Think "Creature from
the Black Lagoon" and you're
most of the way there, though
dagmen (like both delphmen and
humen) breathe air through
the mouth and process it
with lungs; dagman fins
are fishlike in
appearance (ribbed
and pointy), with
rigid fins atop the
head, behind the ears,
and on the back, and
also collapsible fins on
the reverse of every
joint; hands and feet
have the same skeletal
structure as human hands
and feet, complete with
fingers and toes, but webbed
for underwater propulsion;
despite the fish-likeness of
some of these features,
dagman skin is pebbled
instead of scaly.

25

Delphmen

Ollivarian classification: **Del>del**

Base Race cognate: **Dolphins**

Traditional liege lord: Underlord of Caymerdelphia

Nilands occupied: **Delphyrd**, Caymerdelphia

Culture: Delphmen are widely considered the friendliest and most welcoming people in this area of Overtwixt. They are known as care-free and fun-loving, but their play has less of an edge than the dagman pranksters. By their lifestyle, delphmen illustrate their belief that responsibility must be taken seriously, and that life contains many serious moments—but that life should never be taken TOO seriously.

Anatomy: Identical to the bottlenose dolphins of Earth, with smooth gray skin covering a thin layer of blubber; the males of the species exhibit a broad, dark gray band from nose to tail along the back, while the females are distinguished by thinner, lighter gray stripes running in wavy lines along their sides; similar to eqwomen, delphwomen also have a small horn just above the eyes, but very short and stumpy, barely breaking the surface of the skin.

Mermen

Ollivarian classification:	**Hu>del**
Mythological cognates:	**Mermen/mermaids**
Traditional liege lord:	Underlord of Caymerdelphia
Nilands occupied:	**Merpool**, Caymerdelphia

Culture: The merpeople hold beauty in high esteem, and are sometimes considered vain and self-important as a result. But they care as much for inner beauty as outer, and much of their culture revolves around the creation of artistic masterpieces. They are famed for the masterful glassblowing they perform on their hot sandy beaches, which results in small works of art as well as delicate underwater towers.

Anatomy: The upper body of a human attached to the lower body of a dolphin; for the females of the species, the transition occurs just below the shoulders, while the males transition at the waist, exposing a muscular human torso; in both cases, the lower body is covered in the blubbery gray skin of a dolphin; only the females have a dorsal fin. Both the men and the women wear their hair long, either loose or in dreadlocks.

29

Drachmen

Ollivarian classification:	**Spu>del**
Mythological cognate:	**Dragons**
Traditional liege lord:	Kaiser of the Shadowlands (historically a drachman)
Nilands occupied:	**Drachölm**

Culture: Bombastic and always the largest person in a room, drachmen are used to being the center of attention. In a social setting, that makes them the life of the party; in a political or military setting, they have a thirst for command. The Kaiser of the Shadowlands was always a drachman, ever since the days when the first Kaiser conquered Impstead and Spookwood, making its inhabitants his minions. It is no coincidence that all three races now serve the Vizier, led by a drachman Warlord.

Anatomy: The largest of the races I've observed in Overtwixt, drachmen are best described as huge bats, their muscular bodies long, slender, and sinuous from shoulders to tail, covered entirely in thick black hair; drachmen have two sets of shoulders, the lower equipped with meaty forearms and prehensile hands, the upper with immense wings that fold along the back; the drachman's ears are huge and side-facing, and its long body ends in two pairs of crossed, dolphin-like fins that give it the appearance of having a barbed tail.

31

Impmen

Ollivarian classification: Spu>hu

Mythological cognate: Gargoyles

Traditional liege lord: Kaiser of the Shadowlands
(historically a drachman)

Nilands occupied: Impstead

Culture: Impmen have strong clan ties and typically flock in large groups. Much like the ducks and geese of Earth, they are fond of long flights during which they sing in five-part harmony while flying in rotating formations. Impmen do not have strong leadership tendencies, and historically have been quick to accept outside authority. Some few impmen break the mold, forming small companies and hiring themselves out as mercenaries that fight or offer airlift services.

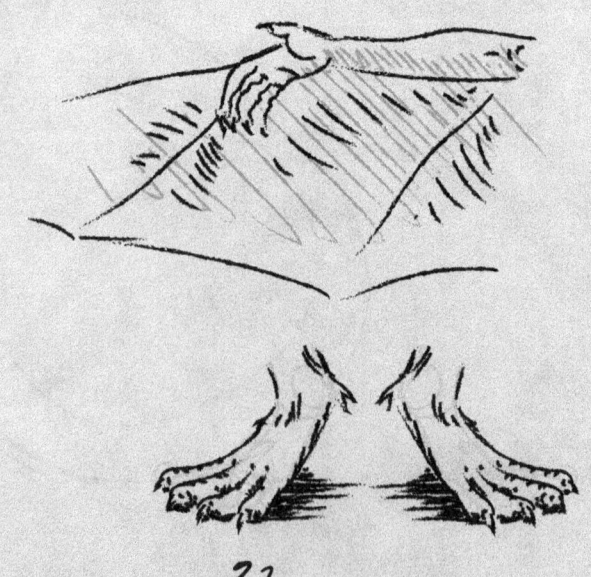

Anatomy: Closely resembling the body of a human, with a well-muscled torso, but the head of a bat; the bat-like wings attach directly from the creature's back to its strong human arms (as opposed to being mounted on the back, as with the gargoyles from human stories); impmen have very human hands, but with sharply taloned fingers; most impmen wear nothing more than patterned trousers in bright colors, with ripped cuffs, while impwomen add colorful strips of cloth to protect their modesty; most prefer to go without footwear, except when flying into battle.

Phomen

Ollivarian classification:	**Spurea**
Mythological cognate:	various
Traditional liege lord:	none
Nilands occupied:	**Pholand**

Culture: Phomen are the most bizarre and frightening of Overtwixt's peoples. It isn't only their physical appearance but also their strange ability to hear one another speak across vast distances, as if standing side-by-side. Perhaps their apparent eccentricity is accentuated by the fact that only two exist in all of Overtwixt at this time, twin brothers who serve the Vizier... but it is difficult to imagine these creatures as anything other than villains.

Anatomy: The body of a horse, so gaunt that every bone shows beneath the hairy black skin; while equine in shape, phoman heads retain bat-like features (oversized ears, upturned nose, exposed fangs); phomen have two sets of wings: vestigial webbing beneath the forelegs and a larger set folding behind the back when not used for flying; phoman tails are hairless like a rat's; size-wise, phomen are comparable to horses and theoretically could be ridden; as such, I imagine they are the inspiration for Pegasus from myth... though how these monsters ever inspired such a beautiful creature, I'll never know.

35

Spookmen

Ollivarian classification: **Spu>spu**

Base Race cognate: **bats**

Traditional liege lord: Kaiser of the Shadowlands (historically a drachman)

Nilands occupied: **Spookwood**

Culture: Much like humen, great variety exists in spookman social patterns; some prefer to live in large groups (called "legions") while a significant minority have loner tendencies. Incredibly crafty and dexterous, with prehensile hands and feet both, spookmen have a well-deserved reputation for being thieves and con-artists. They are not to be trusted.

Anatomy: Most similar to the vampire bat of Earth, roosting upside down (in caves, but more preferably from the upper reaches of forest trees), spookmen are also capable of walking/running on all fours and of course flying; spookmen or "spooks" are the smallest of all the races I've observed in Overtwixt, ranging in size from that of a rat to that of a small lapdog.

36

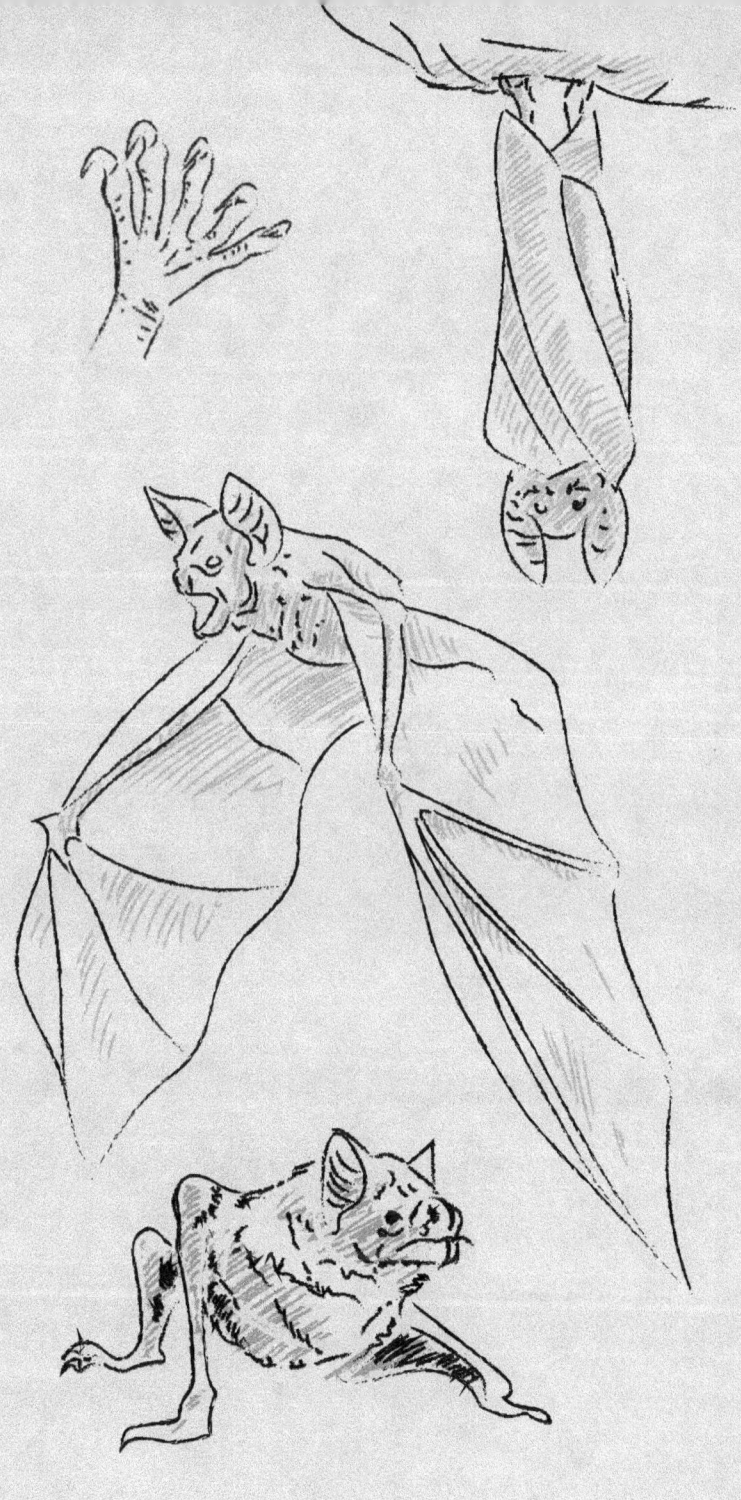

37

acknowledgments

Writing is, in so many ways, a solitary exercise; yet story crafting is never accomplished alone. There are so many people who inspire me in one way or another, so many who assist through constructive criticism, and so many who simply encourage me—and I could not do this without them.

As usual, my wife tops the list of individuals deserving gratitude. Sarah, you cheered me on throughout the seven long years of this project, as you have with all others since our relationship began. But I needed it this time more than ever before, considering how much of a departure *Overtwixt* was from my normal fare. Your genuine emotional response to each draft of every chapter was lifegiving as I sought to capture the essence of our children in the characters of Nachton, Amélie, Cécilie, and Ewan. (I hereby bestow upon you the role of "Countess" should some version of you ever visit Overtwixt!)

Which leads me to Nate, Emme, Sadie, and Ian—my real children, and the greatest loves of my life. Thank you for being you. Thank you for inspiring the positive aspects of these four characters, and thank you for not stoning me when they make bone-headed mistakes in the story (remember that they're only *based* on you, not meant to actually *be* you!). Thank you too for the unique signatures you each created for 'your' character, to be used at the beginning of 'your' chapters; they really add a lot! Special thanks to Sadie in particular for giving me the idea for

Overtwixt on that date night so long ago, when you regaled me with your own fantastical tale about princesses, unicorns, and mermaids (even though you've now outgrown such things). In honor of that contribution, you got to be the point-of-view character in the first chapter of this volume.

No one has done more to bring Overtwixt to life than Jesse Lewis, whose illustrations perfectly capture the look and feel of the nilands themselves, not to mention their many citizens (and denizens!). Thank you, Jesse, for all your hard work and longsuffering patience as I requested tweaks, changes, and the occasional fresh start. I know I'm a pain to work with at times, but you truly delivered.

Immense gratitude goes out to a new all-star on my proofing team: Heidi Burch (role: Sorceress), who offered so many fantastic suggestions, a fair number of grammatical fixes, and a very important save with regard to the name I was originally using for impmen. Thanks to you, all the Diamond Relics are now capitalized and systemized as well!

Long-time team member Beth Paul (Minstrel) was reliable as always, catching faux pas big and small, and reining me in this time on: semicolons, ellipses, and dashes... which I had even begun using—*gasp*—interchangeably! Joking aside, I don't know what I'd do without your timely feedback on each new story I write.

I remain indebted to my parents, Les and Ruth Akers (Salesman and Lounge Pianist), who still read everything I write, even when it's outside their preferred genres. Dad, thanks for reminding me about the difference between "that" and "which." And Mom, the dagmen appreciate how you insisted on protecting their modesty (they really did deserve to be clothed in each sketch). *I* appreciate your encouragement regarding the Five Fundamental Laws. You're right; we *could* all stand to be reminded of those truths, especially during this current era of distrust.

Thank you to Whitney Naylor-Smith (Wanderer) for all her insightful comments and suggestions, and the continual encouragement to "show" instead of "tell."

Special thanks to Faith Reeves (Chronicler) for an *incredible* amount of detailed feedback. You obviously "get" this story at a fundamental level, and so your suggestions for improvement carried great weight. You also kept me from overdoing the Ewanisms to the point of distraction.

Thanks as well to the Marrs, the Matthews, the Cobbs, and the Amblers for trusting me enough to test this story on your kids. You offered compelling consensus about the need for pictures throughout the book (not just at the end), pronunciation cues for difficult words (whether made-up or real), and more explicit indicators as to which character's point of view was reflected in each chapter. Extra special thanks to Kylie, Ryan, Kaeden, and Ben for the specific suggestions you offered (even scribbling encouraging notes directly in the margins, which I will forever keep and cherish).

I'm also grateful to the members of my 2018 men's leadership development group, whom Ewan would probably refer to as jay-dudes: Greg, Matt, Cody, John, Rob, Rob, Scott, and Seth. Thank you for the interest and encouragement you offered throughout the year I spent conceptualizing and writing this story. This is probably my most meaningful writing project to date, and your involvement in my life helped influence that.

Monica Robinson (Defender), I'm sorry for the trauma you endured in chapter 19, when exposed to Nachton's utter lack of respect for both Louisa May Alcott and *Anne of Green Gables*. Just remember it wasn't *me* who burned those books; it was Nachton! (To which Nachton retorts, "The author made me do it!" Ahem.) But seriously, for the record (and before I receive any hate mail), I happen to like those books just fine. And don't forget that Nachton is still a work in progress, even now. There's no telling; he may live to regret some of his past mistakes, and someday decide to make restitution for them...

Thank you to Ella Lyle for providing a final round of proofing, and for coordinating with several of your friends to do the same. And thank you once again to entertainment lawyer Kevin Levine for assisting me with legal questions and copyright concerns for this novel and the entire Overtwixt series.

Last and foremost, I must always acknowledge my Lord and Savior Jesus Christ. I hope and believe that this novel honors you, having spent more time on my knees inviting you into this project than I ever have before. Thank you for the talents you gave me. I hope that, by the choices I make, I continue to develop those abilities and use them only for your glory and the greater good.

about the fonts

The text of this novel was set in 11-point Asul Regular, a baroque humanist typeface designed by Mariela Monsalve. With its subtle semi-serifs, Asul is perfectly suited (in the author's opinion) for younger readers.

Since Asul lacks an italic variant, italicized text was set in Amerigo BT Std Italic, a typeface designed by Gerard Unger in 1987, which complements Asul nicely.

"Nachton Hand" and "Nachton Hand Title" were designed by the author using real quill and ink, scanned and digitized and packaged into a font with multiple variants per character to make it feel more natural. Nachton's handwriting is based on the author's own, which has not improved much in the three decades since HE was fifteen.

Section headers, illustration text, and many place names on the maps were set in Mercator Regular, designed by Arthur Baker in 1995. Mercator's calligraphic strokes give it a hand-scribed feel that's ideal for this application.

Finally, all hublands on the maps were beautifully identified using ITC Locarno Italic (in all caps), designed by Alan Meeks in 1922.

about the author

R.L. Akers loves stories. He loves hearing them, loves telling them, loves embellishing them, and loves forging them from raw materials. He is convinced that every person who ever lived has an interesting story, and he's only met one person in his life who came close to proving otherwise.

Holder of an undergraduate degree in computer science and a master's degree in business administration, Akers has worked in software development as well as non-profit fundraising and publicity. His love for children has led him in the past to be a foster parent and a coordinator of the K-5 ministry at his church. His interests include graphic design, orchestral movie soundtracks, and anything remotely creative.

Akers lives in West Virginia with his wife Sarah and the four children he loves most in this world. Visit him online at RLAkers.com.

about the illustrator

Jesse Lewis is an award-winning published illustrator and graphic artist, who specializes in breathing life into worlds beyond our own and the characters that reside within them. After studying for and attaining his bachelor's degree in fine arts at Savannah College of Art & Design, Jesse went on to expand his skills through numerous book-, video game-, and animation projects both within the U.S. and around the world.

While always pursuing continued development of his own skillset, Jesse has also kindled a passion for sharing his knowledge and experiences by educating new generations of aspiring artists.

Instagram: jnoah.art
Facebook: jesselewisdesign

www.ingramcontent.com/pod-product-compliance
Lightning Source LLC
Chambersburg PA
CBHW050921030726
47503CB00007BB/2405